"

They
ing. He
His mou
He put h
could sp

"If you insist on starting this thing, I won't back down. I don't tell fairy tales."

"Good, because I'm not a child," she hissed.

He touched her chin, not meaning to be gentle, not meaning anything, but feeling suddenly gentle toward her despite himself. She didn't pull back, and he didn't take his hand away. "There is no happy ending to this story, Nina."

"My decision is already made." She still hadn't pulled away from his touch, as if they'd become fused.

But they had, because he couldn't pull away either.

He closed the hairbreadth of distance between them, and kissed her...

Praise for *How Sweet It Is*

"A delightful romance that introduces an intriguing quartet of women...a uniquely entertaining story."

—*RT Book Reviews*

"The writing here is crisp and astute; the dialogue crackles with witty charm."

—*Library Journal* (starred review)

"A charming story of love, forgiveness, and redemption...I look forward to book two, SWEET KISS OF SUMMER."

—FreshFiction.com

"A terrific opening act as Sophie Gunn provides an engaging tale in which love helps heal emotional wounds."

—*Midwest Book Review*

Sweet Kiss of Summer

SOPHIE GUNN

FOREVER

NEW YORK   BOSTON

Copyright © 2011 by Diana Holquist
Excerpt from *How Sweet It Is* copyright © 2011 by Diana Holquist
All rights reserved. Except as permitted under the U.S. Copyright Act of 1976, no part of this publication may be reproduced, distributed, or transmitted in any form or by any means, or stored in a database or retrieval system, without the prior written permission of the publisher.

Forever
Hachette Book Group
237 Park Avenue
New York, NY 10017
www.HachetteBookGroup.com

Forever is an imprint of Grand Central Publishing.
The Forever name and logo are trademarks of Hachette Book Group, Inc.

The publisher is not responsible for websites (or their content) that are not owned by the publisher.

Printed in the United States of America

First Edition: August 2011

10 9 8 7 6 5 4 3 2 1

ATTENTION CORPORATIONS AND ORGANIZATIONS:
Most HACHETTE BOOK GROUP books are available at quantity discounts with bulk purchase for educational, business, or sales promotional use. For information, please call or write:

Special Markets Department, Hachette Book Group
237 Park Avenue, New York, NY 10017
Telephone: 1-800-222-6747   Fax: 1-800-477-5925

To my writing buddy. You know who you are.

Acknowledgments

*T*o everyone at the Natasha Kern Literary Agency for their enthusiasm and insight...

To everyone at Grand Central publishing, for their intelligent comments and awesome covers...

To all my beta readers, especially Ellen Hartman, for always being right...

To my friends and family, who somehow put up with me and all my deadlines...

And finally, to my readers, who have been so supportive and kind...

Thank you all! I could never do this alone.

Chapter One

Dearest Nina,

You don't recognize this handwriting because a beautiful army nurse named Sally is writing this letter for me. I don't think I'm going to make it, little sis. That's okay. Hell, if I don't pull through, I died fighting the good fight and I'm damned proud. So no moping around and getting sad. I could have died a million stupid ways when I was a kid. At least I got to go out doing something that matters.

But, Nins, you know I'm going to milk this dying-young crap.

There's two things you've gotta do for me.

First, you gotta move on. Find a good guy. Start a family. And name your first son after me. Promise me that. Little Walt, *NO MATTER HOW MUCH YOU HATE THE NAME.* (Ha! See, I still get to be the boss even after I'm gone.) I want a little Walter *growing up in Galton, giving the teachers hell, just like I used to. Remember, it was our promise to each other after Mom and Dad passed that we'd move on and not let anything stop us. Don't stop now, little sis.*

Second, I want to do something for a buddy. His name is Mick Rivers. Listen, I want him to have my house in Galton when he gets out of here. I know he'll say I should go *#$% myself, but, Nins, can you make it happen?

Thanks, sis. I'll see you on the other side. I miss you already.

*Private First Class Walter Stokes,
U.S. Army*

Chapter Two

Two years later

$\mathcal{N}$ina Stokes was in her garden searching her tomato cages for the perfect beefsteak when a sporty red car roared halfway up her driveway and stopped. She spared it half a glance, then went back to her vegetables. It was reunion weekend at Galton University, the elite college that dominated the tiny town of Galton, New York. This was the third car she'd spotted this morning using her driveway as a turnaround. It could be annoying having the first driveway on the first road that was clearly marked as leading out of town.

Nina went back to her tomatoes, ripping out the hairy galinsoga that had crept into the cages. She felt bad that she hadn't been taking as good care of her garden as she usually would have, but she was deep into the process of illustrating a cookbook, *The Vegetable Virgin*. It was demanding all of her attention. If she nailed it, hopefully she'd get the job for *The Meat Menage*. Then, if she was lucky, *The Soup Slut*. So finding the perfect plump tomato to nestle next to the green beans for the Italian Veggie Casserole illustration was essential. She moved down the row, carefully peering under leaves.

When she spared a second glance, the car was still there, idling in the middle of the long drive that wound up her hill. She ducked a little lower. She hated giving directions, as she never remembered the names of roads. She might say, *Go right at Mrs. Gradon's amazing cornflower blue hyacinth,* surely drawing a blank stare from a person in a car that flashy.

She was inspecting the last tomato plant when the driver floored the gas. The car jumped forward, then braked hard, fishtailing up a cloud of dust mere feet from her tulip border.

The crazy-loud engine revved a few times, then cut.

She had ducked back into the garden in alarm, but now she dared a peek over the vegetation.

The front door of the car opened.

A man unfolded from the front seat, a flash from his aviator sunglasses momentarily blinding her. Her vision cleared in time to reveal him stretching his arms above his head, as if he'd just woken up from a truly excellent dream.

Nina put a hand on the nearest tomato cage to steady herself. Good thing she'd staked *and* caged the bushes for extra support. *Talk about the perfect beefsteak.*

The man pulled his T-shirt over his head in a swift, one-armed movement. She ducked low, tried to swallow, pulled the brim of her sun hat low to cover her blush and her ridiculous smile.

The most beautiful man I've ever laid eyes on is stripping in my driveway. God, I love this town.

She took a deep breath, the whiff of compost grounding her. *I am a serious artist, a respected yoga teacher, and a sporadic, inattentive, but sincere gardener. I am an orphan, an optimist, a lover of quiet and peace. But I am in no position to be a woman who swoons over a good-looking man, even if he appears like a god in my driveway and seems determined to disrobe.*

Still, she couldn't tear her eyes away from his tanned, trim physique. She couldn't quite get the beginning of a wicked smile off her lips. *Be careful of things that look too good to be true.*

The man turned to lean through the driver's window of his car, and she tried again to shake off her response. Obviously, her boneheaded reaction was due to too little sleep and too much work.

And then everything changed.

She saw it.

His tattoo.

Everything disappeared in a rush of tunnel vision. Gone were the tomatoes, the vague aroma of car exhaust, the fat robin keeping an eye trained on her from the maple tree. Only the tattoo on his shoulder was clear in the shining whiteness of her sudden dizziness: the downward-pointing bowie knife with a flowing white ribbon wrapped around it. She couldn't read the words on the ribbon from this distance, but she knew them by heart. After all, they had been inked into her brother's arm too.

Duty. Honor. Country.

Nina's body went cold with dread.

He could be anyone from the unit.

He might not be Mick Rivers. Sure, she'd stared at the

guy's picture for two long years, wondering about him and his relationship to Walt. But military men all looked alike from a distance. The close-cropped haircuts, the square jaws, the wide chests that tapered to narrow waists. This guy could be any G.I. Joe Shmoe who had just happened to be passing through when he remembered this was Walt's hometown. It had happened just five months before. A soldier named Bill had looked her up to drop off a few mementos of Walt he had saved.

Anyway, if this man *was* Mick Rivers, she had to keep a cool head and hold her ground. She had given him an entire year after Walt's letter arrived to respond to her endless correspondence. She had promised herself that after the year had passed, the house was hers. Now that she was alone in the world, she wouldn't put herself at the whims of others. Her first duty was to herself, and she was going to stand by it.

If Mick Rivers was here for his house, he was a year too late.

While she panicked in the garden, trying to hold firm to her resolve, the man had calmly walked around to his trunk, dug around a bit, then come up with another T-shirt.

He looked around the place, and she ducked lower. His eyes, thankfully, glazed right over the garden.

She sat down, butt in the dirt.

She loved her brother and respected his wishes, but she had to get this guy to leave. She'd just tell him that he was too late.

The house was all she had left.

Chapter Three

*T*wo thousand six hundred and forty-eight miles in five days in a wasted hunk of metal he had won on a dare, and Mick Rivers felt every one of those miles in his ass.

He looked up at the house in front of him and shuddered. *Not good.*

The garden gnome eyed him suspiciously.

Mick tried not to curse—but failed. He threw open the car door and sank into the white pleather passenger seat, rifled through the glove box for the address he'd scribbled on the back of an old phone bill envelope, then cursed again. He felt like a green recruit caught in his first firefight.

Rule number one: never assume anything.

He'd assumed he could stomach the ordeal of talking Walt's sister out of her house. He'd driven across the country, then halfway up the drive before he'd realized his mistake with a sickening lurch that had stopped him in his tracks. No way he could do this, no matter how badly he needed this house.

Yes, I can. She is not my concern. Stay on mission. In and out. Get the job done.

Rule number two: assess the facts.

He knew that Walt's sister still owned the place; he'd checked the public records before he'd set off. So the first question was, Who lived here now?

The house was lived in. By someone who liked vegetables. And flowers.

The only people Mick knew like that were female.

An ancient but well-cared-for green Subaru wagon sat in the drive. The bumper sticker read *Galton Is Gorges.* From the look of the hanging-off bumper, no man was involved, unless he was the kind of man who couldn't fix a car. That is, the kind of man Mick was pretty sure he could dismiss as a concern.

He reconned the yard. The vast flower garden in front of the house vibrated with every color of flower and at least a hundred buzzing, happy bees. Hell, there were even frolicking butterflies. *Frolicking.* He didn't like the word any more than he liked the insects, but there was no other word for it. All this place needed was a rainbow to complete the obvious message: *if you want the house, you're gonna have to go in and rip it out of a very happy person's hands.*

Could this place be more picture-perfect? Cat in window—check. Flowered welcome mat—check. Ridiculously lush garden that spilled over into a sloping yard of perfect green grass—double check. On one side, the grass led to woods that circled behind the house. On the other, to a meadow that disappeared down the hill. The meadow was dotted with every color of wildflower.

Figured.

Flowers made him edgy. Tidy houses made a sheen of

sweat break out on his brow. It was one of the thousands of reasons he loved the army. Barracks, tents, sleeping under the stars with guys who'd blow off a garden gnome's head just for the fun of it. Everything in the army was what it was, didn't pretend to be anything more. Not like trim, pretty houses, which could shelter any kind of unspoken horror.

He took the steps two at a time. Knocked. Rang the bell. No answer. He tried the knob. It turned. *Unlocked*.

"Hello?" he called into the foyer, taking a sneak peek around to assess what he was dealing with. The pin-neat foyer was empty save for a small, compact table holding a vase of red flowers. Pictures of flowers lined the happy-yellow walls. A red and yellow braided rug accented the shiny wood floor.

He slammed the door against the rush of déjà vu that assaulted him. *Home is where the crazies are*.

He went back to his car and back-kicked the door. This house was dead-on for the happy-looking little house he'd grown up in.

He turtled his head into his shoulders to shelter from the ghosts that were still raising goose bumps across his flesh.

Goddamn Walt.

He leaned against the hot metal of the car, letting the heat soak into his skin, into his tired muscles. *Okay, think*. If no one was home, it was a chance to take care of what he had thought would be the tough part of his mission but now saw might be a cakewalk next to getting the house.

He looked to the barnlike garage that was set off to the side, tucked behind the house. He could be in and out in three minutes. If the front door to the house was unlocked, the garage probably wasn't locked either. Not that a lock would've stopped him.

He extracted the tattered letter from his back pocket and dropped the tiny key folded inside into his palm. He didn't need to reread the letter. After two years, he knew it by heart:

Mick,

You still alive? Good for you, buddy. If anyone gets out of this place alive, it's gonna be you, man. Listen, I'm giving you my house in upstate New York. It's not much of a place, but it's something. Hell, you don't have to live there or anything. Sell it if you want. I wrote my sister to let her know that you'll come as soon as you get out of this hellhole. She'll make it happen. She's okay that way.

These keys are for the place. The first is for the front door. The second is for a box. It's in the garage, on the top shelf by the back right corner. It's small, like a shoe box, red rusted metal. There's a couple of them, but you'll know you've got the right one if the key fits.

Destroy it, Mick. I'm counting on you to make it go away. Never let my sister know about it or what's inside. Can you do that for me, buddy? After all, you owe me one for Fallujah, right?

> *Take good care,*
> *Your buddy, Walt*

You owe me one . . .
For months, laid out in an army hospital in Germany, then another in Santa Monica, Mick had no way to do Walt's bidding. Then, his body finally healed, he'd ignored

Walt's request and his sister's letters, her calls, her messages, while he got his head back together. He couldn't get his head around Walt's letter, and frankly, he had enough to deal with without taking on a buddy's mystery. Why him, after all? Why hadn't Walt asked a buddy back home to take care of the box? Why hadn't Walt asked another guy in the unit, one who actually liked him? What was in the box that was worth a house? Why did Walt think Mick owed him? Did he? Questions with answers buried in the muck of war and the haze of a memory that was blown to smithereens.

He really should have answered at least one of Walt's sister's letters. But he never thought he'd need to take Walt up on his offer.

Now here he was, fifty feet from solving at least part of the mystery. By doing this errand for Walt, he'd somehow earn the house.

But how?

His skin was clammy despite the intense, brutal sunshine.

What the hell was he going to find in that garage?

In the daylight, he'd picture a rusty, faded thing crammed with dirty money, or drugs, weapons, maybe even ammo. But in the pitch dark of three a.m., he'd imagine it grossly encrusted, as if it had spent time on the bottom of the ocean. Or worse, he'd see it in his mind's eye marked by a bloody handprint. On bad days, he'd imagined it big enough for a human skull. On even worse days, small enough for a single, severed finger.

What had Walt done? Why was *he* responsible for protecting Walt's sister from what Walt had done? Was Walt's sister so delicate, she couldn't handle Walt's secrets? She had sounded delicate in her first letters. But as time passed, her words had toughened, her resolve set, until she finally told him to answer her now or go to hell.

Welcome to hell.

Mick hoped she didn't live in the house. In a perfect world, she'd have rented it to a happy-flower-butterfly lady, who'd turn out to be eighty-seven, deaf, half blind, and ready to move on to the nursing home anyway.

No more procrastinating. He started toward the barn.

Then stopped.

Something rustled in the vegetable garden, about thirty feet southwest.

He froze, the already-cold sweat on his skin icing over. *There are no snipers in upstate Nowheresville.* He knew better than to react with a combat response to a noncombat situation. He quickly tried to talk himself off that familiar ledge.

But it didn't work. The hairs standing up on the back of his neck told him that was no bunny in the lettuce. Someone was watching him. Someone besides a clay-bearded statue in the daisies or an army of ghosts reminding him of the domestic horrors neat little houses could hold.

You know better than to sit out in the open, waiting for a bullet to the brain.

He took a deep breath. He'd spent a good year getting his head together after agonizing months of getting his body together. He knew what losing his shit felt like, and he knew how to hold it together. He was past this.

He strode across the lawn, toward the vegetable garden.

A ridiculous pink straw hat poked up, then disappeared.

He stopped at the edge of a row of green beans clinging to a web of string tied to poles. The beans hung like a modesty screen between him and a small woman crouching behind the tomatoes.

He cleared his throat. "Hello."

"Oh! Hello." The woman stood, nervously wiping her hands on her denim shorts as if she had just now noticed him. She took off her hat, and an explosion of red hair jolted him backward.

Mick was trying to play it cool, but he didn't feel it.

He was face-to-face with Walt.

Not Walt. Walt is gone. But the redheaded woman looked just like Walt, if Walt had had the body of a knockout. She had the same glowing-ember-colored hair. She had the same button nose, buried in a sea of freckles. Just like Walt, her freckles matched the coppery brown of her eyes so exactly, it was as if hundreds of the things had slid off her tiny nose and flooded her irises.

"Are you lost? Need directions?" she asked, a little too eager to sound normal. Her voice cracked despite her effort. She held a green tomato in one hand and a basket lined with an orange bandana in the other.

Fact one: she was obviously Walt's sister—maybe even his twin.

Fact two: she was picking the veggies, which meant she lived here.

Fact three: she must have been watching him for a while, which meant she was avoiding him.

Fact four: she was sexy as hell.

He ignored fact four. Not at all relevant. In and out. A surgical strike.

He took a deep breath.

"Hi." He held out his hand. "I'm Mick Rivers. Sorry I'm late."

Chapter Four

She stared at him from behind her green-bean veil, struggling to keep a bewildering play of emotions off her face that kept circling back to mad. *Where have you been all these years? Don't you know how to pick up a phone?*

Then—*You're finally here. I can get on with my life. I can learn the truth about what happened to Walt.*

Then—*But what kind of man ignores pleas for contact for an entire year, then shows up out of the blue on a beautiful summer day like it's no big deal? Get rid of him. Quick!*

She stepped out from behind the beans, not sure where to start. A rush of panic welled inside her, like the blinding whiteness of the day those two army guys in full dress uniform had rung her bell.

Everything is about to change.

She felt as if she might faint.

She had to get ahold of herself. She'd known that despite his two-year silence, this day might come.

She managed a choked, "Come inside," accompanied

by an indefinite hand wave that felt as foolish as she was
sure it looked.

She had to sit down somewhere cool.

She moved in a haze toward her house—

Walt's house.

Mick Rivers' house.

Whose house was this? Where would she go if she
gave it to this man?

No, she would *not* give it to him. It was her house now.
First, because he'd missed his chance. Second, because
even if she wanted to hand it over to him, which she
didn't, how would she ever know for sure if he was honest
or if he was another con man who had written the letter
himself? Or worse, how would she know if he had bullied
Walt into writing it on his deathbed?

It hurt just to think about. But she had to think about it.
She couldn't let herself be conned again.

She should get rid of him fast. Except there was something she wanted from him first. What if he knew how
Walt had died? He could be her last link to Walt, to knowing. She'd waited two years for the truth, and now she
didn't want to hear it on such a beautiful day, from such
a beautiful man. Face-to-face with him she realized what
she'd always known but had somehow ignored in order to
keep her heart full of hope: she wanted answers, details,
stories. But this man could lie about everything for his
own gain and she'd never know.

Her mind was numb. *Keep your head.* She floated,
somehow, into the house and down the hall, and she found
herself in her kitchen. She sat down at the kitchen table.
*He came. Years of waiting, and he shows up today like
it's no big deal.*

Her fingers tingled against the cool, smooth wood of the table.

She looked around her.

What was she doing in her kitchen?

Walt's kitchen...

Mick's kitchen...

She tried to fight the icy ball of doubt that was building inside her. *Give the man the house. Walt wanted it that way—*

No. Two years was too long for him to ignore her.

Walt was an impetuous, reckless fool sometimes. He'd left her a mess. He always left a mess behind.

Doesn't matter. This is his last wish.

Unless the letter was a con put on by this beautiful man.

Lemonade. There was something to do as if this visit were normal. She'd serve him lemonade. Pitcher. Glasses. Ice. She went through the motions, determined to remain calm, to ignore the sweat forming on her brow. *Tell me about Walt. I want to know. Don't tell me. I don't want to know.*

Reckless Walt, spontaneous Walt, unpredictable Walt.

Roe, the shy cat, jumped onto the kitchen table. Nina gave him a gentle stroke, but he felt her anxiety and leapt away from her trembling hands to a safer spot just out of her reach.

What was she going to do about this man?

She looked around her.

Where was this man?

She peered out the window to see him right where she'd left him, talking on his cell phone.

While Mick waited for Sandy to pick up his call, he scooped up the basket Nina had dropped in the grass on her dazed trip across the lawn. He put the lone tomato carefully inside.

Now what? He should follow her inside, but too much time in war-torn Islamic countries still made him edgy around an open invitation from a lone woman. Especially a lone distracted, obviously shaken woman. And it was clear that he'd shaken her. Badly.

Nice job, Rivers.

She had left the front door open behind her, and it swung back and forth ominously in the gentle wind.

Sandy finally picked up her phone. "Mick? Are you there? Do you have the house yet?"

He sucked on his cheek. "Can't do it, Sandy," he told his sister. "*She's* here. And, Sandy, this house is just like our old place. I feel like Dad's gonna jump out any minute with a belt and start whaling on me 'cause there's a speck of dust on the couch. I feel like Mom's gonna be upstairs, yelling for us to get ready 'cause he's in the driveway."

"Mick, grow up, would you? Bella is leaving the country tomorrow with Baily for her operation. We need the money. Stop being morbid and get the house."

"Right. I know. I will. I just needed a kick in the butt."

"Consider yourself kicked, Mick. Bella is going to die if we don't get the money. That house is our last hope, baby."

"Well, that sure makes me feel better. Good-bye, sweetness and light," he said.

"Good-bye, Mick. Do it. We're counting on you. Call me tomorrow. And, Mick—"

"What?" He looked to the picture-perfect house.

"Don't you dare fall in love with her."

"What? I won't. Jesus, Sandy."

"You might. So don't. Your duty is to us, Mick. Don't muck it up. You're a soldier. Get in there and fight."

Mick clicked his phone shut and looked up at the open door. He didn't want to go inside, but she'd left him no choice.

Smart woman.

Now he had to enter the heart of her territory.

He knew better than anyone that once you set foot on enemy terrain, you had better start watching where you stepped.

The instant he crossed the threshold, the oppressive perfection of the clean, dusted foyer pressed in on him. He winced as if his kid sisters were there, scrubbing, sweeping, steadily ignoring as best they could the calls of their mother upstairs, mired in bed, in cigarettes, in pills. *Daddy's coming. I hear the car. Why isn't dinner on the table? Mick, hurry!*

He had to get this place, sell it, and get out before it consumed him. Mick moved carefully into the living room, hoping for Walt-like chaos but finding more domestic perfection. He put the discarded basket on the wooden coffee table, then picked it up again.

Water ran in the kitchen, then stopped. Ice clinked. Footsteps down the hall.

"Mr. Rivers." She carried a tray, but her hands were shaking so hard, the ice rattled in the glasses.

"Call me Mick."

"I'm Nina. I'm Walt's sister." She put down the tray and handed him a glass that was as frosty as her tone. "The one who tried to contact you nonstop for over a year."

"Right. Sorry about that. Unavoidable."

She moved around the room carefully, the ice in her glass still clinking, her eyes on him. She set her glass on an artsy cork-and-wood coaster on the coffee table and slid a coaster toward him. Then she sat down on the couch, crossing her legs under her. Her posture was so upright and compact, her movements so economical and spare, he felt absurdly rubbery and enormous as he sank into the chair across from her. A sleek black cat jumped up behind her and settled on the back of the couch. A fluffy orange cat watched from the windowsill.

"So," he began. Then ended. *I'm here to make you homeless and steal a mysterious box from your garage. Thanks for the lemonade.*

"So," she said.

"Right," he responded, unable to begin. Mint leaves nestled in the ice. Pulp floated on the surface. She'd hand-squeezed lemonade, and he'd never felt like a bigger asshole. This was why he'd never come for the house: he knew it was a fool's errand to think he could take a house from Walt's sister without hating himself forever.

She inhaled. "Mr. Rivers, two years ago I got a letter written by a stranger that might have been from Walt or might not. It arrived three weeks after he was killed. It said I should give you his house. I tried to find you. You didn't answer any of my calls, my letters, my texts, my e-mails. You didn't accept a single one of the certified affidavits from my lawyer."

He was relieved that there wouldn't be any small talk. He had to get out of this living room before the walls caved in around him. His nerves were shot. He'd gotten up at six this morning and driven almost straight from Ohio, stopping only for gas and the head. He was dying of thirst, but he felt like an intruder and he wanted to hold on to that feeling so that he wouldn't let down his guard. He had to leave with what he came for—a mysterious box and enough cash from selling the house to get his sister the operation she needed. It didn't matter how beautiful Nina was, how fragile and sad and confused she looked despite her best efforts to appear invincible. "Yeah, well, the letter was for real. Walt gave me the house. I'm sorry for ignoring you for so long, but now I need to have it."

Her eyes flashed annoyance, for which he didn't blame her one bit. "When you didn't answer my letters, I got desperate to understand Walt's request. It was his last wish, you know, and it was a mystery. I don't like mysteries."

"You're not the only one. Believe me."

Her voice rose. "No, Mr. Rivers, I don't believe you. Why should I believe you?"

"You probably shouldn't," he admitted.

She looked ready to spring off the couch and wring his neck. "You ignored me," she went on. "So I tried to find the nurse who transcribed the letter for Walt, so she could tell me what had happened. Maybe he'd said something to her that wasn't in the letter, right? At least she could have told me that Walt had asked her to write the letter without duress. I hoped she could explain to me who you were and why you were ignoring me. I needed someone to help me figure out what was going on, what this was all about, since you felt no need to contact me or to return my contacts with even an e-mail."

The nurse with the gray eyes. The one who had slipped him Walt's letter with the keys and the address folded inside, his sole memory after the blast and before he woke up in a hospital bed in Germany. The image always surfaced accompanied by a slashing pain in his gut. He grasped to remember the nurse's name. Susie? Sally? It was gone, like the rest of his memories. That was reason number six hundred and twelve why he shouldn't have come here. He had to do this and get out as quickly as possible.

"The nurse was killed three weeks after Walt." She paused. "Friendly fire."

Her emphasis on the last two words sparked a flame of protest inside him that ignited his dry, tangled memories. *She's dead too. Poor kid. Poof, another one gone.* He tamped down his thoughts, putting out the fire before it could rage.

Nina's eyes were filled with hatred. He was grateful for her attack. Being adversaries was something he understood. If she'd been meek, he might have fled, consumed with guilt over the fuzzy justice of what he intended to do. But her anger made him bold. "Are you implying that I killed a nurse to get this house? That I'm a murderer?"

"I have no idea what you are, Mr. Rivers."

He fixed her with a cold stare. "This place is nice, but it's not that nice."

"Mr. Rivers—"

"Mick."

"Mick. I intended to honor Walt's last wish. But that was a year ago."

"Yeah, well, I didn't intend to come to ask for the place, but some important things have changed."

"What?"

"I'm not sure that's your business," he told her. He wasn't about to play the sympathy card. He'd rather rob a bank.

"Good, because honestly, I'm not sure I care."

At least they were on the same page there.

"Look, Mick, even if I intended to give you the house, I wouldn't just hand it over unless you could prove that Walt's letter was for real. Can you at least prove that? Not that it matters anymore. But is there anything you can offer me about Walt that will make me believe you're for real?"

During his mad dash across the country, this sticking point, among a million others, had occurred to him. But he figured he'd deal with it, somehow, when he got here. He didn't have any choice. He'd hoped she'd have worked it out by now.

Now here he was, face-to-face with her, and he could see as clear as day that there was no way to prove a thing. Sure, there was the letter in his back pocket, all the proof in the world of something. But it was off-limits if he was going to keep Walt's secret about his mysterious god-damned box. And at the very least, he had to do that.

Duty. Honor. Country.

"So we have a problem," he said.

"You can't prove it," she said. A light in her eye flicked off like a switch.

"Nope. Can't prove a thing."

"Then we're done here," she said.

"Okay. Nice to have met you." It was a bluff, but it worked. She wasn't much of a poker player. He could see the distress in her eyes. She wanted him to stay. So he rose. "It was an honor." He held out a hand.

"Wait!" she cried. Then she took a deep breath. "At least have your lemonade. And while you do, tell me something to make this all make sense. You must have some insight into why Walt offered you the house."

The letter in his back pocket might as well have been pulsing and blinking. *Tell her the truth.* What was the point of keeping a dead man's secret? Especially since Mick didn't have time to mess around. If Bella got on that plane tomorrow, then her initial treatments could start. And from that point, he had three months to get the money he needed to pay for the second installment. Could he even sell a house that fast if he started today? Maybe not, but at least he'd have collateral to borrow off of if he had the promise of the deed.

But he couldn't betray Walt.

"I'm sorry," he said. "I have no idea why Walt wanted me to have this house. Believe me, I wish I knew."

Nina let the shock of that statement settle, hoping her piercing disappointment didn't show on her face. Late at night, so many nights, she had lain in her bed and imagined listening to the tear-inducing story about how Mick Rivers had saved Walt's life, how they'd become bosom buddies, how they'd found the meaning of life from each other in desperate times of adversity, the only suitable payback being the gift of a place to call home.

Instead, she got this near-silent man who had nothing to give her but *nice to have met you...*

She tried to stay steely despite her encroaching dismay. She needed him to not just disappear. He was her last link to Walt, and she was growing angrier and angrier at him and his smug dismissal of their situation. "I've been living in limbo for two years. Can you imagine how that made me feel?" The cats' ears flicked in alarm, unaccustomed to her sharp tone. Roe jumped down and slunk off into the shadows.

He shrugged. "Look, I'm sorry. I'm trying to be straight with you. Believe me, I wouldn't be here if I could help it. I need the money."

Money. Walt's home was nothing to this man.

She stood and began to pace. "This is like waiting for Christmas, being good all year, then getting a stocking full of coal." Tears threatened. *Why this man, Walt?* She hadn't realized until just now how much she had expected from him. *Meaning, warmth, connection, the last link to Walt—*

She turned her back to him and looked out the window. Her beautiful yard, her gardens, her hopes, her dreams. She would never hand this over to an ungrateful stranger who needed cash. Her grief gathered, churned, formed into a cloud of anger. She spun back around. "There is only one person on this earth who knows the truth about Walt's last, deathbed wish. Unfortunately, that person is you, Mr. Rivers. I'm very sorry that you don't give a damn."

"Unless I don't know either," he said, his voice so flat, so empty, it sounded like it came from deep within a terrible dream.

She sank back onto the couch, her anger raining down around her shoulders, forming puddles of grief and hopelessness. What should she do now? Just let him go? "If Walt weren't already gone, I'd kill him," she murmured, more to herself than to him.

Mick tried not to care that he was ripping out this woman's heart with his bare hands and then stomping on it, but it wasn't working.

Luckily, he still had enough of his soldier's sense about him to regroup and replan, no matter how much he hated the mission. Obviously, she didn't intend to give him the house. But she also didn't want him to leave until he gave her some kind of answers about her brother.

So before this went any further, he had to extricate himself from this orderly living room and this bittersweet lemonade and this beautiful, abandoned woman. Then he had to sneak into her garage and get the mystery box. Hopefully, with that intelligence in hand, he could figure out the rest of his plan from there.

He'd been making deals with himself on his marathon drive from California. *If it's drugs in the box, I'll flush them down the toilet but still fight for the house. If it's evidence of a worse crime, one with a specific victim, I'll forget the house and get the hell out of here and not look back…*

He tried not to think about the horrors the box could contain. He couldn't deal with Walt's sister until he knew how devastating Walt's secret was. Once he knew, maybe he'd have something to say to her, some kind of explanation he could share, some way to convince her to hand over the house.

Or maybe he'd discover he'd come on a fool's errand and he could get out—fast.

The important thing was not to waste time. Bella was leaving for Israel tomorrow.

Time for a tactical retreat. "Look, this is a bad situation. You're upset. I'm sorry I ambushed you like this." He stood. "I shouldn't have. I'll give you some air. I'll come back tomorrow."

"That's it? You're leaving?"

"Yep." He put the key to the front door on the coffee table. He considered the tomato basket he'd left on the floor and put it on the table too, in case she went looking for it back outside where she'd dropped it. He understood the panic that followed confused, dazed actions and didn't want to upset her any more than he already had.

"Where'd you get that key?" she asked.

"Walt gave it to me."

"Maybe that's something—" She paused, her voice shaky. "Proof of—" She cleared her throat. "Something."

"Or maybe I stole it from Walt's gear after faking that letter and killing that nurse."

Her face closed in on itself. "Right."

"I'm sorry about your brother. Walt was a good guy. Is a good guy. I wish I understood him. I'll give you some time, some space. I'll come back tomorrow and we'll talk then. Okay?"

He stood up, nodded to the remaining cat, then made for the door.

Chapter Five

She watched him retreat, disbelief filling every atom of her being. The coward! Something wasn't right, but she couldn't put her finger on it. A man didn't ignore a house for two years, finally show up out of the blue in a car with California plates, then back down to *give her space*.

She was tired of space.

She stared at the spot on the chair where he'd been. Space.

Anger at Mick swirled with anger at Walt for planning this gift to this man in such a random, impetuous, Walt-like fashion. Whom did she expect Walt would pick for his house? A prince? A knight in shining armor? A good guy who'd tell her everything and they'd fall in love and live happily ever after?

Oh God. She felt sick to her stomach. That was exactly what she'd been imagining.

She was such a fool. What everyone always said about her was true: she was a naïve fool when it came to life. She should let him go.

Mick was out of the room, into the foyer. Mick, who'd had the nerve to make her wait two years and now wanted her to wait even longer.

She heard the swish of metal against metal as the doorknob turned against the stem, then the grind of metal against wood as the latch slipped from its hole in the doorframe.

She exploded, emitting a sound something like a growl, nothing like any sound she had ever made before in her life.

Somehow, she was beside him, knocking his hand aside. Somehow, she had wedged herself between him and the door. Someone who sounded like her but couldn't possibly have been her growled, "You're not going anywhere, Mick Rivers!"

He let himself be pushed back, his hands up in mock surrender. Or maybe it was shock. She didn't care. This wasn't about him; it was about her. He'd waited too long to be worthy of her consideration. She punched her finger into his chest, backing him to the foyer wall, away from the door. "Two years I've waited for you to get your butt over here, Mick Rivers! Two years I've been paying taxes and repairs and snow removal and everything else that it takes to keep a house from falling down on itself. Do you have any idea what it takes to keep a house from falling down on itself? And not for one minute did I feel as if this house was really mine. Can you imagine how crappy that felt?"

She jabbed his chest to stop his answer, letting her frustration and righteous indignation flow like an unstoppable river. "And then you show up out of the blue and you say you're sorry? Sorry! I'll give you sorry. Why did Walt give you this house? If you don't know, you better at least try to figure it out. Make something up, dammit. Because you aren't leaving here until I know what Walt's last wish was all about, Mr. Rivers. Not that I plan on granting it, mind you. But I still deserve to know."

He tried to protest, but if she stopped now she might tangle into a snarl that could never come undone. "You're all I have left of my brother, Mick. You're the last stinking piece in an unfinished puzzle. You can't walk away like it doesn't matter."

Her body was mere centimeters from his. Heat waves hummed between them. He started to say something a third time, but she held up a warning finger to stop him. She so wasn't done with this man. She wanted to wring him out like a rag. She wanted to grab him and shake him and kiss him—

Kiss him?

No. Not that. Well, maybe that. He had been in her fantasy for so long, she felt she deserved it. But she didn't want to give him the satisfaction. She shoved him away to keep herself from clinging to him. "The nerve of you to treat me like a delicate flower, not worthy of a fight. *Oh, I see you're troubled. Excuse me, ma'am. Didn't want to disturb you. Let me give you space!*" It felt divine to rant after waiting so long to confront this man who had ignored her for two years. She was aware that she was flying off the handle. She was being completely irrational, and she didn't care. She wanted him gone and she wanted him to stay. She wanted to hit him—and also to grab on to him and not let go. "I waited years to find out about Walt's last days. I waited years to get out of this ambiguous living situation that Walt stuck me in. I've been taking care of a house that wasn't fully mine, or maybe is, or who the hell knows?" She threw up her arms, and he took the opportunity to back away.

Oh no. He wasn't getting away that easy.

She grabbed him by the collar of his shirt as if he wasn't towering a good half a foot over her and pulled him close. She raised her face to his. "You owe me, Mick Rivers. So get your stuff out of your flashy car and I'll throw some sheets on the bed in the spare room. You better plan on settling in for a few days. Because you're not going anywhere. Not until you tell me what the hell is going on. I want the truth. And then once you give it to me, I don't want to see your pretty, smug face ever again."

Mick considered the very angry woman blocking his escape route. The heat of her was intense. He had enough sisters to know better than to mess with a woman on fire.

But she wanted him to *talk*.

A chill ran through him from head to toe.

She wanted to put *sheets on a soft, comfy bed* for him.

Another icy blast.

There were no Geneva Conventions against this particular kind of feminine torture. Still, he'd rather be shot in the leg than endure *a few days* of talking (lying, obscuring, whitewashing) with Walt's sister, no matter how good she looked, no matter how badly he needed her house.

She was holding on to his shirt as if he might run if she let go.

And he might.

Except that he was right about her. The truth of their situation was simple. *She wants me here. I'm her last link to Walt. My best weapon is making her think I'm prepared to walk away.*

She'd shown her cards, and he still had his, possibly all aces, close to his chest.

It was time to bluff and bluff hard.

Damn, Walt. Making him use a beautiful, innocent woman. But he had no choice. Bella was sick. He had to exploit every advantage. This was war. War, he understood.

He drew himself to his full height, which next to hers was substantial.

She didn't shrink back an inch.

"You done?" he asked, leaning in.

"Yes," she said, still holding her ground.

Their faces were practically touching.

He considered her a few seconds too long, hoping, but failing, to make her squirm. Carefully and slowly he said, "First, no one bosses me around. No one. So here's what I'm going to do. I'm hungry and I'm tired and I really, really need an ice-cold beer. I have a feeling I'm not going to get one here."

"Nonalcoholic," she threatened.

"You're a cold woman."

"Gluten free," she added cruelly. "With a hint of raspberry."

He groaned. "Which is why I'm leaving to find a dark bar that serves bloody burgers and real brew. Then I'm going to eat and drink until I feel human again. Which might be a good long while. Then I'm going to find a place to spend the night and I'm going to have my first good night's sleep in a week. Then I'm getting myself a little breakfast. Maybe I'll take a walk around this town. Sightsee. Pick up a few souvenirs. A Galton University sweatshirt, maybe."

Her mouth twitched, as if she was ready to slap him across the face. Or, maybe, as if she was ready to kiss him.

He understood her dual impulses because he was fighting them himself. *I don't want to hurt you; I have to hurt you. I want to explain; I can't explain. You're beautiful; you're too dangerous to touch.*

He closed the distance between them another fraction of a centimeter. Her breath was warm on his face. He could practically taste her, and he wanted to, but he wasn't going there. No way was he going there with so much at stake. He had to play this through to the end, to threaten to leave, no matter how lousy it felt to lie. She had to think he was ready to walk away. It was his only advantage until he found the box and could come up with a better plan.

"Then and only then, when I'm good and ready, I'll check back here. If you still want to start this thing, tie that bandana from your tomato basket around the porch rail. I'm going to give you a nice long night to think about this. If I don't see that bandana tied out front when I come back, I'm gonna turn around and you'll never see me again."

He knew she'd tie the bandana to the rail. She was stuck without him and she was tired of being stuck. Knowing all this made him feel so lousy, he almost gave in and told her everything.

Stay on mission, soldier.

"Go back to your tomatoes and your kitties, Nina," he warned.

"I'm not afraid of you," she whispered.

They were so close, he could feel her heart pounding. He could hear the blood rushing hot in her veins. His mouth was dry and his body dying to touch hers. *I'm sorry I have to do this, but I have to.* He put his lips to her ear and whispered all the truth he could spare her.

"If you insist on starting this thing, I won't back down. I'm a soldier. I fight. I don't surrender. So think long and hard before you throw your hat in this ring. Because if I come back and see that you want to fight, I'm taking your house and I'm not giving you a damn thing that you want in return. I don't tell fairy tales."

"Good, because I'm not a child," she hissed.

"No? You sure? Because I've seen your type before. You think you want truth. You think you want answers. But really, you want flowers and butterflies and rainbows and happy garden gnomes." He touched her chin, not meaning to be gentle, not meaning anything, but feeling suddenly gentle toward her despite himself. She didn't pull back, and he didn't take his hand away. "I don't have those things. There is no happy ending to this story, Nina."

"My decision is already made." She still hadn't pulled away from his touch, as if they'd become fused.

They had, because he couldn't pull away either.

Life sucks. War sucks. Losing a brother sucks and getting blown up so bad you can't remember what happened sucks. Having a house or not having a house both sucked when the house reminded you of death and lies and loss and the impossibility of turning back time. Lying sucked for both of them, but that was life, and he was sorry but that was the way of the world. He needed cash—a lot of it, fast—and that was the way of the world too. He was giving her a choice, and that made him feel a little better because it was becoming unbearable to be this close to her without...

He closed the hairbreadth of distance between them and kissed her.

It wasn't a passionate kiss. A touching of lips. But it

was enough. Sadness passed from his lips to hers, from hers to his.

Then he turned his back on her, opened the door, and strode out and down the steps, not allowing himself to look back.

If he'd made her cry, he didn't want to know.

Chapter Six

Nina watched him back his ridiculous car down the long drive, going in reverse as quickly and freely as a sane person would drive forward. He disappeared down the hill. She could hear his tires protest as he spun the car into the street. His motor gunned in the distance, until it faded to nothing.

Birds chirped. The house was silent around her. Sylvie joined her at the window, rubbing against her hand with her head as if she understood.

Maybe it hadn't really happened. Maybe she'd imagined his pale lips and his blue eyes and his close-cropped blond hair. But how could she have imagined the vibrating heat of him? And that kiss—what a kiss. She'd never been so close to a man who made her so furious, so agitated, so conflicted. He was like a cat, furious and hissing, pulling close, but then dashing away—

No, she was grasping at straws. There was nothing to him. She had imagined a good guy would show up, one who understood what a house meant, what this gift meant, what her brother meant. She was desperately trying to make him into a man he wasn't. *He's a man who wants to make a quick buck on Walt's death, and I'm not going to let him.*

She stroked Sylvia, trying to slow her rapidly pounding heart.

When she could breathe normally again, she went to the phone, picked it up, and called the diner. Lizzie picked up on the first ring. "Last Chance diner, pickup or deliver?"

Nina couldn't speak. All the emotion of the last twenty minutes caught in her throat. Walt was gone; he was never coming back; and no one could help her unravel the mystery he'd left behind but an impossible stranger with icy blue eyes who didn't give a damn.

"Nins? I see you on the caller ID. You want the usual? Turkey club on wheat, no mayo, no turkey, no bacon?"

"I. Oh hell." The dilemma crystallized. How did you know if someone was telling the truth if there was no proof? It wasn't even he said/she said. It was he said/she listened. No—even worse than that. It was she asked/he refused to answer.

Lizzie's voice softened. "You okay, hon? Did something happen?"

"Mick Rivers." Nina barely managed to get the words out.

"Oh. My. God. Did he finally call?"

"Just left."

Lizzie inhaled sharply, letting out a little gasp. "Left? He's in town! Did he come for your house?"

"No. Yes. I don't know. It was very confusing."

Lizzie inhaled again. "Hold on. Don't move. I'm getting the Enemy Club together. Emergency meeting. Shit, I'm not off for three hours, and Judy and Emily both called in sick so I can't leave Ally here alone. Can you wait? Seven o'clock. Can you hold on till then?"

Nina nodded. "No. Don't come. I'm okay. I just wanted—"

"Shut up. We're coming whether you like it or not. I'll call everyone. Maybe Jill can get over there now. Whatever you do, don't do anything until we get there! Don't you dare give him that house!"

That shouldn't be a problem. Because Nina finally understood the truth. For two years, she thought she'd been waiting for Mick Rivers to show up to try to claim what might be his. But that wasn't the situation at all. She was the one waiting desperately for him to come so she could claim what she wanted more than anything in the world: the truth about her brother's last days.

Officer Tommy Wynn stood on the sidewalk, looking up at the white wall on the side of Garcia's Pharmacy. The first rays of the sunset cast a soft red glow over the paint, and on any other day the play of the light on the wall would have looked like something out of a Norman Rockwell painting. But not today. Today the serenity was interrupted by the revolving red and blue lights of his squad car and by the scrawl of letters and two ugly black swastikas. The spray paint had dried, but not before it dripped grotesquely, adding to the frightening, gothic effect of what was written on the wall.

If fear was what the graffiti artist was after, the job was well-done. These graffiti guys might be petty criminals, but they weren't half-bad artists.

Mr. Garcia stood behind Tommy, shaking his head.

They'd discovered the graffiti first thing in the morning, but Mr. Garcia had been waiting all day for his son, Johnny, to get back from wherever he'd been so he could paint over the wall. Johnny was kneeling behind his father, stirring the white paint. Again.

Mr. Garcia kept up his ranting. "Do they think we're Nazis? They didn't even spell that right. *Natzis!* And anyway, we're third-generation Mexican Americans, for Lord's sake! I've never even been to Europe except when I was a little kid and my dad took me to France to show me where he fought *against* the goddamn Nazis!"

Tommy liked Mr. Garcia. He liked his huge concho-style pewter and turquoise belt buckles. He liked the red lizard-skin cowboy boots that he was never seen without. Tommy had been on the Galton police force for more years than he liked to remember, and he knew all the merchants by first name, knew their kids, and in the case of Mr. Garcia, even knew his two grandkids by his eldest daughter, Jessie. "I don't think it was directed at you or your store, Mr. Garcia. I think it was just kids. I don't think a swastika means a thing to them." He thought of Noah Cohen, his partner, who had come this morning to take pictures for the police report. Noah was a man who knew what a swastika meant. But did it mean anything if it was made by bored kids trying to get a rise out of the town? Didn't matter. This would be a big deal by tomorrow morning, all over the front page of the *Galton Daily*.

Mr. Garcia shook his head with the soul-splitting sadness only a man over sixty can muster as he watched his son lug the white paint to the wall. "I tell you. Tommy, if you could talk to Nina. She needs to get this memorial mural going. The white wall is just too much for the young ones. It's like a giant space shouting, *Come and desecrate me*. Last month it was all that fraternity nonsense. And before that, the animal rights people. It's like a white wall is too much to resist."

Tommy agreed, but he knew there wasn't much he could do. Nina did things her way and in her time. He'd known her since they were kids. She was three years younger than him, but his sister-in-law Lizzie and Nina were practically best friends. Maybe Lizzie could talk to her. He made a mental note to talk to her as soon as he got off duty.

"I'm thinking of hiring someone else to do the memorial," Mr. Garcia said. "Maybe an art student from the college. I can't keep having Johnny repainting this wall. And I want Matthew's memorial up before Johnny joins up." Matthew was Johnny's older brother, the one who'd died in Afghanistan.

Johnny paused midstroke. "I don't mind repainting it, Dad. But—"

Mr. Garcia cut him off. "Sure you do. You got better things to do than mess around here."

Tommy said, "We'll find out who did this. Meanwhile, I'll talk to Nina. She'd be heartbroken if you take her off the job. I know it means a lot to her."

"Well, then why doesn't she do it?" Mr. Garcia asked. But then he recanted quickly. He held up his hands in surrender. "I know, I know. She's had a hard life with being all alone up on that hill in Walt's house, losing her brother."

"He was her only family left."

Mr. Garcia sighed. "And she's an artist and they're just, you know—temperamental. Heads-in-the-clouds types."

His voice was filled with scorn. "Gotta tell you, I'm glad my kids aren't like that, but then, they've had a solid family to make sure they keep their feet on the ground." He looked to Johnny, who didn't look back, although it was obvious he was listening. "But we've been waiting a whole year. No one bothered the wall when it was just redbrick. I can't unpaint the white."

"I'll talk to her. Give me a few days, okay?"

"Okay. For you, Tommy. But then I'm going to talk to Nina myself. And if she's not going to be able to do this, I have to find someone else." His cell phone chimed. He looked at it and sighed again. "It's Maria. She's texting that supper's getting cold. Not that I have an appetite." His shoulders slumped. "Hurry up, Johnny. It's just a wall, for God's sake. You don't have to make it into the Sistine Chapel. Just slap on the paint and let's get out of here."

Chapter Seven

The doorbell rang for the third time in twenty minutes. Jill, the final member of the Enemy Club, had finally arrived.

"Sorry I'm late. Had to make a few calls to rearrange things." Jill crashed through the foyer, a force to be reckoned with. She wore her powder-pink real estate agent power suit. Her blond ponytail, pulled so tight it looked like it hurt, bounced behind her like a small dog. She texted as she followed Nina down the hall. "Tell me everything," Jill commanded. "Start with his butt."

Nina led her down the hall and into the kitchen, where the rest of the Enemy Club was already rummaging through the cabinets, gathering supplies. "I will not. His butt isn't important. Will you put that thing away?"

Jill lowered her phone and raised her eyebrows, as if the two were connected with an invisible pulley system. "His butt is supremely important. I need a mental picture of the man so I can correctly advise you."

"Okay, just to satisfy you, he's a very trim, fit man," Nina said, plopping down into a kitchen chair. "But there are more important things at stake here."

Jill rolled her eyes, as if mention of anything other than body parts was ridiculous.

Lizzie snatched Jill's iPhone, turned it off, and stuffed it into her black Prada purse. "Nina's right. This is serious. So no electronics and no speaking of the man's assets."

"Amen," Georgia said from deep in a lower cabinet. Georgia was dressed for work, which meant despite the summer heat, she was in a knee-length skirt, man's-style jacket, too-fussy blouse, and tan hose. She abandoned the cabinet she had burrowed in and climbed onto a chair to reach the upper cabinets, her heels falling out of her size-six black pumps. She pushed cans and bottles around impatiently. It was no use—she was too short to get at the top shelf. She kicked off her shoes and climbed onto the counter. She pushed aside the buckwheat flour. "Aha!" She pulled out a bag of M&M'S she had stashed there after their last meeting at Nina's months ago.

Nina sat limply in the center of the kitchen, her arms at her sides. She loved these women, their ease in her house, in her life, and with each other. They had been through so much together, they all could say and do and wear exactly what they felt like. That was what it meant to be a member of the Enemy Club. They had been the four biggest enemies at Galton High back in the day. Now they were all grown up and the best of friends.

But friends with a difference.

They promised to tell each other the truth, the whole truth, and nothing but the truth as only natural-born enemies can, so help them Gracie (the woman who baked the pies at the Last Chance diner, where they met every Wednesday morning). These women and Nina had nothing in common except for a shared past spent despising each other and the shared triumph of forgiving each other years later and finding friendship in the most unlikely of places—each other. Nina knew that no matter how crazy her feelings were about the man who'd just turned her world upside down, they'd each come up with an interpretation of her situation that was unique and unexpected. She could say anything, and they'd run with it in the oddest, most fascinating directions. It had gotten to the point that she'd almost forgotten what it was like to be friends with women who shared her outlook on life.

They were priceless and she adored them all and was counting on them to help her sort out her conflicted feelings about Mick Rivers.

"Wait till we get settled so we can discuss this with a glass of wine in our hands," Lizzie counseled, her hand on Nina's arm. She was the only mother in the group and tended to be the first one to notice when a person was about to crumble.

"Great. Until then, just one more detail about his looks. Pretty please," Jill pleaded. Nina loved Jill, but she was definitely the last one to notice other people's distress.

And yet. "You can't believe this guy's teeth," Nina told them, unable to stop herself. "They were practically glowing."

"You know what Freud says about teeth." Georgia jumped down off the counter, holding tight to her M&M'S. Nina would have tossed them out if she'd known they were there contaminating her all-natural kitchen with processed sugar and artificial colors.

"Of course we don't know what Freud said about teeth," Nina reminded her gently. Georgia didn't mean to be pretentious, but being brilliant made it hard to avoid.

"Death, ladies. Teeth represent death. The only visible part of our skeleton. The rawest part of our anatomy. Loving a man for his teeth is like loving death. Your lusting for this man, Nina, is an act of pure self-destruction."

"I am not lusting for this man," Nina reminded them all, including herself. "Yes, he is a lust-worthy man. But I will not give in to the urge."

"Why not?" Jill asked.

"Because he wants to make her homeless, dummy," Lizzie said.

"Exactly," Nina said. *An act of pure self-destruction.* She tried to hold her resolve, but she had to admit that their shared kiss had been intense. But not lusty. It had been almost the opposite of lust. What was the opposite of lust?

Love?

No, that wasn't right. Not for a man she'd just met who was so maddeningly disappointing in every way.

"Which is weirder—thinking teeth are sexy or thinking that thinking they're sexy is a sign of a death wish?" Lizzie asked. "And where is your corkscrew?"

"Do I own one?" Nina asked. "I don't think I do."

"Yes. I bought it for you last Christmas." Lizzie rummaged through another drawer.

"You're both nuts," Jill said. She had pulled out everything half decent she could find in the fridge. Lizzie eyed her platter with a raised eyebrow, and Jill said, "What? I drank a diet shake for breakfast ten hours ago and I've been running around showing houses to an Ottoman history professor ever since. I'm famished. Even for this mouse food." She arranged carrot sticks, hummus, and whole wheat crackers on a tray. "And even though you misguided women are too dense to ask—yes, my client was gorgeous and single, and he had a very, very nice ass and excellent teeth. Teeth *to die for.*"

Lizzie finally found the corkscrew tucked behind the juicer in the bottom drawer. She grabbed four glasses and the wine she'd brought and led the crowd into the living room. Nina was the last one in.

They all assembled around the fireplace. Nina positioned herself so that she had a clear view of the front door. The basket with the orange bandana and the tomato was on the coffee table between them. Sylvie and Roe arranged themselves just inside the doorway to the hall, as if standing guard.

"Okay, let's get the rest of the incidentals out of the way before we get started. Nice butt. Good teeth. Hair?" Jill asked.

Nina tried to hold her patience. "Blond. Blond like a little boy—white, almost. Cut short, buzzed, soldier style. But it's so blond, you can still see the glow."

"Oh God, I love that," Jill enthused.

"He's still a soldier?" Georgia asked, concern in her tone.

"I don't know. He wasn't in uniform," Nina said. Then she took a deep breath and added resolutely, "And his eyes are Caribbean Sea blue. Now, can we please move on?"

They all observed a moment of silence for the dangerous circumstances represented by Caribbean blue eyes, glowing hair, perfect teeth, and soldiers.

"Tell us exactly what he said, word for word," Georgia said.

Nina did. She left out the kiss, as it hadn't been exactly words, even if it had felt that way.

Georgia passed Nina the M&M'S. "He put the ball in your court. Total con man. Call the cops." Georgia almost always opted for mistrust and the authorities.

Lizzie said, "Tie the bandana on the rail, grab all your valuables, then come and stay at my place till he realizes that Galton, New York, is the most boring place on earth. A guy like him in a car like that will be gone in a week. You'll have met your obligation to do right by Walt, and he'll be history. Problem solved." Lizzie's solutions often involved her mothering someone to death while hoping for the best.

"I could move in with the two of you," Jill suggested. "Neutralize the threat."

"You mean screw the threat," Georgia said.

Jill's solutions almost always involved new lingerie.

"I'm selfless," Jill said. "C'mon. When was the last time a decent man showed up in this town?"

"Tay Giovanni," Lizzie said, naming her husband.

Nina took a single M&M from the bowl and dropped it into her mouth.

They all exchanged worried glances. Nina didn't eat candy casually. She hadn't had that much sugar since high school.

"Look," Georgia counseled, getting serious. "You promised yourself and you promised us that you won't give away your house. You have no idea what Walt really wanted. Maybe this guy pressured him. Or maybe it all happened after Walt was already, you know—" She stopped. "Maybe it's a scam is what I mean. So tell this guy to split and never come back."

They'd been over and over this a million times since Nina had gotten the letter. Nina said, "I want him to tell me what he knows about Walt. I hadn't expected to want that so badly."

Lizzie said, "Walt made a lot of rash, stupid decisions in his day." She put her hand on Nina's. "Don't put the house in danger. You need it."

They all considered Nina's precarious financial situation in silence.

Okay, so dealing with money wasn't her strong suit, which was why she'd moved into the house even when Walt was still in the army. When Walt had died, she'd come into a lot of insurance money, plus more from the army—a death benefit, his pension—all sorts of things that should have kept her going. But she'd lost it all in the stupidest scam anyone had ever fallen for. She didn't want to think about that now, though. The only thing that was important now was that she wasn't falling for another con man.

Now money came in when she needed it. She'd had one hundred and six dollars in the bank when her book illustration job came in. She'd always had luck like that— something in the nick of time to keep her going. She liked to think it was good karma. But maybe it was just dumb luck. She tried to care more about savings, retirement plans, annuities—whatever the heck annuities were. But mostly, she obsessed over finding the perfect tomato, the just-right ocher, getting her copperplate nibs from Germany on time. The job in front of her at the moment took away all thought of the past and future.

They all stared at her, waiting. Nina said, "Asking him to stay a few days to talk isn't the same as giving him the house."

"You're too nice, Nina. You'll break down and give it to him," Lizzie said.

"And you can't do that. You need the house," Georgia added.

"I'm not keeping the house because I need it. I'm keeping it because it's the right thing to do," Nina reminded them.

"Right," Jill said.

"Right," Nina emphasized. "I could totally live fine without the house."

No one spoke.

"I could."

Silence. They knew as well as she did that the scams had ruined her credit ratings, even put her into debt for a while.

"I might even have a big job coming in," she said, defending herself. "I'm meeting with a guy tomorrow. His name is Bob," she added, hoping to make it sound impressive. It didn't. She really should have gotten Bob's last name.

Lizzie looked at the rug. Jill inspected her perfect manicure. Georgia coughed and said, "How's the memorial project coming?"

"That's a low blow," Nina said. They all knew that the memorial project had been eating her time and energy for the past year. It was a huge part of the reason that her finances were so dire. Georgia bringing it up was her way of saying, *See, you can't be counted on to be practical, so for God's sake, don't break down and give away your house.* True, Nina had turned down some plum jobs—anathema for a freelancer—because she'd been so obsessed with finishing the mural.

But she couldn't finish it. Heck, she couldn't even get

started on it. She was still in the preliminary planning stages. Sketching, crossing out, resketching. Every study she did was a disaster. She just couldn't get a handle on how she wanted it to be.

Lizzie said gently, "Honey why not let him go? Why tempt fate by asking him to stay?"

Nina picked up the bandana. "You guys will never believe in me, will you? You still think I'm the artsy flake from high school. Well, I am going to stay in my house because it's mine and I'm going to invite him to stay for a while because I want to hear about Walt's last days in Afghanistan. I certainly can resist falling in love with him and giving him my house while I do that. I'm not that big a sucker."

They looked doubtful.

Nina wanted to throttle them.

Lizzie said, "This house changed your life. You've finally been able to give up teaching yoga."

Nina loved yoga, but she hated the stress of teaching it in a town where yoga studios lined the streets like weeds.

"You've been able to quit that bagel shop chalkboard menu gig you despised. You've worked hard to get to this place, Nins. Why risk it? Let him go," Georgia said.

Jill joined in. "Can you give up the mural? For some jerk who wants to make a quick buck because Walt got softhearted during the most vulnerable time of his life? Walt was spontaneous, which was great, but it was also, you know, a problem of his sometimes. And it's sort of a problem of yours."

"I think Mick's hiding something that concerns Walt," Nina said.

"Why do you think that?" Lizzie asked.

"A feeling," Nina admitted.

Georgia rolled her eyes. "He's a scam artist, all right."

"If I let Mick leave, then I'm right back where I started. Wondering. For the rest of my life. I can do this, ladies. Without getting soft."

"Maybe he has a good reason not to talk," Georgia said.

"You think I'm too soft to hear what he has to say," Nina said, on her last nerve.

"There's nothing wrong with soft," Georgia said.

Nina was done here. Sure, she was an optimist. But that didn't mean she was a fool. Not anymore. "He's staying, he's talking, and I'm not giving away the house."

Chapter Eight

The Enemy Club continued to argue, but their lack of faith in her made her even more adamant. Nina had made up her mind.

She grabbed the bandana and went out to the front porch. She looked out over the lawn she'd so carefully tended for the years Walt had been overseas, then the years after his death. She ran her hand over the railing she'd scraped and painted, then repainted two more times until the green she'd chosen was the exact perfect shade in the morning *and* evening light.

She'd done it all for Walt, and then he'd gone and gotten killed, and now it was all hers. Or not. Who knew what the right thing to do was?

"You're impossible, Walter Stokes," she said to the evening sky. "Why this messenger? Why this man? What should I do? Do you owe this stranger? Do I?"

But there were no answers. Just the silent night, the endless stars in the evening sky.

She tied the bandana to the rail and went back inside.

After they had drained the last bottle of wine, Nina said good-bye to her friends, refused their offers to stay over, went back inside, turned out the lights, and lay in bed.

But she couldn't sleep.

She tossed and turned.

Roe sat at the end of the bed, curled against her feet. But where was Sylvie? Sylvie was never late for bedtime.

Nina got out of bed and searched the house, calling for her. Had she slipped out when everyone was leaving? Or worse—

She opened the back door and went out onto the deck. "Sylvie! Where's my baby?" she called into the black night.

She heard a noise in the garage.

Oh no. Had she somehow left the door to the garage open? It wasn't a typical garage. It was a two-story barn left over from the days when her house was a farmhouse set in the center of acres of cropland, before the area had been built up into a typical rural-suburban community, ten houses now on the land where her one had once stood. The barn had space for a car when the snows came, and room for a summer studio when the car could stay outside.

It also had a huge attic loft. When Sylvie got in, the lure of mice and other loft creatures was too much for her. She scrambled up the vertical ladder like it was a tree trunk. But then she became too frightened to get back down. She got herself treed, as it were, sometimes for days.

Nina sighed. She went back in for her slippers and to change into a pair of jeans so that she could go into the dark night to rescue her dopey kitty.

Chapter Nine

$\mathcal{M}$ick stubbed his toe on a rusted shovel and stifled a curse. He'd snuck back to get the box to get at least half of his mission accomplished. But the garage wasn't what he expected. He'd been prepared to pick the flimsy lock, but of course it wasn't locked, so he'd slipped inside. But instead of the mess of a man's workshop, everything was pristine.

Nina had converted the barnlike garage into an art studio.

There was no rusted red metal box in this place; he knew it before he looked. But he went straight for the shelf that the cursed thing was supposed to be on anyway. Art supplies in neatly labeled plastic containers lined the shelves—oils, thinners, paints.

But no red metal box.

Canvases were stacked against the walls. One huge canvas was propped in the center. It must have been six feet tall. He risked flashing his light on it, and he bit the inside of his cheek in consternation. Had Nina painted this?

It was a patriotic picture, the background all reds, whites, and blues. Walt was in the center of it, looking a little like Superman, a little like his true, slightly goofy self. It wasn't the most effective mix. The Walt in the picture held his gun like it was a newborn baby, not at all the way a soldier would hold a real gun. He had seen this exact same picture a million times in a million different places—the superman soldier with the square jaw and serious eyes. It was the kind of war memorial a person might paint if everything she knew about war she'd read in a children's book.

Mick cringed.

It was just...off.

He couldn't believe that Nina had painted such a ridiculous thing. He couldn't believe that she of all people didn't understand that Walt was a lot of things but—

...*She of all people?*

Why did he expect anything more from her? What did she know about war? About Walt? What did he know about her? But he did expect more from her. Something about their kiss had convinced him that they had a connection—an impossible connection, sure, but still. He thought she had an understanding of how deep the pain could be, how scarring the violence. He thought she knew that her brother was not this grim-faced caricature of a hero, but a slightly goofy kid who'd died doing the best he could in an impossible situation.

He felt her presence an instant before he heard her footsteps.

Every cell of his body cried out for a place to hide, but

he had strolled to the middle of the barn and now he was trapped in the open, a sitting duck, as if years of being shot at by strangers hadn't taught him a thing.

"Sylvie? Did you get yourself stuck in here?" Nina called softly, pushing through the door.

He darted behind the Super-Walt canvas. Luckily, Nina was green at entering and securing a building. She barely looked around. She went straight toward the back wall. "Sylvia! Here, kitty!"

Kitty?

Now he just had to hope she found the blasted furball before she found him.

"Here, Sylvie! Sylvie-girl!" Nina flicked on the overhead fluorescent lights and tried not to shudder as she heard the rustle of mice and other nighttime creatures she didn't want to contemplate darting into hiding. She was diligent about keeping the door latched tight, but it had been ajar. Strange. Maybe the wind. She really ought to lock it, but it seemed like too much trouble. In any case, the open door meant that Sylvie could easily have pushed inside.

No matter how many times the cat climbed the ninety-degree vertical ladder into the loft and got herself stuck, she never learned. The first time, she'd been stuck up there for five nights before Nina had figured out where she'd gone. She'd never forget the flood of relief and frustration she had felt looking up and seeing those two glowing eyes staring down at her.

Goofball cat didn't even think to make a noise.

Now whenever Sylvie disappeared, Nina always checked the barn first. "C'mere, girl. You up there?" She peered into the semidark of the loft. No matter how bright the fluorescents, they barely managed to penetrate the darkness of the loft above them.

She glanced at the last canvas she'd tried for the mural and looked away as quickly as she could. Mr. Garcia had been patient, but she didn't know how much longer he'd wait. She wanted the war memorial mural to be special, important, and meaningful. But it wasn't working out that way. In fact, it wasn't working out at all.

But she didn't have time to worry about that now.

She grabbed the flashlight off the hook by the light switch and went toward the ladder. She'd been meaning to do something about it for ages. Each rung was set directly into the wall, so it was completely upright, with no slope to help fight gravity. The cat could climb up in a wink, as if it were a tree, but she wouldn't dare the trip back down.

It wasn't an easy climb for Nina either. With the flashlight in one hand, she struggled for a grip with the other. When she got to the lip of the loft, she shone her flashlight around as best she could. "Sylvie, mush-for-brains. C'mere, honey." The cat always freaked herself out and went into invisible-cat mode when she had trapped herself.

Nina balanced the flashlight on the loft floor, hung on with one hand, and fished a cat treat out of her jeans pocket. "C'mere, dummy!" Her hand where she was holding on to the top rung was starting to ache.

Two glowing eyes appeared, just out of reach. "Sylvie-girl. There you are." This was the tricky part. Even though the cat was stuck, she still didn't like to be grabbed and wrangled down the ladder.

Sylvie crept a whisker closer.

Nina tried to be patient, but her grip was really starting to tire. She should leave the cat up here. She'd be

fine for the night. Nina could come back in the morning
when there was more light in the loft and she wasn't so
exhausted and maybe also just a wee bit tipsy from the
wine. Plus, it was starting to feel a little dangerous, out
here alone at night. But she'd never sleep knowing that
Sylvie was stuck, and it had been such a crappy day, she
wanted the security of the cat on the bottom of her bed,
purring softly.

Sylvie crept another inch forward.

This was Nina's chance. She held the treat out a little
farther. The cat's nose was an inch away as she cautiously
sniffed the offering. One more step, and Nina would drop
the treat, grab the cat, and wrestle her down the ladder.

She held her breath. "C'mon, kitty. Good kitty—"

She shot her hand forward and caught the scruff of
Sylvie's neck. "Aha!"

Sylvie wrenched her body to the right, and Nina lost
her grip. She managed to get a grip on one forepaw,
which was awful, as the cat-paw tug-of-war felt as if she
was going to rip out the small creature's whole leg. "Sylvia! Stop it!" She dragged the protesting, screaming cat
toward the opening, dreading the feel of the tiny paw
stretching to its limit. She had to get a better grip. She
released the leg and went for the scruff, but Sylvie took
her opportunity to swipe at Nina's arm. "Ow!"

The claws went deep and Nina jolted backward. She
lost her grip on the ladder, desperately grappled for traction. But it was no use. She fell backward toward the hard
dirt of the barn floor, bracing herself for impact.

Chapter Ten

Mick had been watching Nina from his spot behind the painting with rapidly growing anticipation. What was she doing climbing a dangerous, downright stupid ladder in the middle of the night by herself? She was just like Walt—reckless.

Mick had been creeping out of his hiding place step-by-step, dreading the worst. When she fell, he was under her, trying to catch her. But he was a split second too late, and she hit his shoulder at a bad angle.

"Shit!" she cried.

"Dammit!" he said.

"Ouch!"

"Meow," softly, plaintively from above.

He was on the floor, Nina on top of him, screaming her head off. A sharp, shooting pain from his shoulder radiated down his back and into his leg, and like an idiot he thought, *This is nice.* It had been that long since he'd touched a woman.

"Relax. It's me. Mick."

Her breasts were pushing into him, her legs and arms tangling with his, her yelling shattering his eardrums.

"Nina! It's me!" He tried to still her arms, but she pulled them away in desperation.

"What? Who? Mick?" She had finally gotten her limbs separated from his, and she scooched away from him on all fours, scurrying butt-down like a crab.

She stared at him, breathing hard. "Mick?"

"Hi." He tried to move his shoulder, but the pain was bad. Or maybe that was the pain of her pulling away, which was a whole other kind of pain, deeper, more permanent. Nothing like fleeting human contact to remind a guy how supremely alone he was. He wanted to touch her again, pull her to him, and ask what was up with her Super-Walt canvas, with her coming out in the dark to wrestle a cat. Hell, he badly wanted her body against his again, but this time, without the screaming. "You okay?" he asked.

She had scrambled to her feet and was still backing away from him, her eyes moving in disbelief from him on the ground to the cat still in the loft. "What are you doing here?" She wiped sawdust from the floor off her arms and legs.

"Apparently, catching you." He pulled himself gingerly to a sitting position. He tried the shoulder carefully.

Sylvie had come to the lip of the loft and was happily chomping on her treat.

"I'm a black belt, so don't try anything stupid," she said. She was still a little out of breath.

"Stupid like climbing the world's worst-designed ladder with one hand while attacking a dangerous beast with the other? Who embeds a ladder in the side of a wall? That's against the rules of gravity."

"Sylvie isn't dangerous," she said.

"Who said I was talking about the cat?" he asked. He stood slowly, so as not to frighten her again, and moved his shoulder carefully. It wasn't broken or dislocated, but he'd pulled something. Probably a tendon or two. Nothing a little aspirin couldn't handle. He said, "Anyway, you're not a black belt. If you were, you would have fallen better, then ruined my spleen with a back-kick. What were you doing to that poor animal?"

"The cat gets stuck. Something about that loft just tempts her, and then she can't get down. It's like she trees herself and—" She stopped midexplanation. "More to the point, what were *you* doing here?" she asked.

He shrugged. "I thought I heard something in here, and it seemed odd since it was so late, so I came to investigate," he lied.

Sylvie looked down at them, her glowing eyes disappearing every time she blinked.

"I thought you were coming back tomorrow morning," she said.

"Couldn't find a hotel," he lied.

"Oh right. Of course. I should have told you. It's reunion weekend."

"How about that," he said. *Lucky me.*

"Is your shoulder okay?" Nina asked.

"It's fine," he lied again. He wondered if all this lying was going to start getting easier anytime soon.

"I need to get her down." She started up the ladder again.

"Okay. No problem. Go for it. I still have one good shoulder."

She shot him an annoyed look and kept climbing. She

got to the top and coaxed the cat some more. He watched, fascinated, as the cat crouched just out of reach.

After much too long, she gave up and came back down. "Shoot. She's too cautious now. She doesn't trust me."

"That makes two of us."

She looked so disappointed about her cat, he couldn't help himself. He really shouldn't. It was none of his business. He was here for a box, not a cat. Mission creep. Always led to failure.

Although it wouldn't hurt to have a peek into the loft. Could the box be up there? It was so dark, he was pretty sure he couldn't see a thing anyway. Stupid idea.

Nina worried her hands, and the look of desperation on her face made him temporarily insane. He hoisted himself up the ladder, every wrung he climbed setting off a new fire in his shoulder. Least he could do before he made her homeless was save her cat.

"Mick—no! She hates to be—"

He lunged at the cat with his bad hand before she knew what hit her. He tucked the howling, clawing beast under his arm, lowered himself as much as he could, then dropped her. Naturally, being possessed by the devil, the animal didn't fall. Instead, she embedded her claws firmly into his thigh, where she hung, struggling for traction, still howling.

"Sylvia!" Nina cried.

"*Sylvia?*" Mick had to restrain himself from smacking the animal clear across the barn. The cat must have weighed twenty pounds. He got her by the scruff of the neck, his shoulder sending silver hot slivers of pain through his body, paling the pain of the claw holes, which were beginning to seep blood into his jeans. Sylvie released her claws, and he dropped her before she managed to get her claws into any other part of him.

"Sylvie!" Nina cried again as the cat fell, lightly, on all fours the way cats do. She shook herself a bit, then walked away, her nose in the air.

He awkwardly, painfully made his way down the crazy ladder. He couldn't help wishing Nina would direct a drop of her concern his way, even if he had more or less been burgling her barn. "They always land on their feet," he said, landing on his own two feet with an ungraceful thud that jolted his arm with new lightning bolts of pain.

Sylvia, completely recovered from her ordeal, was licking her paws a few yards away as if nothing at all had happened. When she noticed them looking at her, she raised her head proudly and slunk out through the open door.

Nina was still looking at him like he was a ghost, or possibly a rapist, definitely an animal abuser. He searched for something to say. "A soft landing is more than I can say for you. That was one spectacular plunge you took. Are you really okay?" he asked. "I'm not the softest landing pad."

"I'm fine. Thank you," she said, closing the door behind the cat. "Sylvie has been known to dart right back up the ladder after a rescue," she explained. "I don't know why."

"Because you give her treats?"

Nina turned red. She opened her mouth, closed it, tried again. "I'm lucky you showed up, Mick. Thank you. I don't want to think about what might have happened if—"

"No problem." He cut her off. He didn't want to be thanked for breaking into her barn, most likely letting in the cat as he did it, creeping around, failing at finding the box, hating her artwork, and then injuring himself after possibly almost killing her. "What is this place, anyway?"

"My art studio. It used to be Walt's workshop. But I needed a place to work on bigger projects, so I moved his stuff out and moved myself in."

Mick had his back to her, so he let himself wince. If she'd moved Walt's stuff out, the box could be anywhere. Or nowhere: gone. Maybe he was too late. Maybe she'd tossed it. Or maybe she'd already hired a locksmith and opened it. He strolled back to the right-hand corner as nonchalantly as possible and peered behind the plastic bins. He opened one that was filled with paints and brushes and every kind of art tool. He'd have to come back later to check if Walt's box was lurking there, behind all the art supplies. But the place was so neat, he doubted he'd find anything.

She was squinting at her ridiculous painting.

"It's not that bad," he said, responding to the pained look on her face.

"It's awful," she said. "Clichéd and silly. Admit it— you've seen it a million times before. Plus, it looks absurd. Walt just wasn't . . . I mean, I wanted it to be him but bigger than him, and then it turned into—this."

He'd lied enough in the past ten minutes. "Okay, true. But still, it's well-done."

She shot him a withering look. "Who wants to look at a war memorial and think, 'Still, it's well-done'? I want people to cry. To feel pain. I want them to look at my memorial to the soldiers of Galton and *feel* something. Something real."

"So this is a memorial?" He was confused.

"It's a study for the side of Garcia's Pharmacy. The actual wall's two stories high."

He pawed through a few more, smaller canvases. They were more of the same—Walt alone, Walt with another boy who looked like Robin to his Batman. They ought to both be in tights with capes the way they were standing, chests puffed. "I know this isn't my place to say, but you don't seem so inspired."

She crossed her arms. "My brother died. Of course I'm inspired!"

He shrugged, then thought better of it as pain shot through his shoulder.

"Oh geez. We ought to get that thing looked at. I can drive you to the emergency room." She crossed to him and put her hand on his shoulder. She felt along his clavicle. "The bone's not broken. That's good." She prodded his shoulder tenderly. She was so close, it was all he could do to not sniff her. Too late. She smelled like cat treats, M&M'S, and wine—a strangely sexy combination.

"You a doctor?" he asked.

"No. Part-time yoga instructor. But I deal with a lot of injury in my students. Anatomy is part of the study."

He said, "Just a pull. I've had worse."

"Shhh." She touched some more. He tried not to notice how good it felt to be close to her. Her touch was gentle, precise. "Right here," she said.

He tried not to bellow at the top of his lungs. "Yes," he said with a grunt. "There."

She smiled. "Tough guy, huh?"

"It's not so bad. Just needs some time," he managed to get out as the pain went from fire to ember to ice.

She released his shoulder and started to walk away, toward the barn door. "I know some yoga postures that'll help you with that."

He didn't follow.

She stopped and turned back to him. "Well, come on," she said. "It's late."

"I don't think I can manage any yoga—"

"Bed," she said, and his mind exploded with all the possibilities, even if he knew she hadn't meant it that way and he knew that his shoulder couldn't take the stress of a single one of his imaginings. He blew out an even breath. If there wasn't a box in the barn, the house was the next most logical place it might be. But being near her felt even more dangerous, now that they'd had this contact. He was attracted to her in a way that felt urgent and important, a way he wasn't sure he could resist even if he wanted to. He wanted to help her.

They left the barn, him following a step behind.

"I wonder how Sylvie got into the barn," she said, not so much to him as to herself.

The cat slipped in with me and I almost killed you. What if she'd noticed the cat was gone half an hour later, and he had been long gone? Every action caused unexpected reactions that were out of his control. No matter how hard he tried to go through life without touching booby traps, they were everywhere.

They got to the house, cozy and perfect in the moonlight. *The house he wanted to take away from her.*

The orange bandana was tied to the rail.

Now what, cowboy? He steeled himself for the ordeal of going into the house. His tent was in the trunk of his car, but the idea of sleeping on the hard ground with his shoulder pounding was too much. Plus, he had to get inside to charge his phone if he wanted to call Sandy in the morning.

She stood in the open doorway, looking at him like he was a badly behaving cat refusing to return for the night. "Are you coming?" she asked. She wore a light strappy nightshirt over her jeans, and to complicate matters, it was just about the sexiest thing he'd ever seen.

The ordeal was, clearly, to not get involved. It was that simple. He liked her. Not just the way she looked, but the way she stood, glaring at him, angry and frustrated at his stupidity.

He liked that in a woman.

But if he got involved with her, he'd have to keep lying to her. Or worse, tell her the truth about Walt, whatever the truth was. Best to protect the locals, keep them out of harm's way by not implicating them in his actions. "I should find a hotel."

"Thought you already tried and failed," she said, yawning.

"Oh yeah." He was a lousy liar. Always had been.

"You don't have a chance, Mick. It's reunion weekend. Everyplace from here to the highway's been booked for months. I thought you were a lost reunion boy when you pulled up my drive this afternoon."

At least she'd gotten the *lost* part right.

"I don't want to impose," he said. "I have a tent in the car."

"Forget it," she answered. "You have no choice. So come inside and get used to it."

She was right. He had no choice. In more ways than she could know.

So he went inside, closing the door behind him. He'd call Sandy in the morning so that she could remind him that this was a battle he couldn't afford to lose.

Chapter Eleven

That night, Nina lay in bed, listening to Mick's footsteps as he moved from the guest bedroom to the bathroom back to the guest bedroom again. A stabbing sadness hit her, the likes of which she hadn't felt since the day she'd learned that Walt had died. *Footsteps like Walt's, but not Walt's. Never again Walt's.* They had lived in the house for a month together, before Walt left the last time for overseas. Her apartment lease had been up downtown, and it had seemed silly for her to rent when the house was empty. Plus, the cats were so much happier here, and they needed someone to look after them. She had told herself then that it was a temporary arrangement.

For the cats.

But of course it had grown into something more.

She drifted in and out of sleep, thinking of how little she knew about how her brother had died. The army had given her the basics—firefight, bravery, and honor.

But like her mural, the story they'd told her felt clichéd, empty, unformed.

What did Mick know about it? Anything?

Finally, the house was silent again except for the whir of the fans. Walt hadn't liked talking about his time in the army. When he was home, he said he wanted to forget "over there."

She hadn't pushed. Truthfully, she hadn't wanted to know. She had tried to read a book about the war once, when Walt first went overseas. She had to stop during the first chapter, at the part about the soldiers having to peel their socks off along with the bits of their skin that had fused to the fabric in the stifling, unbearable heat.

The image reentered her dreams. After almost a whole year of not dreaming of Walt, she dreamt of him. At first he was okay, eating and playing cards with his buddies. But then he was nearby, screaming. She ran from room to room, unable to find him as the hills and valleys of Afghanistan merged somehow with her house. She opened doors that hadn't been there before, discovering rooms in her house she had never known existed. Some were filled with beautiful gardens; others were dark and ominous caves filled with crying women and children. But she couldn't find Walt and the screaming wouldn't stop. If she could just find him, she was sure she could make it better. The screaming got louder, unbearable. She tried to leave the house, but there was no way out. Every door led to another room.

She jolted awake.

There was still screaming.

But it wasn't Walt. It was Mick.

She climbed out of bed and crept down the hall, her heart pounding.

"Dammit it. No! Walt!" he commanded.

She knocked lightly. No response. She carefully opened his bedroom door, her hand shaking.

He was in the guest bed, facedown, her daisy sheets tangled around his torso. His hands were fists, pressing into his forehead. He leaned on his elbows, his shoulders just slightly raised as if he were shouting into a hole in the mattress.

She stood at the door, petrified.

"Stop, you fucker. Don't you dare. Get back."

For an instant, she thought he was talking to her, and she took a step out of the room. But he wasn't talking to her. He was away, gone.

She had to bring him back. She crept toward the bed, rigid with fear.

"No. No. Stop." Then all at once a roar, barely human, came out of him. "Walt!"

Her impulse was to flee, but she couldn't. She was frozen, as if she were in a dream. She forced her legs to move, and finally they did. She rushed to the bed and put a hand on his bare shoulder. "Mick," she whispered as she shook him as roughly as she dared. "Wake up. It's a dream." His skin was fiery and slick with sweat under her ice-cold hand.

The ghastly scream stopped as he jerked away from her. He rolled to his side. His eyes flew open and he stared at her. "Where the hell am I?" His voice was hoarse.

"Walt's house, remember? I'm Nina, Walt's sister. It's okay. You were having a nightmare."

He blinked once, twice, three times. The third time, his eyes didn't reopen. She watched his body relax back into sleep. His fists uncurled, his shoulders slumped. His hand tucked under his head. His face looked like a child's.

But his body was a man's. A very beautiful man's. She took the time to study his form in the moonlight. Thankfully, the sheet still covered his midsection. But she could see every chiseled inch of his stomach, the outline of his abs evident even in sleep. His torso blossomed up into beautifully molded shoulders. His profile was so serene, it took all her energy not to reach out and trace the lines of his face with her finger.

Sylvie jumped up onto the bed, startling Nina. But Mick slept on. The cat settled against Mick's chest. She looked up at Nina as if to say, *It's okay; I've got him now. You sleep.*

So Nina started to creep out of the room.

But then she stopped and went back to the bed with the softly sleeping man.

She bent down and kissed his forehead lightly.

He didn't wake up.

She kissed his cheek.

Then, overwhelmed with an emptiness that she couldn't explain, she raced out of the room and back into her bed. She was crying and she didn't know why and she didn't like it. She forced her wet eyes closed, forced herself to stop the parade of emotions that were assaulting her: desire, repulsion; sadness, hope. She felt as if she were on a cliff, looking over the edge. She didn't want to jump. Here, she was safe. With Mick—she felt the danger of him as if it were seeping into her room.

She wiped her eyes in frustration. She didn't have time for melodrama. The cookbook job. The memorial. She was meeting Bob, her potential new client, tomorrow morning, and she had to get the job to prove to the Enemy Club that she wasn't helpless.

The image of Mick naked on his bed wouldn't fade. She fell back to sleep and dreamt he was sleeping peacefully, his perfect chest rising and falling in rhythm with her own. In her dream, she was curled up by his side like the cat, and it felt divine.

Chapter Twelve

*N*ina woke up to the smell of bacon.

She sat up in bed, frantic. *There's a beautiful, tortured, wounded stranger in my house and he's frying chemical-laden pork.*

She thought of him tossing and shouting last night. The feel of his hurt shoulder under her fingertips in the barn. The kiss in the foyer, the stolen kisses in his bed—

She had to get to the bottom of what Mick knew about Walt's death, and then get him out of here. Had he really been there? Had he seen it? What would he say today? She was excited, close to answers she'd waited for so long.

And also—terrified.

The clock read eight ten. Being up half the night had made her sleep through her alarm, and now she was running late for her meeting with her possible new client, Bob. She didn't have time to obsess.

She threw on a robe. Smoothed her hair as best she could. Smeared on a coat of lip gloss. Smeared it back off.

It was awkward to have him in her house. It didn't help that she couldn't work the blush out of her cheeks or the images of him in his bed out of her mind.

Mick was at the stove, whistling. Shirtless. Shoeless. *Pantless.*

A pair of faded striped orange boxers was all that stood between him and the stove.

Guess he wasn't feeling awkward about last night.

She cleared her throat and he looked up from his pan. "Good morning," he said cheerily, as if last night hadn't happened.

"Hi," she said. "How's the shoulder?"

"On fire," he said. "But I took some of your Advil. Found it in the bathroom. Hope that's okay."

She sat down and he put a steaming mug of black coffee on the table in front of her. "Milk and sugar?"

She kept her eyes on the coffee to keep them from straying elsewhere. Where did she look when talking to the mostly naked man whose mostly naked body she'd seen just hours ago, rigid with anxiety in his bed? The man whose rock-hard, slick shoulder was still imprinted on her fingertips? The man whose panicked eyes had stared at her like she might mean him harm? The man who might have been one of the last people to see Walt alive?

"I don't drink coffee," she said carefully. She also didn't eat breakfast until after she had finished at least a dozen sun salutations in her yoga studio upstairs, but it didn't seem polite to tell him that just now. Especially since a huge stack of blueberry pancakes was already on the table, along with an industrial-size bottle of real maple syrup, a huge bowl of strawberries, freshly whipped cream, and a jug of orange juice. He was still flipping pancakes and he had at least a quart of batter still in the bowl.

"Expecting guests?" she asked.

"No. Why?"

"To finish all this, we'd each have to eat a dozen pancakes, a half pound of bacon, and a pint of strawberries."

He shrugged, then winced at his shoulder, then sat down across from her. It was the seat that Walt took when he had come home on his last leave. *Back to the wall, eyes to the door,* he'd told her. *Old habits died hard.* "Guess we better get to it, then." Mick looked from her to her mug of coffee, then back to her. "You're really not going to drink it?"

"No."

"Everyone drinks coffee."

"Not me. I don't eat bacon either. Sorry. Nitrates."

"More for me, then," he said, jumping up to tend to the stove.

His calm cheerfulness this morning was so incongruous with his torturous thrashing last night, she didn't know what to make of it. Or of the mountain of food he was preparing.

He went to the fridge and got out the milk. He poured it into her mug of coffee. Added three spoonfuls of sugar. Stirred it. Put it back in front of her. He sat down across from her, waiting like a little boy.

She tried to reconcile the loose, easy movements of his body, the open, playful twinkle in his blue eyes, with the man she'd woken up last night—or had she woken him? Maybe he'd never been awake. "I'm not going to drink it, Mick. Thank you, though. This is lovely. It's very thoughtful." She pushed the mug away.

He pushed it back, the corner of his lip quirking up in an enticing sort of way she was trying not to notice. "It's not just thoughtful, it's *good*."

"I'm an herbal-tea-and-oatmeal kind of girl."

He winced. "Okay, I'll give you a pass on the bacon. And I dare you not to eat at least one of my special-recipe blueberry pancakes. But I can't trust a woman who doesn't drink coffee. A woman who doesn't drink coffee is like a woman who doesn't have sex. It's not natural." He lowered his voice seductively. "I make very good coffee."

Did he not remember last night? The possibility that he had never been truly awake after she'd shaken him from his dream was beginning to solidify. "No, thank you. I prefer tea." She met his eye with what she hoped was a stern stare.

"When was the last time you tried it?" he asked, getting up to turn the pancakes. "They say the first time is awful, but you develop a taste for it if you give it a chance."

"Sex?" she blurted, unable to banish the image of him last night in his bed.

"Coffee," he said with a flirty smile.

She felt her face heat and she floundered for something to say. "I drank coffee for the first time in middle school. Hated it then; hate it now." Why did she feel as if they were still talking about sex? With a half-naked man like Mick, a conversation about the Dewey decimal system would feel as if it were about sex. Images of him last night were further muddling her thoughts.

"The coffee is never any good in middle school," he said, implying great meaning with his sly tone. He added more pancakes to the teetering stack and more batter to the pan.

The memory of Davey Branner slipping her tongue behind the gym came to her like it had happened yesterday. *Ugh*. She jumped up and put the kettle on for tea before she lost her appetite. "How'd you sleep last night?" she asked as casually as she could, watching his face.

"Like a baby." There was no guile behind his eyes, no sense that he was avoiding or trying to hide anything.

He didn't remember. She was sure of it. She considered saying something, but it felt too tender, too personal, her secret. She felt like he had a secret he was hiding, so why not be even? Plus, in the bright light of the morning kitchen, she started to wonder if *she* had dreamt it all. Maybe it hadn't happened. She looked to Sylvie for some kind of confirmation, but the cat, as usual, wasn't talking.

"Mick, I know you don't want to be here, but I hope you'll stay for a few days at least. I really want us to talk. I'm not giving you the house, but still, I'd appreciate hearing what you know about Walt."

He felt his shoulder. "I don't want to be a bother, but I think the arm might need a few days before another marathon drive. I'll set up my tent tonight out back so I don't bug you."

"You don't bug me."

"I bugged you yesterday. I thought you were going to take off my head as soon as I finished my lemonade."

"I'm satisfied for now with ruining your shoulder," she said. "But if you're going to stay a while, we need rules."

Mick said, "Good idea. I like rules. Makes things clear."

"Rule number one: we wear clothes," she said.

"I'm wearing clothes," Mick pointed out.

"Underwear doesn't count."

"I sleep naked," he said.

I know. She tried one more time to penetrate his friendly, playful gaze, but if there was anything behind it, he was very, very good at hiding it. "We wear clothes outside the bedroom," she said.

"So you'll be naked in the bedroom?" He flipped the batch in the pan onto a plate, added more batter, and went to the table.

Not if you keep having nightmares like that, she almost said. "Naked if you like. In your bedroom. With the door shut. Or in your tent. Or wherever. Alone." This conversation was getting away from her. "Your bacon is burning."

He stared at her for a minute, then jumped up. "Oh, I thought that was some kind of sexual innuendo." He flipped his bacon with a pair of tongs. She moved back to the relative safety of her seat at the table. She couldn't take her eyes off the way his torso tapered to the waistline of his boxers or the shaded outline of his abs under his tanned skin. Even his feet struck her as powerful and tempting.

The man's bacon was definitely burning.

He waved the tongs at her. "Two can play at this game. Rule number two is that if I have to get dressed up for breakfast, you have to try new things too. Like coffee." He switched off the gas under her teapot.

"You don't get to make the rules. This is my house."

"Careful, that might not be the case for long," he said.

She checked herself. This wasn't fun and games—even if she was enjoying their playful teasing. This was serious. At least to her it was.

He brought the bacon to the table, sat down, and started eating the strips off the serving platter like they were potato chips. "I left the army two years ago, and I still wake up praising the heavens for real bacon and decent coffee every morning."

She pushed last night out of her mind. Whatever had happened, it didn't matter because he had no memory of it at all. She speared three pancakes and covered them with whipped cream. She put a few strawberries on top. She never ate so greedily, but this morning, she didn't care. She needed strength to deal with this almost-naked man.

He watched her eat. "No syrup? Good God, woman. Rule three: no one wastes my secret-recipe blueberry pancakes by eating them without syrup."

"I'm not taking food advice from a man who eats a pound of bacon for breakfast. Where did you get all this stuff?"

"Bought it this morning. I'm an early riser. Army habits. But I'll have you know that I'm completely healthy, so the food can't be that bad for you."

"Appearances aren't everything," she said, then blushed.

He smiled slyly and said, "Kind of you to notice."

They ate in silence for a few minutes. She hated that she was already warming to this guy. She had to be strong, to resist his charm. She had to remember that he wanted something from her that she wasn't prepared to give.

"Where'd you learn to cook?" she asked.

"As a kid," he said. "My sisters cleaned; I cooked. It was a good deal."

"What about your parents?"

"They weren't such a good deal," he said.

He didn't seem inclined to say more, so she let it drop. "You made an awful lot of food," she pointed out. "Like you're cooking for an army."

He looked at the piles of food on the table. "Old habits

die hard, I guess. We'll have leftovers." He jumped up to flip more pancakes onto the plate; then he turned off the stove. He sat down again and munched more bacon.

"I was surprised to see the bandana," he said after half the bacon was gone and she had polished off all of her pancakes. "I didn't think you'd want to take me on."

"You shouldn't have been surprised. I told you what I wanted. To know about Walt."

"Yeah. About that—"

She looked at her watch. "Shoot. I have a meeting in less than an hour. We'll have plenty of time to talk when I come back. Lunch. We can have leftover pancakes. For the next week. Maybe two."

He stood up, stretched without an ounce of embarrassment. "Great. See you around the hood."

Nina looked around the wrecked kitchen. "Aren't you cleaning up?"

"I cooked." He scratched his belly. "The cook never cleans. Rules, babe. And that one is a cosmic rule, obeyed by all for all time."

She was speechless. The bacon grease alone was a twenty-minute job.

"Unless—" He paused.

Yes, I'll sleep with you, hold you when you have bad dreams, kiss your brow to make the nightmares go away, and we'll talk about Walt and make it all right...

Gah! Where had those ridiculous thoughts come from? She wished he'd put on some clothes. It was hard to think straight around those shoulders, especially after feeling them shake under her fingertips just hours ago.

"You take a sip of coffee—one sip!—and I'm dish boy," he said.

Nina looked down at her untouched mug. She had to get ready for her meeting with Bob. She had to remember that Mick wasn't just her houseguest; he was her adversary. "Why do you care so much if I drink coffee?" she asked. "And no jokes. I mean it, Mick. Who cares?"

He sat down and deflated. "I don't know why." He didn't meet her eye. His evasiveness reminded her of the Mick of yesterday, of last night.

Her opinion of him shifted. The pancake stacks, the mounds of strawberries—all his cooking was overdone, almost frantic. Like him, last night. What had Walt seen in this guy that was struggling to surface? "Because you love coffee so much? And you want me to experience what you love? You want to share it?"

"I hate coffee." He said it so thoughtfully, so sadly, the shift in the room felt physical. He looked into his mug as if it held the answer. "We all drink coffee," he said finally.

"We? All those invisible people you cooked up a hundred pancakes for?"

His eyes met hers the way they had last night, when she'd woken him. "Yes. All of us. It's part of the way of things."

"So if everyone jumped off a cliff, you'd follow?"

His mood shifted again, ominously. A shadow passed over his face. He stood up, walked to the window, and looked out. "In the army, that's exactly what we do. One man goes, the others follow, no matter what. You don't let anyone go over a cliff alone. Ever."

She didn't know what to say. The conversation had gone from light to dark so quickly. The mounds of uneaten food on the table seemed a testament to a man trying much too hard to cover for something. But what?

He doesn't have to go over the cliff alone. She picked

up her mug and sniffed it. The sugar didn't help disguise the bitterness, but she was no coward. She had spent so many mornings at the Last Chance diner, forcing down the coffee so as not to offend Lizzie.

She put the mug to her lips and gulped.

Thankfully, the liquid was cool enough to slide down her throat without incident. When the cup was empty, she slammed it down on the counter triumphantly. "Happy cleaning. We talk at lunch."

Chapter Thirteen

Nina swung through the door to the Brewhaha, spotted her potential new client, and the floor fell out from under her.

She steadied herself with a hand on the condiment bar. *Soy milk, half and half…*

Bobby Ridale.

No wonder he'd avoided giving his last name when they'd set this meeting up. *Bob,* he'd written in his contact e-mail. *Everyone calls me Bob.*

She could think of a few more descriptive words people called him. *Criminal*, for instance.

Or worse, *Walt's best childhood friend*.

Bobby had been by Walt's side for as long as Nina could remember, nudging him in the wrong direction. He'd been the boy willing to do anything for a good laugh or a few bucks. The irresistible bad boy to an orphan like Walt, stuck in a house with his kid sister and old-fashioned aunt who had been thrown into raising two kids. Nina had thought that the army had saved Walt from Bobby. Now Walt was gone and here was Bobby, smiling his charming smile at her across the crowded room packed with happy, caffeinated students and chatting professors.

"Four Troops Killed in Afghanistan" the lead headline of the *USA Today* on the closest table read. The man at the table was ignoring it, playing a game of solitaire on his open laptop.

Shaking, she walked toward Bobby, every step amplifying her rush of memories. She sensed that Walt was here too, as if she and Bobby coming together had conjured him. Not that Nina believed in ghosts. Heck, she hoped the afterlife offered more than hanging around a trendy Galton coffee shop watching your little sister fumble for traction. But still, where there was Bobby, there was Walt. It was inescapable.

She really, really wanted to go home and climb into bed. Except there was another man in her house, just as ghost inducing as this one, scrubbing bacon grease from her frying pan.

It couldn't be a coincidence that they both showed up just a day apart. She shook the unlikely thought from her mind. Of course it could be—when it rained, it poured.

They shook hands and she endured a chaste, awkward kiss on each cheek. He smelled like cigarettes.

"I didn't know you were back in town," she ventured. She sat down across the small table from him, the boy most likely to ruin Walt's life now grown into a man she'd have recognized from across a football field. He still wore his leather jacket in the heat of summer. He still had the five o'clock shadow he'd lorded over his classmates at fifteen years old. He hadn't lost a strand of his wavy black hair, hadn't lost the dangerous glint in his black eyes.

"Twenty years," he said, his voice deeper and rougher than she remembered it. "Senior year was the last time I showed my face in this town. I just got back." He pushed a small plate of cookies toward her. His paper coffee cup was already empty, and the edge of it was unrolled and torn, an old nervous habit of Bobby's that she remembered like yesterday.

"C'mon, you're too skinny. And much too healthy. Eat."

She shook her head. The pancakes from breakfast this morning were already too much for her clenching stomach. "Are you back for good?" Would she run into him at the grocery, the mall?

"Maybe."

"Why didn't you tell me who you were in your e-mail—?" she began.

"Would you have come if you knew it was me?" he asked, picking up a cookie and biting into it, the small circle ridiculously dainty in his huge hand.

"Sure—"

"C'mon, Nina. You never liked me."

She didn't have the stomach for placating him. "This feels rotten, Bobby. Like Walt should be here. Like he is here. It's just a lot of memories in a rush. I wasn't ready for this. You should have told me the truth."

"Listen, I want it to be okay between us. You want something? Coffee?"

"No. Yes. Okay. Tea. Chamomile."

She let him get her tea, giving her time to pull herself together. Two men in two days arriving like blasts from the past. She had no intention of reminiscing with this man. What would they talk about? All the petty crimes he and Walt had done together, hooting and hollering after they got back from shoplifting candy bars at the Kroger's when they were twelve years old? Or, at thirteen, cutting school for a whole month. Or, at fourteen, scoring six-packs of beer from old Eddie Crosswell, who bought for underage kids for a few extra bucks and cigarettes. She'd spent countless nights alone, hating Bobby for getting Walt in trouble. Of course, Walt had been able to take care of himself. She knew that. And she knew that part of her anger had been because she had been jealous of Bobby for taking Walt away from her on those long, lonely Saturday nights when he'd come home at two in the morning stinking of cigarettes and beer and cheap cologne. But now that they were all grown-ups, she ought to be over it. Walt made his own choices. It wasn't Bobby's fault.

"I miss Walt like a kick in the gut," he said when he came back and settled himself across the table from her.

"I do too," she said, accepting the tea he pushed across to her like a peace offering. She concentrated on squeezing the tiny lemon wedge so that she wouldn't have to look at him.

"I was in prison for the last three years," he told her. "Stupid stuff. I heard about the funeral, but it didn't feel right sending flowers or a card, you know? Not my style. But I want you to know, I would've come if I could've."

"It's okay." She waited for elaboration on why he had been in prison, but he didn't say anything more. "Walt had a big crowd," she said. "It felt like the whole town was there."

"Well, I'm glad. He deserved it." He lowered his eyes. A shadow crossed his face and she braced herself for whatever was coming. "Walt was my best bud," he said. "But he wasn't me. He always kept his options open, you know? I didn't. No one in this town would come to my funeral."

"I would," she admitted. "For Walt."

"Thanks." He straightened a little at her words.

An awkward silence bloomed between them. She was doing it again: reaching out even when she didn't mean to. Like drinking the coffee this morning. She meant to be strong, and then she felt a closeness to a person, and she gave in to the person, gave the person what he or she wanted. But what she'd said about his funeral was true. She didn't like Bobby, but he had been a huge part of her childhood, and she'd honor him when he was gone.

It was while he was still around that was problematic.

"Is that your work?" he asked, nodding to her portfolio, which was tucked under the table. "I'd like to see it."

She had forgotten she'd brought her black portfolio and her computer along with her. Also, that she was dressed up in a skirt and heels for a client meeting. She could feel her face go hot with embarrassment, any connection they'd achieved falling away. Not only had she been fooled by Bobby, but she'd told the Enemy Club that she had a big job coming in. She didn't have any job coming in. This was the way of a man like Bobby, the small lies that hurt almost as much as the bigger truths, clouding everything. She had been conned again. When would she ever learn? "Bobby, what do you want? I'm really busy today."

"I came back to Galton for a woman," he said.

Nina felt a pang of pity for the woman. But then, maybe she was an ex-convict too. Someone for everyone in this world.

Then she froze. What if he'd come back for her?

"Georgia Phillips," he said.

Nina choked on her tea, relieved and amazed.

"I know, I know. She's out of my league." This was the charming side of Bobby that was hard to resist.

"No. Of course not." She took a sip of her still-too-hot tea, then said, "Yes, actually, Bobby. Way out. I'm sorry. She's a friend of mine. She's—"

"She's a friend of yours? I remember that you hated her. Wasn't she the one who—?"

"Long story," Nina said. She didn't want to go into the story of the Enemy Club with him just now. "But it's beside the point. The point is, Georgia is—"

"Smart," he said.

"She's brilliant. You know that. She was the valedictorian. She went to Galton University after high school."

"And she's beautiful," he said.

"*You* think so?" she asked, putting stress on the first word. Bobby had always been a man for the fast girls, the ones in tight clothes and too much makeup.

"Aw, give me a little credit. I'm not eighteen anymore," he said. "She's accomplished. Cultured. Beautiful. I've loved her since she was in the fourth grade. But I always knew she was out of my league." He put down his coffee and his lips narrowed, his eyes focused on something over her shoulder. "Listen, Nina. When I heard that Walt had, you know, gone, it was like a bullet to the head. I knew I had to change my life. To make up for—" He stopped.

"For being alive?" she asked, knowing it was cruel. But she was tired. She needed him to cut to the chase.

"Yeah. Exactly." He put his huge bear paw of a hand on hers, and surprisingly, she didn't mind. "I mean, why should I be here when he isn't? It really tore me up. I'd made all the wrong choices and he went out and made the right one, and then—look what happened."

"Look what happened." She waited, trying to loosen the tightening in her throat.

"When I was still inside, I spent a long time thinking about what I needed to do to make up for all the mistakes I'd made. Then it hit me. First I came back here to make it up to everyone I hurt and to try to start again. But I figured while I made things right with the world, I also had to make things right in my heart. I had to try to go after my heart's desire. See? To be honest with myself. So I started to write to Georgia."

"She never told me."

"She sent back my letters unopened," he said. "But if the letters were in calligraphy like you can do—"

"You called me for an art project?" Nina put down her tea. "Back in the day, your idea of romancing a woman was buying a fifth of rotgut whiskey and a few dozen condoms."

He smiled. "I told you, you're looking at a new Bobby Ridale. Yes. I have an art project." Bobby leaned forward. "You have to help me. This is even better than I thought, since you know her. You know what she likes. I just need her to open the envelope, see? To give me one chance."

"She's not so big on art, I gotta tell you," Nina said. "I mean, she likes museums and old masters. But beyond that—"

"I can pay any price you name," he said. "I really need this chance, Nins."

She flinched at hearing her childhood name. Was he manipulating her, or was he for real? How could she trust a man like Bobby Ridale, especially since he'd already not been up-front with her in his e-mail? "Bobby, before I even consider this, which I don't know about, I have to ask you, are you—?"

"Clean?" he asked. "Look, it's not so simple—"

She held up a hand. "I can't do this."

"I don't do drugs. No alcohol. I'm not a bad guy, Nina. But, well, it's hard to explain. I'm not dangerous."

"You love her? I'm sorry, Bobby. It just sounds a little ridiculous."

"Why? You don't believe in first love?"

"But you guys never—" She stopped.

He didn't say anything.

She didn't mean to gape, but it was impossible not to. "No way."

He watched her, a tiny, sly smile emerging, then darting away.

"Really? When?"

"I'll let her tell you if she wants to."

"You and Georgia. I don't believe it. I—"

"Look, forget all that. Let's just say it's not totally out of the blue. We have a history. Nina, I'm trying to make something good come out of Walt's being gone. Isn't that what we're all doing? Trying to find some meaning in it? And this is my meaning. I'm not a monster. I'm trying to fix my life. I passed up a great thing, and I want a second chance. The irony of me being here and Walt being gone feels so damn wrong. I want to make it right by doing what he can't do, not letting life slip by me."

She breathed in and out slowly, deeply, trying to slow her heartbeat. "What exactly do you want me to do?" she asked.

Bobby looked both ways, but the Galton students who packed the place weren't the least bit interested in a couple of over-the-hill thirtysomethings talking about impossible love. He pulled some dog-eared, crinkled papers out of his jacket pocket, unfolded them, and handed them to Nina like they were blueprints for a bank heist. "I've been writing her, but she won't respond. If the letters were fancy, I think she'd have to at least read them. Right? I mean, wouldn't you? Who can't open a gorgeous envelope?"

She looked over his poems. She counted: six poems, each at least ten lines, plus a little illumination maybe, down the margins. This was a big job. He'd just go out and hire another calligrapher if she wouldn't do it. Probably that awful Sue Seemly in Trumanstown, who didn't know her uncials from her Spencerian.

Plus, Georgia was a big girl. She could make up her own mind.

But what would working with Bobby mean? How often would she have to see him? Could she handle that? "Did you write these?" she asked, stalling.

"I did. Do you like them?"

To her astonishment, the boy who had once mooned the mayor at the Galton Thanksgiving parade was blushing. "They're very—touching." It was hard to read pronouncements of love and passion, to look at Bobby, and to think of Georgia at the same time.

"I studied Shakespeare in the hole," Bobby said. "We read a different play every month. I learned about iambic pentameter. Metaphors. The whole bit. We even performed *Romeo and Juliet*."

"Don't tell me—," Nina began.

"Yep. I was Romeo." Bobby's sly grin slid across his face. "And in the second performance, Juliet. We didn't have any women inside."

Nina was terrified he was going to start reciting lines of Shakespeare to her, so she rushed ahead. "So these will be letters?" *Be careful sending letters,* she thought. She knew how dangerous a letter could be. Especially one written in another person's hand.

"One a week, for however many weeks it takes, I figure. I won't stalk her. If these don't work, I'll give in."

"This is a lot of work. I'd have to charge you a lot."

"I told you. Price is no object."

Nina looked at the man across from her. She imagined Georgia getting a calligraphic love poem in the mail, swirls and illuminated caps and maybe even some gold leaf down the sides. Georgia would be pounding on her door in an instant, demanding to know why Nina had done this, and Nina would have to hold out her hands in mock innocence and say, "I had to be a responsible freelancer and take the work," and Georgia would—

Fall in love? With Bobby Ridale? Again?

It was possible. Who was Nina to interfere? Wasn't her duty to make enough money to support herself, first? Plus, who was she to say that Georgia and Bobby weren't a perfect match? Life worked in mysterious ways.

She thought of Mick, in her house, probably done scrubbing the bacon pan and—doing what? She felt an urgency to get back to her house. What had she been thinking when she left him there? What was he doing there, alone?

"Okay. Let's pick an alphabet and talk paper."

"I knew I could count on my little Nins!" Bobby smiled and rubbed his hands together. "Let the first day of the rest of my life begin!"

Chapter Fourteen

Mick loaded the last of the plates into the dishwasher and surveyed the gleaming kitchen. His work here was done. Which meant it was time to quit stalling and look for the box.

He'd start here. He liked kitchens.

He looked to the deepest corners of the dark cabinets over the fridge. These were the kind of inaccessible cabinets Nina might have thrust a box into that she was too sentimental to throw away but too scared to open.

Nothing.

He tried the upper reaches of the built-ins, his shoulder protesting the stretch. He found all the usual not-often-used stuff—oddly shaped pans, a deviled-egg plate, ten champagne glasses covered in dust.

He looked through the pantry closet, filled with way too many whole grains for his taste. He resisted tossing out the bulgur on principle. No red metal box. He sat down at the table to fortify himself and rest his aching shoulder with a final chug of black coffee. *C'mon, soldier....*

Truth was, he didn't want to leave the kitchen. When he'd gotten up this morning, he'd gone straight here and taken a quick inventory. This was the one place he could offer her something, since he couldn't offer her the truth. He'd driven around the still-dark town at six a.m., looking for an open store. He'd grabbed anything and everything that promised comfort at the twenty-four-hour mart while the deliverymen loaded the shelves around him. Blueberries, real maple syrup, strawberries, cream, coffee.

Coffee.

He should get to searching the house. She'd be back soon. He was surprised she wasn't back already.

He drank another cup, stalling some more. Why had he gone off on that ridiculous coffee crusade? *Drink the coffee!* It sounded like he wanted her to drink the Kool-Aid. *There are things a person has to do. Duty.* You didn't question; you did. You joined, and once you joined, you gave yourself over to it; you didn't ask why. You followed your men down an unsecured alley in the slums of Kandahar. You found a mysterious box and destroyed it. You took a house from a kind, thoughtful, beautiful woman who liked herbal tea and cats and flowers because you had no choice. *Duty.*

She'd downed that cup of joe like a champ. She'd hardly hesitated. She dove right in, reckless and aggressive in the face of his dare. But why? What was her sense of duty? To herself? Or would she do anything to get away from cleaning bacon fat?

He had dreamt about her last night. In his dream, she had come into his room, leaned over his bed, touched him gently the way she had in the barn. He had pulled her to him, and she had come willingly, her soft skin white against his tanned, rough flesh. They had made love, and it went on forever, the way it often happened in dreams, a circle of softness and hope. It had felt so real that this morning, he had almost reached out and pulled her to him. *Good morning, gorgeous. I made you breakfast.*

Ridiculous.

She'd have socked him across the jaw.

Which would have been good. He had no place getting close to her when he needed to take things from her. This had to be a strategic, surgical strike.

Too bad he'd been in the army too long to believe that such a thing as a clean hit existed. There were always unintended casualties.

In this war, he was sure that the casualty was going to be Nina.

Because now he had to put on his soldier face and go through her house like a thief, whether he liked it or not.

Searching houses was a familiar affair from his years in war zones. They'd go in looking for guns or insurgents, but mostly find women and babies shuddering in back rooms. At least here, he wouldn't have to look into a child's dark, terrified eyes.

And yet, he stopped in front of the door to the last room on the upstairs hall, where he intended to begin his search, and considered forgetting the whole thing.

Coward. Just do this.

It was a small room, almost empty. A yoga mat was rolled out dead center on the hardwood floor. The walls were painted a soft, soothing gray. A few of Nina's flower pictures hung on the walls, but otherwise, the room was bare.

If the box was in here, he'd see it from the hall. Unless it was in the closet.

He forced himself into the room, disgusted with himself for being so soft. This wasn't wrong, he assured himself. He was on a mission. He had to do this for Walt. Going through her house was—

Stinking lousy.

He'd have to cook her a hell of a dinner to make up for this.

He stood before the closet door. Put his hand on the doorknob. *Maybe he'd do a chilled soup....* He threw open the door, his heart pounding, his head spinning with contradictions. He imagined Nina coming up behind him, demanding he tell her why he was going through her things. He glanced out the window. Just another beautiful summer's day in paradise.

She permeated every inch of this house.

He rifled through the first shelf of sheets, a search-and-seize machine powered by willpower and determination.

Then he stopped.

He shut the door in disgust. This was going to be harder than he'd expected.

Her bedroom was the next room down the hall. Was he really going to rifle through her bedroom? Go through her drawers?

There had to be another way to find the box.

Except he knew that there wasn't.

He stormed into her bedroom, hoping the box would be in full sight, sparing him a decision on whether to search or not.

He stopped in the center of her bedroom. Her scent, sweet with an edge of something foresty, assaulted him. The room was like every other room in the house: simple, plain, with one splash of intense color that drew his eye. In this case, her deep, rich red bedspread.

He went to the antique chest of drawers—threw open the top one.

Her underwear drawer.

The lace and satin, the virgin whites and the racy blacks, the one pair of cotton panties with tiny red strawberries—

He slammed the drawer shut and hustled downstairs, looking for a distraction, anything to give him time to think. But there was no TV. Who didn't have a television? Had he seen a computer in the house? There was no newspaper to read. It was as if the rest of the world didn't exist. This was her paradise, her refuge, and if he had his way, he was about to bust it open and toss her out of it.

He flopped onto the couch, took out his cell, and dialed his youngest sister, Sandra. She picked up on the first ring.

"Did they get on the plane okay?" he asked as soon as she got out "Hello."

"They're at the airport now. Did you get the house?"

"Um, not yet. It's complicated. Might take longer than we bargained for."

"Complicated! Oh, Mick!"

"No worries. I'll work it out. I'm just saying, I might need more time."

"Mick, this thing has started. They're getting on the plane in two hours. There's no time to mess around."

He heard the desperation in his baby sister's voice. They were all counting on him to come through. Bella wasn't in an American hospital that let in anyone who needed aid. The experimental treatment that was her last hope for her brain cancer wasn't approved yet in the States, so they had to fly her to Tel Aviv, where they were working miracles—expensive, cash-only miracles for foreigners like Bella. It had already cost them everything to get her and Baily there and get them settled. Sandra had taken out a second mortgage to cover it. Baily had exhausted her savings and quit her job to go along on the yearlong trip. The next installment, the money they didn't have, was due in when the initial tests were done and the vaccine ready. That would take three months. If Bella made it that long.

"I'm going to get the money. Don't worry." He rubbed the ache that was forming behind his temples.

"Mick, it's the sister, isn't it? That's the problem. You can't fall for her. We discussed this."

"Why would you say that?"

"Because you're a sucker for needy women. Is she needy?"

"No. Well, not yet. Guess she might be when I'm done here."

"I knew it. You're already caving. I can hear it in your voice. Keep your head, Mick. This is no time to fall for someone. Especially her."

"I won't. I'm not."

Sandra moaned. "I should come out there."

"No. I got this."

"Don't let her seduce you."

"I'm not that kind of guy, Sandy."

"No, not for women. I know that, Mick. But for duty. You'll get all soft on her, feel like you have to protect her, to be a big, strong soldier for her. But you don't, Mick. You have to do your duty to Bella. To us."

Mick got off the phone as quickly as he could before Sandy got started on that again. *Duty*. He went back upstairs with new determination and forced himself to cross the threshold into the small room next to the yoga room.

It was another art studio, smaller than the one in the garage.

To his dismay, this room felt even more intimate than her bedroom. Her work was everywhere, framed on the walls, tacked to a huge corkboard that covered one wall floor to ceiling, on the worktables.

A still life of vegetables piled on a draped table was set up in the center of the room. An easel sat facing it holding an empty canvas. No, not empty—a few light pencil marks sketched the outline of the food. Next to that was a drawing table, scattered with sketches of the vegetables, each with a different arrangement or from a slightly different angle.

He looked more closely at the sketches. They were good. Not at all like that awkward, overblown painting of Walt he'd seen in the barn. These had a whimsical style, realistic, but with an ethereal lightness.

Kind of like her, come to think of it. Real, but not grounded. Floating a little above it all. He liked this lightness about her. It gave her a peculiar kind of beauty, as if she glowed.

But it was exactly that quality about her that also pissed him off. It was what made her seem so innocent, vulnerable, and as unpredictable as someone from another world. It was the part of her that didn't link with the outside world. As if she were above it. No, not above it exactly. The opposite. As if she was in it, the here and now, completely. What happened a world away didn't matter. She was one hundred percent *present*.

He went back to the sketches pinned to her corkboard. He was impressed. She'd pinned up pencil sketches of small, simple things. A fork. The orange cat looking out the window. The light hitting the front porch. He had the sense that this was her real work. The work she wasn't doing for anyone else.

He unpinned a picture from the board. It was of Walt, sitting on the back deck in a plastic Adirondack chair, drinking a beer, a shit-eating grin on his face. His feet were slung up onto the rail. Her pencil sketch was fast, light, and yet she'd captured Walt to a tee. He had that mischievous twinkle in his eye that meant he might sit there forever, or he might jump up and set the whole damn place on fire. Completely unpredictable Walter Stokes.

A wave of emotion hit Mick, but he bit it back with irritation.

Shit, he hadn't even liked the guy, and here he was getting soggy over his picture? It was just hard to think that the guy would never have another beer on the back deck.

Why am I here, Walt? Too bad the picture couldn't answer. *What am I doing ransacking your sister's place?*

He pegged the picture back to the wall, a little harder than necessary.

He looked around the studio at the images everywhere, real but not real. What had happened that last day in Kandahar when the truck exploded? Mick knew what the guys who'd come to clear the area had been able to tell him, but it wasn't much. His mind was a complete blank. Gone. Just like almost a year of his life.

He went through the cabinets, the closet.

He'd never known an artist before. Never known someone who could capture the past. Maybe that's why she painted and sketched and drew, to get it all down on paper. So if she forgot, she had a record. Proof.

He had shit. A letter from a guy he barely knew telling him to find a stinking box so he could get a house he didn't really want to help his sister by destroying Walt's sister.

Walt grinned out at him from his spot on the wall.

He had to get out of this room, this house. He had to clear his head.

But he wasn't going anywhere. Nina's car had just pulled up in the drive.

Chapter Fifteen

Nina came into the house to find Mick still in the kitchen, still drinking coffee. "Did you even move?" she asked.

"Hey, I'm dressed, aren't I? Just for you, by the way. Following the rules like a good soldier. How'd the meeting go?" He had thrown on a T-shirt and a pair of jeans before he'd charged down the stairs to meet her, but he was still barefoot.

"Bad. I mean—okay. I got the job. So good." As much as she wanted to talk to him about Walt, she wasn't sure she could handle it after the rush of memories that Bobby had brought back. She wanted to go upstairs, lose herself in painting the perfect tomato, and forget this was happening while she got her head back together.

"You wanna talk?" he asked. "I won't nag you to drink my coffee again. Promise." He pushed out a chair with his remarkably sexy toes. They'd have to make a new rule about naked toes.

She was frozen with indecision. Could she spend another minute sitting across the table from another man who conjured Walt's ghost?

She reminded herself that she was the one who wanted Mick here. She was the one who'd said they'd talk over lunch.

"You look shook-up. Did something happen? Are you okay?" He leaned forward.

The concern in his voice touched her. But she didn't want to be touched, especially by the man who was here to take her house. She tried not to respond to his sympathy, tried not to respond to his excellent toes or his ice blue eyes with their translucent lashes blinking at her.

And yet she sank into a chair, folded over, and rested her forehead on the cool wood table. "My new client turned out to be Bobby Ridale, Walt's best friend from when we were all kids." The hard table grounded her a little, but now she had a very fine view of his toes. Why did tanned feet emerging from jeans look so sexy? The way the hem draped the rise of his foot was worthy of a painting—a sketch at least.

"And a friend is a bad thing?"

"It brought back a lot of memories. I wasn't prepared. Bobby could have told me who he was in his e-mail, when we set up the meeting, but he pretended to be a stranger needing a job so I'd show up. I'm such a sucker."

"He ambushed you!" His toes flexed. "He should have called first. Warned you."

She raised her head, raised one eyebrow.

He crossed his arms over his chest, then said, "Completely different situation."

"Oh. Okay. That clears that up, then." She put her head back down and added, "Hypocrite."

"Okay, so I ambushed you too," he said. "But you have to admit, you ambushed me right back. I was prepared to admit my mistake and leave."

"So now we're even?" she asked.

"Not a chance. Now you owe me for the cat rescue and the messed-up shoulder. Give me the house and I'll call it a deal."

She smirked at his feet. "Dream on. Face it—you're worse than Bobby. At least he's not trying to kick me out of my home." Sylvia jumped into the cave formed by her head and her lap, forcing her to sit back or have a mouthful of cat hair.

Mick's face was contorted in a combination of frustration and indecision, as if he wanted to tell her something that he couldn't.

She stroked the cat, feeling so tired, she could barely stand the thought of going upstairs to work. It was nice here in the kitchen, staring at this beautiful soldier, pretending that he might be a friend. "Bobby just got out of prison," she told Mick. "So I guess you get some points for not being an ex-con."

"What was he in for?" Mick asked. "Rudeness?"

"Didn't ask," she said. "Truth is, I didn't want to know."

"Well, I'm sorry," Mick said. "At least you won't have to see him again."

"Oh, I will. I took his job," she said.

"He actually had a job?"

"Yeah. It's a big one too. I expect you'll meet him. He'll be here now and again to look at the work."

"Why did you take his job?" His eyes had strayed to her hand stroking the cat. His eyes followed her hand back and forth, back and forth, giving her the sensation that he was reading subtitles, translations of what her words really meant.

"He was Walt's friend. I felt like I owed him," she said. "Plus, I need the money since I'll be homeless soon." She watched him watch her hand move over the cat.

"Walt didn't trust him," Mick said after a bit. "You shouldn't either."

She stopped stroking. "Why do you say that? Did Walt tell you something about Bobby I should know?"

"Walt didn't have to tell me anything. He gave me, a practical stranger, his house. Why not give it to his best childhood friend if he's a good guy, an ex-con who deserves a second chance to get back on his feet again? Wouldn't a house be the perfect bequest for a guy like that? Walt obviously didn't trust this guy or didn't like him—or both." He leaned forward and took her hand, sending a wave of electricity through her.

She tried to ignore his hand on hers, as if it wasn't making her heart pound. "If the trustworthy one gets the house, I should have gotten it," she pointed out.

"Walt left you something, right?" His voice was tinged with anxiety. "There should be a death allowance. Some salary odds and ends from the army. Pension."

She looked grim.

"Didn't Walt have insurance? He must have half a million or so coming to him—to you."

She sighed. "Well, that's sort of a long story."

He waited.

"I got scammed out of all of it."

Mick's eyes went wide. "No."

She sighed. "Yes. You know me well enough by now,

right? You had me pegged at hello. I'm all rainbows and fairy tales."

"What happened?"

"Walt was married to a woman named Mary."

"Married?"

"They were kids. They met when they were in basic training, mistook lust for love, and got married. They realized it pretty quick and got divorced. I only met Mary once, after they'd eloped. Anyway, Mary showed up. Or at least a woman who told me she was Mary. She had the same brownish hair. What did I know?"

"Oh no," Mick said. He looked as if he felt sick to his stomach.

"She brought a kid with her. A redheaded kid. She told me that those three months they had been together had been enough for her and Walt to produce a son. She'd said she'd named him Walt, since she'd never really stopped loving my brother. I don't know why I believed her. The boy, whatever his name really was, looked so much like Walt. I think I wanted Walt to have a son. Wanted it so badly, I gave her everything. Everything but the house." She pushed back her hair. "By the time I realized that the lady wasn't Mary and there was no son and—Well, the FBI is still looking for her. But Walt's money is all gone."

A shadow passed over Mick's face. "I'm really sorry for that."

"Well, it was my own dumb fault. I was grieving. I didn't want to be alone in the world, and then, suddenly, I had a nephew and a kind-of sister-in-law. I was an idiot. I just wanted to believe so badly."

"So all you have is the house," Mick said, his voice flat.

"Yep."

He stared at her a long time; then he said, "Look, Nina, this Bobby guy—he's trouble. I can see it in your face. Tell him you changed your mind and you don't want to work with him. You have enough problems with one jerk hanging around who doesn't know better than to show up without calling first."

She shook off his hand, lowered Sylvia gently to the floor, and stood, trying to control her annoyance at Mick for butting in, for caring. "Bobby dredged up a lot of muck I wasn't ready for, but I can handle it. I'm a big girl. You dredged up muck too, Mick."

"So you admit you have muck?" he asked. "I'm surprised."

"It's not my muck," she said. "It's Walt's muck."

"We all have muck," he said.

"Not me."

"Right. You're the sunshine girl. I forgot."

She started to protest, but he interrupted.

"Look, since I'm stuck here for a few days with this bum shoulder, let me be around for your next meeting with Bobby. I don't trust him, and I don't think you should either."

"That's ridiculous. You never met him; how can you not trust him? Plus, Mick, you're not my protector. I know that story of losing everything sounds bad, but I'm a different person now. I can handle myself."

His mouth hardened. But then he grimaced as if he couldn't help but say more no matter how badly he didn't want to. "I'm trying to figure out why Walt gave me his house. Maybe this is it. Maybe he wanted me to keep you from being too nice to guys like Bobby."

"That makes no sense at all."

"I have to trust my gut. And my gut is telling me to tell you to watch your back around this guy."

• • •

Now Nina was really too tired to talk about Walt. She went upstairs to work.

Mick set to work making a cold potato and leek soup for dinner, along with an avocado salad with raspberry vinaigrette.

Despite the food, he was dreading dinner. They couldn't avoid talking about Walt much longer.

Who was Bobby? The name was familiar to Mick, like he'd heard Walt talk about the guy, but he couldn't remember any details.

When Nina came downstairs from her office, where she'd been holed up all afternoon, he could see in her red-rimmed eyes that she was about as up for a tough conversation as he was.

"I propose a truce tonight," she suggested. "No talking about the house or Walt."

"Okay." So he still had time to find the box tonight, after she went to bed and before they started talking tomorrow. He planned on going back out to the garage and doing a thorough search as soon as he was sure she was asleep.

She smiled weakly. "You wanna go out on the deck? It's a gorgeous night," she said.

"Nah. I like it here," he said, taking his usual seat. He pushed the garnishes toward her. "Grated Vermont cheddar, sliced scallions, sour cream—and not the low-fat kind that you had in your fridge." He shuddered.

"I'm starting to think that you want this house for the kitchen," she said. "You haven't left this room except to sleep and shop for groceries."

And to ransack the place. He'd gone through most of the downstairs rooms quietly and efficiently between making the soup and spinning the salad. The elaborate meal was a lame attempt to assuage his guilt.

So far, it wasn't working.

"I like kitchens," he said. "I did all the cooking in my family."

"Right—you cooked; your sisters cleaned." She tried the soup and sighed. "Oh. Wow. Thanks."

He tried not to respond to her positive response. "My sisters were all hopeless in the kitchen."

"All those sisters, and the boy doing the woman's work? Walt couldn't boil water."

"But we're not talking about Walt tonight," he reminded her.

"Right. No Walt. Tell me about your sisters. Did they chop the wood? Take out the trash?" Her soup was already half gone. "Join the army?"

He pushed away his bowl and sat back. He was enjoying watching her eat, maybe a little too much. The way her lips curled around her spoon was lovely. "They cleaned. Lots and lots of cleaning. My father liked the place in perfect shape."

"Division of labor, then."

"My mother tried to teach them to cook, but they were all hopeless. Sandra was the baby. She could never remember she had rice on the stove, or beans, or whatever she was making. Her ruined pots were epic, smoking and black. We'd soak them for days, then give up and throw them out where my dad couldn't find them. Baily, the oldest girl, refused to count or measure. The only person I've ever met who could make spaghetti into inedible mush. Now that I look back on it, she must have done it on purpose to be so awful. Bella was the middle girl. She swore she'd never touch raw meat—and stood by it, so that was a no-go in our

house. We had red meat at every meal. Including breakfast."
He stopped. Talking about Bella made his throat tighten. He
guzzled his water to get the sour taste out of his mouth.

She watched him closely. "So you were the oldest?"

"Yep. And the wisest."

She looked doubtful but didn't say anything. That was
the power of an excellent soup.

"So my mother eventually gave in and taught me to
cook. She'd been reluctant because she knew my dad
would be pissed that I was doing something so girly."

"Was he?"

"Yeah. But he liked the food. And I was manly enough
to complain bitterly to anyone within earshot. Kept up my
macho exterior."

"Your secret is safe with me," she said.

"You can shout it from the rooftops. He's long gone
and buried."

"I'm sorry."

"I'm not." He kept talking to cover the awkward pause.
"Anyway, my mother was secretly preparing us for a
future without her." The words had come in a rush, and he
instantly regretted them. Why had he told her that?

Nina was serving herself seconds, but she stopped
midladle. "She left your family?"

Her eyes were so honest, so open. She seemed so genuinely interested, he couldn't stop himself from blabber-
ing on. "She'd gotten her diagnosis three days before she
taught me to flip my first omelet. Three months after I
mastered the Sunday night roast, she was bedridden. I
was grateful I could cook while the cancer did its final
work. I brought homemade broth to her bed for a month
and a half before it was over."

"That's a lot of broth."

"Yeah, it was." He hated himself for telling her all that. What did she care about his mother? His asshole father? Was he actively trying to get her sympathy? It was a cowardly, despicable way to proceed and he promised himself he wouldn't tell her anything else about his family. Especially about Bella. He didn't want her to give him the house out of pity. That was more than he could bear.

"I'm sorry, Mick."

"Yeah, well, it's life, right? What can you do?"

She looked at the soup she'd just served herself as if she didn't want it anymore. "My parents also died when we were young. Car crash. I was nine."

This was the trouble with talking: warmth, closeness, trust, stuff in common. He couldn't risk it. "I'm sorry."

"It's life, right? What can you do? Walt and I had a single, childless aunt who came and stayed with us. We got by okay."

They looked at all the food on the table. As usual, Mick had made way too much.

"Where are your sisters now?" she asked.

"All over. California. Nevada. Tel Aviv."

"Tel Aviv?"

"Long story."

"Tell me," she said.

"I will, but not now," he lied. *Must never tell her.* She couldn't feel even more sorry for him. He already felt lousy with her pity.

There wasn't enough soup in the world to make up for how he'd feel if she gave him the house for that.

Chapter Sixteen

Georgia said good-bye to her eleven o'clock patient, a sweet professor who was having panic attacks before his lectures. She shut the door lightly behind him, looking forward to her quick lunch before her next patient came—a senior volleyball player with bulimia.

She considered calling Nina. She was worried about her. Nina hadn't ever fully faced her brother's death, and with this man arriving, she'd have no choice but to confront the fact that he was gone. Georgia had been a psychiatrist long enough to know that it wasn't going to be pretty.

Her office was in the back of her house. She walked to the front door and checked for the mail, which came at ten on the dot every morning. Sometimes she hated that her office was in her home. It made it impossible to escape work. Other times she liked the submersion that she was able to achieve with her life being so contained. Being Galton's only psychiatrist was a responsibility she took extremely seriously.

The mail was the usual batch of junk and—

She paused at the hand-addressed envelope.

She got one every month. Return address, Upstate Correctional Facility.

She considered opening it but didn't. She tossed it into the recycling along with the credit card offers.

She'd opened Bobby's first letter, over a year ago. Big mistake. She hadn't even considered writing back. A relationship with Bobby Ridale was impossible. He was a convict, for heaven's sake. Plus, their past was too complicated to reopen. Their brief high school affair had cost Georgia her virginity, but at least it had cured her of her childish curiosity about bad boys.

He had written in that first letter that he'd loved her since fourth grade.

He said he'd be out soon and wanted to see her.

He didn't say that he was after her money, but then, that wasn't exactly the kind of thing you put in a love letter. She had to be careful.

She went into the kitchen to fix herself a tuna sandwich.

Nothing wrong with lunch alone.

She sat at her table. Read the *New York Times* cover to cover. Did the crossword.

She wasn't lonely.

Okay, so she was in these quiet moments.

But these moments passed. No reason to get sentimental.

She ate her sandwich and a few handfuls of M&M'S.

She still had time before her twelve thirty.

She went back to her office and tried to look over files, but the silence and her loneliness kept taking her thoughts back to Bobby Ridale.

• • •

Mick walked the streets of downtown Galton, looking for something to get his mind off of Nina, the house he had to take from her, the box he couldn't find, and his sister's plane touching down in a foreign land. Would she leave the plane in a wheelchair? Had the trip been too much for her? Could she deal with the Middle Eastern heat?

The town wasn't much. The one main street was lined with quaint small businesses. A diner, a dry cleaner, a flower shop, a drugstore—

Garcia's Pharmacy.

It was a tiny place with a red neon sign. He turned the corner and was taken aback by the huge blank white wall that loomed over him. The pristine emptiness of the expanse reminded him of Nina.

Emptiness. It was a word that suited Nina well.

A word that suited him lately too. He was looking at his life. What was he going to do next, after the box and house were settled? He'd rush to Tel Aviv, be with his sisters. And then? He'd go back to California and start earning again—but how could he ever earn enough to pay Nina back? He'd been a soldier most of his adult life. What else could he do? This empty white expanse of nothing. Nina had nailed the perfect memorial for soldiers everywhere.

Cut it with the self-pity, Rivers.

He escaped the wall and his thoughts by ducking into the cool refuge of the drugstore. It was the usual array of magazines, skin creams, candy. Something about the place's predictability soothed him. He could walk into any drugstore in any town in America and find the same arrangement of basics. He grabbed a plastic basket from the front and collected odds and ends for a care package. He tried to send one off every week to the hospital in California where he'd spent four months recovering from the blast.

"Soldiers get twenty percent off everything. Wounded get twenty-five."

Mick spun around. A man of about sixty with darkened, sun-damaged skin stood behind the counter. The guy looked made of leather. He stepped around the counter, his red cowboy boots clunking on the worn linoleum floor.

"Not a soldier anymore," Mick said. "And definitely not wounded." The ache of his shoulder was still a shooting pain, but he straightened as much as he could manage. *Wounded in the line of cat retrieval*...

The man nodded. "Lucky you."

"Yeah, guess I am." His eyes flicked to the thin yellow band around the man's wrist. "Sorry for your loss."

The man nodded. "Thanks. It was my son."

"Iraq?"

"Afghanistan."

"Was there for six years. Saw a lot of good men go down." He let the anger of watching good men go down pass over him. So many good men; no chance against hidden IEDs. It was the kind of warfare where prayer and luck were more important than skill and knowledge. Every day a gamble. But this guy looked like he knew that.

"His name was Matthew Garcia. He was out of Kandahar mostly." The man pointed at a framed picture of a boy in a uniform next to the cash register, and Mick forced himself to look at it.

He winced. Matthew Garcia was the model for Nina's

Robin to her Walt-Batman. He looked better in photos than in her pictures. Mick nodded. He put his stuff on the counter.

"I'm having a mural painted," the man said as he rang Mick up. "A memorial for the lost. For my boy."

"Saw the wall," Mick admitted. He felt for him, but the man's grief swirled like a sour mist around him, and Mick couldn't get caught up in it. He took the plastic bag and his change. "Good luck with it." He turned to go.

"Yeah, well, I'm gonna need luck at the rate I'm going," the man said.

Mick waved, nodded, and reached for the door.

"Flighty artist types," the man muttered.

Mick spun back around, stunned by the wave of anger that filled him, as if the man had insulted a friend.

The man went on. "I hired a local artist, but she can't seem to get going on it," the man explained. "Think I'm gonna have to fire her."

"What's the rush?" Mick had to struggle to keep the anger out of his voice. *He lost a son; take it easy...*

A boy who looked a lot like the boy in the picture appeared in the doorway to the back storeroom. His eyes went to his father, then to Mick. His face hardened.

The man ignored the boy, who was obviously another son. "I'm having trouble with graffiti. Last week, someone defaced the wall with Nazi nonsense. Third time in three months."

"They defaced a war memorial?" Mick let his anger show.

"Well, no. They defaced a blank wall. See, if the thing was painted, I don't think anyone would bother it."

Mick shook his head. "I would hope not."

"That's why I think I'm gonna have to fire the girl. I mean, how hard is it to paint a few flags? Not like it's fighting a war or anything. It's stupid paint. Just do it!"

The boy slipped away back into the storeroom.

As badly as he wanted to slip away too, Mick couldn't help himself. "Fire Nina?"

"You know her?" The man's face flashed surprise. He took a step backward.

"I'm—" He paused, looking for the right description of their relationship. "Staying with her. Just for a few days. I knew her brother."

"Well, why didn't you say so straight off?" Despite the man's dark skin, Mick could see his blush rise. "I'm sorry. It's just—It's been almost a year I've been waiting." His tone had turned conciliatory.

"She's working hard on it," Mick said. "In fact, I'm helping her." As soon as the words left his mouth, he knew he had just found another way besides fattening her up to pay her back for taking her house and walking off with Walt's last secret. He couldn't paint, but he could do something. He didn't know what he could do exactly, but placating Mr. Garcia was at least a good first step. "That's why I'm in town, actually. Part of the reason. To help her out. It's coming along great. We've been discussing it."

Mr. Garcia stumbled over himself to cover for his gaffe. "Oh, good, then! Excellent! So definitely, I can wait a few more weeks. But then—well—winter's coming. I don't know where you're from, son, but winter here comes early and fierce."

"Don't worry about a thing. Give us a little more time. You're going to love it. I promise. It's, um, not going to be the usual kind of thing. It's gonna be something—deeper."

"I'm glad there's a soldier working on it," the man admitted. "You know the score."

Yeah, he knew the score. And he was losing. He'd been here three days, and already he'd gotten himself tangled up in Nina's life. Every step closer to her felt like a step farther from where he needed to be.

Chapter Seventeen

*S*he was going to gain ten pounds before Mick left. All the food Mick had made, combined with the stress of having him here, plus having two major art projects going with her veggie oil paintings and Bobby's letters, plus the memorial—

She'd been eating like a horse.

All morning, she'd shut herself in her upstairs art studio, coming down every so often to defrost pancakes in the microwave. She alternated between working on her vegetable painting for the cookbook, finishing the first letter for Bobby—which was so beautiful, she dared Georgia not to open it—and stuffing her face with Mick's blueberry carb bombs.

But no matter what she did, her mind was firmly on Mick. Where the heck had he disappeared to this morning?

She looked at her studio clock. Two twenty in the afternoon.

Two twenty-two.

SWEET KISS OF SUMMER   119

Two twenty-five.

She gave up trying to work and devoted herself to straining to hear the roar of Mick's car in her driveway.

He was coming back, right?

The silence of the house had never bothered her before. Now it made her feel on the verge of panic.

She looked out the window at her empty yard. His tent was still set up by the garden. Ridiculous that he'd slept outside last night, but he had insisted he felt better out there. She had thought that he was starting to warm to her, even to open up a bit—

Wait. No. She reminded herself that their relationship was about Walt, not him. She reminded herself that she was going to get Walt's story out of him, let his shoulder heal up a bit, then send him on his way. She very, very firmly reminded herself that she wasn't going to give him anything—especially the house.

She went downstairs and devoured her fifth pancake, then climbed back upstairs to resume her lonely vigil.

Finally, at the first rev of his car in the driveway, she raced out of her studio and down the stairs. She met him at the car. "Where have you been?" she demanded before he'd gotten free of the driver's seat.

He climbed out and eyed her askance. Then he got two bags of groceries out of the back. "Hi, honey. I'm home," he said. He moved past her and started for the back door.

"I've been worried all day. I thought maybe you'd left town." She followed him around the back, then stopped. "What is wrong with the front door, for heaven's sake?" she called after him.

"Old habits," he said. He took the steps to the deck two at a time with both bags under his good arm. He managed to open the door with a complicated arm and foot combination and slipped inside.

The screen door swung shut behind him.

She didn't follow him inside. Instead she stood on the back deck, looking into the dark forest past her backyard. Was this how it was going to be? She desperately wanted him to talk about Walt when he wasn't around, then she wanted to stay on the deck and stare into the forest when he showed up? Was he right, and she wanted to hear only good things? To live in her fantasyland?

She forced herself to follow him inside.

He was unloading the groceries in the kitchen. Ground beef, frozen veggie burgers, buns, more coffee, herbal tea.

The tea touched her, but she had to stay strong. "We have to talk," she demanded.

He winced, trying to put cans of refried beans in the upper cabinets.

"Also, we should work on that arm. I can help," she said.

He kept stubbornly unloading the groceries. "I'm a big boy. I don't want your sympathy."

She was surprised at the harshness of his words. "It's not sympathy, Mick. It's human kindness."

He folded the empty grocery bags and put them in the recycling bin by the back door. "I don't want your human kindness, Nina. I want your house. I'm sorry. Your kindness while I hang around waiting for you to admit it's my house isn't feeling so hot. I'd rather we keep this business. Can we keep it business?"

"Oh, so you get to cook and shop and be all nice, but I can't be nice back?" she asked, exasperated.

"Right," he said. "Exactly."

"That's crazy," she protested. "No more food! No more

cooking! If this is business, then it has to stay business for both of us."

"That's a problem," he said, sitting down at the table with a sad sort of sigh.

"It's not. You eat your food. I'll eat mine."

He scrunched his lips. "I just met a man named Mr. Garcia."

"Okay." She sat at the table across from him. "What's he have to do with this?"

"I told him I'd help you with the memorial."

"What?" She jumped back up, confused. "Stay out of my business, Mick!"

"Yeah, I thought you'd say that."

"So why did you do it?"

"Because I'm here to take your house," he said. "And it's making me feel shitty. So please, Nina, eat my food and let me help you on the mural, and we'll get through this without me feeling like the world's worst asshole."

"First off, don't feel shitty, because you're not getting the house."

"I think I am."

"What makes you think that? Besides, obviously, bull-headed stubbornness."

"You'll give it to me because I'm honest and you know it. Plus, it's the right thing to do. You know that too. I'm just waiting for you to admit it."

She shook her head. "Not that easy." She paced to the window, then back to the table.

"We'll see."

"So how do you intend to help with my mural, smart guy? Can you paint? Sketch? You saw what I had in the garage. It's terrible. I need Michelangelo, not some worn-out, emotionless army vet with a bum shoulder."

"I can help you get an idea going. I was there. The war? Remember? Maybe that'll help. Shake something into place."

The idea of sketching him flitted into her head. It made her blush to think about concentrating on the exquisite lines of his lips, his eyes, his jawline. This man on the side of a two-story wall would have the women of Galton lining up to join the military. Or at the very least, it would have them falling all over themselves to send some pretty awesome care packages. But he was right about having to keep their relationship neutral. They couldn't cross lines that would confuse the issue of the house. She said, "My business is my business. It's not okay to snoop around in it. If Mr. Garcia has a problem with me, he talks to me." She leaned against the counter and crossed her arms over her chest.

"He was ready to fire you, Nina," Mick said. "I wasn't about to let you go down when I was right there to have your back."

"Is this part of your drink-the-coffee, lemmings-over-a-cliff thing again?" she asked. "Mick, this isn't the army. We're not a unit or a troop or whatever you call it. We're enemies."

"We're all on our own, you mean?"

"Yes. That's exactly what I mean."

"You needed my help," he said. "And I wanted to give it. I don't get why you're so upset."

"Because you're supposed to be here talking about Walt. It's been three days! It's about time we got that conversation started."

"Yeah, about that," he said. "I've been doing a lot of thinking about that. Look, Nina, I'm sorry, but I'm not going to talk about the past. Not the good stuff, not the bad. None of it."

Her mouth fell open. "Then how do you plan on convincing me that Walt's letter was for real? That this house is yours?" She started pacing again.

"By just being me."

She stared at him in disbelief. "Did I mention to you that I lost everything else Walt had in a scam? And now you think I'm just going to *fall* for you?"

"You want me to tell you my sob story?" he asked. "Would that be better?"

"I don't want to hear it, Mick."

"Good. Because I'm not about to tell it."

They stared at each other across the kitchen.

Finally, he said, "I never talked Walt into giving me this house. He just did it. I have no idea why. I'm just going to have to hope that it'll be like brother, like sister. It's the best I can do. I told you in the beginning I don't have answers. You have to believe me on that."

"You think I'll be like Walt and decide to give you this house because you're you?" she cried. She couldn't imagine being more exasperated at this man.

"It's all I've got. I'm sorry, Nina. I've spent the last three days thinking about this. I don't like dwelling in the past. Afghanistan was not a nice place, and I don't feel like talking about it. Especially about Walt. Especially to you."

"So you're scared," she said. She sat down next to him. Close to him.

"Scared?" He looked shocked at her accusation. "I

spent six years in a hellhole getting shot at, and you think that you scare me?"

"Yes. Me and this house. I saw it the first minute I saw you, looking up at my house like it was on fire or full of ghosts or something. You're a coward." She leaned forward. "Why? What's so scary about me? About this house? About talking about Walt?" She leaned in even closer, crowding him.

He didn't answer.

"You'll hang around in the kitchen, but I never see you anywhere else. You won't even come in the front door. You sleep outside in a stupid tent. Why? There's a reason." She was so close to him now, she could feel his heat, hear his breathing.

He didn't move.

"Or is it not the house? Are you afraid of yourself? Because you know what you're doing is wrong."

He tried to remain rigid, unresponding, but she could feel the vibration off his muscles as he struggled to hold himself back.

She whispered in his ear, "You won't talk about the past; you won't fight for the future. You're a wimp, Mick Rivers. Maybe that's why Walt gave you the house. Because he knew you'd be the only one in the unit too chickenshit to take it."

Chapter Eighteen

$\mathcal{M}$ick spent his third night in Galton in his tent in the yard. His shoulder didn't like it, but he didn't give a damn. That house and that woman were making him dizzy with regret.

And lust.

Just a little lust, which he would studiously ignore. She was beautiful, and he was a man reacting to female beauty. That was normal. But even as he told himself that, over and over and over again, he knew there was more to it than that. *She understood him.* She'd called him on how he felt about the house as if she'd seen straight into his soul.

Which was why he had to find the box and get out.

A little after eight the next morning, he saw the light in her upstairs studio click on. Hopefully, he could go inside now, and she'd be hard at work, not up for another attack.

He certainly wasn't up for another fight. Yesterday, he'd left her in the kitchen and wandered around the house just to prove to her that he wasn't afraid of a damn house. She didn't have a TV, so he'd sat and stared at the black cat for a while, stewing. Eventually, even the cat had had enough. He'd curled into a ball, turning his back on him. So he'd left, finding the nearest bar and watching some game on the television that he couldn't concentrate on enough to remember. He had called Sandy, but there was no news except that they were taking the week to settle in. Worse, he had no news for them.

Later that night, he'd searched the garage again, careful not to let in any cats.

He hadn't found a thing.

Which was why today he was going to search this place as if it were a known insurgent's den, to hell with politeness.

He paused outside his tent.

Shit.

He went back inside, grabbed his jeans and a T-shirt, and threw them on.

I'm a rule-following wuss, he thought as he let himself into the house through the unlocked back door. *Why doesn't she lock her doors? The world isn't all rainbows and nice guys...*

In the kitchen, she'd left a note on the center of the table. *Come upstairs, last room on the left. DON'T EAT!*

Don't eat?

He opened the fridge. Another note, taped to the milk. *I said don't eat! And don't drink either. Come upstairs!*

This was what happened when you let a woman call you a coward and you couldn't defend yourself without giving away the farm. She started ordering you around. Telling you what to do. Calling you names.

She was in the yoga room, bent completely in two.

"That hurts just to look at," he said. But the truth was, the only way it hurt was an increasingly upsetting and impossible arousal in his groin. She was wearing skin-tight yoga gear that outlined every smooth, sleek muscle.

"Too bad. Because we're working on your shoulder. I can't watch you gimping around anymore. If you get to cook and be my artistic advisor, I get to fix your arm."

"It's better," he said, aware that he sounded like a child.

"It's not. You can't even stand up straight after last night sleeping on that stupid hard ground." She shot him a look of pure scorn from her upside-down position.

He stood up straight and winced.

She raised her eyebrows.

He gave in. She was right. It was only fair that if he was going to offer her help, he should let her help him. "Just this once."

He came into the room and she rolled out a green mat next to her blue one. "Lose the jeans," she said.

"Yes, ma'am."

He did, then lost the shirt too, just to piss her off.

She scowled at him. "You didn't eat, did you? You need an empty stomach to do yoga properly."

"Not a bite." He stepped onto the mat. Her toes were really nice. Good grippy toes. He wasn't sure he'd ever noticed a woman's toes before, but hers seemed extraor-dinarily strong, almost like fingers. "Never done this before," he warned. He meant the yoga, but he might as well have meant that he'd never felt quite so docile and willing. What was happening here? He didn't like it.

"I'm an excellent teacher. Just follow. We'll get you limbered up; then we'll move to the shoulder and see if we can free it up a little." She started to turn this way and that. He watched, but he didn't move. She was gorgeous, yes. There was that. But more important, he didn't want to follow. He wanted to lead—

"Mick!" She straightened. "Right foot forward, left foot back, and bend here—" She came to his mat and reached out to bend him.

But he was through taking orders. "Like this?" he asked, catching her arm and pulling her to him.

She froze in his arms but didn't speak.

"Or is it better like this?" He kissed her on the lips—hard.

She stiffened in his arms. Then she relaxed. Then she kissed him back. "Yes, like this," she murmured. Her hands were on his bare back; her fingers ran up his spine; her awesome toes nestled next to his. He deepened the kiss. Pulled her closer. Her thin, clingy, spaghetti-strap shirt and tight black leggings might as well have been nothing. The fabric was so thin, he could feel every inch of her through it as if it weren't there.

And she definitely could feel every growing, insistent inch of him.

She pulled back. "Mick."

"Who's the coward now?" he asked.

She ignored him. "Your shoulder is tight. I feel it."

He let her go. "Oh, so this is a clinical examination we're undergoing here?"

She shot him a sideways glance and moved away from him. He felt the docile helplessness rush back into the space she'd occupied. "Yes. Exactly. Now, follow along."

She stepped primly back to her own mat and began contorting again. He watched her a minute. *Stubborn woman.* "I'm not going to let you deny what's going on here, Nina."

"What's going on here?" she asked, bent and twisted and gorgeous.

"You tell me." He sat down on the mat. Then he lay on his back, put his hands behind his head, and stared up at her, waiting for her to admit the inevitable.

She stopped and harrumphed. "Mick. Your shoulder."

"I already told you, I'm not going to follow along," he said.

Her eyes passed over him, her pupils widening as she scanned his bare chest. She seemed to like the view from up there as much as he did from down here. Her legs looked a mile long from this angle. He wanted to pull off her pants and kiss every inch of her, starting at her toes and ending—

"What aren't you telling me, Mick?"

Her nipples had gone hard under her thin shirt. "What aren't you telling me?" he asked.

"You first," she demanded.

"I can't tell you. Classified information."

She scowled, turned her attention away from him, and contorted a while longer into all sorts of impossible shapes, each one more enticing than the last. Finally, she gave up and sat down beside him, on her mat.

He stared at the ceiling and she stared straight ahead, tapping her remarkable toes.

After a while, she tentatively reached for his shoulder. She prodded it, finding just the spot that made him jump. She murmured something, moved on her knees onto his mat, and touched him again, more softly this time. She leaned over him and pulled his arm forward gently across his chest, pushing down on it with her shoulder. After the initial burst of pain, it felt good. She manipulated it, back and forth, slowly, easing the soreness out of the tight tendons.

He closed his eyes. "You can't help being nice, can you? No matter how big a jerk I am?" he asked, pain alternating with release.

"You're not a jerk. You're a coward but not a jerk. There's a difference."

"I'd rather be a jerk."

"Most men would."

He could feel the blood flowing in his veins. "I want to kiss you again," he said. "That makes me a jerk, right?"

She bent low to him and kissed him, openmouthed and hungry. He tried not to moan. She surfaced and said, "No, that doesn't make you obnoxious. It makes you human."

Maybe that was his problem. Humanness. It was a hard one to shake. "I'm planning on making love to you, and then taking your house. I can't think of anything ruder."

She considered. "Okay, the house part is kind of jerky. But the sex—" She kissed him again, and this time he did moan. "Yeah, that not so much. Morally neutral."

She worked on his shoulder a little more, deeper, more tenderly.

"If I'm not mistaken, you're softening me up for something," he said.

"If you're planning on taking my house—which won't work, by the way, but still—and you won't tell me about Walt, then I deserve something out of this." She met his gaze and held it.

He had no idea how serious she was. "I made a year's supply of blueberry pancakes already," he said.

"True. But not good enough." Her eyes were on his chest again, then down, down...

"I rescued your devil cat," he reminded her.

"Two more points," she allowed. She let her hand drift

to his chest. Tentatively, she drew a finger down it, to his belly. "I want you to make love to me, Mick."

"I feel like this is some kind of trick," he said. He closed his eyes to better feel the trail of her finger from chest, to belly, to—

She was gone. He opened his eyes.

She was standing over him. She had pulled her shirt over her head. Shimmied out of her pants and panties. No—not her panties. He looked at the heap of clothes on the floor.

There hadn't been any panties.

Oh help me, Lord.

She stood before him, stark naked and gorgeous.

"Now, that's not following the rules at all," he murmured.

"So punish me," she said.

"Why are you doing this, Nina?" He was barely able to get the words out.

"Because I waited two years for a fantasy. For a man who'd give me answers about my brother. For a man who deserved my brother's last, dying wish. You're a terrible disappointment, Mick."

"I said I was sorry."

"Yeah, well, sorry isn't good enough. You owe me. So pay up." Then, without waiting for the answer that he was too tongue-tied to give anyway, she lowered herself and straddled him on the small green mat, and he knew the rules had stopped applying and that despite his aching shoulder, he was going to enjoy this hard floor very, very much.

It was a trick on Nina. Not a purposeful trick. Not pre-meditated. But the way it worked out, it might as well

have been. A trick of the universe. Or of fate. Because
by the time she leaned down, her small breasts brushing
against his bare chest, she was a goner. She knew she was
supposed to resist getting close to him, and yet she felt
inexplicably close to him. She wanted to share his secrets.
She wanted to ease his pain. She kissed the corner of his
lip, then down his neck, nuzzling his ear.

She wanted to make love to him now.

Here.

Hard.

She filled herself with him. She moved, rhythmically,
on top of him while he held her hips firmly in his tanned,
strong hands, his eyes closed, his face bathed in ecstasy.
Forget her promises not to care. She wanted him here.
Then there. Then—oh yeah—right there.

"Don't you dare stop, Mick."

"Wouldn't dare," he groaned.

"You owe me this." She threw her head back. "For two
long years of being an asshole, you owe me."

"I do. I know. You're right. We have a lot of catching
up to do." He pulled her hips into him violently, and she
pulled away just as urgently, trying to fight the sensation
that was building too fast inside her. She wanted to slow
it down, but he was unstoppable. Two years she'd waited
for this—no, not this. Not exactly. But maybe—yes, yes,
oh God. She had been waiting for this. Not the sex, but the
connection. She had to get through to this man, somehow,
and if this was the way, then, oh God, yes . . .

He put an arm around her and they rolled so that he
was on top of her. He growled with pleasure or maybe
with the pain of his shoulder—she didn't care which. He
wanted to control her, to control the rhythm. She knew

this as surely as she knew that she wanted him to dominate her, to use her to reach something—what?

Who cared? No more thinking.

She gave in to him, spreading under him, gasping. "Mick. Don't stop."

He held her wrists roughly over her head, pinning her to the hard floor. The floor hurt; his grip hurt. But his plunging, feral rhythm hummed, and she wanted more of that hum. This was what she'd wanted from the moment she'd first laid eyes on him. This was what a man like him could do, should do. And there was nothing wrong with it. Except that she couldn't let him fool her into something—

What?

Who cared?

He was moving faster, closer. She could feel her small breasts trapped against his chest, moving with every plunge as if they were huge. Maybe they were. Maybe she had turned into some kind of Amazon. Maybe she was growing in his grip. It felt that way. Growing into a goddess. Faster, harder—

She gasped and she pressed up into him, sealing his body against her vibrating clit until she thought she might die of the pleasure of it.

And then she did.

She felt him come inside her an instant later. He collapsed over her as thoroughly as she had collapsed under him.

After a while, she picked up her head to look at him. "Hi."

"Hi." He paused, then said, "Please tell me you're on the pill."

"I am. Please tell me you're not a whoring bastard who just gave me some unspeakable disease."

"I'm not. I won't. I know this doesn't look good, but I swear, I'm not usually this kind of guy."

"Why should I believe you?"

"This is the story of the two of us, Nina, isn't it? You just have to believe me. It's all I've got."

"I believe you. After all, I was the one who jumped on you," she admitted. She let her head fall. Then picked it up. "I'm still not drinking your damn coffee."

"Oh yeah?" He rolled off her so they were side to side. She rolled to face him, the hard floor digging into her hip. He pushed a strand of her hair back, tracing it with his touch as if it were smooth and luscious, not impossibly wild and kinky. She felt as if even her hair had grown with their passion. "I did your yoga. You should drink my coffee," he said.

"You did not do yoga!"

"You sure?" he asked. "We were on mats. And those were some pretty damn ambitious positions."

"How's that shoulder?"

"I think we did permanent damage."

She looked stricken.

"Kidding."

"Liar."

"It's just a shoulder. I have another."

"I'm making breakfast. Tea. And oatmeal."

"And more sex?"

"Maybe."

"Sounds delicious to me."

Chapter Nineteen

They sat at the table, oatmeal and tea in front of them. He was trying to be polite, making little sounds of appreciation.

"You're such a liar, Mick," she said. "Be straight with me. Just tell me you hate what I eat for breakfast, and we'll move on."

"No way. I want more yoga. This is the best oatmeal I've ever had."

"Really?"

He locked eyes with her. What had happened between them? Sex like that didn't come along every day. But what had it been for her? Just sex? Did she do this all the time? She was on the pill, after all. He didn't know a thing about her. "The best. Bar none."

"Are we talking about oatmeal?" she asked.

"Nope."

"I didn't think so."

They ate for a while. He could live on mush if he got to

supplement it with a few healthy servings of her. If only they were strangers. If only they'd met in the back of a dark bar somewhere, he'd propose to her right now. God, her hair, her freckles, her perfect pert body. The way she'd not cared that this was an idiot thing to do, but just done it anyway.

But it was soft to think *if only*.

"Mick, there's something we need to talk about."

If only. He let his fantasy evaporate. "I said I wouldn't talk about—"

"No. Not about Walt. It's about something else." She took a deep breath. "You have bad dreams."

He didn't move.

"That first night. When you slept inside. You said things. A nightmare. And last night, I heard you again. From all the way out on the lawn."

He stood, walked to the window. *Shit.* Did he talk about the box? About Bella? *If only...*

"I don't understand what you're saying, mostly," she went on. "But you talked about Walt. Like you were reliving something. The first night, when you slept inside, I tried to wake you up, and you seemed to wake up, but I don't think that you really did, since you didn't seem to remember it."

He didn't answer. Didn't turn around. He wasn't in control. Not if he turned at night into a mumbling, incoherent mess, then couldn't remember it in the morning. "Did we just have mercy sex? Do you feel sorry for me?"

"No. Of course not. The two things aren't related. I just wanted you to know. I don't want us to have secrets. Especially now."

Secrets are all we have. He turned to her. "What do we have, Nina? What happened just now?"

"I don't know. I guess we have—loneliness."

The word struck him cold.

No. That wasn't what had just happened on that hard floor.

That was the flowers-and-rainbow version of what had just happened. "You think we made love because we're lonely? You think we're nothing but two lonely, sad, desperate people with bad dreams, fucking on a hardwood floor?" He wasn't used to being seen as the weak one. He hated that she saw him that way. He'd seen things, done things, that she could only imagine.

"Isn't that how it always starts out?" she asked.

"Not in my world," he said. "In my world, it starts out with me being pissed. Pissed that you were trying to push me around. Pissed that you want something out of me that *I can't give*." He stressed the last three words as strongly as he could. "I was pissed at you, Nina. I didn't want to take orders from you. *Don't eat. Don't drink.* I wanted control. I wanted dark, dirty, evil control over you, and I knew exactly how to get it. That's what we just did in there. Fuck loneliness. That was a power grab, and it felt good. For both of us. For me to take and for you to give."

Her eyes grew wide in anger. "I fucked you too," she said, her voice defiant.

"We fucked each other," he allowed. "And it was good. It wasn't love and it wasn't soft and it wasn't kind. And we both liked it. Needed it."

But now what?

The unspoken question hung in the air between them.

She said, "Tell me why you're here, Mick. The whole truth." She looked exhausted, worn-out, the fight in her gone.

"You really want to know?"

"Yes." She put down her spoon. "No." She scrunched her lips. "Yes. Tell me."

He had to get back to Bella. He had to stop this selfish nonsense that was making him weak with lust and self-indulgence. He was falling for Nina when he was supposed to be taking from her. "Walt asked me to do something here in exchange for the house. He didn't want you to know what it is."

She deflated. "Tell me you didn't just fuck me because that was Walt's last wish. Was *I* the mercy fuck?"

"No. Nothing like that."

"Then what?" she demanded. "No, wait. He didn't want me to know?"

"Right."

"But I want to know."

"And I want to tell you. But I can't without betraying my duty to Walt. See the rub?"

"He put us in an impossible situation," she said.

"Well, it's possible if I don't mind sneaking around and lying to you. But honestly, Nina, after—" He paused, and images of them just moments before, their bodies slamming, stirred his body back to life. "Secrets are hard to keep if we're going to keep up—this."

"Are we?" she asked.

"I don't think I can stop," he admitted. "Although we really should."

"Walt sucks. Sucked. Damn him!" She brought her empty bowl of oatmeal to the sink and rinsed it out.

"What was he thinking?" She spun back to face him. "No more of this. Of us. This is out of control."

"That's probably smart," he agreed, even though it made him want to rip his head off. And other body parts.

Stay on mission, soldier.

"Keeping this up would be dumb," she said.

"Idiotic," Mick agreed. "I think Walt knew that if anyone would come and do his dirty work, it would be me. I'd do it and keep my nose clean and not betray him."

"Guess he was wrong about you," she said. "Well, the keeping-the-nose-clean part."

"I believe in duty," he said. "Walt knew that."

"And I believe in duty too," Nina said. "Up to a point." She took his hand, and the gesture almost made him come undone. "He gave you the house in exchange for whatever it is you can't tell me?"

"Maybe. I don't know if it's that simple. I guess when I find what I'm looking for, I'll know."

"You could prove to me that Walt's letter wasn't a fake if you told me."

"Yeah. I think so."

"Is this why you didn't come for two years? Why you didn't answer my letters? Because there's something awful waiting here?"

"I don't know what's waiting. But yeah, I didn't want to do Walt's dirty work. I had my own issues."

"Okay, don't tell me what he wanted you to do. Just do it."

"You sure?"

She hesitated. "No. But do it anyway."

Mick nodded. "Yes, ma'am."

"Promise you won't tell me. You'll finish whatever your secret mission is without me knowing," she insisted.

"I thought you wanted to know everything."

"I do. But I get that you can't tell me this." She paused. "I also know that I want you again, and that is pissing me off because it's really beside the point and is messing with my head."

"You're sexy when you're pissed off."

She smiled weakly.

He felt better now that his dilemma and their attraction were out in the open. It was better to face these things, then deal with the consequences. "Okay, let's play it like this. I have to ask you something. But I can't tell you why."

"Okay." She nodded. "That's good. What do you want to know?"

"What did you do with Walt's stuff from the garage? I need to find something that was supposed to be there."

He could see the wheels of her mind spinning. "I threw out the junk; sold the tools and other stuff that wasn't personal and was worth something; gave mounds of clothes and whatnot to charity; put the rest of it in the basement."

"I need to go through what's left in the basement."

"Okay."

"Good."

"Good."

"And then what?"

"Well, that's the million-dollar question, isn't it?" Mick said.

"In other words, you don't have a clue."

"Not a damn clue. But I sure hope it involves more of that yoga."

Chapter Twenty

Nina read a year-old issue of *Marie Claire* magazine while she waited for Georgia to finish with her patient. Finally, halfway through "My Life as a Mail-Order Bride," the back door opened, then closed with a click. Then the door to the waiting room opened and Georgia stuck her head in. "Ms. Stokes? Right this way."

Nina came into the office with her usual sense of awe. African masks covered the walls. Fertility gods and goddesses from every culture sat on tabletops, bigger ones manning the floor. Toys for fidgeting—intricate worry dolls from Mexico, smooth stones from Cape Cod—waited in bowls and trays within easy reach.

Nina eyed the assortment of comfy chairs. She opted to lie down on Georgia's couch.

"Wow, this is serious," Georgia said. She sat down in her armchair and crossed her legs.

"Kinda. Thanks for making time for me," Nina said.

Georgia had squeezed her in between patients, and they didn't have much time to talk.

Even though she wasn't a real patient of Georgia's, Nina knew that when they were in this office, Georgia wouldn't break out of her therapist role. It was up to Nina to do the talking, and Georgia would keep her secrets, even from the Enemy Club. "Mick has nightmares," she told her friend. "He says Walt's name. He yells, screams, sweats—it's terrible to hear. The stuff he says makes me sure he was there when Walt got injured, Georgia. I think there's something he doesn't want to tell me about Walt's last mission."

Georgia didn't seem surprised. "What do you do when he has the nightmares?"

"The first time, I woke him up. But the next morning, he didn't remember. Not the dream. Not me being there."

"It's common for soldiers," Georgia said. "They've seen a lot that we can't even begin to imagine."

"I think he doesn't just forget what goes on in the night, Georgia. I think he's forgotten what happened to him and Walt in Afghanistan. Is that possible for him to forget like that?"

"Sure," Georgia said. "Totally possible. Too much stress. The mind protects itself from what hurts too much to face."

Nina thought of him accusing her of living in a rainbow world, wanting everything to be roses. Did Mick also block out the worst of his world? What parts of him were blocked out along with those memories? "I want him to remember," Nina said. "I want him to tell me what happened to Walt. What really happened."

"Be careful," Georgia said. "He might not be ready. And you might not be either."

Nina said, "But isn't it important to remember? Walt gave Mick his house, Georgia!"

"You don't know that."

"I'm starting to believe the letter isn't a con."

Georgia didn't say anything.

"Mick must have done something heroic. He must deserve it. Why wouldn't Mick want to remember that?"

Georgia stayed silent.

Nina sat up and looked at her friend. "We should face the past," she insisted.

"Sometimes," Georgia said. "But you can't force him, Nina."

"I know that." She picked up one of the worry dolls. They were a family: mother, father, brother, sister, even a baby. She picked up the brother. "But shouldn't he want to know?"

Georgia pursed her lips. "You want tough love? Enemy Club treatment?"

"The truth, the whole truth, and nothing but," Nina said, not at all sure that she meant it.

"Close your eyes. Clear your mind. Then think of the absolute worst scenario of what could have happened to Walt. The worst, most terrible thing you can think of. Then ask yourself, *What if this was what happened to Walt?* Could you live with that? Would you rather live without it? It's the past; you can't change it. So maybe you might decide that it's best not to know. That's a totally valid, healthy, rational decision you'd be making. Maybe he's making a similar choice."

Nina closed her eyes. Georgia was nothing if not rational. But Nina refused to be that way. She was emotional. *She cared.* She didn't want to make valid, rational decisions.

She wanted the truth—like her memorial. She wanted to get to the bottom of it. She called up images of grim-faced soldiers in heavy gear. Terrible heat, dust everywhere. The sound of guns, the sound of bombs. Stray dogs, crying children, alone, barefoot and dirty. And there was Walt. Standing in the middle of it, holding his gun.

She opened her eyes. "I can't do it. Oh hell. This is why I can't paint that damn mural. I can't face it."

"Right. And that's okay. Because it's too hard. Think of Mick. He was there. Who are you to force him back there?"

"I'm someone who cares about him," she said, shocking herself a little with the obvious truth of her words. "Walt I can't save. But Mick still has a chance."

"Save?" Georgia emphasized, repeating Nina's word.

"Why not?" Nina asked.

"Because it's not your place," Georgia said. "He has to save himself. You're acting like you're his mother. You're not. You can't save him. Work on saving yourself."

Nina closed her eyes, refusing to give up. She could let the darkness into her world. She wasn't as innocent as everyone thought she was. *The absolute worst thing.*

The images quieted, cleared, until it was silence, the hot wind blowing, the unrelenting Afghan sun bearing down. She saw Walt, alone, on the ground. He was in pain, but worse—

She opened her eyes. "The worst thing I can think of is Walt thinking that he was going to die alone. No friend near," she said.

Georgia sucked in her cheeks. She let her eyebrows rise a fraction of an inch.

"What?"

"From what you told me about Mick's dreams, it

sounds like Mick might have been there when Walt got injured," Georgia pointed out.

"So?"

Georgia spoke slowly, carefully. "The worst situation you can imagine for Walt is the very situation you yourself are in. Alone, hurt and confused, with Mick."

Nina sat up. "That's not true."

"You believe that what Mick said in his nightmare means that Walt wasn't alone when he was injured. He was with Mick. But maybe being with Mick feels like being alone to you because emotionally, he's not there."

"You mean I'm really thinking of myself when I try to think of Walt? I'm not that selfish!"

"We all are, Nins. We can't help it. Putting yourself in someone else's situation is one of the hardest things in life to do. Most people don't have the capacity at all. But it's not a bad thing that you can't get into Walt's head, hon. It's more important to get into your own. Look at me—"

Nina did. She didn't want to, but she did. She had to know what to do when she got back to her house and to Mick, besides tear his clothes off and forget everything else but how good it felt in his arms.

"Walt is gone. It doesn't matter what happened to him because you can never understand it. You can never put yourself in his head the way you would need to in order to understand. He's a soldier. It's a very specific, unique mind-set. So maybe it's better not to try. That's okay. But you're in danger, Nina. You're in danger now, in your house, and your unconscious is trying to tell you that. You are alone. You are facing a crisis. A man you know you can't trust is by your side—"

"I slept with him," Nina said.

Georgia didn't even flinch. "I want to hear every sick, dirty detail. But not right now." She adjusted her gray pencil skirt and composed her face into its neutral, maddening blankness. She glanced down at her watch. "Nina, we're running out of time. Listen to yourself: you're scared of being with him. That makes sense: what's worse than making love to a man who isn't really there? There's a reason 'orgasm' in French is *la petite morte*. The little death."

"It is? God, Georgia, you can put a morbid spin on anything."

"Why are you afraid to *die* with him? What is dangerous about him?"

"He's got a secret. He's looking for something in the house. Walt sent him to do it and told him not to tell me, but he told me this morning."

"Looking for what?" Georgia sat back, unable to hide her surprise.

"I don't know. He says that it's Walt's wish that I not know."

"Nina! He could be a con man. Maybe Walt was dying and let slip that he'd stashed a million bucks under the floorboards!"

"I don't think so."

"Because you trust everyone. Because you don't see the dark side. Because your worst fear is to be alone, and so you want to trust everyone, even though you know it's better to be alone than to be with someone untrustworthy. Listen to your unconscious and beware."

"You think I should call the cops? Or at least Tommy?"

"No. Not that kind of beware. At least, I don't think so. Maybe. We'll see. But what I mean is, beware your heart." A chink broke in Georgia's therapy face, and she let escape pure exasperation. "And your pants."

"He's in my basement now, looking for—whatever."

"What's in your basement? Do you know?"

"Of course I do. I put it all there. It's all junk."

Georgia's watch started to beep. "Shoot. I have a patient coming any second." She stood. "If he decides he wants to delve into his past, tell him to call me. I know a lot of people in the veteran community here. They're not psychiatrists, but they're good. Very good. It's not an easy thing you're asking him to do. He shouldn't face what happened to him alone."

Nina put the small doll back in its bowl with the rest of its family. "This sucks, Georgia. I still have no idea what to do."

"Yeah, I know. The worthwhile things are always hard. But I think you do know what to do. Just listen to yourself."

"You mean listen to you."

"Well, naturally. But I'm only repeating back to you exactly what you just told me. Almost word for word." Georgia stood up.

"I have something else I have to tell you," Nina said. She wanted to get the Bobby situation out into the open.

"Not now. Later," Georgia said. The door from the driveway to the waiting room opened, then closed. "Now I have to kick you out. We'll talk more later."

Chapter Twenty-one

Mick turned the basement upside down.

There was no red metal box.

He was starting to believe that one had never existed.

He closed the green trunk, half empty with Walt's carefully folded dress uniform, his worn-out boots, a few tattered tan T-shirts, socks, work gloves, two duffel bags, long underwear full of holes.

There was nowhere else to look unless he started tearing up floorboards. He had to ask Nina about the box specifically. There was no other way.

He sat down on the trunk. He rubbed his eyes, stretched his sore shoulder. He wanted to rip out the basement pillars with his bare hands. The house would fall in on itself, on him. He and Nina could split the insurance money, go their separate ways, be done with this—whatever it was.

He stood, paced, tried not to look at the pillars, which, of course, he couldn't budge if he tried.

I could let everyone down if I don't find the box. Bella, Nina, Walt...

He felt nauseous. He couldn't do this another day. The huge unknown of it was clouding every waking moment. He wanted to get back to California because it felt closer to Tel Aviv. *Nothing I can do there; my work is here.*

Nina's car rumbled up the long drive. The car door opened, closed. The house door opened, closed. Her light, shoeless footsteps padded over the hardwood floor above him.

"Mick?" she called down the stairs.

He stood slowly, as if he weighed a million pounds. Then he sat back down. *It's a red metal box with a lock. Have you seen it? I have the key. I won't tell you what's inside. Just tell me where it is.* Was that too much of a betrayal?

She called again, "Mick?"

He listened to the silence, then her footsteps descending the stairs.

She wore a green cotton sundress, no shoes, and no makeup. She was incredibly sexy. First because of her beauty, but also because her serene sadness matched his own.

She sat down across from him on the boxes filled with Walt's old Hardy Boys books. She crossed one leg under her. "Hi."

"Hi."

She gestured to the boxes all around them. "Did you find what you were looking for?"

"No."

"So now what?"

"Now I ask you if you've seen it."

Her lips clamped together. "What if I haven't?"

"Then I did my best but failed. It happens. I did what I could. I've searched the garage, the house. I don't have anywhere else to look."

"What if I have seen it and I refuse to tell you where it is?" she asked.

"Now, why would you do that?"

"Because having you around, rummaging through my life, refusing to talk, isn't all that bad for some crazy reason."

"No?" He could feel his blood heat. He had to change the subject before he crossed to her and kissed her. *Every step closer to her makes my job harder.* "Where'd you go?" he asked.

"I saw my friend Georgia. She's a psychiatrist. The one I'm writing Bobby's letters for."

"Does she think you're crazy for letting me do this? Or am I the crazy one for doing it?" The space between them seemed to shrink. Maybe if it shrunk enough, they'd be alone in the world and nothing else would matter, not Walt, not secrets, not houses, just the two of them. Was that what he wanted?

"What are you doing?" she asked.

"My duty."

"Right." She tilted her head. "Georgia thinks that you're dangerous. That you're a con man, scamming me for some treasure Walt told you about."

"What do you think?"

"I think," she said, standing, crossing to him, "that we should go back to bed." She stood before him, her skin glowing in the dim overhead light. All he had to do was reach out and pull her to him.

"I thought we decided this was a terrible idea."

"It is. But I want to anyway. Now."

"Me too," he said. "But after, I'm going to ask you what I need to know."

"Have you been in the attic?" she asked, pulling him to his feet.

"There's an attic?" He closed his eyes, inhaled her scent, pressed against her.

"You have to climb through the fake ceiling in the linen closet." She pressed her lips against his neck, then nipped the skin, then kissed it. "You haven't failed yet."

"I'm still going to ask you," he murmured.

"Ask me what?" she asked, tracing her fingers down his back.

"I have no idea," he said, lost in her. "Doesn't matter anyway."

The bed was softer, but everything else was just as hard. She let her eyes close as she basked in the comforting heat of him. *This man has no future; this man has no past; this man is here, in the moment, with no tomorrow and no yesterday, and there's nothing in the world that is more lost than that...*

She loved the way his hard muscles grew soft under her touch. She understood that he wasn't the man she was making him into—the man she'd been waiting for, the man with the answers, the man who could be her last link to Walt. She told herself sternly as he made love to her that he was who he said he was, a man with nothing to give her but this.

This would have to be enough.

He moved inside her, her fantasy man. Here, now, she could close her eyes and make him into whomever she needed him to be. And she needed this fantasy, just for a little while. A little while longer. One more moment...

He was so good in her mind, in her bed.

The reality of him could come later.

But now it was her turn to come.

Then his.

Then she fell asleep in his arms, putting off reality just a few moments longer.

The next morning, he didn't ask her about the box. After all, he had one more place to look.

He hoisted himself painfully through the small opening in the closet and into the attic.

He knew immediately that the box wasn't here.

The cramped, almost empty space looked as if it had been untouched for decades. He sifted through two boxes of old photographs, a box of forgotten books, and a trunk of clothes that must have belonged to Nina's parents, if not her grandparents. Long silk gloves, men's shirts with hand-sewn collars and pearl buttons.

As he rummaged through the boxes, he tried to convince himself that he didn't ask her where the red box was because he didn't want to trouble her with his responsibility. But it was a lie. He didn't ask because he didn't want to find the box and shatter this thing they were building together. He knew it was impossible; he had to find a way to take her house, and as soon as he found the box, he hoped he would know how to do it.

He pushed away the cobwebs from the last box in the attic, a fancy wood and felt container that held a set of ornate silver.

Nothing.

He climbed down from the attic. Nina was in her office, working, so he made her lunch. Made her dinner. Made love to her again that night. Their lovemaking had a manic, desperate feel to it, and he couldn't push that one word out of his head: *loneliness*.

After she fell asleep, he let his hand slide down her side and she spooned into him without waking. Her warmth melted every ounce of resolve he still had.

Maybe there was no box. Maybe it was all one of Walt's sick jokes, to get him to come here and—what? Fall in love with his sister?

Was he falling in love with Nina?

That couldn't be possible in just a few days. He felt as if he'd been here for years.

Mick tried to sleep, but he couldn't. Every time he started to drift off, he jolted awake with thoughts of Bella, of war, of Walt.

Of Nina.

He tried the bed in the guest room, but it didn't help.

He slipped out of the house and into his tent.

No dice. A new fear had occurred to him that he couldn't unstick from his mind: Nina might think he was sleeping with her to get the house.

Was he?

What was he doing? Whatever it was, it felt intense, life changing. It wasn't the sex—well, it was partly the sex. But more, he was entranced by her cool acceptance of him in her house, even after he'd told her that he couldn't give her what she wanted. She didn't want anything from him but him.

She just wanted him.

There was no duty involved—just desire. When had he

ever just followed his desire? When had he ignored his best instincts and let loose, damn the consequences?

Never.

He gave up on sleep. He backed his car down the drive without starting the engine so as not to wake her, then drove to town.

He walked the empty streets. A group of drunk students, a solitary jogger, an old, bent woman with an equally old, bent dog passed through his otherwise solitary wanderings. The town was crisscrossed with bridges that spanned outrageous gorges. He followed a narrow footbridge that ventured out over a huge, gaping gash in the earth. Water roared below. In the dark, he couldn't see the stream, could only hear as the water flowed by.

The bridge led from the gaping scar in the earth to the fancy coffee shop, a used record store, the Last Chance diner. Everything was closed, dark. The changing landscape matched his mood—roiling, dangerous, perilous depths linked to a peaceful, happy, flat, sleeping world. Back and forth, across the bridges, cliff to street, war to peace, everything coexisting as if it were the natural order.

So why did he feel so edgy, so out of place?

He went down the main street, through a little park with an old war memorial at its center. A brass sculpture of a noble man on horseback, his sword raised, gleamed in the moonlight. It used to be so simple when war had clear-cut enemies that you could see, who followed rules, conventions. Enemies who didn't hide behind civilian populations, who were linked to states, not gods or ideas or straight-out hatred.

He looked across the park to Nina's white wall.

There was someone there. A shadow.

Mick ducked low. He crouched, feeling his way silently across the park. He dashed across the silent street.

The shadow was a man. A man with a spray can.

Mick considered his options. No weapon. No backup. No choice but to go forward, alone.

He moved closer, silently, slowly.

And then he attacked.

The man was down in an instant, completely unprepared. "Shit!"

Mick pinned him. Yanked the hood of his sweatshirt off his head.

"Bastard! What the hell—"

Mick stopped.

This was no man. It was a kid. A boy. A very tall bean-pole of a boy. He looked familiar, but how could Mick know anyone in this town? He moved off him but was ready if the boy tried to flee. "Illegals go home?" he asked, reading the half-written words on the wall. "What do you know about illegals?" He looked at the boy more closely. His brown skin, his black, straight hair. "You legal?"

"I'm a United States Citizen," the boy said, full of scorn for Mick's question.

"You're a punk." Mick pointed at the wall.

"Don't turn me in. Are you gonna turn me in?" the boy asked.

"Maybe. Unless you give me a good reason why I shouldn't."

"Because I'm Johnny Garcia. It's my dad's wall. He'll kill me."

Chapter Twenty-two

Mick and the kid sat in the park in the dark, side by side on a bench under the night-dark maples. This was the silent boy he'd spotted in the drugstore. Only now he wasn't silent. In fact, the kid wouldn't shut up.

"I never meant to do this," Johnny said. "It's like, I don't know. It pisses me off. I was out with my friends and we were—" He stopped.

"Having a few beers. It's okay. I get it."

"Yeah." The boy smiled shyly, and Mick caught a glimpse of just how young he was. Fourteen? Fifteen? "I mean, my brother—I miss him like crazy. Like, every day, I miss him. It's not like I'm an asshole. I'm just—I don't know. I get so mad."

Mick nodded. "I get it. Look, kid, these things are complicated."

"Exactly. And the stupid wall. It's like—"

"Too simple?"

"Yeah. And it'll go up, like a two-story picture of my

brother, and I'm supposed to think that's great, and I do. Hell, I do. Really. But—"

"But you're pissed. You're angry. It's not fair that your brother's gone and no damn picture on the side of a wall is going to change that. But there's nothing else to do, so your dad's doing this and you're getting drunk and doing, well, *this*."

The boy looked out into the night. "I'm gonna join up. Just as soon as I'm old enough. Show them fuckers a thing or two."

"Which fuckers? Your dad?"

"No, man! Them!"

"Them?"

"Yeah."

"All of them?"

"Yeah. Every goddamn last one."

Mick sighed. "How old are you?"

"Sixteen. I can sign on when I turn seventeen if my parents sign for me. And they want me to go. Believe me, that's all my dad wants me to do. I'll be out of this dumb town as soon as I graduate."

"You've got it all planned out."

"It was easier when my dad was a kid. He just lied when he was sixteen and the navy took him on. No way I can do that. They check now. It's different. If it wasn't, I'd be gone already."

"A whole lotta things are different now, Johnny," Mick said. "You don't always know who you're fighting. There's no rules, and they'll blow you to bits with a roadside bomb. It's a different war." Mick felt his rage build. This kid couldn't go. His brother had already given everything. This kid needed a chance. Even if it was just a chance to be sixteen and not be angry every minute until he was seventeen and could do something about it.

"I gotta get home," Johnny said.

"Not until we figure out what we're going to do about the wall."

A police car drove slowly by. It passed the wall. Then stopped. Then backed up. The policeman got out. Stood a moment, then went for his radio.

"You're gonna turn me in?" the boy asked.

"Nah."

"Thanks, man!" Johnny got up to slink off into the night, his eyes on the policeman.

"Sit," Mick said.

Johnny looked around, considered running for it.

"Don't," Mick said. "I'm bigger than you and faster than you, and all I have to do is yell out to my friend over there. The one with the gun."

Johnny thought better of it and sat back down.

"I have an idea," Mick said.

They watched another police car drive up and park behind the first. The blue and red lights rotated, throwing a psychedelic show against the white wall.

Mick said, "I have a job for you. How can I get in touch?"

"You're not a sicko, are you?" the boy asked.

"No," Mick said. He knew this was going to get him into trouble with Nina. Big trouble. "Guess you'll just have to trust me on that."

"No way."

"Look, kid—" Mick pulled up his sleeve.

Johnny leaned in so he could see in the dark.

"Nine years in the army. Last six in Afghanistan," Mick said.

"Oh." Johnny sat back. "Okay. I didn't know you were army. I trust you."

Damn, this kid had a lot to learn.

"I'll give you my cell," the boy offered pulling out his phone, waiting for Mick to pull out his.

But Mick hadn't brought his cell.

"Enter this address," Mick said.

The boy shook his head in disbelief at the unprepared-ness of old people. But Mick told him Nina's address, and Johnny entered it in his phone.

"Meet me there tomorrow, twelve o'clock."

"At night?" he asked. His face lit up at the idea of a secret army mission.

"Noon," Mick said. "I'm putting you to work."

"Okay," Johnny said, deflating. "I know the street. I've got a buddy who lives a few houses down."

"Good. Don't be late."

Johnny took off into the shadows. Mick watched the police cars' light show until it ended, the cops driving off into the dark, quiet, empty night.

Mick went back to Nina's and let himself into the sleeping, unlocked house through the back door.

When he got upstairs, he paused in front of Nina's bed-room door. He pushed it open softly, hoping it wouldn't squeak.

She lay on the bed, one cat curled into the bend of her knees, the other against the curl of her back. Her closed eyelids seemed translucent, like something out of one of her pictures.

He couldn't make himself go in to disturb her peace.

He walked to the guest room down the hall. It was

two in the morning. Surely now he'd be able to sleep. He peeled off his jeans, his shirt, and tossed them on the chair in the corner.

A pile of his laundry was neatly folded on the chair. Nina must have done it sometime this afternoon, while he was up in the attic with the dust, the spiders, and Grandma's silver.

He stared at the pile of neatly folded clothes. He raised a tattered T-shirt to his nose.

Lilac.

He didn't expect the rush of emotions, a flower bomb exploding in his face.

His cell phone on the nightstand caught his eye. There were three texts from Sandra.

Mick, pick up! I need to talk to you.

Then, *Mick, where RU? Bella took a bad turn.*

Then, *Mick, I'm going to Tel Aviv. Call me.*

He called her. She picked up, wide-awake despite the hour.

"I can't not be there," she said.

"Me either. But we can't go. Baily is with her. It'll just eat up resources, Sandy. We can't spend more money that we don't have."

"But what if—"

"Don't think 'what if,' Sandy. Stay on mission."

"What's happening there, Mick?"

He sat down on the bed and tried to breathe. What was happening here? *I'm helping a mixed-up graffiti artist, falling in love with a beautiful woman who's making my laundry smell like lilac.* He was becoming like Nina, just looking at the slice of world in front of him, forgetting the rest as if it didn't exist, forgetting his duty.

"Mick?"

"Sorry."

"You're sleeping with her, aren't you?"

"It's not about that. I'm—I think I'm falling in love with her."

"Oh God. You're sleeping with her. How could you? What is wrong with you?"

His eyes went to the folded laundry. "I'll handle it."

"You better. Get out of her head, Mick. And for God's sake, get out of her bed."

"I can't find the box, Sandy."

"Forget the stupid box."

"I can't. If I find it, I'll know how to prove to her that Walt gave me the house. Also, I'll have done my duty."

"What if there is no box?"

"The thought had occurred to me," Mick said.

"Oh, Mick. Bella said it's so hot there. She's so uncomfortable. And the food is upsetting her stomach."

"I'll find it," he told his sister. "And I'll get the house and I'll get out."

"What if she won't give you the house?"

"I'll figure that out when it comes to that."

She was unconvinced, but then, so was he. She told him about Bella and her fever. How they were going to start the tests in two days, but now it was uncertain. She cried a little and he didn't. But somehow, he talked Sandy out of leaving the country, for now, and hung up, more awake than ever.

He let himself out the back door, climbed into his tent, and eventually fell into a troubled sleep.

Chapter Twenty-three

Two hours later, Nina woke up alone in bed.

Mick was gone. She jumped out of bed, panic racing through her veins. They were just getting started on something—

On what?

Whatever it was, he had gotten up in the middle of the night and split.

She looked out into the yard, and her heart started beating again when she saw his car, the small tent, its drab brown incongruous with the vibrant reds and yellows and blues and purples awakening in her morning garden.

Her emotions veered from confused to sad to furious. She hated needing him here when she also wanted him gone. She stalked outside, picking up a stick on the way. She pounded on the outside of the tent.

"Rise and shine, soldier," she said.

A hand unzipped the mesh tent flap, and Sylvie strolled

out, looking refreshed and ready for her day. She sat to lick a paw.

"You let Sylvie out last night!" she said. The cat's collusion with the enemy added to her frustration. "What is wrong with you? This is real life, Mick. We sleep in houses. This isn't the stinking army."

His voice from inside the tent was sleepy and thick. "I'll come out if you put the stick down."

She dropped the stick. "I'm unarmed."

He stuck his head out, then emerged, too trim and tan in his boxers to make this a fair fight. But she was determined to fight anyway, no matter how beautiful he looked in the morning light. She scowled. "Put some clothes on, soldier."

"I'm not in your house. Your rules don't apply." He stretched. The morning dew was all around them, clinging to the blades of grass and the spiders' webs. But apparently he was immune to the chill. Of course he was, Mr. Toughguy. Summer was halfway over; fall was already starting to crowd the nights. By September, they'd get their first frost. She imagined his tent in the yard, covered in wet leaves, then snow. How long could this standoff go on? She wanted to beat him over the head with a stick, and she wanted to make love to him. She wanted to take care of him and she wanted to push him away.

"Okay. Hit me. What are you doing out here? We're friends now. Friends with benefits. You can sleep inside," she said.

"I can't."

"You don't want me to hear your nightmares," she guessed.

"No. My dreams aren't important. They're just dreams. A person can dream anything. Dreams don't matter."

Men. They were as thick as bricks.

They stared at each other.

"You did my laundry," he said finally. "Thank you. Really. It was very sweet. But I wish you hadn't."

This was it. She was going to have to go for the stick. "You're welcome. I think. God, Mick, what's your problem? Can't we be friends?"

"No. It feels rotten."

"Is this about you thinking you're taking my house and feeling guilty about it again? You're not getting the house, Mick, so cut the guilt."

"We're adversaries, Nina. There have to be some lines. Sleeping apart seemed like a good one."

"I didn't see any lines last night when we—"

"You know what I mean."

"Really? Do I? You know what I think? I think you have no idea how to leave the army and enter normal civilian life. You want to be a savage in the desert forever, and it pisses you off that I'm giving you a glimpse of civil society, of human kindness. You want rules and lines, and then you don't want rules and you break through lines. I did your laundry, Mick. I like you. I want you to stay and tell me about my brother. It's all very normal and sane, and you want to make it a battle with winners and losers." She pointed at his tent. "In upstate New York, little boys are the only ones who sleep in tents in the front yard."

"Afghanistan isn't a desert," he said from between narrowed lips.

"Whatever. You know what I mean. Welcome back to civilian life, Mick. Here we wear clothes, use nice laundry detergent, cook less than a dozen of whatever we're making. Here we sleep inside, on soft, comfy beds. And we make love, and then in the morning, we wake up next to the person we've made love to and say good morning and have a conversation."

She stopped yelling and looked at him.

He wasn't defending himself.

She took a step closer. "Mick?" She leaned in. "What is it? Why are you really out here? Why won't you let me be nice to you?"

He shook his head as if he didn't know where to begin.

"Okay, let's start here: why do you hate the house so much?"

He stared over her shoulder toward the house, but his eyes were unfocused. "I don't hate it. I just don't want to be in it. There's a difference."

"You do hate it. I already told you that I saw you that first day, Mick, when you drove up the drive. You looked like you wanted to set the place on fire. Why? Why are you outside in a tent with that bad shoulder of yours on the cold, hard ground?"

He was still staring toward the house, his eyes a million miles away.

"Mick."

He teetered on the edge of something. She was desperate to push him over. She rose on her tiptoes and kissed him softly on the cheek. The scruff of his unshaved face scraped her lips. "Tell me. Just do it. Talk to me. Please?"

He didn't move a muscle. "I hate the house because it reminds me of my house, as a kid," he said. The words were laced with irritation. He looked around as if he'd just missed a bus and was considering alternative transportation options. "It was not a happy time."

She felt as if she were running toward a rapidly closing door. "Okay. So why do you want it if you hate it?"

"I told you. I need the money."

"Why?" She pressed her body against his stiff, rigid one. He didn't flinch away, but he also didn't put his arms around her or soften a muscle. She didn't care. He was finally talking. It felt like a miracle.

"I have a sister," he said finally. "Her name is Bella."

"The one who wouldn't cook meat." She laid her head on his chest, listening to the beating of his heart. His bare skin was covered in goose bumps, so she ran her hands over his back and shoulders, trying to warm him. He stayed just as rigid, just as cold.

He had stopped talking again. She willed herself to wait. It helped that his chest felt so good against her cheek. His pounding heart soothed her. Despite his outward agitation, it beat steady and strong.

"She's sick. Brain tumor."

"Oh, Mick." She glanced up at him, then away again, afraid to break the spell. *Keep talking.*

"I was off fighting. No one told me how bad it was. I didn't know. I'd have come back if I'd known. I'd have worked to save her sooner. Now it might be too late." His voice was hard, matter-of-fact.

"I'm so sorry." She glanced at his face, but it was a mask. "I understand you're upset. But doctors save sick people. We can't. There's nothing people like us can do."

"No. That's not true. The doctors did all the usual treatments, and they failed. But there's another option. It's not approved in the U.S. Bella has to go to Israel to get it. There they have it all worked out. They make a vaccination from the person's own tumor. It takes a while because they have to make a specific vaccine for each patient, but once they get it, they have an amazing success rate. The hospital in California has a deal with the guys in Israel. They call it a compassionate-care agreement. They send their U.S. patients who are beyond cure here to Israel. But you still need money. A lot of money. Since it's not approved, it's not insured."

"If it's so good, why isn't the treatment here?" Nina asked, trying to keep up with him. *Tumors, vaccines, agreements*—she'd have to ask Georgia what she knew about this sort of thing.

"The government moves too slow here. They have to do studies and tests and trials. Bella couldn't get into the studies because by the time they caught her tumor, they were only taking first-stage patients. She was past that. There was nothing here for her, and her insurance won't pay for an experimental treatment overseas, and the whole thing takes time—a lot of time. She's over there now, counting on me to get the money to keep her there."

"No wonder Walt gave you the house."

"No!" he insisted. "He didn't know about Bella. I didn't even know about Bella till after I got back. I should have known. I should have been told, and then I would have rushed here for the house, and then gone to Israel and gotten it done. But no one let me know how bad it was. So I wasted months in Afghanistan. They all thought I was doing more important things—"

"You were, Mick—"

"More important than saving my sister?" he asked, his voice rising. "I only got out of the army because I was injured. Then my stupid sisters let me lie around for months getting better, while Bella was getting worse. When I could have helped."

Her first impulse was to pull back, but she fought it. "You didn't tell me about Bella because you thought I'd think it was another scam."

"Do you?"

"No. I don't know." She believed him. But then, she'd believed the woman who had pretended to be Mary and look where that had gotten her.

Mick said, "I don't want you to give me the house because you feel sorry for me. I want you to give me the house because you should. Because it's mine. Because Walt gave it to me. Because it's the right thing to do, even if I was an ass for two years. I don't even know why I'm telling you this now."

"Because you care about me and I care about you."

He grimaced.

"Look, Mick. I'm sorry for Bella," she said. Her head was spinning. Did she feel sorry for him and his sister? Sorry enough to go back on her promise to herself to hold firm? She could feel herself caving already. *It could still be a scam.* His story had all the hallmarks of a con.

He shook his head and pulled away from her. "I didn't want to tell you any of that. I feel like a shit, Nina. It's like you doing my laundry, like I'm a kid to be taken care of. I'm not a kid. I'm a man, here for what's rightfully mine."

She steeled herself against his words, against his beauty, against the memory of him in her bed. *Take the house.* She was so ready to say it. But if she lost the house, then she'd have lost everything that had been Walt's. She didn't want to be a sucker again. Even if he was telling the truth, she had to stand up for herself.

She could almost hear Georgia and Lizzie and Jill urging her to hold firm. But hadn't everything just changed? *If she cared about him.*

"So you need the money right now?" she asked.

"My sister Sandy took out a second mortgage on her place. That got Baily and Bella to Israel, and it paid for the first phase of the treatment. I need the second installment in three months. I don't want to do this, Nina. If you give me the house, I'll pay you back as soon as I can."

Famous last words. She might never see him again. He might be pulling off the biggest scam of them all.

She closed her eyes, trying to shut off her heart so that her mind could take over. But she couldn't. "How much money do you need?"

"A hundred thousand, more or less."

She willed herself to focus. It was a lot of money, but the house was worth more than twice that. She could borrow against the house without selling it. She could probably have the money in a week or two if she took out a home equity loan. Maybe. She'd have to talk to someone who knew something about these sorts of things.

But should she? Hadn't she sworn that she'd look out for herself and not be a sucker for another good-hearted stranger with a sob story? Nothing had changed since she'd made that decision but the fact that she might be falling in love with Mick. Which of course made her even more suspect of her motives.

He was watching the ground, his face rigid with self-disgust.

"You have time," she said.

"A little time. But getting money out of real estate takes time."

"I have to think about this," she said. She'd talk to Jill and find out exactly how much time they had. What was possible.

"I know. I have to think about it too. Honestly, Nina, if I could take back telling you what I just told you, I would. I don't want your sympathy."

It was exactly what Mary had said before she took everything and disappeared into the night.

Chapter Twenty-four

Georgia said good-bye to her ten o'clock and went to get her mail. The oversize envelope in swooping, looping calligraphy caught her eye immediately.

She restrained herself from ripping it open and went to her office for her letter opener. Was it a wedding invitation, bar mitzvah, engagement—?

It was a poem.

A sonnet, for heaven's sake.

Shall I compare thee to a charge-ed fence?
Thou art more lovely and not made of wire
The height that forces us apart ere hence
Is like that fence, whence touch'ed—fire!

Georgia lowered the paper. It wasn't signed. There was no return address on the envelope. But she knew exactly who it was from. *Bobby Ridale.* The postmark was local.

A shock of fear ran through her.

He's here?

Not necessarily. Someone could have sent it for him. Only one person in this town could write like this.

She punched Nina on her speed dial.

"Is this some kind of joke? Is he here? Why didn't you tell me?"

"Hi, honey," Nina said. She sounded tired.

Georgia tried not to lose steam. *"Sometimes too hot the heat of spotlights shine,"* she read.

Nina picked up the next line. *"And suffr'ing in its glare, I cannot bear."*

"Nina!"

"The electrified din of your current so fine—"

"He's a criminal!" Georgia said. "He's comparing me to an electric fence."

"By chance or nature, so close, but unaware."

"Nina! This isn't poetry. This is a crime against poetry!"

"I knew you'd be upset," Nina said. "But what could I do? He was Walt's best friend. He said he loved you since fourth grade. He means well." She paused. "He pays well."

Georgia scoffed. "You're sleeping with the man who's trying to take your house *by any means necessary*. What do you know about meaning well?"

"Are you implying that Mick's sleeping with me to get the house?" Nina asked. The usual spunk was gone from her voice.

"I'm implying that you can't just pretty up words and expect them to be full of goodness. That's not how life works, Nina."

"I know that," Nina said.

"I don't think you know that," Georgia said. "I think that you think that if you wish it's pretty, if you make it pretty with your paints and your pens, it'll be okay. That's not how the world works, Nina." Georgia heard the light knock of her next patient on her door. "I have to go. We're talking about this later. Next Enemy Club meeting. I'm getting the girls on my side."

"Give him a chance, Georgia."

"Hmph!"

"And, Georgia—we have to talk. About Mick. He wants the house because his sister is dying and he needs the cash."

"Don't you give in to that man!" Georgia said. "Pretty words don't make it right!" She clicked the phone shut and shoved the poem in a drawer, ignoring the tingle of anticipation that played through her veins.

It was nice to be wanted, even if it was by a criminal who wrote unforgivable poetry.

A very good-looking criminal. Her very first school-girl crush.

Oh hell. She was getting as soft as Nina.

Mick searched the barn for the last time. The attic. The downstairs. The basement. He'd gone through the yoga studio while Nina worked next door in her art studio, the only sound her chair scraping against the wood floor.

The only rooms left to re-search were her art studio and her bedroom.

There was no reason to feel like he was doing something wrong. She'd given her permission to search the house.

And he'd been in her bedroom before.

Naked.

On that bed.

But never again. Time was running out. He had to focus.

He went to the bed, stood before it. *She'd be glad when he was gone.* Well, of course she would. He had refused to tell her happy stories about her brother, and then he had dumped all his misery about Bella on her as if she were the one who was responsible for fixing it. And now here he was, searching her bedroom for a secret that was so bad, her brother wanted it destroyed.

He was starting to get damn sick of himself too.

He glanced under the bed for the third time.

Nothing. Not even a dust bunny.

Went through her closet again.

He hadn't realized how sexy it was going to be, shuffling through Nina's closet now that he knew the scent of her, the outline of her body under her clothes.

Think of Bella, idiot.

Her closet was arranged by color, or maybe by season. The soft pinks and yellows she'd been wearing hung next to autumn's oranges and browns.

He'd like to still be here to see her in those, but how could he be? The box would be found. The house would be sold. He'd be in Tel Aviv, by Bella's side. And Nina would be here, homeless, wishing she'd never met him.

So what if he'd never see her in that orange dress? What redhead would look good in an orange dress anyway? Didn't they not do that? Or was it that they didn't wear red?

No, she was wearing red today. A crinkled, silky, sleeveless fire-engine-red shirt that fell open slightly at the neck when she bent, showing a glimpse of exquisite cleavage.

He shook the image from his mind.

She was sick of him. He had to stop this.

He halfheartedly looked through her bookshelf.

Her books were mostly fiction. Romance novels mixed in with literary stuff. Some poetry. And art books. Over-size doorstops, piled on one another. Matisse, Picasso, Monet, Chagall.

He pulled out the Chagall and opened to a picture of a man and a woman floating in the sky, the man's languid, fluid limbs wrapped around the woman like he was her cloak.

He wanted that with Nina. To wrap himself around her, to float in the sky, feet nowhere near the ground.

He'd looked everywhere. The box wasn't going to be found unless he told her exactly what he was looking for.

He went to her office.

He'd just have to ask her, whether Walt wanted her to know or not.

The door to Nina's office was ajar. He raised his hand to knock, then paused. Her profile was still as she stared at an easel set up in front of her, a brush in her hand. Her attention flicked between a still life of vegetables and her small canvas.

She looked, dabbed at her canvas, and looked some more, dabbed.

Watching her, he understood Walt's impulse. Why ruin a perfectly good world with something best forgotten? Why mess up the present with what's long past? *You can't ask her for the box.*

She spun around and gasped, her hand flying to her chest. "Mick! Don't sneak up on me like that."

He pushed through the door. "Sorry, didn't mean to spy. You just looked so serene, I didn't want to disturb you." He came in and stood behind the canvas, surprised it was all browns and grays. "I expected a little more color," he said, looking at the colorful vegetables arranged on the table.

"It's the undercoat," she explained, her mouth curving into a frown as she turned back to regard her canvas unhappily. "The shapes and shadows. I build the color on top of it when it's right. If it's ever right."

"Looks good to me," he said to her back. He could smell the strawberries of her shampoo mingling with the acrid turpentine of her paints. He took a step back, hoping the space would induce her to turn back around.

"It's coming along." Her attention was back on the tomatoes. They sat on a draped table with an eggplant, three zucchinis, and a mystery vegetable he couldn't name. "I'm sorry I yelled at you this morning. I was out of line," she said, still not looking at him. "I really am sorry about your sister. And I'm sorry that I can't just hand over the house. I wish I could. But I have to look out for myself too."

He leaned on the windowsill, watching her dab at the painting. When she painted, he could tell that she forgot everything else. He wished he had something like that to distract him. Well, something besides bombs and sex and beer. "I have to ask you something," he said finally.

She didn't even look up. "Make it quick. You're blocking my light."

He moved from the window to the wheeled chair in front of her drawing table. He sat on it backward, his arms over the chair back. "I need to tell you what Walt wanted me to find because I can't find it and maybe you know where it is, and I know you don't want to know, but I'm out of options." He picked up a tomato.

"Mick! Put that back! My painting!"

He looked at the tomato in his hand. "Sorry." He looked to the arrangement. Where had it been? He put it next to the zucchini.

"No. It's next to the other tomato."

He looked at the table. The fruit was on different levels, like steps draped with white cloth. He knew he shouldn't have touched it; he'd kept his hands off it before, but now he'd been lost in thought.

He looked closer at the arrangement. Tomato on the step—

No.

Not a step.

He peeked under the white cloth.

"Mick! You're ruining everything. Don't touch! Every fold in that draping took me ages to get right." She put down her paintbrush and scowled at him.

Under the cloth was a small red box with a lock. He let the cloth fall back. His heart pounded. He desperately tried to keep his face neutral. "Sorry." He handed her the tomato.

There was the box. Just like that, practically out in the open.

His whole body was tingling with anticipation. He wanted to show it to her, open it with her, prove to her that the house was his and then—

Then what?

He felt as wrapped up in this woman as the man in the Chagall painting had been wrapped around his love. But

Mick was rooted to the earth, while Nina floated above him, alone. He had no right to drag her down to his level.

"So how long will that painting take?" he asked.

"Depends. I have lots of other stuff going on." She eyed him as if he was the main problem. "I'm guessing two weeks."

"Two weeks!" He'd have to sneak the box out tonight, damn the painting.

"It's oil paint, Mick. I have to let every layer dry completely before I do the next. It's a long process." She eyed him suspiciously. "Why do you care?"

As soon as he knew Walt's secret, everything would change. He might learn something so awful he could never tell her.

Nina was painting again, her attention withdrawn from him, leaving him cold.

He wanted badly to tell her about the box on her table.

It would bring them closer.

But he had a duty to Walt.

He wasn't sure how long he sat there, watching her paint. It was hypnotic. So hypnotic that before he knew what he was doing, he found himself telling her a story. "I was in basic training with these three incredible women," he told her.

She looked up, then back down at her canvas. "Hmm..."

"I'll never forget them: Patty Smith, Lancy Hawke, and Elizabeth James. First day of training, Patty sucker punched me in the jaw when I tried to help her over a wall on the obstacle course. Me and my jaw will never forget that little lesson. A week later, Lancy told me she'd set my bunk on fire if I kept letting her get away with half push-ups when I did her count. Elizabeth was different, though."

Nina had stopped painting and was looking at him as if he'd lost his mind.

"She let the guys treat her like a girl. That went on maybe a week or so before the other two women let her have it. After that, Elizabeth pulled her weight like Patty and Lancy—like a man."

"What are you saying, Mick?"

"If there's one thing the three of them drove into my thick skull, it's that trying to protect a woman, trying to treat her like a delicate flower, is insulting and condescending."

"I agree," she said. "But why are you telling me this?" She had gone back to her painting and was only half listening to him. Which was good, because he was babbling. He didn't know what he wanted to say to her, only that he didn't want to do Walt's bidding anymore. He wanted his duty to be to her.

He thought of his sisters. He had a duty to them. Sandra had warned him not to let his duty shift. This wasn't about him. It was about family. It was about Walt. He was becoming a selfish person, wanting Nina and wanting her to want him when that wasn't the point.

He saw all this, and still he couldn't stop himself.

"Nina, I don't think that you're a delicate flower who can't know things. I think it's wrong to treat a person that way. I don't know why Walt didn't learn that lesson at basic, but I'm sorry he missed it. If it were me, my brother, my house, I'd want to know what secret some strange guy was looking for."

"Bullshit. There are things you don't want to know. That you won't face. Why should I face Walt's secret if you won't face your own? Who's the delicate flower, Mick?"

"It's not like that."

She stared at him for a long time, then said, "I don't want to fight anymore, Mick. But face it—you ignore your nightmares like they don't exist. I hear you at night, even when you sleep outside in your stupid tent."

"Nina—" He took her by the shoulders and she looked at up him, and he thought, *Destroy the damn box and save this innocent girl*. "I don't feel right not telling you. I want to tell you. I feel as if it's my duty."

"I have work to do," she said. "So do you." Her voice was defiant, but she didn't shake his hands away.

They stared at each other, locked in their impossible standoff.

And then the doorbell rang.

Chapter Twenty-five

Nina went downstairs and opened the door.

Johnny Garcia was on the porch, looking like he'd rather be anywhere else than here. He said, "I showed up."

Mick came up behind her. He nodded at the boy. "Johnny, you know Nina? Nina, Johnny Garcia."

"Hi, John," Nina said. "How's your dad?"

"He's super," Johnny said, not willing to give an inch.

"So can I help you?" Nina asked.

"He's here to help you," Mick said.

Nina took this incomprehensible piece of information in. "Um, what exactly is he going to do to help me?"

"Yeah, what exactly am I going to do?" Johnny asked. "I got stuff to do."

"Stuff like vandalizing blank walls?" Mick asked. "I caught him at it last night," he explained to Nina.

"John!" Nina said. "It was you?"

The boy turned red. "Not every time," Johnny said. "The first time it really was the frat guys. They kinda gave me the idea, though. So yeah, whatever. It was me. Shoot me." By the time his speech was done, he'd swallowed his blush and resumed his tough-guy stance.

"I don't think they still do that around here," Mick said. "Too bad, though."

"Whatever happened, Johnny, I'm not a cop," Nina said. She wasn't sure what Mick had in mind with this kid. Was she supposed to punish him herself? "But thanks for telling me the truth."

"Let's go out to the barn," Mick said. "I want you to see something."

"No! What are you doing?" Nina pushed in front of the door, blocking Mick's way out. "There's nothing to see in the barn."

Johnny looked from one to the other. "This is weird," he said. "I'm outta here." He went down the steps and righted his bike.

"Wait. Hold on." Mick turned to Nina. "C'mon. What's the big deal? Show him your plans for the wall. He's gonna help."

"I don't have plans for the wall," Nina said. "You know that." She wasn't going to ask in front of the boy how he could possibly help, but she was thinking it.

"That's why my dad wants to fire you," Johnny said. "He knew you weren't doing anything."

"I'm doing things. They're just not working." God, this kid was a punk. Why would Mick bring him here?

"Exactly," Mick said, striding down the steps and past the two of them. He grabbed the handlebars of Johnny's bike, yanked it away from the boy, and casually started wheeling it toward the barn.

"Hey!" Johnny and Nina cried at the exact same moment.

Mick didn't look back. Nina couldn't help smiling just a little at the sight of Mick wheeling the too-small bike away from them. No matter how much this guy pissed her off, she still had a soft spot for him. She'd really have to work on that.

Mick got to the barn, left the bike, disappeared inside.

"Well, c'mon," she said to Johnny. "I don't suppose it's so bad you can't see it. But don't tell your dad, okay? This has to be between us three."

Johnny softened, although he pretended not to. "Okay. Whatever."

When they got to the barn, Johnny looked at the painting for a split second before he said, "That sucks, man!"

Nina inhaled sharply. "Never had an art criticism class, have we? Constructive criticism?"

Mick put a hand on the boy's shoulder. "It's not finished, right, Nina? It's still in the conceptual stage."

"Was the concept corniness?" Johnny asked. "Walt looks like he's supposed to be Superman. Like he needs a cape and a giant *S* on his shirt."

"Constructive criticism means," Nina said, "if you can't say anything nice—"

Johnny made a zipping motion across his lips.

Nina rolled her eyes.

Mick tried again. "Look, here's the thing, Johnny. I kinda owe Nina a favor for her letting me stay here a few days. And you kinda owe her a favor 'cause you tagged that wall and pissed off your dad."

"Why do I owe her?"

"Because it's better than owing the Galton Police Department," Nina suggested.

Johnny nodded. "Okay."

"So we're gonna help her come up with a better idea for the mural. And then, if we can, we'll help her execute it."

"I'm not an artist."

"Neither am I. We're just the concept guys for now. What should go on that wall? What will make a difference?"

"On a wall? Nothing," Johnny protested.

"So why'd you write on the wall if it didn't make a difference?" Nina asked.

"Because—that's different," Johnny said.

"Why? You knew that your work with a spray can would communicate something. So why can't my work with a brush do the same?" She paused. "Our work."

Mick shot Nina a grateful glance.

She tried not to let it please her. It was one step forward, two miles back with this man. But somehow, something was working. "I have work to do. *Paying* work," she emphasized. "You boys get to work here. Earn your keep. I'll be inside."

Mick and Johnny sat in the barn the rest of the afternoon. Maybe he was avoiding the inevitable opening of the box. But maybe, just maybe, he and the kid could come up with something to pay Nina back at least a little for all the grief they had caused her.

Mick had pulled in the Adirondack chairs from the back porch and an easy sort of silence had descended on them. Mick hadn't realized how much he missed the company of men.

He looked at Johnny. Okay, of boys.

Still, his whole life, he'd grown up surrounded by women he felt he had to protect. Being with Johnny let the burden roll from his shoulders, at least for an hour or so.

He reminded himself that Nina didn't want protecting.

Or rather, she wanted to be protected from some things, not from others. It reminded him of Walt, the way he'd rush into minefields, daring them to blow. Then he'd creep through secured towns like they might be ready to explode.

He'd tried to explain Walt's odd recklessness to himself lots of times. He'd even asked Walt once or twice what was up with him.

Once, he'd come upon Walt in his bunk, and when he spoke, Walt had jumped a mile into the air like he'd just been caught with his hand in the cookie jar.

And maybe he had. Mick hadn't pursued Walt's strange reaction that odd afternoon. Funny that he should think of it now, staring at Nina's picture of Walt as a superhero. It had seemed at that moment—at lots of moments, now that he thought about it—that Walt had a secret in Afghanistan. One that he wanted to keep from Mick and the other guys.

Mick stared at the picture, drank a Coke, and ate chips.

Neither he nor Johnny said anything more than, "Want another soda?" or "I gotta go pee."

At five o'clock, Mick stood up. He stretched. "A pretty good day's work," he said.

"But we didn't do shit," Johnny said. "We just sat here like morons."

"You did. I was thinking."

"You were? Of what?"

"Sorry, kid; you wanna know, you've got to ask me when I'm working. Now I'm off duty. You too. So go home, think about our project some more, and come back tomorrow."

"Aw, man! No way."

"Way. You owe me two weeks."

"I have stuff to do, you know."

"Yeah, like what? Video games? Hanging out with your buddies? Defacing private property?"

Johnny gave up without a fight. Almost as if he didn't mind sitting around any more than Mick did. "Okay, noon. But next time, you better have ginger ale. I hate Coke."

"Bring your own, buddy. And make sure you shut the door behind you when you leave. Whatever you do, don't let the cat in!" Mick said, and he walked out of the barn, making sure to shut the door behind him, leaving Johnny behind so he could spend a few minutes alone with the painting.

Who knew? Maybe the kid would actually come up with something.

Chapter Twenty-six

The next morning, thank heavens, was Wednesday, which meant the Enemy Club would meet at the Last Chance diner. Nina needed to straighten out her incredibly tangled emotions about Mick and about the secret he wanted so badly to tell her.

But the moment the overchilled diner air hit her, she realized Mick would have to wait.

Georgia was in full war mode. She had tossed Bobby Ridale's poem on the counter, and Lizzie and Jill were reading it, trying to contain their amusement.

"He compared you to an electric fence," Lizzie said. "That's so—" She paused. *"Electrifying."*

"I told you to get your hair straightened," Jill said. "But you never listen to me. You think that things like having frizzy hair aren't important, and then you get this! Electric fence! Bzzzzz!"

"Ladies," Nina said, sliding onto the stool next to Jill, nodding hello. "I don't see any admirers writing iambic pentameter for you, then hiring Galton's top calligrapher to seal the deal."

Jill rolled her eyes. "I prefer diamonds."

Georgia said, "Can you believe Nina did this? Accepted this job? Without telling me first? Can we start there?"

"Good for her!" Jill said. "It's business, honey."

"It's dirty money," Georgia said.

"Not necessarily," Lizzie said. "Let's not jump to any conclusions."

"Exactly. He might be a good guy now, Georgie," Nina said.

Georgia stared at her in disbelief. "You hated him the most, Nins. You hated how he pulled Walt the wrong way. You know what this guy is capable of. Remember the time he got Walt to help him paint the water tower to look like a giant penis?"

"People can change," Nina insisted.

"So he's not a criminal anymore?" Georgia asked. "Remember the time he got Walt to go along with him to steal Mr. Barley's truck?"

"We all knew he kept the keys in the ignition so he wouldn't lose them. It was just a joyride. They brought it back."

"Covered in mud with no gas," Lizzie said.

"Well, Walt stopped doing stupid stuff," Nina said. "Now Bobby's out of prison. He did his time. So maybe he's matured too."

"You never let yourself see the bad side of anything," Georgia said, looking pointedly to Jill and Lizzie for reinforcement. "You and your *life is good* vibe. It pisses me off sometimes."

"Well, maybe you never look on the good side of things," Nina said. "Maybe you should give him a chance."

"A known criminal?" Georgia cried. "I don't think so." She glared at Nina. "I can't believe that you agreed to write that poem up for him." Georgia looked around the diner suspiciously. "What if he's stalking me? Is he in town?"

"What if he's still cute?" Jill asked.

"Oh no. You're not on her side too?" Georgia spun around to face Jill.

"What if he's kind?" Nina asked.

"What if he's criminally insane?" Georgia asked.

"What if he's really in love?" Lizzie asked.

Georgia jumped up. "What is wrong with the three of you? Do you know what it means to be a criminal? A convict? It means you can't get a decent job. It means you have a deficient personality disorder. Most likely, it means a person is too dumb to function in society legally. Do you know what the average IQ of a resident of the United States prison system is?"

"Of course we don't," Lizzie said with endless patience.

"It's low," Georgia said. "I'll have to look it up," she admitted. "But I'm sure it's low."

"Okay, okay. I get your point," Nina said, coaxing Georgia back to her stool. "But I think you've got to give the guy a chance. He wrote you poetry. Just meet him somewhere public. Talk to him. Do it for me, so I can write the rest of the letters and get paid."

"No way. Never. I'm a professional, Nina."

"Oh, and we're not? So we can't understand how important you are?" Lizzie asked. "Your job has nothing to do with whether or not you should meet this man."

"My career, not my job," Georgia corrected. "I can't jeopardize everything I've worked so hard for, for a man."

"I'd jeopardize anything for the right man," Jill said. "And I have a *career* too."

"I think you're scared," Lizzie said. "I mean, honestly, George, it doesn't have to be marriage and kids. Maybe it could just be fun. You could use a little fun, you have to admit."

Georgia scoffed. "I have fun. I have you guys. I have my chamber group every Friday night. I play tennis on Tuesdays. My psychoanalytic book group meets every other Monday afternoon."

"Shoot me now," Jill said, holding up her hands in surrender.

"We drink wine!" Georgia insisted. "Very good wine."

"I'm not supposed to say anything, love, but there's another letter coming soon," Nina admitted.

Georgia shook her head. "You have to stop. To tell him to stop. You have a duty to me, as a friend, not to do this."

"You tell him," Nina said.

"I'll call the cops," Georgia said.

"Fine. Do what you like. But, Georgia, I think that it's kinda sexy being compared to an electric fence."

Jill sighed. "Beats being compared to nothing."

"So it's okay for me to hang out with Bobby, but it wasn't okay for Walt to hang out with him?" Georgia asked.

"Yes," Nina said. "Because you're responsible and you'll take care of yourself. You won't be reckless. You'll consider and do the right thing. If Bobby says, let's go steal Mrs. Eilten's lawn flamingos—"

"God, I remember that," Lizzie said.

Nina nodded sadly. "You'll say, 'No. Let's watch a DVD and then make love.'"

"Make love!" Georgia shouted.

Heads turned.

She lowered her voice and said to Nina, "I'd rather steal lawn flamingos."

"You would not. Not even you," Jill said.

"You're a Pollyanna," Georgia said to Nina.

"Believe me, I'm not," Nina said, holding her chin high but doubting her words as she spoke them. Was she? Was she ignoring every sign that people around her were dangerous? Was she pushing her friend into a bad situation?

Georgia rolled her eyes.

Nina said, "Give yourself the chance to think about it. That's all I'm asking. Just a chance."

That night, Johnny Garcia sat in the park across from his father's pharmacy, studying the empty wall.

This sucked.

There was no way he could get out of this. He had to show up tomorrow or Mick would turn him in for sure. That guy, whoever the hell he was, didn't mess around.

But there was no way he could keep showing up and staring at that picture of Walt looking so dumb. No way he could sit there for another five hours of silence with that guy, drinking, pissing, drinking some more.

He had to get out of this.

And the only way out was to solve the problem: what to put on the wall.

But he wasn't an artist. Sure, he'd considered maybe being one. In fact, picking up the spray-paint can had reminded him that he could do some cool stuff when he let himself. But hell, if he ever told his dad that, he might as well just dig himself a hole and climb in it. If he said, *Dad, I want to go to art school,* his dad would know for sure that his only worthwhile son had died doing something important.

Plus, his dad would think he was gay.

His friends would think he was gay.

And he wasn't gay. He liked Samantha and she liked him even though the sex was, well, kinda nerve-racking, an uncomfortable combination of sweat, skin, and apologies. Still, he couldn't go, like, more than a few days without it, so definitely not gay.

He had to solve this and get on with his life and then get out of this stupid town. The way out definitely wasn't art school.

The only way that counted in his family was to join the army.

He had to remember who he was, where he came from, and in whose footsteps he had to follow.

No matter how much it scared him to death.

Chapter Twenty-seven

$\mathcal{M}$ick stood in Nina's studio, his heart pounding.

It was two in the morning.

The problem is, I'm falling in love with Nina.

It was a very big problem.

He was about to ruin her vegetable arrangement and then, maybe, her life with some sort of awful news about her brother that she didn't want to hear.

Was his duty to her or to Walt? To her or to Bella?

He said a quick apology to the zucchinis and tomatoes and snatched the box.

He went back to the small guest room and stared at the box, his heart pounding.

He could take it to the lake, row out to the middle, and drop it to the bottom. He didn't need to know what was inside. Hell, he didn't want to know Walt's secrets. He still didn't have the slightest idea why of all the guys in the unit, Walt had decided that he was the one to be trusted with this task, but from the nonstop emotional pinball machine that he'd been trapped in since he'd come here, he was pretty sure he didn't want to find out.

The box grew heavy in his hand.

He thought about Walt. Walt getting drunk in Germany before they all shipped out to the hills and valleys of Afghanistan. Walt had been melancholy that night. A sad drunk. Never trust a sad drunk, Mick's father had always told him.

Mick's father had been a sad drunk, so he knew.

Fact one: he and Nina hadn't come to any kind of agreement about what to do about the box.

Fact two: they hadn't come to any sort of agreement about what to do about their relationship.

Fact three: he had to open the damn box. If he didn't, Nina would be right that he was a coward. His past was somehow tied to Walt, and he didn't know how but he knew that he had to find out or—

Or what?

Or he'd never be able to get any closer to Nina.

Was that what he wanted? To get closer?

He had to deserve her.

The key worked smoothly. The top creaked open.

Walt's Boy Scout merit badges were on the top, tiny threads hanging off some of them where they'd been cut off of whatever they'd been sewn onto. Camping, canoeing, basketry, first aid.

Mick put them on the bed, feeling his stomach constrict as he thought of Walt as a Boy Scout, innocent and hopeful and full of promise. Mick hadn't ever thought of Walt as the scouting type.

He leafed through a few crayon-on-construction-paper birthday cards. A straight-C report card.

Okay, so he wasn't brilliant. But why would Walt want this destroyed? Nothing wrong with a C.

He unfolded a sheet of loose-leaf.

It was a love letter, in purple ink with smiley-face dots over the *i*'s. *You are the cutest boy in fifth grade by a hundred miles…meet me on the track after school today under the big maple tree…*

Pretty heavy stuff for fifth grade from a girl named Mallory, but still, nothing worth hiding.

Under Mallory's letter was a newspaper clipping of boys in baseball uniforms. The Garcia Pharmacy Tigers had won the league championship, and they had the trophies and grins to prove it. Mick found Walt in the front row smiling like mad, his arms thrown around his mates. It could have been an army picture of their unit, except for the backward hats and cleats. Poor guy never even got the chance to grow up. That's what it was with Walt in the army; he still acted like an out-of-control kid.

Mick pushed away the negative thought and kept digging through the box.

He unfolded a short newspaper article.

Across the article was a word, scrawled in pencil.

Bullshit.

Mick read the article underneath.

It was a news story in the local paper about Nina and Walt's parents, Shelley and Ron Stokes. They smiled out at him from the fading picture, their arms around each other. It was obviously not a professional picture, but a personal snapshot given to the paper by an aunt or a friend. Mick counted back the date. Walt would have been twelve, Nina nine. He skimmed the details. They'd died suddenly in an "unfortunate and unexplained car accident." There weren't many more details. Donations could be sent to the food bank at the Galton Catholic church where Shelley volunteered every Tuesday and Wednesday night.

Okay, so the word across the article was a little strange. *Bullshit.*

Had a twelve-year-old Walt written that? The gray lead fading against the yellowing page, he tried to come up with other options. *Bullet? Bullshot?*

No, it read *bullshit.*

Walt had scribbled *bullshit* over the article about his parents' death, then tried to erase it, then put it into a box with his prized possessions.

It made sense. It was bullshit to have your parents die. Walt was an angry kid, lashing out at the randomness of the universe, then being sorry he'd defaced this important artifact.

Still, hardly anything to give a house away for.

There were two other words, erased, at the bottom of the article. Mick held the clipping up to the light. Two words—*sticks and stones*—had been written across the bottom, then erased.

Sticks and stones.

Mick put the strangely defaced article aside and continued through the box. More report cards. Three snapshots of a school-age Walt with a black-haired girl. Mick wondered if it was Mallory from fifth grade, but there were no notations on the back. She had short hair that grew longer as they both got older. Sometimes there was a brown-eyed boy with them. Was it Bobby?

Mick was relieved that Walt had a girl. And a friend. At least he'd had that before—

He pushed away the thought.

Maybe Walt had wanted him to destroy the box because he wanted to spare Nina the pain of walking through this minefield of memories. Hell, he hardly knew the guy, and he was feeling pretty lousy rifling through this stuff. So much promise cut short.

A few more letters, these from Nina to Walt overseas. Mick skimmed them, but there didn't seem to be anything beyond town gossip and descriptions of her art projects and vegetable gardens and wishes to see him soon.

That was it.

Except for a small black rock.

Sticks and stones.

He was grasping at straws, looking for anything to explain this odd disappointment.

He flipped through everything again, annoyed. He read the letters from Nina more carefully. Nothing.

Okay, so it was a little hokey that Walt had gotten a Boy Scout merit badge for basketry, but that was hardly a reason to give a guy a house.

There were only those three words, barely visible on the newspaper article.

Bullshit.

Sticks and stones...

For some reason, it made Mick think of war, which he spent most of his time trying pretty damn hard not to think about.

It made his heart go cold.

He closed the box and lay back on the bed.

It was both better and worse than he had imagined.

On the one hand, it wasn't like Walt had committed a crime that he wanted covered up. There weren't any body parts to discard. No drugs. No weapons.

But had there been a crime committed?

Bullshit.

It looked like the frustrated scribble of a kid who'd lost both his parents to a freak accident. No bigger bullshit in this world than something like that.

But then, why did he want the box destroyed if it was nothing? Was this whole box thing just a ruse to get him to come here and fall in love with Nina?

Not that he was falling in love with Nina.

I am so losing it for that woman.

He went through the other mementos in the box, looking for something else that was out of the ordinary.

Nothing seemed strange.

Now what? Did this box prove that the house was his? Or did it do the opposite? Did it make Walt's letter seem too dramatic to correspond to the box, and so make it seem like a fake?

He'd have to do some investigating.

But how?

And did he have to? Or could he just destroy it? Do what Walt wanted, clearing the air between him and Nina at least a little. He'd done his duty by Walt. Now it was up to her to decide whether or not to do hers.

He thought of her sleeping in the next room. Thought of the way she'd treated Johnny. She had been so gentle for no good reason other than that she felt for the kid. It was part of her way, to see the potential in him when most people would have chased him away. Who wanted a punk hanging around their house, messing with their stuff? But she hadn't even flinched. It was as if she didn't even care what he'd done to her wall, to her career, to her precious memorial. He hadn't told her about Johnny beforehand because he thought she'd be mad and it would cause another fight.

But mad wasn't Nina's reaction to people.

Well, maybe to him.

Or maybe not.

Not really.

Even when he'd been furious at her, she'd taken him to bed, soothing them both. And when she'd lashed out at him, she'd said she was sorry, and she'd let him watch her paint.

He really liked that about her.

He really liked *her*.

He relocked the box, slipped into Nina's studio. He would put the box back and redrape the fabric, being careful to put the vegetables back exactly the way they had been.

How had they been? He stood, the box in one hand, a tomato in the other.

However he would put it back, she'd be pissed that he messed up her wrinkles, but not too pissed. In fact, she'd just smooth them over and get on with her picture.

He'd put money on it.

How did a person get that way? Not angry? It made him remember his father, always angry, always flying off the handle. All of them spending their lives trying to avoid his wrath. The house had to be in perfect order, not a speck of dust, nothing out of place. The food had to be served on time, then cleared. It was as if they all believed that by painting a perfect picture of a domestic life, it would be true. As if they could paint over the pain of his father's insane rages and beatings when anything at all went wrong.

He hadn't thought about his father in years, and now

these past few days he couldn't get the man out of his head. He believed that his father had somehow killed his mother, caused the cancer, as if cancer could grow from fear or terror or lack of love. He knew it couldn't, that his mother's illness had been just one more random thing to deal with.

Still, his father had ruined his childhood. All their childhoods.

"What are you doing? What's that?"

Mick startled. He looked up. Nina stood in the doorway. She stared at the box that was still in his hand.

Chapter Twenty-eight

*H*e wondered how long he'd been standing there thinking about his father. The man had died of liver damage when Mick was twenty-two, but he was still messing up his life, getting in the way.

"Mick?" Nina repeated.

"How do you do that?" Mick asked Nina.

"What?" She was wearing a T-shirt and loose pink cotton pajama bottoms. Naturally, she looked amazing.

"Sneak up on me like that?"

"That's it, isn't it? The thing you're supposed to find? That box? Don't deny it. I can tell by the look on your face." She stepped into the room slowly, as if she were seeing a ghost and couldn't look away. "I use that box all the time for still lifes; I don't even think about it anymore. I found it in the garage, but I brought it in before Walt—" She paused. "You know, I love that box." She pointed at a small picture on the wall behind her desk. "The patina is so interesting. I think I've painted it twenty times."

He looked at the canvas in its unassuming black frame. Sure enough, there was the box, positioned behind a vase filled with daisies. Two smaller blue boxes were stacked on top of it.

She took the box from him, inspected it, shook it. It didn't make a sound, since everything inside was packed tight. "I hadn't even thought about taking it to a locksmith to get it opened. I never considered it personal, if I'd much thought about it at all, which I didn't. I guess I figured it was full of garage stuff. I don't know, sandpaper or rags or garage-y things. Why would a person leave something important hanging around a garage? It was on a shelf with nuts and bolts and junk way in the back, covered in cobwebs. It looked industrial." She handed it back to him quickly, as if it had suddenly become too hot for her bare hand. "I loved how it looked," she said sadly. She paused. "I am shallow, aren't I? That stupid box is the story of my life."

He could feel the key in his pocket. He could open the box for her, show her the article, the stone. Or he could pretend he didn't know what was inside and offer to destroy it. "No. Not shallow. How would you know it was important? Why would you suspect?"

"Mick. Don't you see? It was locked and I never wanted to open it. That was what you said the very first day I met you. It's what everyone says about me. That I just want the world to be pretty. I didn't want to look inside. I still don't! Now I really, really don't want to know what's inside."

He put the box back under the draping, not bothering to get it right, just wanting the box to go away. He crossed to her, took her in his arms, and pulled her close. She was still warm with sleep. His skin felt chilled against hers.

He wanted badly to protect her. He felt awful she'd seen the box. But a small part of him was also glad. He had expected answers from the box, and instead he'd gotten only more mystery.

She let her head fall on his shoulder. "I didn't suspect that Walt had secrets. Walt wasn't a saint, but he was an honest guy. When Bobby got deeper and deeper into bad crowds after high school, Walt pulled away, got serious about staying out of trouble. He felt like he had me to look after, you know? He tended bar downtown at night. Worked some construction. It was hard because our parents were gone—"

She drifted out of his arms and sat down on her wheeled chair. She looked great—sleepy and sexy and sad. "Our aunt Melody moved in, but we didn't have money for college or anything. The day Walt turned eighteen, Aunt Mel took off back to Florida. Walt had to tone down—for me."

"She left you two alone?"

"Walt was of age. I was fifteen. Aunt Mel was old and she hated the winters here. Brutal on her arthritis, she said. We didn't need her. We did fine. We had my parents' house to live in and the insurance money and some social security every month. Plus, we were both good workers and pretty independent by then. We sold my parents' house the day I turned eighteen, and we split the money. That's when Walt bought this place. I moved downtown, used my share of the money for art school, and worked wherever I could. But Walt didn't want to go to school. He never had any ambitions besides serving his country in the army and serving beers to his buddies in Galton. He bought this house on the cheap, kept to himself. He still hung out with Bobby from time to time, but he was

almost more like a father to him, bailing him out when he
needed it. Cleaning him up when he didn't. I didn't think
about secrets."

Mick was struck with her rosy picture of Walt. Like her
picture of him in the barn, it was a little off, something
key missing. The Walt he knew was wilder, more out of
control. The kind of daredevil who tried to tempt fate. But
he didn't want to get into all that with her. Not when she
looked so sad. He said, "I'd have bashed the thing open
with a sledgehammer. I'd have wanted to see what was
inside just because it was locked. I'd have been curious."

"I wasn't."

"What do you want now?"

"I have no idea."

"So you don't care if I destroy it? That was his request,
Nina. That I find this box and destroy it. I'm sorry. I wasn't
going to tell you. I'm sorry you had to see it."

"No. It's good that I know. Now that I know, I know it's
not something worse."

Or is it?

"So destroy it," Nina said. She pulled it out from under
the draping and handed it to him.

"Your picture will be ruined."

"Nah. I'll put something else under there. It doesn't
matter." She messed with the vegetables, not looking at
him. "Did you open it?"

He made a split-second decision not to answer her. It
didn't matter. "Walt gave me the key. And this." He pulled
Walt's letter out of his back pocket and handed it to her.

She read it. Held it to her face. Closed her eyes. "I hate
this."

"I'm sorry."

"So you're for real. He really gave you the house. He really has a secret in the box that's so terrible, it's worth a house." A tear trailed down her cheek. "I kind of wish you were another con artist."

"I'm really sorry." This was awful. Everything he'd wanted to avoid, he'd run right into. "I was supposed to keep it all secret. I blew it."

"No. It's good," she said. "It's over. Over is good. Now I know he meant for you to have the house. You proved yourself. It's good for you and good for Bella and good for me too, because I can move on. I'll talk to Jill. Find out how to get you the money you need."

"It's not over, Nina. I'm going to give you a few days to think about this, okay? To think about all of it—the box, the house. I won't destroy the box right away. Once it's gone—"

"Once it's gone, then you fulfilled your duty to Walt. So I think I should fulfill mine by giving you the house."

Mick headed for town. He walked the main street, picking up a few necessities just like he'd done every week since he'd left the army hospital in Santa Monica. A bag of pink hard candy wrapped in a red ribbon, a horoscope book for Libras, a *Galton Is Gorges* T-shirt.

He felt like crap. He'd done his duty, just about, and didn't achieve an ounce of satisfaction. He'd given up pretending it was Walt's house he was trying to take. It was Nina's, pure and simple, and he didn't want to take it from her.

But he had to have it. And now she was going to give it to him.

Sandra had called at the break of dawn. Baily was

worried because Bella was getting weaker. They hoped it was just the change in climate and stress from travel, but who knew?

They might even have to stop the tests that were the first steps to making the vaccine till she got stronger.

If she got stronger.

And the first thought he'd had when he heard this terrible news was: *good, I have more time to work things out with Nina.* He hated himself for thinking of himself and his problems when he should think only of Bella. It was like when he'd taken off for the army, leaving them all behind. He had acted out of duty to his country, sure, but he'd also known that joining the army the day after his father died was the first damn thing that he'd done for himself. He'd put himself first. And look where it had gotten them—broke and struggling to save the family he'd abandoned way back then.

He constructed one of the mailing boxes from the pile in his trunk, put his purchases inside, and carried the box to the post office to send it off to the VA medical center in Santa Monica. He addressed the package to Georgette Meyers, the nurse who'd taken care of him during those long months of recovery from the blast he couldn't remember. She'd get it to the patient who needed it most. Didn't matter what was in it, just so long as he got it off, and she passed it along to whoever needed a smile.

He stood in the long, barely moving post office line and thought about the trap he'd walked into. Whatever in Walt's box that was worth a house meant nothing to Mick. Hell, he should ship off Walt's box too, with no return address. Be done with it. Be done with Galton. Take Nina's money and go.

But he'd botched his side of the deal by letting Nina see the box. Nina shouldn't have to know the truth about her brother, whatever that truth was. Whatever the damn secret was. How could he take the money with this failure hanging over him? He had to make it right here in Galton somehow.

The line inched forward. A foreign student with three enormous boxes labeled to a faraway country dumped his first box on the counter and tried to converse the best he could in his broken English with the clerk. The clerk measured, then tried to explain size and weight requirements. Mick might never get out of here.

"Are you Mick Rivers?"

He turned to the woman in line behind him. She wore a brown pencil skirt with matching brown jacket, reminding him of just about every schoolteacher he'd ever hated.

"I saw your name on your box. On the return address," the woman said. She held out her hand to shake. "Georgia Phillips. I'm a friend of Nina's. Have been forever, so I know all about you." She was looking at him carefully, the way a collector might appraise a painting she was considering buying.

"Nice to meet you." He shook her hand. This was the woman that poem writer Bobby was in love with. He wasn't sure how much he was supposed to know about that.

Conversation stopped, so he turned back around to face the front of the nonmoving line. The student at the counter argued with the clerk in English that was so bad, Mick could hardly recognize it as his native tongue. The clerk argued back, her arms crossed over her chest.

After a few minutes of watching this, Mick turned back around. "Did you know Walt?" he asked Georgia.

"Sure," she said. "We all grew up together. This is a small town. He was three years older than us, though, so you probably knew him better than I did. After all, you went through a lot together." She let that hang in the air.

"Yeah, probably," he said, trying not to think about what they'd been through together.

She was watching him with that careful look again.

He said as casually as he could, "Did you know their parents?"

Georgia hesitated a moment, considering. "Sure. Why do you ask?"

The line moved forward, and they eased along with it. "No reason. I've just been trying to figure out Nina. Her parents died when she was young, right?"

"She was nine. It was awful. Out of the blue. A complete surprise." Georgia's eyes became veiled.

"A car accident," he said.

"Nina told you about it?" Georgia asked.

He shrugged. "A little." He took a deep breath. He was pushing his luck, but it seemed important to find out if people already suspected something was off about their parents' death. Some kind of *bullshit*. "Was it just a car accident?"

Georgia's eyes narrowed. "What are you getting at?"

The line moved up again. "Nothing. Just what I heard."

He couldn't read Georgia. Her face was a mask. But her silence seemed to indicate something chilling. "Georgia, tell me if there's something I should know. I won't tell Nina. Walt sent me here to destroy a box and—" He stopped. "I'm saying too much. Georgia, I care; that's all. I want to do the right thing by Nina, and I'm having trouble figuring out what the right thing is."

The line moved forward again.

"Look, Mr. Rivers. I'm a psychiatrist. People think that we do talk therapy, but the truth is, we specialize in the things people don't say. The silence between the words. The silence is what matters. The things we don't discuss are the most important. So forget what's in the box. This is not about a stupid box or a long-ago accident. If Nina told you to toss the box—"

"She did."

"Then she's not ready to face what's inside. You can't force her. In fact, I suspect I might say the same thing about you. You can face what's inside—or not. Inside you—not inside some stupid box that a reckless kid left behind."

The hairs rose on the back of his neck. "Walt asked me to destroy the box," he repeated.

"Screw Walt. Walt's gone. What do you want?"

They had gotten the attention of the elderly woman in front of Mick in the line. He smiled at her, nodded, and lowered his voice. "I have to do my duty. To do what he asked. It's not about what I want."

Georgia's gaze was hard and steady. "Ask Nina your questions. Don't ask me. This is between the two of you. I've already said too much." She clamped her mouth shut and got out her phone. She started texting as if it were the most interesting thing in the world. She really didn't want to talk to him. Okay, he got that. But there was something more, something odd about her.

"You know something about the accident, don't you?" Mick asked. It was just a feeling, but the feeling was strong.

She looked up, her mouth a perfectly shaped *O*.

"Answer me, Georgia. I need to know." He was next

in line. The elderly woman in front of him tottered to the window. He hoped she had a lot of confusing business to address very slowly. He heard her say, "Just three stamps today, Betsy. I have exact change!"

Georgia clicked her phone shut. "Look, Mick, you're an army guy. You're looking for an order. For someone to command you to do what's right. But this isn't war. It's life. You have to figure it out. You have to do the right thing, and that thing is foggy and confusing. There's no general here to give orders. There's no secret intelligence that I have that'll bust open the battlefield."

The old woman at the counter closed her purse after carefully tucking her three stamps inside.

"Next!" the teller called.

Mick didn't move. The people behind Georgia in line shot him evil looks. "Just tell me one thing, then. What's your professional opinion on fulfilling deathbed wishes?" he asked her. "Isn't my duty to Walt?"

"Walt is gone," Georgia said. "Anything Nina thinks she's doing for him, she's doing for herself. I'd say that pretty much goes for you too. So try to see things clearly, Mick."

The man behind them harrumphed loudly.

"Next!" the teller called again.

"Thanks, Georgia." Mick moved away, but Georgia caught his arm at the last possible moment and pulled him close.

She leaned in and whispered, "Mick, Nina told me about your nightmares. You have no right to dig in her past unless you're brave enough to dig up your own. You just might not like what you find in either place."

Chapter Twenty-nine

A week! You caved in a week!" Jill cried.

Nina had gone to Jill's real estate office to talk to her about her options for selling the house, or at least taking out a home equity loan. "Eight days," Nina pointed out. "And I didn't cave. I'm just exploring my options. Jill, his sister is dying."

"And Walt has a son named little Walt—"

"Walt didn't promise little Walt his house."

"If he had, little Walt would have been grateful. He wouldn't have ignored you for two years."

"You'd do the same thing, Jill. Mick is a good guy. His sister is sick."

"I wouldn't. You're a sucker."

"I can lend him the money and he'll pay me back."

"Just like you arranged with fake Mary?"

"Stop. This isn't the same."

"You don't know that." Jill started to pace her tiny office. "And what if he is for real? You'll put yourself into

crippling debt that you can't afford. You'll have to pay
off a home equity loan, hon. You don't have that kind of
income. And neither does he. What does he do, anyway?"

"He was a soldier for a long time."

Jill considered. "I suppose he could go back."

"No!" Nina cried.

Jill's eyebrows rose.

"He did his duty. He can't go back. Three tours was
enough. He was wounded, Jill."

"Then he's a guy with no real-world skills, Nina.
He's not going to be able to help you much with a huge
loan. Nina, look at me: you don't have a steady income.
Fake Mary destroyed your credit. You're not going to get
a good rate even if you get the loan. And you still don't
know if you can trust him. What if this sick-sister story
is a con?"

"I don't think it is."

Jill made a sour face at her. "I have to tell it like it is,
Nina. I've heard this story before: you giving up everything for a good cause."

"How's the market?" Nina asked. "If I can't get a loan,
then I have to sell the house."

Jill shook her head. "It's okay. You know Galton—not
enough housing stock, especially near campus. But don't
do it, Nina."

"Will you do this or do I have to find another Realtor?"

Jill considered. "Look, talk to Mel at the bank. See if
you can get the equity loan. They only take a week or two.
They're fast. You don't have to rush on anything. And
meanwhile, promise me you'll take this slow. Think on
this."

"Okay. I'll think on it for a week."

"One week. And I'm going to spend that whole time trying to talk you out of this."

Johnny came to the barn at noon.

Mick dragged the plastic Adirondack chairs from the back deck into the barn. Johnny sat in the blue one. Mick took the yellow.

"Nice chairs," Johnny said. "They make this almost bearable. Now if we could just move them to the lake and get some fishing poles, I think we might be getting somewhere." It was the first words they'd spoken in the half hour they'd been in the barn.

Mick looked up from the rock he was tossing up and down in his hand. "Almost bearable?"

"Almost."

"I can *almost* call the cops if you want," Mick suggested.

"Did I mention how awesome it is to sit around all afternoon in a stinking barn with an old pissed-off guy?" Johnny said morosely. "It rocks."

Mick nodded. "That's the spirit. Anyway, the sooner we solve this, the sooner we're out of here." He took aim at a post. He missed.

"We may be here forever," Johnny said. He finished the ginger ale Mick had broken down and bought for him and set the can on the ground by his chair. He picked up a stone and casually tossed it at the post. It hit dead center with a satisfying thud. He grinned at Mick, sat back in his chair, and cracked open another can. Mick had bought him a six-pack. He could stay all day. "So why are you here, really?" Johnny asked after half the can of ginger ale was gone. "You in love with Nina Stokes?"

Mick looked up. He had let his mind wander to a kid

he'd known in a run-down village in Afghanistan named Mohammed. He looked a lot like Johnny must have looked when he was eight or nine. "I'm helping Nina; that's all."

"No offense, dude, but you don't look like you're doing much helping." Johnny hit the post again. "Ten for ten. You're four for twelve. Not that I'm keeping score or anything."

"I'm trying to help her," Mick said, ignoring the score. "Anyway, it's none of your business." He missed the post again.

Johnny let out a victorious burp. "You're trying to put spin on a rock, dude. You gotta throw fastballs if you wanna hit it. It's a rock, not a leather, ten-dollar Rawlings."

"I'm hitting some."

"Four for thirteen," Johnny said.

Mick scowled, but he tried a fastball. He hit it dead-on.

They ran out of small stones within reach, and they had to get up to gather stones from around the barn's crumbling cement foundation. While Johnny had gone for a second load of ammo, Mick found some black paint and a brush. He painted a three-ring bull's-eye on the post. Let the cocky hotshot hit that.

"What was it like coming home?" the boy asked. They'd taken up their positions again. Johnny hadn't hit the bull's-eye in seven throws.

"Which time?" Mick asked. "I came home three times. Once after every tour."

"The first," Johnny said.

Mick hit the bull's-eye dead-on. "The first was good. We got off the plane, but it was still the army, right? So we lined up in formation. There's all these moms and wives and kids crying and busting out at the seams. They've got balloons and teddy bears and all kinds of shit. But we stood at attention forever till they told us to fall out. Then all hell broke loose. I'll never forget it."

Johnny thought about that, and Mick guessed he was thinking about his brother not coming home.

"So you had a girl waiting?" Johnny asked.

"Three. All of them gorgeous," Mick said.

"Yeah? Three? How'd you handle that? They were really hot?" Johnny asked.

Mick coughed.

"Big boobs?" Johnny asked, undeterred.

Mick ignored that. "They were sweet too. They even brought me a teddy bear and balloons. I have no idea why."

"'Cause you're a wimp?" Johnny suggested.

Mick hit the post with his next rock. "It was a tough teddy bear."

"I'll bet."

"Yeah. Sisters are cool."

"Sisters!" Johnny cried. "I thought—" He shot Mick a look, and Mick pursed his lips and hit the bull's-eye a second time. "Never mind," Johnny groused. "God, you're old *and* boring!"

Mick smiled. "Just you wait. You'll be me before you know it."

After a while Johnny asked, "What about the second time you came back?"

"It was the same deal. Big speeches. All of us lined up. Families waiting. Only this time, when they told us to fall out, there wasn't anyone there to welcome me back. Finances had gotten tight, and the trip was too much."

"That sucks. But still, better to come home to no one than not to come home."

"The thought had occurred to me."

They threw some more rocks.

"What about the third time you came home?" Johnny asked.

"Dunno. I was on a stretcher, wiped out with meds."

"No shit."

"No shit."

"But at least you didn't have to stand there at attention, knowing there wasn't anyone to give you a teddy bear," Johnny said.

Mick looked at him. *From the mouths of babes.* "Yeah. At least there was that."

"So what was wrong with you? You look okay now. I mean, except for the ugliness."

"Yeah, that they can't cure. Yet. As soon as they can, though, I'll be sure you're the first to know." He opened a can of Coke, then polished it off in one swig. He stacked the empty on the can he'd drank before. "Three months I was out of it, stuck in a hospital in Germany. Then I finally got stabilized enough to get out of there to a VA hospital in California."

"That sucks." Johnny eyed the stacked cans.

"When I came to, first thing I did was count my legs. Then my arms. After that, it didn't suck so bad."

"So what happened?"

"I got better."

"I mean *over there*, stupid. What happened to you over there to land you in the VA?"

"Oh. Yeah. That. I don't remember."

"You don't remember?"

"Nope. I remember riding in the Humvee. We were listening to the Stones, 'cause that's what our driver liked.

There were four of us. Walt was in the Hummer in front of us. And then I remember waking up in California."

"Shit. So you were there when Walt, y'know . . ."

"Went down? Yeah. I guess. I must have been."

"But you don't know what happened? That is so fucked up. Can't someone tell you?"

"Everyone else who was there is gone."

That gave Johnny pause. But not for long. "Is that why Walt gave you the house? Like, maybe you saved him— for a little while anyway. Or something." Johnny's eyes had gone wide. His voice grew excited.

Mick frowned. Everyone wanted a hero, a happy ending. "What do you know about Walt giving me the house?" Mick asked.

"Oh, everyone knows he gave it to you. Lizzie at the diner told my mom. My mom eats lunch there every weekday, and Lizzie's part of the Enemy Club with Nina. We all just figured you were some kind of hero and that's why he gave it to you." The boy paused to take a breath. "So you were Walt's buddy? My mom says he used to hang with a pretty fast crowd. I've heard stuff about him."

"He was wild. Wild wasn't okay when people are try- ing to blow you up."

"So why'd you save him?"

"Who said I saved him?" *Can't save a dead man.*

"You must have done something heroic," Johnny said. "You said yourself you don't remember, so who knows? My mom thinks it's cute that you'll fall in love with Nina and you guys'll end up together, because of Walt. Like that his death brought something good."

"Yeah, because of Walt." Mick tossed a stone, and it was so off, it hit Nina's canvas. The dead, empty thunk of the stone against Walt's pink cheek seemed fitting. He had to stop himself from throwing a second stone.

Johnny shot him a sideways glance. "You don't think you saved him, do you?"

"No one saved him. He's gone." He took aim at his stacked Coke cans and hit the top one dead on. It fell to the floor and rolled away.

Chapter Thirty

*B*obby Ridale showed up at four o'clock to look at the second letter Nina was writing for Georgia.

Mick was in the kitchen, cooking up a dinner of rice and baked chicken that smelled so good, she was having trouble concentrating. He poked his head out of the kitchen to watch them go up to her studio. She shot him a warning glare not to interfere.

When they came down, Mick came out of the kitchen, wiping his hands on a yellow kitty-print dishrag.

"Hi," he said. It was a voice Nina hadn't heard from Mick before. Rough and low and challenging, as if he were trying to start something.

Bobby looked at him, his face neutral. "Hi. Bobby Ridale." He held out his hand.

Mick shook it, but he didn't smile or offer his name. The tension between them was almost physical, as if testosterone was zinging off the walls.

"Mick Rivers, this is my client," Nina said. She felt like

a kindergarten teacher, trying to model good behavior to children. "Mick is also a friend of Walt's. Was. Is." She stopped, flustered.

Bobby nodded to Mick. "Walt was a good man. We all miss him."

"I remember him talking about you," Mick said.

Bobby's eyes narrowed. "Yeah?"

Nina looked from man to man. What was Mick doing? He had told her before that Walt had never mentioned Bobby.

"Yeah. Well, we were good friends."

Mick pursed his lips and nodded. "Right." He said it as if what he really meant was *You better get out of here before I take your head off.*

"Well, I better get moving." Bobby said his good-byes. Mick didn't say another word.

Nina shut the door behind him, then turned to face Mick. "What is your problem?"

"I don't like that guy," Mick said.

Nina rolled her eyes. "Yeah, I noticed. Oh, for heaven's sake! Just because you and I—" She paused. "Because we did whatever it is we did together doesn't mean you get to go all macho man on me. Especially with my clients."

"I don't trust him. He seems shady."

"He's a felon. I told you that."

Mick shook his head and started back to the kitchen. "Well, he doesn't love Georgia. That's for sure."

"You don't know that." She followed him. The kitchen smelled divine, like garlic and lemon and rosemary. "That's why he came back to Galton. It's all very straightforward and honest and lovely of him."

Mick shook his head again. He checked something in

a pot on the stove. Her stomach grumbled. "If a guy like that is in love, he doesn't write poems and hire an artist. A guy like that moves in with two dozen cheap red roses and a wallet full of condoms."

"Mick! That's terrible." She had to stop herself from crossing the room to him, leaning over his shoulder to see what was in the pan.

He shrugged. "Don't you think it's a weird coincidence that he shows up the day after I do?" He opened the oven and pulled out a gorgeous golden-brown chicken. Steam rose off it filling the kitchen with lovely smells.

"How would he even know who you are?"

"I have no idea. I'm just saying, it strikes me as odd."

"You don't know anything about Bobby," she said. She had no idea why she was defending a man she also didn't trust. She had thought it was a weird coincidence in the beginning too.

"Look," he said. "I'm a guy. I know guys like that guy. That guy is not in love with your friend Georgia."

"How do you know anything about Georgia?" she said to his back.

"I met her. In the post office." He leaned back on the counter, his arms crossed over his chest. "She's not his type."

"Okay, so she's not traditionally pretty," she allowed.

"She's very pretty. But men like him don't like pretty. They like big and busty and vulgar. But all that's beside the point. What matters is that a man like Bobby doesn't behave like this guy is behaving. It doesn't add up. Especially for a woman like Georgia."

"Like Georgia?"

"C'mon, Nina. Don't play dumb. She's not a bimbo," he

said. "She's smart and she's cultured and she's so over that guy's head, he couldn't touch her with a ten-foot pole."

They stared at each other, the tension between them almost painful.

"So you're saying that you can smell a con and I'm still an idiot?"

"I'm saying you should open your eyes to the possibility."

"Mick, did you get rid of the box yet?"

"No, but I came to a decision."

Her head was starting to ache. "Okay. What is it?"

He sat down at the kitchen table. "Here's the thing, Nina. I'm starting to really like you."

She waited, her heart pounding.

"And that's kind of mucking this all up."

She didn't say a word.

"Walt was your brother. So you decide. If you want the box destroyed, we do it together."

Chapter Thirty-one

Nina slid into the car beside Mick, wondering what she was getting herself into. He had refused to give her any clue about how he intended to destroy the box. He'd said only that they'd leave at six in the morning, in his car, and that she should wear comfortable, warm clothes.

"Ready?" he asked.

"Ready." Panic was beginning to creep into her skin, but she was determined to ignore it. This was the right thing to do because it was what Walt wanted.

They drove down the hill to town, then through town and toward the lake. The stores were still asleep, unlit and silent. The roads were mostly empty in the predawn light. A police car passed them going the other way. Mick pulled into the small marina.

"Oh no, Mick. I get seasick," she said as they drove in past the rows of small sailboats and motorboats parked to the side of the lot, still in their trailers. Were they going to drop the box in the lake? Lake Galton was long and deep, formed millions of years ago by glaciers. She didn't like to think about being out on it, especially on a windy, chilly morning like this one. The water was choppy with tiny waves.

"No problem. We don't need a boat." He parked the car and went around to the trunk. He pulled out the box. "C'mon."

"You're going to throw it into the lake from the pier?" A sliver of the moon still visible in the sky reflected in the back window.

"No. You're going to throw it into the lake from the pier." He started walking toward the water.

She followed him out onto the long wooden deck. The platform was wobbly under her feet, and she went only a few steps before she was nauseous. She looked back to the shore to get her bearings. A family of deer drinking from the water's edge watched them warily. Somehow she made it to the end of the landing.

"You still want to do this?" he asked. "We could go back to the car and open it first. We could just take it back to the house, put it back on the shelf."

She shook her head. She was dying to know what was in the box—and also dying never to know. Tiny waves lapped against the dock, fueled by a wind that made her shiver almost as much as her fear of knowing—of not knowing.

"Toss it." Her voice sounded steady, but her mind was reeling. *Damn, Walt.* "You should do it, though. That's what Walt wanted."

"Coward." He looked back to the parking lot. A white van towing long, narrow crew boats pulled in. College kids with Starbucks coffee cups and baggy sweatpants piled out looking sleepy and cold. "Okay. We better hurry. I didn't think it would be a crowd out here." He held the box under his left arm. He started stretching his right shoulder like a pitcher warming up for the big game.

"How's the shoulder?" she asked.

"I think it'll do," he said.

Panic had claimed every inch of her body. "Wait!"

He waited.

She couldn't breathe. Behind her, the crew team had started to unload their boats and carry them to the water's edge. The deer had disappeared along with the sliver of moon as the sun rose on the horizon. *Walt's last secret would be the next thing to disappear.* Did she want to know what was in the box? "If there's something he wanted to hide from me, then I have to honor that wish. It's not up to me."

"It's always up to you."

"Throw it," she said, her voice so soft she repeated her words, just in case he couldn't hear her. "Do it!"

Just like that, he tossed the box as far as he could into the water. It flew through the air, a red square against the gray sky. Then it arced and fell and landed with a splash in the icy water. It disappeared into the choppy water in an instant, not even leaving behind a trail of bubbles. It was gone. Just like Walt, gone. Just like her parents, gone. Just like everything, every damn thing, including, soon, Mick—gone.

Damn it. She was staring at a freezing lake at dawn, tears streaming down her face.

She didn't want to be crying. Not here. Not with Mick and the Galton U. crew team and no hope of ever knowing anything more about Walt. Why had she let him do that?

Mick took her into his arms and held her close, telling her softly over and over that it was okay. That it was all going to be okay.

But she wasn't so sure.

"Mick, I think that was a terrible mistake," she found herself saying. She pulled away from him. "Oh God. Why did I let you do that? I want it back, Mick. I need to know."

"It's too late, Nina. It's—"

The icy water hit her like a bullet.

"Nina!" she heard Mick yell. But she ignored him. She had to get that box back. She started to swim, the coldness making every movement feel like stabbing needles through her skin. Her jeans were heavy on her legs. Her sneakers were pulling her down.

She heard a splash behind her, but she didn't turn. She didn't want to take her eyes off the spot where the box had hit the water. How deep was the water this far out? It could be twenty feet. Thirty. Impossible to reach the bottom or to see through the water's murky, choppy depths.

"Nina!" Mick's voice was close. Then he was right beside her. "Are you nuts?" He had jumped in after her, and he didn't look happy about it. But she couldn't worry about him now. She kept swimming. Her teeth were chattering. Her feet were going numb. "You shouldn't have listened to me."

"Nina, stop."

"I was wrong! Why didn't you know I was wrong?"

He caught her arm and they bobbed in the water, their teeth chattering. "I didn't do it for you. I did it for Walt. It was my duty."

"Duty!" She was crying so hard, she felt as if she'd cried the lake. "Well, what about your duty to me, Mick? Don't you feel anything for me?"

"Nina, stop."

"Walt marched to his death in the middle of nowhere because he thought it was his duty, and you threw away my box because you thought it was your duty. Didn't you guys have a duty to me too?"

"Nina—"

"You just do what you're told. Follow the lemmings over the damn cliff. Look at you now, following me—"

"Nina—"

"Like I'm just another duty to you. Just another thing you have to bear to be a tough guy. I'm so sick of tough guys—"

"Nina!"

"No, Mick! I—"

She was underwater. He had dunked her, the bastard! And he was holding her down, his hand on her head like it was a basketball. She started to struggle. He was a maniac. She couldn't breathe. Then he was tugging her up to the surface by the back of her shirt. She sputtered for her breath. She was about to scream at him, but the look on his face stopped her cold. He was furious. "Shut up or you go under again."

She coughed.

"Now, stop talking and listen to me," he said. "The box was empty."

The tiny waves slapped against her shoulders. The crew team had rushed down the dock and were teetering on the edge, calling to them. She hoped none of them would jump in. Or worse, call 911 and have Mick arrested for trying to drown her.

"Did you hear me? Nina? It was empty," he repeated.

"You dunked me," she said. She was breathless, treading water, not knowing which way to swim. Maybe out to the middle of the lake, far away from everything and everyone.

"Sorry. You wouldn't shut up."

"Why was the box empty?" She was struggling to keep up with him. "Are you telling me there was nothing in it all along?"

"Nina, my duty is to you. I took everything out of it before we came down here. I was never going to throw Walt's stuff in a lake. I don't give a damn about Walt."

"You could have told me," she said.

"Keeping the box needed to be your choice, not mine. I didn't know any other way to make you choose once and for all."

"I'd hit you if my arms weren't frozen solid," she said. He had done it for her. He was here, sopping wet in his jeans in a freezing lake, for her. He had jumped in, no hesitation, for her. "No, wait, I'd hug you. I'd kiss you." She threw herself at him and took his mouth in hers. Slowly, they sank below the surface as she wound around him as tightly as she could, ran her fingers over his cropped hair, down his back, then back to his face, feeling it with her fingers. When they couldn't last another second underwater, she separated from him and they came to the surface and gasped.

The students on the shore were shouting to them. She waved, and a cheer went up on the shore. She couldn't have agreed more. She was ecstatic. Elated. And not just because of the kiss or the fact that they hadn't lost whatever was in the box. She was radiant because Mick had gotten it so right. He'd done it for her.

He chose me. His duty is to me.

"We better get back to shore before they call the cops," Mick said.

She started swimming, and he swam alongside, holding his powerful stroke to match hers.

Chapter Thirty-two

When they got back to the dock, a crowd of rowers pulled them up. Nina and Mick dismissed their offers of further help, ignored their expressions of disbelief, brushed off their offers of towels, laughed at their questions about their sanity. They made it as quickly as they could to Mick's car. He blasted the heat. She felt insanely happy. As if she had cheated death. As if she had a second chance. She couldn't stop her teeth from chattering. "I can't believe you jumped in after me, Mick," she said.

"I can't believe you jumped in," he said. "Did you know how deep it was? You could have killed yourself. Killed both of us." His voice was harder than she expected. But then, he was frozen half through.

"Nah. I've jumped off that pier millions of times. We used to go skinny-dipping there in the summer nights when I was in high school."

"That's a small relief." His voice was flat.

"Mick?" She really looked at him for the first time

since they'd gotten out of the water. His face was ashen. "What's wrong?"

"What's wrong?" he asked. He looked up at the ceiling of the car as if the answer might be there. "Nothing," he said finally.

"Something," she said. "Tell me, Mick."

He looked at her, sopping and shivering. "That was crazy, Nina."

"I know. I'm sorry. I didn't mean to do it. I just did it."

"Just like your brother," he said.

If she was chilled before, now she was frozen solid. The edge in his voice was icy with disdain. "What do you mean by that?" she asked.

His face was dark, his eyes darker. He threw the car into reverse and backed out of the parking space. "Nothing. Forget it."

"No. What? Tell me!" Her dripping, soaked clothes suddenly seemed somehow shameful. Everything about the morning felt childish and irresponsible.

"Forget it." He concentrated on driving through the deserted parking lot, through the park, to the main road. It was still early enough that they were the only ones on the road. Still, he drove as if it took all his concentration. "Really. It's no big deal. I'm just a little shook-up; that's all. Forget it."

"At least you had the foresight to kick off your shoes," she said, trying to lighten the conversation and her mood. "I wasn't quite so lucky."

"Lucky!" Mick slammed on the brakes, fishtailing the car to the shoulder of the road. The red brake lights reflected off the concrete, giving the scene an extra touch of eerie glow in the pink of the dawn. He turned to her. "There was nothing lucky about that. You were reckless, Nina."

"I wasn't. I knew it was deep."

"It was still reckless. It was crazy. It was the kind of thing Walt would do—rushing in first, thinking later. You couldn't have gotten the box back. It was gone. Sunk. It was a fool's mission. I was swimming out to you, but I couldn't stop thinking of Walt. Of how he'd pull that shit all the time. Jumping into some crazy shit, and we'd have to go after him. And he'd be all jazzed up and we'd have to practically shanghai him to settle him down. It wasn't cool."

She thought of how he'd dunked her. "That's not fair. This isn't exactly a war zone, Mick. No one was in danger."

Mick put the car into gear and started driving again. After a while he said, "I know it's not a war zone, Nina. I'm not crazy. It was just unreal—the similarities. That's all. How similar you guys are. Were. Forget it."

Nina sat in the passenger's seat, wet and shaking, wondering what had just happened. She had been so high, and now she felt like she was slipping down a cliff, with no end in sight. "So that's bad? To be like Walt?"

"Sometimes," Mick said. "I'm sorry. I'm just shook-up is all. Forget it. He was a good man. A good soldier. I shouldn't have said anything."

"You can't just imply he's a bad soldier and then say he's a good soldier," she said.

"I'm sorry. Forget it."

"No, I can't forget it, Mick. I asked you to stay in Galton to tell me about Walt. So tell me. Details!"

"There's nothing to tell. It's nothing." He paused. "Okay. When you jumped in the water, Nina, and I came after you, I had a flashback to the war."

"Oh my God. You remember what happened?"

"No. It's not like that. It was a wave of déjà vu. Like I'd been in that situation before, but with Walt."

"Did Walt do something to hurt you? Oh God, is that why he gave you the house? Because your getting hurt was his fault? You had to follow him into some stupid situation?"

"I told you I don't remember, and I still don't. I just need a little space, okay? I'm a little freaked-out, is all."

They went home and showered, but they barely spoke. Nina could feel the gap between them growing by the second, as if she were still sinking under the lake, but he had risen alone to the surface and swam away. She wanted to pull him close. She even tried at first, just a touch on his arm, but he moved away.

She wasn't sure which was worse, that he equated her with Walt or that he held Walt in such disdain.

She was going to have to face that Walt wasn't everything she thought he was. She looked at her clean, combed reflection in her bedroom mirror. She refused to be what Mick thought she was: a waif, unable to face the truth. If Walt was a bad soldier, so be it.

After she was dressed in dry clothes, he brought her a small paper bag and handed it to her. "I'm heading out to the barn. Johnny should be here any minute. Okay?" She was relieved he wasn't going to go through it with her. "I think you should look it over alone. It's hard to know what to make of it, and I don't want to influence you."

They heard the rattle of a bicycle coming up the bumpy drive. Mick quickly left the room.

She sat on the bed, staring after him in dismay. She felt like a little girl. She looked at the bag in front of her.

It was time to grow up.

Chapter Thirty-three

Nina considered putting the bag in the closet and never looking at it again. *Am I just like Walt? Is that a bad thing?* She lay on the bed next to the bag, as if maybe, if she lay there long enough, she'd get a vibe from whatever was inside, some kind of answer would come to her about what to do next.

Walt, you up there? You watching all this? You see what you started?

Of course, there was no answer. She didn't expect any answer.

What could be the worst thing she'd find in the bag? That's what Georgia would have asked her. The absolute worst?

Some kind of proof that Walt was a criminal. A drug dealer. Weapons. Cash.

A high-pitched, crazy-sounding laugh escaped her. She covered her mouth in dismay. After the fiasco at the lake, even all that didn't seem so bad. It felt as if Walt had already been pegged by Mick as the worst thing in the world and she didn't need proof in a paper bag to know it: he was a bad soldier. *Reckless.*

Reckless meant irresponsible.

Irresponsible meant death.

What if Walt gave Mick the house because whatever happened to them on that last day had been Walt's fault? What if Walt was responsible for almost killing Mick? What if that was what the gift of the house was all about? Then she'd have to give him the house.

Gladly.

She wished she could make Mick remember that last day in Afghanistan. Other men had died in the explosion. *Four from the unit,* one of the men who had come to her front door in full uniform had said.

What if it had been Walt's fault? And what if she shared his nature? No wonder Mick had pulled away.

The worst thing.

Yes, the worst thing was knowing her brother wasn't a good soldier. That not only had he died, but he had caused other soldiers' deaths. *Had almost killed Mick.* That wasn't the way it was supposed to be. You weren't supposed to think about a fallen soldier that way.

She felt so empty, she wasn't sure she'd ever be full again. The blackness inside her expanded to block her breathing.

No one knows what happened that day. It's wrong to assume.

She got up and looked to the barn. Johnny's bike leaned against the side of the barn. His brother, Matthew, might have died because of a bad soldier like Walt.

She felt sick.

She went to the bathroom but couldn't get a handle on her nausea. Walt had done some bad things when they were kids, sure. He'd been kind of irresponsible, the way boys could be, especially boys without parents. But over there—she didn't want to think about it. She'd assumed that he'd straightened up over there. They wouldn't let him get out of control over there, right? He'd gotten away from Bobby and doing bad, irresponsible things.

She was furious at Mick. He had no right to let her think these kinds of things about Walt.

He had no right to give her this bag.

The worst thing?

Could she really handle another bad thing about Walt now that she felt that she knew Walt was a dangerous soldier? No wonder Mick hated this house—he didn't want to take anything from a man like Walt. No wonder he was frustrated with her—she was just like Walt in his eyes.

She thought about him that first day they'd met. His words were seared into her consciousness:

I've seen your type before. You think you want truth. You think you want answers. But really, you want flowers and butterflies and rainbows and happy garden gnomes. I don't have those things. There is no happy ending to this story, Nina.

He had said that on the first day. And she hadn't listened. She had still thought this would somehow come out okay, no matter how much he'd tried to tell her otherwise.

She wanted to set the bag on fire.

She wanted to set Mick on fire. To never see him again.

She had no idea what to do next.

So she took a deep breath and opened the bag, spilling its contents on the bed.

Chapter Thirty-four

Wednesday morning, Nina pushed through the glass door into the Last Chance diner. She was the first one of the Enemy Club to arrive.

Lizzie came out of the back and stopped short. "Nins? You okay? You look a little—" She paused. "Upset."

Nina held up the brown bag with Walt's stuff to Lizzie. "Booth meeting today," she said.

Lizzie glanced in the bag. "You brought your own breakfast?"

"It's the stuff from the box that Mick was supposed to destroy." Nina had been staring at the contents of the bag for days, wondering what it all meant.

"What was he supposed to destroy? Wait—I'm lost."

"Long story."

Lizzie nodded. "Booth meeting. I'll bring the coffee." She turned to her staff. "Ally, can you cover the counter for me? I'll try to cover the coffees on the floor." Lizzie

moved efficiently behind the counter, bringing two coffees and, for Nina, a cup of chamomile tea.

Georgia came next, armed with Bobby's second poem.
Lizzie intercepted her at the door. "Love letters have to
wait," she said. "Emergency."

Georgia took one look at Nina's face, folded the elaborate calligraphic letter, and slid into the booth across from
Nina.

Jill, as usual, was the last to arrive. "Brown bagging it
today?" she asked. She was dressed in a green pantsuit,
her nails bright pink talons. "Why the booth? And what's
up with the paper bag?"

Lizzie flashed her an impatient stare. "Emergency."
She nodded toward Nina.

"Oh." Jill moved in next to her.

Nina gave them the short version of the events of
the last few days, ending with, "So this is what was in
the box."

"Did you look?" Jill asked.

"Yeah," Nina said. "I've been staring at it for days."

"And?" Georgia looked a little pale.

"And I want you guys to look," Nina said.

Lizzie looked through everything, then passed it to
Georgia, who scanned it quickly and passed it to Jill.
They worked in silence, broken only by the rhythm of the
diner. Three workmen in orange safety jackets came in.
Lizzie nodded them toward any spot they wanted. She got
up to get their coffee, then came back to the group.

When they'd gone through every piece of paper, every
picture, Jill cleared her throat. "I'm totally confused.
There's nothing here. I mean, the basketry Boy Scout
thing is embarrassing. And I'd forgotten that Walt had

such a crush on Mallory Cleog. Ugh, what was he thinking? But that's not worth a house."

"Are you sure this is all that was in the box?" Georgia asked. "Maybe Mick still has something and is holding it back."

Nina said, "I don't think so. I think this is it. He was pretty clear on wanting me to have it."

"I don't get it," Lizzie said. "The only thing that's even sort of interesting is the article about your parents. But it's not revelatory or anything. I wonder, though, why Walt scribbled over it like that."

"Because he was pissed that his parents were gone," Georgia said. "He wrote, *Bullshit*. And it was bullshit, them dying. I don't see anything there."

"But what about the erased stuff? I think it says, *Sticks and stones*?" Lizzie got up to refill more coffees.

They looked through everything again, wondering what they were missing.

When Lizzie came back to the table, she said, "I still think the article is weird. Like it's some kind of clue."

Georgia said, "It's nothing! You can't read too much into things. It'll make you nuts."

"Says the psychiatrist," Jill scoffed. She had finished her coffee from the Brewhaha and was eyeing the carafe of coffee in the center of the table. "Aren't you the one who reads every little thing into everything? Awfully quick to dismiss such an odd scribble."

Nina leaned forward. Georgia *had* seemed quick to dismiss the hastily written, then erased words. After all, it was all they had that was even remotely interesting.

"What could it possibly mean?" Georgia asked. "We're grasping for straws here. You have to look at your own motivation too. How disappointing to go through all this and find nothing. Our minds will create interest."

Lizzie got up to check the tables again. The mood at the table without her was strained, as was often the case between Jill and Georgia. Nina felt annoyed that they were letting their own animosities play into her dilemma. They were the Enemy Club, sure. But they were usually able to focus on what was important.

When Lizzie came back to the silent table she asked, "What was it like watching Walt's box disappear into the lake?"

"It was awful," Nina said. "I thought that I wanted to be done with it all. With Walt's house. With Mick. With everything. I thought that I needed to move on. Then, when it sank, I went a little nuts. That's why I jumped in. And now Mick is mad at me for being too crazy, like Walt."

"Walt was a little crazy," Jill said. Lizzie kicked her under the table. "Ow! Geez! C'mon. We're the Enemy Club here. Right? We're not going to lie just to make the world all rosy. We've never done that. He got into things, that boy. That's why we all were a little in love with him."

"Speak for yourself," Georgia said. "I never fell for him."

"I did," Lizzie admitted. "He was fun—that's for sure. You never knew what he'd do. Remember the time he got all those illegal fireworks and set them off over the lake and let us come and watch? That was awesome."

Nina nodded. "It was. Scary too." She looked at her friends. "I thought about you guys a long time before I went through the bag. I thought about how when Mick first showed up, he accused me of being naive. And you guys did too. And I don't want to be naive. Ever. I like that we tell each other the truth, the whole truth, and nothing but the truth. It's the right way to live. It's what gave me the strength to look through everything."

They nodded. They understood.

"And then it all was so disappointing. I don't know what I expected to find. I thought about all the worst stuff. But this—it feels like a letdown."

"I still think there's something in it," Lizzie said. "You want me to show Tommy? Maybe he has some ideas, being a cop and all."

"Tommy!" Georgia exclaimed.

They all looked at her.

"My brother-in-law?" Lizzie said carefully. "Policeman? I think you remember him."

"What's wrong with Tommy?" Jill asked.

Georgia turned red. "It's just...I wouldn't want him wasting his time. He's so busy, with his new baby and Meghan just turned four."

Two students slouched in, wrinkled and obviously hungover. Lizzie jumped up again and brought them coffee right away. They thanked her with a slurred, heavy, "Oh, coool..."

"What does Mick think of the stuff in the box?" Georgia asked.

"He doesn't know what to make of it either. But we've barely spoken about it. He's been giving me space."

"Will you please let me talk to Tommy?" Lizzie asked. "You might as well settle that at least."

"Yeah," Nina said. "It's a good idea. Ask him if he knows anything that might be interesting."

Mick and Johnny were in the barn when Nina got back home. She went inside the house, made herself some tea, looked at it in disgust, and poured it down the drain.

She went upstairs and tried to work on her painting of the ingredients for a scallion and potato frittata, but she couldn't concentrate.

She hadn't worked on the memorial in ages. Maybe Mick and Johnny were making headway.

She'd check up on them.

When she got near the barn, she stopped.

What the heck were they doing in there?

It sounded like a shooting range.

Chapter Thirty-five

Mick took a particularly excellent rock and felt it between his fingers.

"You can't do it, old man," Johnny taunted. "This one's for the match."

"Keep it down in the peanut gallery, please," Mick said.

He took careful aim at the pyramid of Coke and ginger ale cans that were stacked ten feet away. He didn't just have to hit it. He had to hit it hard enough that his one stone would take down all ten cans to tie with the punk who was taunting him.

Ready. Aim—

Just as he let loose his stone, the door flew open. Nina's voice filled the barn. "What in God's name is going on in here?"

The stone flew wide. Didn't hit a single can. It skidded to a stop in the dirt.

"Woo!" Johnny sang. "Yes! Yes! I am the champion of

the world!" He did a semi-obscene end-zone dance, then stopped when he saw how upset Nina looked. "Um. Hi." He cleared his throat. "Sorry."

"How's the work going?" Nina asked. Her voice was subdued, more sad than angry.

"We were just freeing the creative spirit," Mick mumbled. "You know. Getting the juices flowing."

"Speaking of flowing juices, I gotta pee." Johnny slipped out the door, closing it resolutely behind him. *Coward.*

Mick and Nina stood silently in the barn.

"So. Hi," Mick said.

"Hi."

"Did the Enemy Club have any clue about the stuff in the bag?" he asked.

"Not really," she said. She looked around the barn. "A little. Mick. This is a mess."

He went to retrieve the cans. He thought about throwing them away but instead just straightened the pyramid. "You want a go at it?"

"No, I don't! Honestly, Mick. I thought you guys were working."

"Sorry. Thought you might want at least one shot." He paused. "So what did they think of Walt's secret?"

"They're like me. They have no idea what to think," she said.

She looked destroyed. He wanted to go to her, but everything he'd said at the lake held him back. He was a walking, breathing reminder of everything that she didn't want to face. No, of everything she shouldn't have to face. This was why he'd been avoiding her for days. He'd been wrong to force her out of her comfort zone.

Johnny came back into the barn, looking at them both suspiciously. "So, um. Should we call it a day?" he asked Mick hopefully.

"No. We should not. We should work," Nina said, cutting off a response by Mick. She pulled the easel with her canvas toward them. "Tell me again what you think of it," she demanded of Johnny.

"Oh yeah. It's great," Johnny said. "Really excellent. It's—um, well done."

Mick cringed. *Into the fire...*

Nina bent, picked up a rock, took a few steps back, and winged it at the canvas.

Johnny's eyes went wide. "Damn. Good arm—for a girl."

Mick stepped between the boy and Nina, in case Nina decided to show Johnny just exactly how good an arm an angry, insulted *girl* might have.

"I hate well done," Nina said. She picked up another rock, and to Mick's relief and surprise, she didn't fling it at Johnny, but at the canvas again, all her anger over the past few days evident in the dent the stone left in Walt's oversize forehead. "Who cares about well done? It's empty. Meaningless!"

"Whoa!" Johnny said. Mick could see the boy's esteem for Nina rise a few notches. Johnny bent down to his stash of rocks.

"No, Johnny, don't!" Mick said.

But it was too late, the boy had hit the picture right smack in the middle of Walt's nose. "Five points!"

"Johnny!" Mick said. "Cut it out."

Johnny looked at the two adults. "Hey, she did it! And you did it too, the other day."

"That was an accident," Mick said.

Nina shook her head. "To hell with accidents. Let's destroy this."

She searched the barn till she found the perfect rock and went to the canvas. She held the stone over her head and came down on the picture, ripping a huge hole right down its center.

"Dude," Johnny whispered. "You didn't tell me she was so fierce. No wonder you're into her."

A nugget of pride welled up in his throat. He was proud of her.

"Ten points! Twenty!" Johnny called.

"My turn," Nina said. "I'm so dead sick of looking at this thing. I'm sick of all this rainbows, heroes, sunny skies bullshit." With every word, she tore at the canvas, finally flinging it to the ground. "How's that for reckless, Mick?"

"Pretty damn reckless," Mick admitted. He could see that glint in her eye. Walt's glint. No, her glint. It terrified him, but it also stirred him in a way he couldn't explain.

She looked at Johnny.

He looked at her.

She nodded her chin slightly.

"Cowabunga!" The boy landed with his Dr. Martens square in the middle of the huge canvas. He stomped on it with undisguised relish, a mad tribal dance of freedom. "I've been wanting to do this for days, man! This is awesome! This feels so good." He started to howl as he stomped, a joyful, soulful cry.

Nina joined in on the stomping. By the time they were done, the canvas was completely destroyed, and both of them were gasping and laughing with the effort.

Mick was impressed. She looked genuinely happy beating the shit out of the painting. She'd been spirited and fearless—and yes, reckless. But she was right; this wasn't war. This was the opposite of war—it was life. She wasn't hurting anything but a lousy picture.

She was nothing like Walt.

Nina bent down, picked up a stone, eyed the pyramid of cans, took careful aim, and brought the whole thing down with a dead-on shot to the middle can. She wiped her hands on her jeans. "Well," she said. "I believe my work here is done. If you boys could clean up, I'd appreciate it. Tomorrow, I think we might be able to get this project moving forward."

Mick told Johnny to split and the boy left gladly.

Mick set about cleaning up the barn.

He wanted the time to think. He had to get his head on straight about this situation.

Fact one: Walt had almost gotten himself killed so many times, it was as if he'd wanted to get himself killed.

Fact two: Walt had maybe almost gotten Mick killed. But maybe not. That one was a mystery and might always be. Yes, there had been other incidents when Walt had been reckless. Hell, Mick must have had grounds to write the guy up at least ten times, and they hadn't been together all that long.

Mick finished straightening up the barn, not coming to any conclusions. If he could remember what had happened, then maybe he could tell Nina that her brother had died a hero.

Or maybe not.

He brought the chairs back to the deck.

He heard Nina moving around in the kitchen.

His stomach growled.

He couldn't hang out here all night, avoiding her. It was time to confront this thing. If she wanted him to go, he'd go. He didn't blame her. She didn't need a guy hanging around throwing rocks in her barn and criticizing her nature and her dead brother. Hell, if he was her, he'd want him gone.

He'd have to figure out something else for Bella. The thought made his heart sink.

Nina was frying something brown in a pan at the stove, her back to him. He'd been doing all the cooking since he'd arrived, so seeing her at the stove felt like an affront.

"Hi."

"Hi." She turned, then went back to her meal. "You hungry? You want something?"

"Me? Nah. I'm good." He peered over her shoulder into the pan. She smelled good. The food didn't. "What is that?"

"Tofu. With scallions and soy sauce."

He sat down at the table. "Nina. Please talk to me."

She plated her beige meal and sat down across from him.

"Can we talk about the stuff in the box?"

"I thought it would be something awful. Instead, I don't know what it is. Another mystery."

"The article about your parents is strange," he said. "The way it's marked up."

"Lizzie thinks I should talk to Tommy. He's her brother-in-law. He's a cop, so he could cut through all the red tape and get me the accident report. Maybe talk to some people who might have been there. He'd know the officer who was at the scene, even if by now he's long retired. I never really read the report, never got involved in what had happened. Everyone tried to protect me, you know. I was only nine."

"That's a good idea for us to get in touch with Tommy," Mick said.

"Us?" she asked.

"Us," he answered. "Heck, I might as well do something worthwhile since I'm here."

Nina looked at him a long time. She ate some of her tofu. "I don't know."

He leaned back in his chair. "Nina, when I first came, my plan was to get in and out. I didn't want to cause any trouble."

"But you did," she said.

"I know," he said. "I shouldn't have. I should have just gotten in and out and done my duty."

She pushed her plate away.

"But my duty changed, Nina. Like I told you at the lake. *In* the lake."

She smiled and he felt a chink in her armor opening. Would he be able to sneak through it? Did he want to?

"It felt like my duty to you was more important than my duty to Walt."

She tried a sip of her water, but it seemed a struggle.

"I know I said some awful things," he said. "It's hard to explain, but—" He paused. "I want us to try to make this work."

She stood, threw her meal in the trash. "Make what work? What is going on here?"

"I don't know," he said. He crossed the kitchen to her. "I still hate this house. And I meant what I said about you being like Walt. I can't take that stuff back. It's the way I feel."

"I know," she said. "And I know that Walt was—" He could see the emotion well up inside her. "Reckless." He could feel her pull away from him, and the air in the room retreated with her. "Just like you said."

"Look, Nina. I told you that I don't remember the day he died, and that was the truth. He may have been reckless; he may have been a hero. I don't know."

"But a part of you knows," Nina said. "The part that dreams, that has nightmares and déjà vu. The truth is in there, Mick. You just have to want to get to it."

"I don't know if I can, Nina. I can't let you think that I can if I'm not sure."

"You know what I want?"

"What?"

"I want to go to a bar with you and get really, really, really stinking drunk, and for one night, to forget everything. No Walt. No box. No house. Nothing. Just you and me and a bottle. Or two. I want that for one night. To forget everything."

"And then what?"

"And then we deal with real life tomorrow."

Chapter Thirty-six

Georgia snuck upstairs to her bedroom for the hundredth time to reread the poem Bobby had sent her. Her chamber group was downstairs for a special mid-week practice to get ready for a recital. They were practicing Bach fugues, and they needed her back. But she couldn't help it.

Like as the inmates make toward the line of gruel
So does my sentence hasten to its end.
Each day I waste, I feel the fool.
I have to grasp the day, the minute—when our souls
    might blend.

It was idiotic.
It was awful. Worse than awful.
The meter was off and the idea behind it was unsophisticated and ridiculous. *Gruel?* In a love poem?
But he'd gone to a lot of trouble.

She could hear the violins finish running through their parts downstairs.

"Georgia! We need the cello, love!" Stu Zepalt called. He played beautiful viola, had since he was three years old.

She folded the letter carefully and put it back under her pillow.

It was ridiculous that she'd put it under her pillow. Like she was a silly teenager.

But the truth was, she felt like a silly teenager.

No one had written her love letters in years.

Okay, no one had ever written her love letters.

No man would ever write letters like these, with a hired artist. It was insane.

It made her smile. At least, it made her smile when she was alone in her bedroom. When she allowed it.

She joined the other three at their music stands in the living room. She picked up her Spanish cello that she'd imported from Argentina and spent a small fortune fixing up. She picked up her ten-thousand-dollar bow. How could she even think of letting a man like Bobby Ridale into her house? Into her life?

"Shall we start at the second repeat?" Stu asked.

Georgia had never noticed how nasal his voice sounded.

It wasn't like beggars could be choosers. So? Bobby was a felon.

God, just listen to her.

They started to play. As the tempo picked up, Georgia began to lose herself in the music. Nancy Lempe on violin was hitting the melody dead-on, and Georgia and Stu were harmonizing up a storm, eyes to music, eyes to each other, eyes to the violins that were soaring the melody through the house, out the windows, into the vast universe. This was something beautiful, something real, something true. It didn't always happen in their little group, but when it did, it was astonishing. They aced the repeat, nailed the tricky twenty-fifth to thirty-third measures where they always tripped up on the change in rhythm, and hit the ending with a fire and vivacity that left them all panting and sweating in their chairs.

When they'd caught their breaths, Stu said, "That, ladies, was better than sex."

Georgia took a long, hard look at Stu.

She swore then and there that she was going to meet Bobby Ridale before the week was over.

Nina was drunk.

Not just a little tipsy, but falling-down, seeing-double drunk.

And it felt *good*.

She supposed Mick was drunk too, since his forehead was resting on the table and he was singing marching songs softly to himself. "Another round," he called into his knees. He looked up and tried again. "Another round!"

Chrissie, the bartender at Lucifer's Pub, shook her head. "Sorry, Nins, but I'm cutting you guys off."

"I'm a soldier!" Mick called out, but he didn't seem sure of it. "I sherve our country. So you must sherve me!"

Chrissie smiled and saluted but moved away to the crowd of students who had just come in.

Nina looked around her, the room vibrating in and out of focus. Shot glasses littered their tiny table, relics of their epic attempt to forget, at least for a night, that they had reached the end of something. Or had it been the beginning? Or was it just one big circle that they had to go around in endlessly? The floor was moving, and it was sort of pretty the way it undulated. She looked up at Mick. He was sort of pretty too.

"You know, when you drove up that driveway the first day, I thought you were hot," Nina said.

"And when I spotted you hiding in the garden, I thought you were nuts," he said. "I should've run for the hills."

"Why didn't you?" she asked.

"'Cause I was an idiot and I went and fell in love," he said.

The floor stopped moving. Nina felt suddenly sober. She watched him watch his feet. He was drunk; that was all. Didn't know what he was saying. "So now what?" she asked him. "I can't remember what we agreed on except that you hate me and all my kin and I don't want to be near you much either because you're too much of a coward to face your past. Oh, and you're set on stealing my house."

"That about sums it up. Except for the bit that I think I love you."

She willed him to look up, but it was no use. "Is this going to be like your nightmares?" she asked. "You say a bunch of stuff and then you don't remember it later? Very bad character trait, Micky."

"Remember what?" he asked. He shot her one of his blindingly beautiful smiles.

So there it was. It meant nothing if he didn't remember, if they were joking around. And who knew what she'd remember tomorrow? Wasn't that the whole idea of this night, not to remember? To forget everything? "Where will you go after you're done here?" she asked him.

"To Tel Aviv, if I can get there. Then...who knows? Guess I'll join up again."

She felt an insane need not to ever let him go back to the army. He'd done his duty, after all. She had to keep him here. Not for herself—well, a little for herself because she really, really liked making love to him and if she had more time she could break down his stupid wall and find out what happened to Walt and—

She was feeling the liquor again. Her head had restarted its spinning, along with the floor. "Let's play for the house," Nina said.

Mick raised his head from where it had fallen against the table again. "What?"

"Darts. I think we should play darts. Winner gets the house."

They maneuvered with considerable difficulty to the dartboard. The bar was filling up with students and locals, and he seemed to be slowing as they got nearer to the dartboard. "We could skip the darts and go home and make love," he suggested as they pushed through the crowd.

"No. This is bigger than sex. This is real estate." She chose red and gave him green. She stepped back a few paces and wobbled, trying to keep the board in focus. Her first dart hit the floor. "Oops."

"You want to reconsider?" he asked.

She took another throw, this time hitting the wall about a foot from the board. Her third dart hit the board. She gave a little cry of triumph, but the sudden movement made her dizzy so she settled back down to concentrate.

It was Mick's turn. Despite all he'd drunk, he hit the board with three straight throws, right in the bull's-eye.

"Mick." She turned to him, suddenly overwhelmed. "Life sucks."

"No. Death sucks. Life is great."

She leaned on him a little, enjoying it much too much. "No matter how bad things get, we're still here," she said.

"Yup. Here we are." He leaned in close. "Let's not be here. Let's go."

"So Walt sucked. That's okay. It's life."

"You're drunk."

"Walt was a weenie!" she shouted to the bar. "I'm okay with that, you know," she said more quietly to Walt. "I'm over the hero thing. I don't need no stinking hero."

"Nina." He tried to get ahold of her arm, but she slipped away as she headed to the dartboard. He called after her, "Just by being there he was a hero."

She grabbed the darts out of the wall and off the board. She came back, taunting him. "How do you know what he was? You can't even remember."

"He was there, wasn't he?" he asked her. "He deserves respect."

"Not if he killed a bunch of guys 'cause he was irresponsible." She backed up again and threw a dart. It hit a beefy man in the back. Luckily, it was too badly thrown to do any real damage.

The man swung around as if someone had sucker punched him. "What the hell?"

Nina's mouth fell open. "Oh. Sorry. So sorry! Runs in the family, you know. Not my fault. We're all reckless!"

The man stood up, pushed back his chair.

"Oh my God, he wants to fight," Nina whispered to Mick, mesmerized by the approaching man. Two of his friends had also gotten up. They weren't small either.

"Nina. Now. We're going." Mick had her by the shoulder. He pried the rest of the darts from her hand and handed them to the nearest drunk student, who took them with a "Hey, thanks, man." He looked at them a long time, as if trying to figure out what they were.

"You gonna rescue me too? Just like you did Walt? I can't give you the house as a reward, since I guess it's already yours."

"This your girlfriend?" the man asked. He held out the dart that had hit him. "I think she lost something." His voice was rough and low. He pushed up his sleeves.

Mick put himself between Nina and the man.

"Yeah, Micky. Am I your girlfriend? What am I?" She pushed around him as best she could, but Mick held her back with a very sexy, muscled arm that she couldn't help but take a moment to appreciate. "I think I'm just the chick he sleeps with until he goes back to war," she called around his shoulder.

The man backed down a bit. "You army?"

Mick sighed. "Used to be. Now I'm just fighting on the home front."

The man and his friends laughed. "I think you're losing. You better get a grip on that one." He nodded to Nina. "She's out of control."

"Lost her brother in Kandahar," Mick said.

The man held out the dart to Nina. "Sorry, lady. I ... uh ... didn't know."

"Oh hell!" Nina cried. "You're not even gonna fight him? Give me that dart! I'll fight! I'll fight and I'll be good at it. Not like my loser brother."

She had started to cry. How had that happened? She was crying and all the men were looking at her with sympathy, which she didn't want. But Mick wouldn't give her the dart and he wouldn't hit her back no matter how many times she pummeled his shoulder, and it was his bad shoulder too. But he didn't seem to care, as if she was just some silly, pesky child that he scooped up with one hand and carried out of the bar.

Chapter Thirty-seven

The next morning, Mick woke to the doorbell. He looked at the clock.

Noon.

He looked at Nina, sound asleep next to him. Her lipstick was smeared and her hair was a mess. She smelled of stale beer and cigarettes. Or was that him?

He remembered the first time he'd seen her, a fresh-faced, tea-drinking health nut in a pink sun hat.

Funny how this new Nina seemed...well...healthier, despite the liquor stench. He felt like they had gotten somewhere important last night. He kissed her cheek and she stirred a little, then turned over and groaned.

"Don't worry, I've got it."

He looked at his morning-after face in the mirror.

The doorbell rang again.

He hauled himself down the stairs.

He let Johnny in, then went to the kitchen to put on some coffee.

"Whoa, dude! You smell like a brewery," Johnny said, full of admiration.

"Yeah. Rough night. I'm thinking that maybe we'll call off work today," Mick said. "Free pass. You can scram."

Johnny struggled not to look disappointed. "Cool. Excellent. Good, man."

Mick moved around the kitchen, making coffee, toasting an English muffin. But the kid didn't move. "You want to be here," Mick said. "Don't play the cool dude with me. Face it, we're both trapped." He was dying to go back upstairs.

"I had an idea," Johnny said, looking at a spot on the floor.

Mick sighed. He pushed the image of Nina disheveled in bed aside and sat down at the table. His head ached and it took him a minute to understand that Johnny was talking about the memorial. "Yeah? What's that?"

"Yeah. I brought some stuff. It's just an idea. It's probably totally stupid. Never mind. I'll go. You're busy."

"No. Tell me," Mick urged. If they figured out the memorial, at least he'd have helped Nina in some way that was tangible.

"I can't tell you in words," Johnny said. "I have to show you. Give me a minute to work by myself in the garage. Don't come in, okay? Not till I call you."

"Okay," Mick said. His head was clearing enough to make him curious. But still, there was no danger of him going to the barn. The sunshine alone would make his head explode.

"Promise? You won't bust in?"

"John, my head is made of glass right now. I'm not busting in anywhere till I've had ten cups of coffee and a few hundred aspirin."

"Good. I'll call when I'm ready."

"Quietly," Mick said. "Just call quietly."

Nina pulled herself out of bed, but it wasn't easy. Someone had pounded nails into her forehead and cemented blocks to her feet.

Somehow, she got into the shower. She remembered darts. She remembered stumbling down Main Street on Mick's arm. She remembered barfing in Mr. Allendale's rose garden before they got there.

Oh, those poor roses.

It was one thing to stop looking at the world through rose-colored glasses. It was another thing altogether to barf on the rosebush.

Oh God, what an awful, awful night.

Wait—not completely awful.

Mick said he loved me.

The water flowed down her body, around her toes, down the drain, warm and cozy.

He loves me.

Mick came into the bathroom. She peered around the shower curtain. He was sitting on the closed toilet, holding his head in his hands. Guess his head ached as much as hers did. She turned off the water. "I don't usually drink," she said.

He handed her a towel. "Or play darts, apparently."

"Mick, you had a nightmare last night," she said. "It was a bad one."

"You mean everything that happened at Lucifer's last night was just a bad dream?" he asked.

"No." She wrapped herself in the towel and stepped out of the tub. She cleared steam off the mirror and watched his reflection. "I mean you had nightmares after we got home and you fell asleep," she said.

He didn't respond.

She left the bathroom and he followed, settling onto her bed to watch her get dressed.

"Do you mind?" she asked.

"Not at all. In fact, it's my pleasure," he said.

She shrugged and the towel slipped. He made noises of appreciation that set her skin on fire.

"You know, we're awfully chummy for two people who just met last night in a bar," she said, pulling the towel tight around her.

"That's true," he said. "But it was an eventful night."

It had been. Maybe it was good to be able to back off their discussion of Walt, to let it breathe. Maybe this was just what it took for two people like them: a step forward, two steps back. "I'm going to call Tommy today. See if he can meet me at the police station to look at the accident report. You want to come?"

"I want us to make love again."

"Me too. But you're looking at the new Nina. The one who stares down trouble and doesn't back off. I don't have time to stay naked."

"You don't have to do this, Nina," he said. "Talking to Tommy, exploring the past—you can let it go. I didn't mean to put down Walt. I'm not perfect either. No one is."

"I can't let it go." She sat down on the bed next to him. Traced her finger down his chest to his belly. She laid back, her legs dangling off the side of the bed. "I want to face it, Mick. Whatever it is."

"Why?" he asked. He ran his fingers through her wet hair.

"Because I want to prove to you how tough I am."

"If you wanted that, you could've beaten up that guy last night."

"I tried to beat up a guy last night?" She groaned. "Oh God. I did. The dart guy."

"Forget it," Mick said. "He was a wimp. You could have taken him easy."

"C'mon, Mick. Be serious. I want you to see that I'm not fragile or innocent. That I can handle what life throws at me. Even if it's you."

"You don't have to prove anything to me, Nina."

She watched her reflection in his icy blue eyes. *I love you,* he'd said. She knew he'd meant it. "I want to prove to you that I'm not like Walt," she said.

"I know you're not like Walt." He pushed her towel aside and traced her nipple with his finger to prove it.

"Look, Mick." She sat up and took his hands in hers. The towel had slipped to her waist, making the exchange grossly unfair, but she didn't care. She needed every advantage she could get. "I want you to have the house. Not because Walt wanted it, but because I want it to be that way. This is between you and me now."

"Nina."

"Don't say no. Say thank you."

A sliver of emotion escaped around the corners of his eyes. "I'll feel like an ass, Nina. I'll leave you with nothing. How could I do that to the woman I love?"

She let his words settle. "You'd do it for Bella. I'm going today to the bank to take out an equity loan on the house. The bank guy said it'll take two weeks if everything is in order."

He shook his head. "I don't know what to say."

"Say thank you, Mick."

"I'll hate myself."

"So you'll hate yourself for Bella. And if you want to be impossible and insist, then you'll pay me back. Get a job here in Galton, stick around a while." She pulled him to her so they both lay on their sides. She traced his tattoo with her finger. *Duty. Honor. Country.* This was the right thing to do.

"Thank you, Nina."

"I think I love you, Mick."

"I know I love you," he said.

"You damn well better," she said.

"Let's seal the deal." He pulled off her towel.

"Let's."

For the first time, their lovemaking didn't feel desperate. Mick felt as if a huge boulder had been lifted, and, finally free, he could see her, really see her, for the first time.

He made love to her slowly, carefully.

He owed her everything.

It occurred to him that this wasn't good to owe her so much. But then, he didn't care. She was right. He could stick around Galton, find work, make up for everything that he was taking from her.

He could prove to her that he wasn't a con man, out for her money.

He could make this whole thing right.

"Hey, guys!" A stone hit the bedroom window.

Nina picked up her head from where it rested on Mick's chest. The covers were on the floor; they were both naked and sweaty and exhausted. They'd finally made love like lovers, not frenzied, angry strangers. Nina couldn't have been happier. Or more exhausted.

Another stone hit the window, this one harder.

"Dammit," Mick said, raising his head an inch, then letting it fall back.

"Is that Johnny?"

"I forgot all about him."

She quickly wrapped the towel around herself and went to the window. Johnny was on the lawn. He spotted her in the window and waved to her. "Come down! It's ready."

"It's ready." She turned to Mick. "What's ready?"

"Trust me, I have no idea. But it damn well better be good."

Chapter Thirty-eight

Johnny had taped newspaper over the barn windows and shoved drop cloths into the cracks by the floor, blocking most of the afternoon's light. He led Mick and Nina into the darkened space with a flashlight.

"What is going on?" Nina asked.

"Shhh. Sit," Johnny said.

They sat in the Adirondack chairs. Johnny went behind them, so she couldn't see what he was doing. The barn was dark, the screen from his laptop the only source of light.

"Mick, what's he doing?" she whispered.

"I have no idea," he answered. "But I have a feeling it's going to be good." He took her hand.

An image flickered on a blank canvas Johnny had set up on the easel. It was a home movie of a little boy at his birthday party. He was maybe six or seven. There was no sound. She turned around to see that Johnny had hooked up his computer to some sort of projector.

She looked back to the image. Was the father in the

movie Mr. Garcia? He was. Which meant the boy was Matthew. She gasped. They were watching Johnny's brother. But why?

"Johnny—," she began.

"Shhhh. Just watch," he said.

She glanced at Mick. He wasn't saying a word. He'd dropped her hand and was watching, rapt.

Now Matthew was eight, maybe nine, playing soccer. Then he was on the beach, maybe twelve or so. Then he was with a girl, dressed for a dance. Then he was in uniform. Nina felt a lump form in her throat. The little boy had grown into a soldier in a minute before their eyes. He stood by his mother, who was dwarfed by him. Mr. Garcia held up his father's medals from the Second World War and Johnny held them too. They messed around, mussing each other's hair. Mr. Garcia shook his son's hand.

Nina wiped away a tear, but it was no use—the deluge had begun. She hadn't thought of Matthew as anything more than a fallen soldier in years.

She looked to Mick. His lips were a tight white line.

The image of Matthew in his uniform stayed on the screen. Then his name, his rank, the date of his death, and the name of the town where he'd died scrolled over his image.

The barn went dark as the show ended.

They sat in silence in the dark.

Johnny flicked on the lights and she startled, wiping away her tears quickly, so they couldn't see how moved she was.

"What do you think?" he asked.

"It was amazing," Nina said. "But Johnny, I don't get it. Why were we watching that?"

Johnny rolled his eyes. "Isn't it obvious?"

Mick stepped in. "The police lights," he said.

"Yeah!" Johnny said. "How'd you know?"

"Why do I never know what you guys are talking about?" Nina asked.

"I was there with you in the park when the cars came," Mick said. "What a great idea. I wish I'd thought of it."

"What are we talking about?" Nina implored.

"The police lights at night flashing on that wall were intense," Johnny said. "Better than anything I've ever seen on a wall. Whenever I thought of the wall, I'd also think of those lights. They were eerie and cool."

"They were intense," Mick said.

"Yeah, see, you saw it too. But I'm smarter than you," Johnny said. "I thought that if a blank wall with lights is the coolest thing we could do for the memorial, then why just lights? Why not movies? We could play movies of soldiers, of whatever. People could send us images and we could put them up."

"Where'd you get this equipment?" Nina asked.

Johnny's enthusiasm cooled off a notch. He looked down at the ground. "I sort of borrowed it. But I'll give it back. If you like the idea, I can figure something more, um, *permanent* out."

"I don't know, John. I mean, it's an interesting idea," Nina began.

"Interesting?" Mick jumped up. "It's great," he said. "Perfect. C'mon, Nina. You were moved. I saw you bawling like a babe. You said you wanted the memorial to be moving, to make people feel something. Well, that definitely made you feel something, and it was just a sample."

"But during the day—?"

"We'd have to put something else up during the day. I was thinking that we could make the permanent art like frames, with blank spaces for all the video that we could play at night," Johnny said.

"All the video?" Nina asked.

"The video that people send me. I'll put up a website. I'll edit it together, and everyone can be on the wall. People would come from all over to watch. It would be a forever-changing show. People would love it. They'd sit in the park and really think about things and really feel things and get involved. Multimedia," he said. "And the people who couldn't come could watch it online."

"I don't know, Johnny. There's so much logistics that we'd have to figure out."

"Show up next Friday night," Johnny said. "Just show up and give it a chance."

Tommy had agreed to meet Mick and Nina at the police station the next day. He had pulled the file about her parents' accident. He set up in a small room in the back so they could look it over.

"I have to tell you the truth, Nina. I re-read the report three times since you called yesterday, and I'm not sure what you're looking for is in there."

"I'm not sure either," she said.

"Also, there's pictures," Tommy warned. "It was a violent crash. The pictures aren't so nice to look at."

"I'll look at the pictures," Mick said.

"Thanks," Nina said. There were limits to how much darkness she could handle.

They sat down at the bare wooden table in the small room. The file sat on the middle of the table. It looked so bland, like it should hold household bills or a kid's science homework, not the record of her parents' deaths. Tommy shut the door behind him on his way out.

"Well," Nina said.

"Here we are," Mick said.

"I feel like I should apologize to Walt for this," Nina said.

"No, I should." Mick stood up. He looked at the ceiling. "Walt, if you don't have anything better to do than to hang around, watching us mess everything up, then we're sorry. But you've gotta go and get your own life, man. We're just here, dealing with what you left behind. I didn't want to deal with it, but Nina insisted. So I'm sorry that I didn't follow your instructions. But I just couldn't. I liked Nina too much to do that." He glanced down at her. "I respect her too much to carry out your last wish, 'cause it was a stupid wish. And I'm truly, truly sorry to you. But I'm not sorry for me, because it was the right thing to do. By the way, Nina and I are kinda getting somewhere and it's really, really good, even if it's a little complicated, so maybe you can kinda bug out of here because we like our privacy and we've got stuff to work out. Alone."

Nina tried not to let her mouth hang open. "I can't believe you're joking around about this."

"I'm not joking about anything," Mick said. "I'm dead serious about every word I just said."

He grabbed the folder and they started to read.

Half an hour later, they had gone through the entire folder. They had learned one fact that Nina didn't already know, but neither of them could decide what it meant. Maybe it was just another dead end.

The accident had happened on a dry, sunny afternoon. At four o'clock, her parents were heading north on Route 79, away from the school and back toward town. Nina's dad was driving. Her mom was in the passenger's seat. They must have just dropped off Walt or Nina, or brought them something, or maybe they were just running errands near the school. The report didn't say. Coming around the third curve, just after passing under the Iona Avenue bridge, they lost control of the car. It narrowly missed the guardrail and sailed over the edge of the roadway, plunging twenty feet down a small hill, rolling three times.

There was one eyewitness.

"I never knew there was an eyewitness. No one ever told me that," Nina said.

Mick re-read that part of the report, just to check. "It's Georgia. Your Georgia," Mick said. "Why hasn't she told you?"

"I have no idea. But I think I better find out."

Nina suggested that they go for a walk around the lake, and Mick accepted gladly. He didn't want to go back to the house after seeing those grisly pictures of Nina's parents. He hoped that taking in a little Mother Nature would help get the images out of his system.

It wasn't as if he hadn't seen worse destruction in person, in Afghanistan. But somehow, seeing those pictures felt different. It felt like foul play. And Mick had no idea why he thought that. There was nothing in the file to indicate anything but bad luck.

"So Walt didn't have anything to hide after all," Nina said. "At least, it certainly seemed like he didn't. But the detail about Georgia was strange."

"It was." The trail around the lake was deserted except for them. The trees made the fading light feel even darker, almost stormy despite the blue sky. The water glimmered through the dense foliage.

"Why would she never tell me that she saw the accident? Don't you think that's odd? Does she have something to hide?" Nina asked. She made her way up a narrow rise and he followed, glad she couldn't see his face, because he could feel it darkening with dread, and he was sick of dread.

"She was nine, right? She was just a kid," he said.

"I know. But she's not a kid now. She must remember it. She's had years to tell me."

"You think that she might have seen something that she doesn't want you to know?" Mick asked. The irony that Mick and Georgia both might have witnessed the last living moments of the people Nina loved most in this world didn't escape him. That was all Nina needed, another person close to her who might be full of bad news.

"Kinda like you and me," she said. "Shoot, does everyone have some kind of dirt on my family? I don't think I can take any more. Next someone's going to tell me that Santa isn't real."

He grabbed her hand and forced her to stop on the narrow trail.

"Don't ruin Santa," she warned.

He could see the vulnerability in her eyes. "Nina. Don't joke. You don't have to follow this through. Forget this whole thing. Tie up your veggie paintings and come to Tel Aviv with me."

"I do have to follow through, Mick. I was a rainbows-and-fairies kind of person and it's not enough. It's only half the world."

"Maybe it is only half," he said. "But it's a good half."

"You said you wouldn't try to protect me, Mick. That you wouldn't treat me like a delicate flower. So man up, okay?"

"Maybe I was wrong," he said. " 'Cause now, I kind of want to take you home and take off all your clothes and make love to you the way you deserve to be made love to and never, ever let you out of that soft, safe, comfortable bed again."

"That sounds nice," Nina said. "But first, I have to go and talk to Georgia."

"Right." He kicked a stone in the path. "You know, Nina, that you're showing me up with all this bravery crap."

"Yeah, that's true, isn't it?" She smiled. But then she softened. "Mick, just because I'm doing all this searching, don't feel pressure. I don't want you to tell me anything you don't want to tell me. I don't want to force you to go where you don't want to go. Or where you can't go. I get that you've seen things and done things that I could never imagine. What I'm searching for is other people's pasts, not my own. You're not dealing with the same thing. Plus, you still have your sister to deal with. You have enough on your plate."

Chapter Thirty-nine

$\mathcal{N}$ina sat in the middle of the floor, pictures of her family scattered around her. The early morning sun streamed in the windows, dappling the floor with sun spots. The cats battled the pictures for the sun, throwing themselves over the pictures with resolute, stubborn abandon.

She'd promised Johnny pictures of Walt for his demonstration on Friday night, but it wasn't easy, even without the cats getting in the way. She hadn't looked through the family pictures for years, and she honestly wasn't sure she was up for it now. She stretched her arms over her head. It was just past dawn, and her back was already aching after last night's marathon catch-up painting session.

Mick was on the couch on his back, sorting through a box of early slides that was balanced on his stomach. He held each one up to the light and squinted at it. "You really liked pink," he said.

"I still do," Nina said. She picked up a picture of Walt and Chrissie Polk, dressed for the prom. A string pulled at her heart, but if she gave in to it now, she'd never get through the hundreds of images surrounding her.

Before her parents' accident, they had the usual boat-loads of pictures. Nina eating her first baby food, Walt riding his first two-wheel bike, every vacation they'd ever gone on lovingly recorded in endless shots of them in bathing suits, on skis, on roller coasters.

After the accident, the number of pictures of them both dropped drastically, from hundreds to just a few each year of special events. Birthdays were always duly recorded, with the obligatory cake and candles and stupid hats. The first day of school was a biggie, with backpacks on and sad, hopeless smiles that said everything about summer ending. But the lack of everyday photos made the special-occasion shots feel sad and forced, as if they were try-ing to construct proof of a normal life that didn't exist anymore.

"If I ever have kids, I promise to put photos into orga-nized books every single year and not leave anyone with a mess like this," Nina said.

"If?" Mick asked. "I'd think you'd want kids for sure." Mick held up a slide of Walt with his arm around a little boy. The same boy had been in a lot of the pictures. "Oh heck, that's Bobby, isn't it?"

Nina tossed another picture into the "maybe" pile and looked at the shot Mick held up. "Yep. I'm surprised you recognized him pre–leather jacket."

"It was the five o'clock shadow."

Nina smiled. "Why would you think I wanted kids?" she asked.

"Because you're such an optimist. Optimists like kids. The future and all that." He paused. "I like kids."

The implication of his words warmed her. "I'm an optimist about some things. Not about that. It's hard to think about kids when you know how badly you can hurt them."

"But you and Walt made it. Don't you think that you're stronger for what you went through?"

She stared at a picture of Walt. He was around six, dressed in a pumpkin costume for Halloween that her mom had sewn. Her throat tightened. "I don't feel so strong just now. Now I feel like mush." She gestured to the photos all around them.

Mick nodded. "So let's get this done." He held up two slides. "What's more right for a memorial, a picture of Walt with really bad hair in a terrible powder-blue suit, or a picture of Walt with one of his buddies in Speedo bathing suits?" It was Walt and Bobby again. They were about ten, arms flung around each other. Yeah, ten was about the age where you could just barely get away with flinging an arm around a buddy. Eleven, it was all over. No touching unless you wanted to be called names.

Nina fell back against the base of Mick's couch. She wasn't going to let this make her cry. "This was a terrible idea."

Mick gathered a handful of pictures and slides. He arranged them facedown in front of her. "Close your eyes."

"Why?"

"Just do it."

She did.

"Okay, pick twenty. Fast. Just grab them."

She opened her eyes. "That's not how to do this, Mick. It has to be thoughtful." She paused.

"Nope. It's too hard. Give yourself a break. Pick. Quick,

or I will." He gently put one hand over her eyes and held it there.

The warmth of his hand soothed her. She reached for one photo, then another, then quickly grabbed a random assortment. He took his hand away and kissed her cheek. She handed the pictures to him. "Use these. Don't show them to me. I don't want to see." She pushed Sylvia off her lap and started gathering up the rest of the pictures. "I'll organize these one day. Maybe I'll be ready when I'm a hundred and two."

Nina tried to get in touch with Georgia all weekend to no avail.

Finally, on Monday, she decided to swing by her house after stopping at the bank to apply for the loan.

Mick wanted to go with Nina to talk to Georgia, but she insisted that she wanted to go alone. So he sat on the back porch, drinking a beer and waiting for the sound of her ancient car in the driveway. The heat of the sun made him sleepy. Times like this, he liked to close his eyes and remember Bella the way she used to be. In his mind's eye, she was still his little sister, trying to ride a two-wheel bike. Or crying in her bear costume because her trick-or-treat bag had busted. His thoughts of Bella melted into dreams of Bella. But as he dozed deeper, Bella disappeared and Walt walked up the steps and sat down in the empty chair next to him. The joker was in full dress uniform.

"So you didn't follow my orders," Walt said. "And you took the house anyway." His chest was covered with medals of honor.

"I know this is a dream," Mick said. "So don't even try to freak me out."

"But a new sort of dream," Walt said. "Not the usual nightmare, right? Good for you, buddy. You're making progress."

"Walt, sitting here on this deck talking to you is as big a nightmare as I could imagine." Mick drank his beer, but it tasted like Johnny's ginger ale. "Why'd you do it, Walt? Why'd you give me the house?"

"'Cause I knew that you'd do what I wanted. You were pure army, through and through. But I was wrong. I chose wrong. Dammit, what happened to Mr. Army? You were supposed to destroy the box. Not come here and destroy my sister."

"I fell in love," Mick said.

"That right?" Walt stood up. His medals clinked against one another like a wind chime. "So why are you destroying her life? Taking her house—it's the last thing she had. And now, digging where I told you not to let her dig. Funny kind of love."

"What happened with the accident?" Mick asked.

"The accident? Don't you remember yet?"

"Remember? I wasn't there." Mick wanted to punch Walt in the face, but he couldn't move. He was pinned to the chair. He hated dreams. They felt a lot like war.

"You were there, big boy. You told me not to go in." Walt started laughing. "And you were right!" He grinned. "Nina goes in too, buddy. That's her way, huh? Watch your flank."

"Not that accident, asshole. I don't want to go into that. I want to know what happened to your parents."

"My parents are dead, Mick. Can't you let anyone rest in peace?" Walt became agitated, pacing, his eyes on fire. "You ought to go before you mess up more of her life.

She was happy before you came. You're going to leave her homeless and sad."

And then he was gone.

In the distance, Mick heard an explosion.

He jolted awake, spilling the beer he'd nestled in his lap when he'd dozed off.

It was Nina's car, rumbling up the driveway. He'd really have to get the parts to fix that muffler.

The wind chime rustled softly in the breeze.

As he waited for her to come around the back, he tried to shake off the dream. *Can't you let anyone rest in peace?*

He had stirred up the ghosts of Nina's parents. Was Walt right? Should he have followed orders and trashed the box? What kind of minefield was Nina walking into?

Duty. Honor. Country.

What about love?

Where did love fit into it all?

Nina came into the house and threw her purse on the couch. She should go upstairs to work. She'd already lost half the day at the bank filling out paperwork with Mel and then at Georgia's.

And she hadn't learned a thing.

Mick came in from the back porch, holding an empty beer. "Hi."

"Hi." She studied his pale face. He was so beautiful, especially when he looked sad. "You look like you saw a ghost."

"Nah. Just another dream," he said. "So? What happened?"

"Nothing. I couldn't find her. It was kind of weird.

She's not the kind to disappear." She felt a wave of discomfort wash over her. "I waited for her for an hour, but she wasn't there. She hasn't answered a single one of my messages. Georgia isn't the kind of person who falls out of touch. She wears a beeper on her belt, for heaven's sake." She took a deep breath. "Great, now I'm getting paranoid."

"I'm sure she's fine," he said.

"Right. Me too. It's just odd." She sat down.

He sat down too. "It's late. Did you eat lunch?" he asked.

"Nah. Don't want food."

"Sex?" he asked.

She smiled but shook her head. "I just want to crawl under a rock and make this all go away."

"I dreamt that Walt came," he told her.

"I'm sorry, Mick."

"I sit around dreaming of ghosts, when you're actually going after them. You should give yourself credit. It's brave of you, Nina."

"You're the brave one, Mick. You're a soldier, for cripe's sake. People shoot at you." She touched his hand. "Anyway, you have enough on your plate without digging up ghosts. How's Bella? Did you speak to Sandy today?"

"Yeah. Nothing new. They're still waiting for results of the tests to see if they can make the vaccine. Nina, they want to thank you personally for the money. I told them that maybe they can because maybe you're coming out there with me."

"You must be dying being stuck here, Mick. You should go now. We could put the plane ticket on a credit card and pay it back when the money comes through. Mel said it shouldn't take long. Go, Mick."

"No. I want to see this through with Georgia and the box. When we understand it all, when I know you're safe, then I'll go. And I mean it, Nina. I want you to come too."

Georgia called Nina first thing the next morning, apologizing for missing all her calls and her visit. Nina chided herself for thinking the worst. Georgia invited her over after her eleven o'clock. She even sounded cheery, if that was possible for someone as serious as Georgia.

Nina sat in her waiting room, trying not to let her mind roam to the worst-case scenario.

"Next!" Georgia called, a tiny smile playing around her lips.

She held the door open for Nina.

"You would not believe where I was this weekend," Georgia gushed the instant the door shut behind her.

This was so not Georgia's way. Nina didn't know what to make of her schoolgirlish chatter. "Where?" she asked.

"At Lucifer's."

"No."

"Yes."

"All weekend?"

"It felt that way."

"Alone?" Nina asked.

"With Bobby Ridale," Georgia said.

Nina let herself fall onto the couch. "I don't believe it. What happened?"

"Kind of a long story. But I called him and agreed to meet with him."

"And?"

"And—" Georgia was grinning. "I got drunk."

"No."

"Yes."

"Drunk drunk?"

"Well, tipsy drunk," Georgia admitted. "I turned off my cell."

"Crazy woman."

"*And* my beeper."

"You went mad." Nina stared at her transformed friend. She looked happy. She looked, as shocking as it was to admit, as if she'd had fun.

Nina wanted to ask about Walt. But it was one thing to decide to muck around in her own dirt; how could she ruin someone else's rainbow day? She'd give Georgia time to gush. "Georgia, did you bring him, y'know . . . ?"

"Home?" Georgia asked. "I didn't completely turn into Jill, you know. I still have some standards. But Nina, we hung out all weekend. I even took Monday off and we went to the vineyards. I want you to meet him."

"I've already met him, remember?"

"I want you and Mick to come for dinner. Saturday night. I'm going to make a crown roast."

"In August?" Nina asked.

"I'm not exactly ready to barbecue, hon. I'm not that changed. Maybe next summer. If things work out."

"Oh my God. You're thinking about next summer? You're thinking long-term? After one long weekend?"

"One long weekend and two beautifully calligraphed love poems," Georgia said. "And we did have a bit of a history back in high school, remember. It's not like we're strangers."

"Never underestimate the value of a good calligrapher," Nina said, getting caught up in Georgia's excitement despite herself.

"I never do." Georgia's face was washed with warmth. Nina had never seen anything quite like it on her friend. "Will you come for dinner? Saturday? Six o'clock?" Georgia asked.

"Of course. What should I bring?" Nina said.

"Just your usual sunny self. And that gorgeous man you're shacking up with."

"I couldn't do it," Nina told Mick over burgers later that night. "She was so happy. I've never seen her so happy."

He shook his head. "Didn't she ask you why you came?"

"I made up some nonsense about wanting to talk about our relationship. Mick, you should have seen her. She was glowing."

"You're too nice," Mick said. "There's something off about that guy."

"Stop it," Nina said. "Don't you bring your negative energy into this." She pointed her veggie burger at him menacingly.

"Why do I feel like the angel of death around here?" he asked.

"Because you're an idiot?" she asked. Then she softened. "You're worried about Bella, so your mind is in a dark place. Also, you're trying to find a way to punish yourself for being happy. But you don't have to. Just be happy." She leaned over to kiss his lips gently. "Georgia's happy. Bobby's happy. I'm happy. You be happy too."

"Are you, Nina? After all these wounds I opened up?"

"Yes. Deliriously happy. I love you, Mick. That's enough for me right now. It's all good. Everything is wonderfully good."

He didn't look convinced. "I'll believe that after you talk to Georgia."

"Well, okay. So don't believe me. But I'm not talking to her until after Saturday night. It's just a few days. I don't want to ruin her dinner party."

"I will never, ever understand women," Mick said.

"That's our plan, Mick. We have to keep you menfolk on your toes."

Chapter Forty

$\mathcal{F}$riday night, Nina and Mick had a surprisingly hard time finding a parking place in town. Main Street was so clogged, they had to turn down a side lane and ended up leaving Mick's car a good four blocks away.

"Maybe that new George Clooney movie opens tonight," Nina said.

They were getting closer to Garcia's Pharmacy. "Is it my imagination, or is there some kind of party going on?"

Mick looked at the mass of people converging on the pharmacy and on the park across the street.

Nina's heart had started to pound. "What exactly is going on here?"

A man in front of them heard and turned around. He handed her a piece of paper. "It's the unveiling of the new war memorial."

Nina and Mick stopped short, forcing the people behind them to have to jump aside to avoid hitting them. They read the flyer in the light from the streetlamp:

Welcome to the dedication of the new Galton War Memorial to honor all those lost from Galton and around the world in the fight for freedom. Bring a chair, bring a blanket, and bring a friend. Show starts at nine p.m. Sharp. Weaver Park, across from Garcia's Pharmacy. Memorial design conceived by Nina Stokes, Johnny Garcia, and Mick Rivers. Technical support by Garcia's Pharmacy and Johnny Garcia. In memory of Matthew Garcia, Walter Stokes, and the other brave men and women who died in the service of the country we love.

"Wait, what?" Nina was stunned. "He has no right to put our names on this. He was supposed to show *us* his idea put together first, not to show the whole town."

"Too late for that," Mick said.

The park was packed with people on lawn chairs and blankets. They looked like they were ready for a fireworks show. They were going to be sorely disappointed. Nina tried in vain to spot Johnny in the crowd.

"He's a kid with vision—that's for sure," Mick said, trying to keep up with her.

"Nina!" Jill called. She and Georgia and Lizzie were on a blanket with Lizzie's husband, Tay. Annie and Tommy and their older girl, Meghan, were there too. Meghan was playing with a flashlight.

"You guys knew about this! I can't believe you didn't tell me about this," Nina cried.

"Johnny made us promise not to tell," Jill said. "He wanted it to be a surprise. He told everyone not to tell you."

"How did everyone know to be here?" Nina motioned to the crowds around her. "Who are all these people?"

"It was on the evening news. But we knew you didn't have a TV," Lizzie said. "Sometimes it's good that you're such a recluse."

Her whole world was here. And they'd think that she did this, and she had no idea what Johnny had in mind. Showing home movies of his brother? "This was on the evening news?" she repeated, more a statement of dread than a question. She really had to get a television.

"Yeah. Look, over there," Jill said, pointing across the park to where the Channel Ten News truck was parked. They were interviewing Johnny.

"Excuse me." Nina took off across the park, Mick a step behind her. It was slow going, with everyone congratulating her on her new mural. Nina kept glancing up at the wall, which Johnny had covered with a couple of patched-together drop cloths. What was behind those drop cloths?

When she finally reached Johnny, he called out. "Finally! There's the artist."

The reporters, lighting crew, and cameramen swung their interest to Nina.

"Come on. Get in on the interview," Johnny urged.

Nina backed away. "Oh no. Nope. Thanks."

"She's shy," Mick explained, putting himself between Nina and the advancing news crew. "Back off," he said more forcefully when they didn't budge.

They did. But then someone worse approached.

"Nina! I can't wait to see what you've done!" Mr. Garcia boomed. "Thank you for involving Johnny. I had no idea. It means so much to him to honor his brother."

"No problem," Nina said, floundering.

"He was great," Mick said.

"Came up with the whole concept, actually," Nina

began, but she was interrupted by music starting on the PA system.

"Wow, he's really got this place rigged up," Mick said. "C'mon, let's sit and watch."

"Let's slink away while we still have the chance," Nina said, but she let herself be led to a spot of empty grass.

Johnny stepped in front of the mural and climbed up on a ladder. He spoke into a microphone. "Ladies and gentlemen, welcome. This is a memorial the way you've never seen it before. This isn't my memorial. Or Mick's. Or even Nina's—even though we're all the artists. And it's not my dad's, even though it's on the side of his pharmacy, Garcia's. But if you do need a cool drink, then come on in and pay your respects. We've got a deal on Diet Coke all week." The crowd laughed. But Johnny grew serious. "This is your memorial, Galton. And it's yours too, America. And it's also yours, Afghanistan and Iraq and every other place that American soldiers have gone to fight for what they thought was right. It's everyone's. So without further ado, I give you . . . the Galton War Memorial. Remember, it's a work in progress, so if you want to be included, find us at GaltonWarMemorial-dot-com."

Johnny gave the signal and a few of his buddies on the roof dropped the cloths covering the wall to reveal—

A blank white wall.

The crowd murmured. A few confused, lackluster claps. Then silence.

Johnny looked out at them.

They looked back at Johnny.

A baby cried.

Then, slowly, very slowly, he climbed down the ladder, folded it up, and walked away.

"Oh my God," Nina said. "We're going to be lynched."

Then the klieg lights that had been shining at the wall went dark.

Images began to flicker across the wall. First just one, in the center of the wall. It was Johnny's brother, six years old, at his birthday party.

There wasn't a sound from the crowd as the silent images flashed in the darkness. Then another set of images began to play simultaneously in the upper corner. These were of a kid she recognized from school.

Nina understood what Johnny was doing.

And it was brilliant.

The crowd had gone completely silent.

"Where did Johnny get so many pictures of so many soldiers?" she whispered. She shot a look at Mick.

"Don't look at me. I'm just the ginger ale procurer."

The pictures of Matthew were interspersed with pictures of all sorts of people. Some of them Nina recognized from around town. John Flicker, who'd died in Iraq. Was that Mr. Wilkins? Nina had known his granddaughter, Sherree. He'd been lost at sea during World War II. The pictures were overwhelming. So much loss. So many good people. Men with families. Boys too young. Women with smiling children. Girls who didn't look old enough to date, much less die.

Nina looked around her. Women were crying. Men were patting each other's shoulders or just standing at attention, the world around them melting away.

"Where did he get all these pictures?" she asked again, of no one in particular.

"Didn't you see it on the news?" a woman next to them asked, her voice choked up with tears. "He put out a call. People sent pictures to a website or some such thing."

Nina couldn't believe that Johnny had done all this in such a short time. But then, she'd been holed up in her house, dealing with her work and with the emotional fallout of Walt's mystery. She hadn't noticed anything going on around her. She'd even missed this week's Enemy Club meeting.

But what Johnny had put together was amazing. It was moving. It was absolutely perfect. It had brought in everything good about these men and women, all these wonderful memories. It had united them in something bigger than themselves. It had brought out the whole town.

And then the pictures of Walt began. Walt, ten feet tall on the side of the pharmacy. Walt as a baby. Walt as a kid with Bobby in their Speedos. Walt in his powder-blue suit. She knew they were just pictures, and yet she felt as if he had suddenly reappeared in Galton, just for her. The crowd was gone. Mick was gone. She could see only her brother as he used to be, hamming for the camera. Her mouth was so dry. "Walt." Her voice was hoarse. She felt an arm around her, which was good because she had somehow stood and wandered away from where they had sat down. She was in the street. Her legs were jelly and she lost her balance, and now she was sitting again as Walt in uniform played on the wall. "Oh God, Walt." The lump in her throat would never go away.

And then Walt was gone and another boy was on the wall and then another. She was back on the sidewalk with Mick's arm around her. He was whispering, "It's okay. It's okay. I miss him too." And she somehow sat through the rest of the pictures.

When the show ended, there was silence.

A dog barked, then stopped.

And then, one by one, people began to stand. Soon, everyone was standing. Then slowly, the clapping started.

It wasn't the kind of ecstatic clapping after a concert or a play. It was rhythmic, slow, controlled clapping. The way you clap when you're also crying.

It was the greatest honor, to see people clap and cry and salute and care.

To see Walt again, ten feet tall.

Nina was mobbed by praise, hugs, and kisses. People thrust their hands at her to be shaken, threw themselves at her to be hugged.

"Oh, to see Walt again."

"Oh, to see my Roger."

"It was beautiful."

"So moving."

The news crew had somehow found her, and they shoved a mike in her face. "Nina Stokes, the artist responsible for this moving memorial, has just debuted a seminal work. Amazing. The crowd response was unreal. How did you ever come up with this concept?"

The reporter in her red power suit and too much makeup stared at her, waiting for an answer. Bright lights shone in her eyes. "I didn't. Johnny did."

That didn't seem to satisfy them.

"And Mick."

They waited, the microphone still in her face. They wanted an explanation.

"Really, it wasn't me. It was a sixteen-year-old boy who understands that sometimes, to find the light, you have to look at the darkness," she said.

The reporter blinked at her. Nina knew she hadn't made any sense to this woman. But it made sense to her and to Mick, and that was all that mattered.

Chapter Forty-one

*T*he next day, a very sheepish Johnny Garcia showed up on his bicycle at the house.

Nina wasn't mad exactly. How could she be mad after the triumph of last night? But she did have a million questions.

They sat in the kitchen. Mick made himself coffee and poured her tea. Johnny had brought his own ginger ale.

"I knew I needed more pictures, so I put out a call online. The response was crazy. I never expected to make the news. How cool was that? I kept thinking you'd see the publicity or someone would tell you even though they promised not to and you'd call me. Then when you didn't, I thought you were really pissed off. But I couldn't stop."

"You could have called me," Nina pointed out. She wondered how a person put out a call online, but he was talking a mile a minute, and she didn't want to slow him down.

"Well, I thought you'd take my head off. I mean, I

totally took over your project, and you probably hate it and so you hate me."

"But you didn't stop," Mick pointed out.

"No. Because it was so good. It was just exactly right and nothing else was righter, so I couldn't let it stop just because some old fogies wanted to slow it down."

Nina understood what he meant. When a project caught fire, there was no stopping it. Good art was like love—you just had to get out of the way and let it flow. She looked at Mick and felt a wave of satisfaction wash over her.

"And then Mr. Pauger at the church said he'd lend me their AV stuff. And they have *good* AV stuff, y'know? 'Cause they're that giant church that does the light shows and stuff. The head AV guy there even helped me with all the technical stuff. So then I knew it would really be great."

"That's when the evening news stepped in?" Mick asked.

"Yeah, well, first the paper called, then the TV. That was totally cool."

"Not totally, Johnny," Mick warned.

"So you're really pissed?"

"I'm a little pissed," Nina said. "You should have told me. We could have worked out the details better. Like, what's going to be on the wall during the day?"

Johnny's eyes lit up. "That's the best part! See, we're gonna let the people who send the pictures say what image they want on the wall permanently. And then you'll paint it. Those pictures will create a frame, and the movies will play inside it. It'll be a hodgepodge. And with each image will be a URL, and people can access it—"

"You lost me," Nina said. "A web address?"

"Yeah. And people can come with their smart phones and stand in front of the wall and type in the URLs and watch the video during the day on their own personal screens. It'll be a whole website thing, too. So they won't have to actually *be* at the wall to watch. They can see the whole thing online from anywhere in the world. Like, even the soldiers still fighting—they can see their buddies. We're already getting hits from all over the world. It's amazing."

Nina caught Mick's eye. He shrugged as if to say, *I have no clue what this kid's talking about.*

"It's genius, Johnny. Really. Still—you should have told me. But it's pretty darn genius."

"I know," he said. He was grinning like a little kid.

She tried to scowl at him, but he was so excited, it was impossible to keep a smile off her face.

"But I should've told you, still. I know." He tried to swallow his smile, but it was impossible for him too.

Soon, they were all grinning at each other.

After a while, Nina had to bring them back down to Planet Earth. "I can't be going down to the wall always painting things, John. Every painting will need a study. It'll need to be thought through. It'll be like a hundred little murals. I don't know if I can do it—the time, the cost."

Johnny turned bright red. "You wouldn't have to do it all."

Nina pursed her lips at him. "So who will? Mick?"

"I could," he said softly.

"You could what?" Nina asked.

"I could paint. I can paint. I'm pretty good, you know."

Mick and Nina stared at him.

"Well, why the didn't you say so in the beginning?" Mick asked.

"Because. I dunno."

"Because painting isn't cool, Mick," Nina said. "Right? You didn't want us to know. Johnny—this probably isn't a big surprise, but us old folks, we don't care much about cool."

Johnny kicked his feet around under the table, not meeting their eyes. "I don't want my father to know."

"Why not?"

"His dad hates artists," Mick said. "I've seen it myself."

Nina winced. "Oh. I see. Well, you guys will have to work that out. Unless you want a little help with it."

Johnny looked up. "Yeah? You'd talk to him? I mean— I dunno. No offense, Nina, but I don't know how much he respects you. Geez—I'm sorry. I shouldn't have said that. I'm an asshole."

"No. You're telling the truth. That's okay. I'm good with the truth these days. Even if it sucks," Nina said. One bit of truth she had to face: some people could never respect an artist. That was just the way it was.

"I'll paint too," Mick said.

"Don't tell me you're a secret artist too," Nina said.

"No. See, I'll be awful, and Mr. Garcia will see that what Johnny can do is sort of incredible and be impressed. And if he's not impressed, then I can break his nose."

Johnny grinned. "My dad would take you, easy."

They talked some more about the wall. Johnny had brought a laptop. He opened it on the kitchen table and showed them how the website was set up. "It's still ugly, but it's gonna be sweet."

Mick said, "It would be good to set up some kind of donation thing on the website. That way, we could maybe put up some kind of permanent screen-computer thing so people without smart phones could see it."

"Permanent screen-computer thing?" Johnny asked. "You're a technical wizard, you know?" He pointed at the corner of the screen where there was a button labeled *Donations*. "We're already raking it in, baby!"

"Johnny! You can't do that. It's—"

"Cool as shit," Johnny said.

"We have to find someone to manage that," Nina said. "Quickly!"

Mick patted Johnny's back. "You did good, kid."

"I know."

"Okay, later we'll work out the rest of the details," Nina said. "Now I have some old-fashioned work to do." She pushed back her chair.

"You should really get with the times, Nina," Johnny said. "Digital art is the way to go."

"Well, I still like the old way," she said.

She looked back to shoot him a nasty glare, but as she did she caught Mick high-fiving Johnny.

The boy couldn't have looked more pleased.

After Johnny left, Mick lingered in the kitchen. Nina came back down after a while.

"You did good with him," Nina said.

"He did good with himself," Mick said. "I just sat by and tossed rocks around."

"Don't sell yourself short, Mick. You made a difference in his life. I have a feeling that you're the kind of guy who goes around making a difference in lots of people's lives, and you don't even know it." She came to him and he took her in his arms. "Like, for instance, Walt's life."

"Oh no. Let's not start this again."

"Well, you must have meant something to him since he

gave you the house." She looked at her watch. "Oh shoot. We have to get to Georgia's in four hours."

"So what's the rush?" he asked. "It's just around the corner. I think we should get naked to celebrate the triumph of the Galton War Memorial."

"Quite the opposite, Mick. You need new clothes. You can't go to Georgia's in jeans."

"Why not?"

"Because—it's Georgia. She's going to be fancy."

"Somebody better tell Bobby that."

"Nah, he knows. Trust me. C'mon. We're going shopping."

Mick groaned. "I've never been a fancy guy."

"Well, too bad. It's time you tried something new."

Chapter Forty-two

That night, they arrived at Georgia's palatial house just as her grandfather clock struck six o'clock.

Georgia, as Nina had predicted, was dressed to the nines in a black cocktail dress. It was the first time Nina had seen her out of one of her work suits in ages. Nina wore a red linen sheath dress. She handed Georgia a bouquet of daisies from her garden in a vase she'd painted with twisting vines.

Mick was reintroduced to a very dapper Bobby Ridale, resplendent in black pants and a crisp white shirt. Mick greeted the other man tersely.

What was it about this guy that rubbed him the wrong way?

Nina escaped with Georgia into the kitchen.

Georgia checked the appetizers in the oven. "Yours cleans up nice."

Nina and Mick had driven out of Galton to the nearest

mall, which wasn't near. They'd ended up with a decent pair of flat-front khakis, a light blue linen shirt that perfectly matched his eyes, and brown shoes and belt. "Yeah, he does look good, doesn't he? It wasn't easy. He's been a bear all afternoon. Bobby looks pretty dapper himself."

"Is that why Mick is so cold to Bobby? He was mad about shopping?" Georgia asked. "It almost felt like there was history between them."

Nina wasn't going to tell Georgia how Mick felt about Bobby. All bad news would wait till this evening was done. She knew it went against the Enemy Club creed to not tell the truth, the whole truth, and nothing but. But she couldn't live by that tonight. She needed a break from bad news as much as Georgia did. Which was why even though she was dying to ask Georgia about the police report, she would hold to her decision not to talk about it until tomorrow. "Nah. We probably bought his pants a size too tight."

They carried the small mushroom soufflés into the living room. They smelled divine.

The men were stonily silent. Nina wondered if they'd been fighting already. She put a hand on Mick's thigh. "So how's it been being back in Galton?" she asked Bobby.

"It's nice. Real nice," he said. "I've been doing my rounds, making amends."

Nina raised her eyebrows at Mick, as if to say, *See, he's not bad.*

They stumbled through more small talk until Georgia mercifully announced that dinner was served.

Dinner followed in the same vein. What did you talk to an ex-con about? Even sports talk fell flat, as Mick and Bobby rooted for different teams for every sport. Even a discussion of the pros and cons of the designated hitter ignited a heated explosion. Thankfully, no one tried to bring up Walt.

Finally, dessert was served: crème brûlées that Georgia fired with a tiny torch at the table. They were delicious. But Nina could hardly stand the tension between the two men another minute. They had to get out of there. "We should go," Nina explained, patting her mouth with her napkin and letting out an exaggerated yawn. "It's been a crazy weekend, and we're both exhausted."

"Nonsense," Bobby cried, alarming Nina with his vehemence. "The evening is just getting started. "We haven't even gotten a chance to talk about Walt."

"I don't really like to talk about him," Nina said. "It's all still a little raw."

"I couldn't believe it when I heard he signed up for the army," Bobby said, ignoring Nina's request.

"Why's that?" Mick asked, his tone challenging.

Oh no, here they go. Nina felt her heart sink. She loved Mick, but this side of him, always doubting, was getting exhausting.

Bobby shrugged. "He didn't seem the type, is all." He poured himself more wine.

"Who's the type?" Mick asked, refusing Bobby's offer of wine.

"Mick," Nina warned. She knocked him in the shin.

"No. It's okay." Bobby refilled Georgia's wineglass. "The type who joins up is more wholesome," he suggested. "Not that there was anything unwholesome about Walt," Bobby said. "But what do I know? Look at yourself, Mick. You tell me. Why'd you join up?"

"To serve my country," Mick said. "It was my duty. I felt a responsibility."

"See?" Bobby said. "Now, me, I didn't feel any duty. After my dad got shot in the gut trying to protect our grocery store, my mother tried to raise four kids by herself. I started working full-time at fifteen and never stopped. I love my country—don't get me wrong—but I had responsibilities on the home front. And those came first."

Nina wasn't sure she'd exactly call what Bobby engaged in during his teen years as *working full-time*. More like stealing, shoplifting, petty crime, who knew what else.

"I fought for every thing we got," Bobby went on. "My kid brother got put in juvie at fourteen by a crooked judge. My kid sister died because we didn't have health insurance and my mother couldn't take her to see a doctor when she got pneumonia."

Nina shot Mick a glance to see how he was taking all this. His jaw was set.

"Soldiering is for guys who had it good and wanna keep the status quota."

Nina glanced to Georgia to see how she was taking Bobby's life philosophy and his misspeaking of the phrase *status quo*. She twitched only a little bit, around the eyes, but her smile stayed intact.

Mick cut in. "Or it's for guys who want a leg up, who see the service as a way to get experience and an education. People who believe that no one owes them anything. Or just people who love their families and want to keep them safe."

"Yeah, yeah." Bobby leaned in. "How'd that go for you?"

Mick's eyes narrowed dangerously.

Then, as if remembering something important, Bobby smiled and held up his hands in surrender. "Sorry. Sorry.

Didn't mean to hit a vein." He gave Mick a crooked smile and glanced at his watch.

Nina glanced at her own watch. She felt as if time had stopped. They had to get out of there. She knew that Mick was thinking about Bella, about how he hadn't kept her safe, how he had failed her while he did his duty to his country. Had Bobby known Mick's story and provoked Mick on purpose?

"Let's talk about something happier," Georgia suggested. "Famine, maybe? Disease?"

Nina poured herself more wine after all. "Did you hear about that Ebola virus spreading in Africa again?" she asked with fake cheer.

Mick said, "I think we better go, Nina."

"No. Stay. I'm sorry," Bobby insisted. "C'mon. Tell us some war stories."

"No, thanks."

"Okay. Then let me tell you some prison stories. I've got loads."

An hour later, Bobby wound down his story about sharing a cell with a three-hundred-pound dockworker who liked to knit tea cozies. Finally, Nina and Mick were able to pry themselves away. They said their good-byes as politely as they could. Nina could see that Georgia was upset with the way the evening had gone. But they had tried. What more could they do?

They were silent most of the way home.

When they pulled up at the house, Nina said, "I'm exhausted. That was awful. Why can't you let up on that guy, Mick?"

"I don't know. I just can't."

She got out of the car, slamming the door a little too hard behind her. She headed for the front door, but Mick got her by the arm.

"What?" she asked, shaking herself free. She couldn't wait to fall into bed.

He held up a finger in front of his lips. "Shhh..." He nodded toward the house. Sylvia was sitting on the front step. "Did you let her out?"

"No," Nina said.

"Neither did I. She was on the kitchen table when we left."

A chill ran down Nina's spine.

"I don't suppose you locked the door," Mick said.

"No. I didn't. Maybe Jill or Lizzie or someone came by and we were gone and they took pity on her and let her out."

Mick cocked his head in disbelief.

"Right. Let's call the cops."

Chapter Forty-three

"Wait here," Mick said.

"What happened to 'call the cops'?" Nina asked.

"Do that," he said as he left the car. He crept up the steps and pushed open the door with his foot. Her heart went cold as she realized that he hadn't needed to use the doorknob. He disappeared inside.

She fumbled with her cell phone and dialed 911. A few seconds later, a voice answered. She started giving the details when Mick came back outside. His face was grim.

"Tell them the place is trashed," he said. "Someone did a real number on it."

Tommy was the last of the policemen to leave.

Apparently, nothing had been taken, which was the worst thing of all. If something had been taken, at least this would have made some kind of sense.

"Nina, no offense, but these guys are looking for stuff

they can sell fast. Expensive jewelry, computers, TVs. They left your bulgur wheat intact."

"My rugs are worth thousands. I have art that's priceless."

"These guys don't know from rugs and art. Look, they were a couple of thugs who broke in and were disappointed, so they roughed the place up a bit. We see it all the time. We'll catch them."

"Like you caught the people who were graffitiing on Garcia's Pharmacy?" she asked.

"Hey, that's not fair," Tommy said. "Vandals are tricky 'cause they're usually just one-timers. Kids. And now that the wall is going full steam, it hasn't happened again, right?"

She backed off. "I know. I'm sorry. I just didn't realize this night could possibly get any worse than dinner with Georgia and Bobby Ridale."

"Bobby Ridale is back in town?" Tommy asked. "Now, that's something the police should know about."

"Well, at least we can eliminate him as a suspect, as he's got an alibi. He was with us," Mick said.

"He's dating Georgia," Nina explained.

"No, he's not," Tommy said.

"That's what I told her," Mick said.

"I'm betting that Georgia's house gets knocked off next," Tommy said.

Nina swatted his arm. What was wrong with men? "Not nice! Remember, Bobby was Walt's good friend."

Tommy and Mick met eyes. Nina wasn't sure what testosterone-laden message passed between them, but she didn't care to pursue it. She had her own problems just now.

"I'm going to start cleaning up," Nina said.

"And I'm going to keep an extra-close eye on Georgia Phillips' place," Tommy said.

"Smart man," Mick said. "This is all starting to feel a little off to me."

Nina couldn't believe how awful she felt. She refused to let the tears that were threatening fall. This was just stuff. It wasn't a big deal.

She picked up pieces of broken glass from the pictures that had been knocked off the walls. "Don't say it," she warned Mick.

"Don't say what?" He brought over the trash bag and she dropped the glass in carefully.

"That I shouldn't leave my door open."

"I don't know that a lock would've stopped these guys. They seem determined to find something."

"Why would they destroy the pictures on the walls?" she asked.

"Looking for a safe, I'd guess. Or maybe they're idiots and they thought it was fun. Or maybe they just wanted to be mean," Mick said. A car pulled up in the drive. Mick looked out to see Jill and Lizzie jump out of the front. A man and a teenage girl climbed out of the back. They all hurried to the door.

Nina kept cleaning, so he met them in the foyer.

"How bad?" Lizzie asked.

"Bad," Mick said.

"Mick, this is my daughter, Paige. This is my husband, Tay." They made quick introductions, then went to Nina and embraced her. Before Mick got back into the room, they were getting down to work.

Another car pulled into the drive. To Mick's surprise

it was Bobby. Georgia got out of the passenger-side door. "Oh my God," she said, sweeping past Mick and gathering Nina in her arms.

"Didn't think the night could get any worse," Bobby said to Mick.

Mick watched him carefully. "Yeah, that's what we thought too."

"Anything missing?" Bobby asked.

"Don't know yet. Doesn't look like it." He had to fight to keep his cool around this guy. He didn't want him in Nina's house, but how could he explain that?

"Well, you should let an expert look at it. Maybe I can figure out a thing or two."

Mick was surprised by Bobby's up-front acknowledgment of his profession. Maybe he had misjudged the guy.

The muscles of his gut clenched.

Nah, he was up to something.

Everyone was hard at work. Lizzie and Jill were a team with the broom and dustpan, carefully sweeping up the shards of glass. Tay and Paige had gone to the dining room and were putting what they could salvage back onto shelves. Georgia and Bobby were putting books and knickknacks that hadn't shattered onto the bookshelves. Nina was on her knees, putting the pillows back on the couch.

Mick joined her. They worked together through the living room, into the dining room, then the kitchen, then up the stairs, every new room as upsetting as the one before.

Bobby stuck his head into the yoga room where they were putting sheets back in the closet. "Rank amateurs. What a mess."

An hour and a half later, the eight of them had gotten the house more or less back in order.

They collapsed in the living room, looking around at what they couldn't fix. Mick hadn't realized how much the house's character was made by Nina's pictures. The bare walls felt like a terrible affront to everything she stood for. He remembered coming here for the first time and hating all the flowers on the walls. Now it felt as if someone had ripped out a part of her soul. "I can't believe they wrecked your pictures," he said.

Nina nodded. "Bobby said you were right. They look for safes that people hide behind pictures. Like I'd have a safe."

Jill said, "If you did, it would be filled with granola."

"They were mad," Bobby said. "They came hoping for jewelry and valuable electronics, and when there was nothing worthwhile, they took it out on your house."

Lizzie sat up. "We didn't check the garage. Would they have gone in there?"

"Nah," Bobby said. "People don't keep valuables in a garage. Only kids would break into a place like that, hoping for a nice bike they could sell to their friends for twenty bucks. These guys were more serious than that."

"I have expensive art supplies out there."

Mick said, "I'll go check."

"Thanks, Mick," Nina said. "And if there's anything wrong out there, don't tell me. I don't think I could take it tonight."

"I'll come with you," Bobby volunteered.

"I think we better get back home," Tay said. "I've got to open the diner at five thirty in the morning."

"You guys go," Lizzie said to her family. "I'll stay here with Nina and catch a ride home with Georgia later."

"Thanks, everyone. I don't know how I would have gotten through tonight without you all," Nina said.

"No problem." Tay and Paige said their good-byes and filed out.

"Really," Nina said to her remaining friends, "you guys are the best."

"Of course," Jill said, shutting the door behind Lizzie's family.

"Don't be silly," Georgia said, rubbing Nina's shoulder.

"That's what enemies are for," Lizzie concluded. "Now, let these brave men go out and check the garage while we begin to administer the first aid. Where's that bottle of wine I brought?"

Mick went into the barn first, his body tense. He flicked on the light and let out a sigh. "Looks okay," he said.

"Whoa," Bobby said. "What is this place?" He walked into the studio. "I had no idea."

"Yeah, it's pretty nice."

Bobby walked the perimeter. "Who knew an artist needed so much stuff? I should go into the art-supply business."

"Yeah, when I first came here, I thought it would be full of Walt's stuff," Mick said. "But she moved it all out."

"That must have been hard for her. How do you trash your brother's stuff?" Bobby said.

"Yeah. Well. I don't think she trashed it exactly." Mick was satisfied that nothing in the barn had been touched. "Let's go back to the house." He held the door open for Bobby, but Bobby was still fascinated by the canvases and other paraphernalia around the barn. He looked like a little kid seeing a toyshop for the first time. "We ought to go back," Mick repeated. He was anxious to get back to Nina. Not that he thought anything bad would happen. He just wanted to be near her.

"Yeah. Sorry. Coming. A guy like me doesn't see a place like this every day," Bobby said. He came slowly to the door.

Too slowly.

Because just as Mick was about to give up on Bobby and leave by himself, a streak of orange fur blew in and dashed up the ladder to the loft.

Chapter Forty-four

Shit!" Mick shut the barn door.

"What the hell was that? A raccoon?" Bobby grabbed a nearby broom.

"Nina's cat. She has a little attic problem."

Bobby looked up at the hole in the wooden ceiling. "Damn. The cat went up there? Guess it's full of mice. Lucky cat." He started for the door.

Mick shook his head. "No. We can't leave her up there. Nina will go nuts. I've got to get her down."

"You do?" Bobby asked. "Mick, that woman has you wrapped around her little finger."

"Yeah, well, it's not a bad place to be wrapped, if you know what I mean." Mick started for the ladder, but Bobby cut him off.

"I'll go up," he said.

"No. I'll rescue Nina's cat. You can rescue Georgia's cat when she gets stuck."

But Bobby held his ground. "Georgia doesn't have cats. Allergies. Anyway, I like cats," he said. "I got it."

Mick backed off. He handed Bobby the flashlight from the hook on the wall. Mick was looking forward to watching smooth Bobby Ridale get mauled by even smoother Sylvia the cat. Sure, it wasn't nice to sic Sylvia on Bobby, but he couldn't help it if the guy insisted.

Mick crossed his arms and stood back. He'd go in to get the cat after Bobby failed. He wasn't catching Bobby if he fell, though. This guy wasn't worth another busted-up shoulder.

"What a stupid ladder," Bobby said. "Who builds a ladder dead vertical into a wall? Whoever it was, wasn't a cat burglar. No wonder the animal can't get down." He muttered curses as he looked up the tricky ladder into the dark loft. Sylvia's glowing eyes blinked back at him.

Bobby stuffed the flashlight into his jacket pocket and scampered up the ladder surprisingly fast. Mick expected him to stop at the top rung and peer around the attic, but instead, he lithely pulled himself up with impressive strength and a light hop.

"Here, kitty, kitty, kitty." Bobby disappeared into the darkness. "It's an oven up here," he called down.

Mick listened to his footsteps move around the loft. "You find the cat?" he asked.

"Oh yeah. I almost got her."

Mick waited until he couldn't wait anymore. He silently scaled the ladder.

He almost fell off when he found himself face-to-face with Sylvia, who was waiting patiently by the edge of the opening for her treat.

Bobby was a shadow in the corner, the beam of his

flashlight dancing like a mosquito along the walls. Mick's eyes adjusted to the dark, revealing Bobby on his knees, rifling through a pile of boxes along the far wall.

"I've already been through everything up here," Mick said. "Nothing but junk."

Bobby spun around and shined the flashlight in Mick's face, blinding him.

Mick had seen enough. He snatched Sylvia, who wailed in surprise, then protest. He wrestled her down the ladder, this time avoiding her claws in his leg. He dumped her outside, shutting the door behind him.

He waited for Bobby to come back down the ladder, but the guy was in no hurry.

"Looking for anything in particular up there?" he called.

"Treasure," Bobby said, his voice muffled by the distance. He seemed remarkably unconcerned that he had just been caught going through Nina's stuff. "People put stuff up in places like this, then forget all about it. I've got an eye. I know when there's something like an old vase or painting or something that's worth a fortune."

Mick could hear the thump of big boxes being moved. "So you're like a one-man appraiser? You're thinking of Nina?" Mick asked.

More shuffling from above, then a muffled curse as something tumbled to the ground. "Yeah, as a matter of fact, I am. I'm kinda like you that way. I like to be a hero. Help the ladies out." The pounding of Bobby's footsteps across the loft got closer. His shadow appeared; then the man himself swung over the edge of the hole and scampered down the ladder with the ease of a gymnast. He knocked the dust and cobwebs off his sleeves.

"I'm not like that," Mick said, watching him remove the evidence.

"Yeah, I noticed. Letting me rescue the cat." He hung the flashlight back on its hook, but his eyes were still everywhere, scanning the barn.

"Except I was the one who rescued the cat while you were going through Nina's things," Mick said.

"True enough," he said in a friendly way that Mick didn't feel in return. He clapped Mick on the back. "A true hero. Bet you were excited when you got home tonight and saw Nina's place wrecked so you could get to play the man on the white horse. That's your thing, right? Being the hero? All that army, war stuff."

"It made me sick to my stomach to see Nina's house like that." Mick had to struggle to control his anger.

Bobby shrugged as he took in the barn one last time. "Sure. Sure. None of you army guys have a hero complex."

Mick had started for the door, but now he stopped. "I don't need to be a hero."

Bobby shrugged again. "Like I said, sure. No problem."

He's not worth it, Mick told himself. They let themselves carefully out of the barn, making sure the cat was nowhere in sight.

They walked wordlessly back to the house.

When they hit the front steps, Bobby picked up the pace and got to the door first.

Mick could hear the four women in the living room talking in hushed tones, the clink of wineglasses punctuating their conversation like a melodious fifth voice. Bobby hustled into the foyer, blocking Mick's path like a running back. "Nina. You would not believe what I found in your loft," he cried before Mick had closed the door behind them.

Mick fell back, curious to watch the Bobby Ridale show. He leaned against the doorframe to the living room and crossed his arms over his chest.

The guy was smooth. He was still talking, not letting in a second of pause for Mick to get a word in. The women were sipping white wine and passing a bowl of M&M'S. They tilted their faces up at Bobby with open smiles. Nina looked exhausted but satisfied, nestled in the ring of her friends. Mick envied her for that. He felt both inside and outside her circle.

She held up her hand to stop Bobby's rush of words. "Wait! Slow down. You went up in the loft? For heaven's sake, why?"

"Sylvia," Mick said from his spot in the doorway.

But no one turned to him, and Bobby rushed on. "Right. The cat got up there. My fault. I didn't know what a mess that would be." He smiled back at Mick like they were in this together, sharing a good joke. Mick hadn't wanted to punch a guy so badly since the last time he'd been in the same room with Bobby earlier that evening.

Nina was watching Mick, a puzzled look on her face. She shook her head slightly, as if warning him to back off.

She was right. He knew the night had brought trouble enough. He didn't want to upset her any more by calling Bobby out on—on what? What exactly could he accuse him of that he wasn't already telling them all with great fanfare?

"Mick wanted to go up after her, but I insisted since his shoulder isn't looking so hot and all and that ladder is a doozy. When I got up there—wow! That was my kind of place. So I started poking around," Bobby said. " 'Cause, you know, it's in my blood. Old habits die hard. I see a stash, and I gotta know what's in it. Did you know that you have a case of vintage records up there? It was dark, so it was hard to see, but I think they're in prime condition. I saw a few titles. Stuff from the thirties. I think there was even a Rondel and the Heartbreakers album. If it was, man, those babies are worth a fortune. Nina, you need to bring them down and clean them up and then sell them online."

The women murmured in surprise and excitement over Nina's good luck. Mick couldn't get over how smooth this guy was. He admitted he was a crook but in the same breath parlayed it into a stroke of good luck that was to everyone's advantage.

Or was Mick getting it all wrong, and the guy was just honest? Bobby had played the scene so convincingly, if he was dishonest, he was damn good at it.

Georgia said, "Bobby went through my entire attic. He found stuff that I thought was just musty old heirlooms waiting for a garage sale. He said some of it was worth thousands. We're going to sell my mother's Stangl ware online. We have a whole set, it turns out, which is very rare." She blushed. "I'm going to give it all to charity, of course," she added. "To the American Association for Prison Reform."

Mick tried not to roll his eyes.

Bobby went to Georgia. She made room for him on the couch, and he took her hand and kissed it. He poured himself a glass of wine and threw it back like it was whiskey.

Mick sat next to Nina. He'd give Bobby this round. But he still didn't feel good about the guy.

Lizzie inspected the wine bottle on the coffee table. It was empty. "Well, ladies, I think our work here is done. Nina, are you okay here with Mick? You want us to stay too?"

"No. We're fine. I'm fine. You all go home," Nina said. "And thanks, guys. For everything."

After everyone left, Nina and Mick collected the wine-glasses, barely speaking. The house still felt eerie to Nina, as if whoever had done this was waiting outside for the first chance to come in and wreck the place again. She shook off her fear as best she could. She was so grateful that Mick was here and she didn't have to be alone. But at the same time, the ominous sense that he'd somehow brought this trouble with him nagged at her.

She knew it wasn't his fault. But there still was a part of her that believed that how you looked at life made a difference. She'd spent her life trying to be optimistic, looking for the good in everything. Had the bad always been there, and she'd not seen it? Or, had looking at the dark side of life brought the bad into her world?

Had Mick brought the bad?

My thoughts don't control what a couple of thuggish criminals do on a Saturday night.

She forced herself to look at the good. Mick was here to be with her; her friends came to help; her kitties were safe and sound, asleep by their favorite windows.

After the living room was straightened, she collapsed on the couch. Mick sat down beside her.

"What a night," he said.

"What was that all about with Bobby?" Nina asked.

"What?"

"The macho act," she said. "You looked like you wanted to rip him to shreds. He was only trying to help. You have to let up on him."

"I don't think a guy should go through a person's stuff. Even if his motives are good," Mick said gruffly.

"You went through my stuff, remember?" she reminded him.

"I asked. And even though you said yes, it still felt like crap. I wasn't bragging about it. That guy is too smooth, if you ask me."

"Well, I'm too tired to ask you. I think you hate him because he's a tough guy who let himself fall in love. He let down your team," she teased.

He shrugged.

"I just wish you wouldn't always look on the dark side of things," she said.

He sighed. "I feel like I brought all this darkness on you."

She glanced at a piece of glass on the floor that they'd missed in their cleanup. "I have to admit, I was thinking the same thing. But it's ridiculous. The darkness is out there. We don't control it." She got up to throw out the glass.

"You don't really believe that, do you?" he asked. "I read some of your yoga books, Nina."

She came back to the couch. "Really? You don't seem the type."

"Well, I paged through them. They talk about channeling good vibes, keeping out the bad karma. Do you believe in that?"

She traced her finger over his arm. "I believe it doesn't do any good to look at the negative, but I took it too far. I was naive. Now I'm not."

"I still think that you're putting off talking to Georgia about the accident because you don't want to face it," Mick said.

"No. I'll talk to her. I know I have to. I'm going to talk to her tomorrow."

"Good." Mick nodded. "I'm sorry about the house," he added.

"Well, I should've locked the doors. You only tell me that every day, twice a day."

"And every day, twice a day, you ignore me." He stroked her hair. "I wish I was wrong," he added.

"Do you think the break-in was random?" Nina asked.

"Yeah. I do. Who would have anything against you?"

"I don't know. I really don't. It just feels weird. All this darkness coming on at once." She took his hand. "And all this light."

Chapter Forty-five

That night, Nina couldn't sleep.

She got up the next morning at dawn to do yoga, then worked in her studio till seven, but she couldn't get anything done. Echoes of her conversation with Mick reverberated in her head. Was she doing it again, putting off facing what had to be faced?

Nina knocked on Georgia's front door at nine on the dot.

Bobby answered. "Hi," he said. "Come on in." He was wearing a blue-and-white-striped bathrobe loosely tied at his waist and no shoes.

Georgia came up behind him, dressed in pink cotton polka-dot pajamas. "Sweetie! What a nice surprise." She paused. "Are you okay? It's not the house, is it? You didn't find anything missing?"

Nina followed them both to Georgia's gorgeous kitchen, feeling awkward. Seeing Bobby in Georgia's house felt off, no matter how hard she tried to convince herself it wasn't. The room was majestic, with no expense spared—ivory-and-gray-granite countertops, imported Italian floor tiles, cherry cabinets climbing majestically to the ten-foot ceiling.

Bobby sat down at the table. He was unshaven. His hair was a mess. He picked up a section of Georgia's *New York Times*. Someone had already done the Sunday crossword puzzle in ink and Nina was pretty sure it wasn't Bobby.

"Come to my office," Georgia said. "This looks serious."

Georgia closed the door behind them. "Mick again?"

Nina settled in. "No. Not this time." Nina quickly told the story of the police report and how Georgia was in the report as a witness. "You never told me. Is it true?"

"It's true. I was there," Georgia said. Her therapist face didn't reveal a hint of emotion.

"Why didn't you tell me?" Nina asked.

"We never spoke back then. We hated each other, remember? We were enemies." Georgia's pink jammies were an odd contrast to her stony face and serious words.

"I know. But after we were over all that little-kid nonsense, why didn't you tell me then? Now that we're friends?"

Georgia sighed. "Witnessing that accident made me become a psychiatrist. It changed my life."

Nina steeled herself for what would come next. "Oh, Georgia. I'm sorry. And I'm sorry to make you talk about this. But I have to know."

Georgia smiled weakly. "Well, talking is what I do, right? It's my religion."

If she'd been anyone else, Nina would have crossed the room to her and given her a hug. But Georgia was Georgia, despite the pink polka-dot jammies.

"I was nine years old," Georgia went on. "And I saw death. Right before my eyes, people were gone. I couldn't get that image out of my head for years. Did you know I couldn't ride in a car for my entire fourth-grade year?"

"Georgia! I'm so sorry. I thought—I was only thinking of myself coming here like this. I knew it was nothing. I'm just trying so hard to understand Walt's letter and the stupid box."

"It's okay; I'm a grown-up. I can talk. But it was true. I refused to get in a car after the accident. My parents were furious. That's why they sent me to a psychiatrist. Dr. Zimmerman. Meeting him even the very first time was like a whole new world had opened up for me. I didn't know what he was, but I knew the day I met him that whatever he was, I wanted to be. That man taught me how delicate our psyches are, how the littlest things can throw a person off. But how we can fix ourselves—but carefully. Always taking great care."

"Sometimes a cigar isn't a cigar and all that stuff," Nina said. "Teeth represent death—"

"Yeah, all that stuff. The stuff that's underneath the obvious," Georgia said.

"Tell me about the accident, Georgia. Will you? You saw the article Walt had cut out, the one he wrote on and hid in the box. What do you think? Was it bullshit? Why did it say 'sticks and stones'? It's important, isn't it?"

"Nins, remember when we were talking about the mind protecting itself from knowing too much? And how just now we were talking about taking care?"

"Of course. We had been talking about how Mick can't remember the blast that sent him home."

"Exactly. Well, my mind did the same thing when I

was a kid. I saw the crash, the car flying, but I couldn't put it together. It was too painful and awful. I'll tell you what I saw if you want, but I don't think you should pursue this, trying to dig into whatever it was Walt was struggling with by scribbling on that article. You can't ever really know what Walt was thinking. You can't ever know what he meant. So why chase it? Why try to put it together if you can't change it and it's awful? I'm asking you to consider that I'm not telling you any more because you won't want to know. I want you to take care of yourself."

Nina sat back on the couch. "Everyone keeps telling me that I'm naive. They all say that I want to look on the happy side of life. I want to prove them wrong. I can handle it, Georgia."

"Who cares what everyone thinks?"

Nina considered her friend. "You know what? I don't care what anyone thinks. I want there to be a reason Walt sent Mick to destroy that box. And now you're telling me there might be a reason. I want to face it. I want to understand so that I can move on."

"I'm telling you that you might not want to know the reason."

Nina groaned. She closed her eyes. "You want to hear something pathetic? Talk about me wearing rose-colored glasses. I was starting to think that Walt sent Mick on a bullshit mission so he'd come here and fall in love with me. I thought that Walt knew we'd be good together and wanted us to meet and it was the only way he could think of to get Mick to come here."

Georgia smiled. "Maybe it's true."

Nina opened her eyes and scowled at her friend. "Georgia."

"Okay. But maybe it doesn't matter if it's true or not, because it's good," Georgia said.

"I'm over good!"

"Why, Nina? What's wrong with good?"

Nina stood up and walked to the window. She looked out over Georgia's perfect lawn. "Tell me about the accident. I already did your worst-care-scenario exercise. I imagined the very worst thing that could have happened, and I know I can face it."

Georgia sighed. "I don't think you could have imagined what I saw."

Nina's throat went tight. She tried to turn to look at Georgia's face, but she couldn't make herself. Instead, she watched two squirrels scamper around the trunk of the huge maple. "Tell me," she said, her voice cracking just a little.

"Okay—"

The door opened. Nina spun around.

Bobby poked his head in. "How you girls doing? You want me to bring you some coffee?" He walked into the room as if he intended to stay.

Nina felt as if she were nine years old again, staring at her worst two enemies. Bobby, the boy who took Walt away from her. Georgia, the little girl who pushed her on the playground. She wanted Mick to be here so there was someone on her side.

She shook away her discomfort. It was ridiculous to feel as if she were among enemies, when these people were now her friends. She was going too far to the dark side.

They were her friends, weren't they...?

"No coffee. Thanks," Georgia said.

Bobby sat down next to Georgia anyway.

Nina's skin went cold. *Look for the truth.* She looked from Bobby to Georgia, waiting for the feeling of dread that was descending on her to coalesce into a coherent thought. "You weren't my enemy until after the accident," Nina said to Georgia, not sure what had made her remember that just now. "You hated me after the accident. Did you hate me because of the accident?"

"No. It wasn't that—," Georgia began.

Nina went back to her chair and sank into it. "Before the accident, we weren't friends, but we weren't enemies. After the accident, you were awful. You told everyone I loved Joey Sianai, and then he started torturing me. He and his friends followed me home from school for a whole year, yelling and throwing things and calling me weird. And you and Jane Betties and all those girls came too, yelling that I loved him. Why did you do that?"

"Nina, we were nine. I'm sorry. It was awful. But why bring this up now—?"

"Because I never noticed before that you being mean to me was linked to the accident. Did you have something to do with it?" Nina could hardly breathe. Bobby's hulking presence had added a sinister feel to the air. Nina's throat was dry and tight. Her voice had grown small. "It was an accident, wasn't it?"

"It was," Georgia said. "But not the way you think."

Nina wished Mick were beside her. But he wasn't.

"Georgia," Bobby said. He stood up, putting himself between them. "Is this really necessary?"

Nina stood up too. She said to Georgia, "You're my friend. One of my best friends."

"I am, honey."

"And you had something to do with my parents'

death?" She looked to Bobby. He said he'd loved Georgia since she was in fourth grade. He'd noticed Georgia right after the accident. What was going on here? Were they both involved? Nina felt sick to her stomach. She remembered how Georgia hadn't wanted Nina to go to Tommy for the police report when they'd discussed it at the diner.

"It's not that way—," Bobby began.

"Bobby!" Georgia cut him off. "It's okay. She should know." A look passed between them that Nina couldn't interpret.

Bobby, still in his bare feet and bathrobe, looked dangerous, the way he had when they were younger. Had he been listening outside the door and stepped in to stop Georgia from telling Nina the truth? Why? She shook her rapidly fogging head. Her world was spinning. "Just tell me."

"I was on the bridge," Georgia said. "And I tossed a stone. It hit your parents' car."

"No!" Bobby said. "Stop it, Georgia."

"I didn't mean—"

Nina blinked away the black spots that were forming in front of her eyes. She tried to listen to her friend, but the words were jumbling in her head.

"I'm sorry. I was nine. I was throwing stones. The car came out of nowhere. I was a kid." Georgia's voice didn't rise. She wasn't upset. She was telling a story she'd known for so long, it had lost any drama. "I did it," Georgia said. "And Bobby saw. That's how he knew. And he told Walt. But we'd made a pact not to tell."

"Stop it, Georgia," Bobby said.

"And I've never forgiven myself. But, Nina, I thought it was better if you didn't know."

"I have to go," Nina said. "I'm sorry. I have to go."

Chapter Forty-six

Nina came home to find that Mick had lugged down the crate of records from the loft. He was on the back deck, carefully wiping the cobwebs and dust from each album with a towel.

He didn't say a word when he saw her face, just took her into his arms.

After telling him Georgia's story, Nina sank down in an Adirondack chair. She picked up an album thoughtlessly, The Beatles' *Abbey Road*. She didn't remember listening to it. It must have been her parents', but she didn't remember them listening to it either, which wasn't surprising, as she didn't remember much of them at all.

Because Georgia had caused their deaths.

"Nina," Mick whispered. "You okay?" He was kneeling in front of her, his hands on her knees.

"Yeah. Sure. I'm just a little shocked; that's all. Walt didn't want me to know, but now I know. Mystery over." She smiled.

"What's funny?" he asked, more alarmed by her smile than by her sadness.

"I had actually thought that box was a ruse. That Walt knew that we were right for each other and had fooled you into coming here so that we'd fall in love," she said.

"I like that version better," he said.

"But that version is wrong," she said.

He took her hands. "So what?" he said. "We're still perfect for each other."

"How do you figure that?"

"I stopped trying to find the bad in everything and you stopped trying to find the good in everything and we met in the middle. Some things just are. Not good. Not bad. Just are. Like this news. Nina, the accident was still an accident. Georgia didn't mean anything by it. It doesn't change anything. Not really." He kissed her hand. "There's not a thing we can do about it."

"Make love to me, Mick," she said. "I don't want to talk about accidents and betrayals and good and bad."

"Me neither," he said. He rubbed her thigh. Then pushed up her dress inch by inch. He sighed, and she loved that sigh. *I know Walt's worst secret and I survived.* Things would change between her and Georgia, for a while at least, but their relationship was strong; they'd get past it.

He kissed her inner thigh, working his way upward.

She watched him move along her leg, the expanse of skin exposing itself as he pressed further.

She closed her eyes and let her head fall back.

He pushed her dress up to her waist; then he abandoned that fabric for the tighter, silkier fabric between her legs. His fingers rubbed, stroked, pressed, while his mouth moved in closer, closer.

She loved summer. The heat of the sun on her face, the heat of the man moving between her legs. Maybe it wasn't all good, but it wasn't bad either, so she'd just take a little bit of both.

He carefully pulled off her panties. "Mick—"

"Shhh..." He lowered his head between her legs and he kissed, nipped, pulled, until he found the perfect combination of kissing, nipping, pulling, to make her grab the armrests and plant her feet as firmly on the ground as possible, considering she was floating about ten feet above it in a cloud of Mick-inspired bliss.

After Nina left, Bobby and Georgia went back to the kitchen. "I don't want to talk about it," Georgia said.

Bobby shook his head. "You shouldn't have lied to her."

"Oh, and you're Mr. Truthful? C'mon, Bob. You know Nina even better than I do. Walt is all she had in the world. I did the right thing and you know it."

"You told me that your Enemy Club always tells the truth, the whole truth—"

"Not this time." She cut him off.

"It makes you look bad, Georgia. She'll hate you."

"I'm not important. Bobby, she doesn't have to face what really happened. She's a happy person. She's a true optimist. I want it to stay that way. I don't want to be the one who makes her go over to the dark side."

Bobby shook his head. "You're amazing, Georgia. Willing to take the blame like that for something you didn't do."

"I'm not amazing. I'm just—okay, I'm amazing. But I couldn't do it any other way. Not now, anyway, when things are going so well with Mick. He's a good guy, I think. I think that he can get her past Walt's death."

"Yeah, he's all right," Bobby said.

"Don't lie, Bobby. You hate him," Georgia said. "Why?"

"Because he hates me. Forget it. Not important. I don't need to defend myself to that guy. We'll both be hated. Who cares? Kinda like a last favor to Walt to keep his little sister happy. We'll take the blame, be the bad guys, and leave Walt out of it."

"Exactly. To Walt." Georgia raised her orange juice glass in a toast.

"To Walt," Bobby said. "May he rest in peace."

Chapter Forty-seven

$\mathcal{M}$ick watched Johnny follow Nina through the garage studio. She had loaded the boy down with supplies that they were going to truck out to the wall today. After a week of sketching and conceptualizing, Johnny and Nina were going to start the artwork that would frame the video projections.

Mick had liked watching the two of them work together, but he felt like a third wheel. He brought them sandwiches, made tea. But not being an artist left him out of their loop.

Still, he felt a sense of peace. Nina wove peace around her like a cocoon. It was her specialty and he wanted more of it. He loved the way Nina made beautiful things, grew beautiful things, was a beautiful thing. He had reached—dare he admit it?—a place of rainbows and flowers. *And he liked it.*

Today, the money from the bank should come through, the last of his worries solved. At least, they were solved except for finding a way to pay Nina back. That he was still working on.

"Mick, get off your ass and help us. And don't think that just because you say you can't paint you're getting away with not painting," Nina warned. "You promised you'd try."

Mick heaved one of the plastic bins onto his mended shoulder, and dutifully marched it to Nina's old Subaru. They packed so much stuff, Mick and Johnny followed behind in Mick's car.

Ten minutes later, their caravan pulled to a stop by the side of Garcia's Pharmacy and they unloaded the supplies. Nina kept running her fingers through her hair, the way she did when she couldn't settle. She was nervous about the money, although he wasn't sure why and she refused to do anything but smile and say she was just being silly.

They had held two more trial movie nights at the wall in the past week. Johnny had so much material now, he was having a hard time viewing it all, much less editing it. It was coming in from all over the world, as the news of the unique memorial in a tiny town in upstate New York spread through the Internet, as well as making the *New York Times* and *USA Today*.

Both nights had been huge successes. Not with the evening news and huge crowds, but even better, with somber, thoughtful crowds who came silently, sat, watched, then left just as silently. There was no clapping, no fanfare, and that felt exactly right. It wasn't about the wall at all. It was about the soldiers, about the mission, about the people who came to watch and to remember. Then they went back to their lives feeling a little stronger, a little closer, than they had an hour before.

But during the day, the wall was still blank except for the address of the website. Surprisingly, it didn't seem to matter. Mr. Garcia said that people had been showing up at the wall with their smart phones, standing with their backs to the wall and their eyes to their tiny, private screens as if that were enough, some kind of pilgrimage.

But a blank wall was a blank wall, and they didn't want to tempt any more graffiti, even if they knew they'd already caught—and reformed—the main offender.

The three of them had gotten the car unloaded. They stood, looking at the blankness.

"That's a lot of wall to fill," Johnny said.

"So let's get started, men," Nina declared fearlessly.

Johnny and Nina started to plot their strategy.

Now that his chauffeuring duties were done, Mick knew he wouldn't be much help. "You kids go to it. Call if you need me. I'm going to go see about these records." Since he'd known he'd be superfluous, he'd loaded the box of records from Nina's loft into his trunk. She said he could do whatever he wanted with them, that she didn't care. So he decided he'd take them down to that funky music store on the corner and see if Bobby was right about finding treasure.

"Hello, son."

Mr. Garcia had come out of the pharmacy. He patted Mick on the back. His snakeskin cowboy boots must have felt like ovens in the August sun, but the man didn't seem to mind.

"Sir." Mick nodded his head.

Mr. Garcia motioned to Nina and Johnny. "Good team."

"Yeah. I'm just the hired muscle," Mick said. He felt

something uneasy stirring in Mr. Garcia, just below the surface. He hoped he wasn't going to start talking about his other son.

"Never knew Johnny was arty," Mr. Garcia said after a while.

"He's good," Mick said. "Good ideas anyway. Don't know if he can paint. Guess we're about to find out." Johnny and Nina were opening paint cans, pointing to impossible heights, squinting their eyes looking from their blueprint to the wall and back again.

Mr. Garcia crumpled his nose, trying to swat away an invisible bug.

"This is good for Johnny," Mick said. "He wants to run away and join the army, you know."

"I know," Mr. Garcia said. "Proud of the boy."

"You want him to join up?" Mick asked.

Mr. Garcia looked askance at Mick. "Anything's better than this stuff," he said.

Mick held his tongue as long as he could, which was about three seconds. "You mean, better he risk his life and possibly die than he be an artist?"

There was no way Johnny could have heard their conversation, but the boy looked up as if he had. He looked quickly away from his father and turned his attention back to Nina. He was less animated than before.

Mr. Garcia shrugged. "Call me traditional, but I think a man's gotta be a man. Not forever, but at least for a while before going soft."

"Sixteen-year-olds aren't men," Mick said.

Mr. Garcia sucked in his lower lip and chewed it. "You got a son?" he asked.

"Nope."

Mr. Garcia nodded as if to say, *Argument over; I win.*

Mick watched Johnny. "He'd make a good soldier," he admitted.

"Yes, sir," Mr. Garcia said. "I'd be damn proud."

"But he might make a brilliant, one-of-a kind artist."

"Some things are worth more than others, son," Mr. Garcia said. "You gotta do what's right for your country. Then you can go and paint pretty pictures for yourself. But first, country."

"What if painting pictures is what's right for your country?" Mick asked.

"It don't work like that, son. Never did. Never will."

Mick ducked into the dusty, dark music store. Something jazzy and jarring played over the speaker system. A bell rang when the door closed behind him, but no one appeared. Mick flicked through the albums in the case up front, amazed that they still existed and that anyone cared. Guess there was something for everyone in this world. Most of the albums were a dollar, but the ones behind the counter, displayed on the wall and in the dusty glass case, had astronomical prices. Hundreds, some even thousands of dollars.

Did people even still own turntables?

Could Bobby have been right?

Mick rang a bell on the counter and waited. Music had never been his thing, although some of the guys lived for it, their iPod earbuds constantly jammed in their ears, their own personal soundtracks playing them through the war, one song at a time.

A scruffy-looking man appeared from the back, looking as if maybe Mick had wakened him. "Wassup?"

Mick showed him the albums. "Found these in an attic. Wondering if they're worth anything."

The sleepy man pawed through them. "Nope."

"Nope, they're not worth anything to you? Or nope, they're not worth anything to anyone?"

"I'll take 'em off your hands if you want. List 'em on eBay for you on my site for twenty bucks."

"This whole box is only worth twenty bucks?"

"Nah. It's not worth even that. What I mean is, you pay me twenty bucks to list them. Then we split the profits fifty-fifty if it sells. I wouldn't try to sell 'em one-by-one. I'd do 'em as a lot, list the titles, and try to sell the whole box for five bucks plus shipping. Sometimes, you find someone who has some kind of emotional attachment to a record and they'll pay those kinds of prices."

"Why would I pay you twenty bucks to maybe make two-fifty if I'm lucky?"

"'Cause no one ever believes me. They think they've got treasure, even though they basically want to trash it on me. They think it'll go online and spark an auction and they'll be millionaires. Course, they're too lazy to do it themselves. And it is better with me. People in the biz know me. Trust me. If I say the stuff's good quality, I got a track record, you know? They know it won't be scratched." The clerk yawned. "Look, you wanna list it? Be a millionaire. It's about as likely as the lottery. Why not, right? Don't wanna rush you, but I got stuff to do."

Mick looked around the empty store. "You're pretty busy, huh?"

"I do ninety-nine percent of my business online, buddy. The store is my reward. A cool place to hang with buddies. Talk records. If someone in the world wants one of these records, they'll search 'em out and find 'em. That's how it works. Got a hot lottery going on right now on an old seventy-eight of Elvis." He looked to the doorway leading to the back of the store.

Mick nodded. "You know what? I do want you to list these." He got out his wallet.

The man smiled and took the box. He started filling out a form. "Sucker born every minute," he said, grinning up at Mick. "Welcome to the millionaire's club. Sign here."

Nina looked up from her work at the wall. Mel Skirston was standing behind her, looking uncomfortable. He was the banker who was handling her home equity loan. He held a paper bag from the Last Chance diner in his hand and she could smell the French fries.

"Hi, Mel," she said, putting down her brush. "Everything okay?" She could feel her stomach sink. The look on his face told her everything she needed to know—that he wasn't here to bring her lunch. In fact, whatever was on his mind might just be ruining his appetite.

"Nina. I was just passing by. But I'm glad I spotted you." He wiped the sweat off his brow. "Got a minute?"

She wiped her hands on a rag. "I'll be right back, John."

The boy nodded and she followed the banker away from the wall.

"I tried to call earlier. I have bad news," Mel said. "Nina, there's a problem with the loan."

"What do you mean?"

"When you had that run-in with that woman who claimed to be Mary, when you signed the money over to her, did you sign anything else?"

She blushed. It still stung to talk about getting conned, especially to someone like Mel, who would have known better. "I don't think so."

"Someone already borrowed against the house," he told her. "An equity loan was already taken out just a few weeks ago."

"I don't know what that means," Nina said. "What are you saying?"

"I'm saying I think you need a lawyer, Nina. And the police. I think you've been scammed again. That Mary lady must have had some paper that you signed. I don't know yet. What I'm telling you is that the loan isn't going to go through. Mary must have found a way to get even more from you than you knew. Maybe you signed over a power of attorney?"

She couldn't breathe. Had she? She had no idea. And now Mick was stuck. She'd promised him something that she couldn't deliver.

"Or," he continued, more gently, "maybe she forged something with all your information. I don't know, Nina. But what I'm telling you is, the bank won't issue the loan. I don't think you'll be able to sell the place either until this is all cleared up."

"Oh, Mel. I don't know what I signed. I mean, I know she got Walt's insurance money. I—why wouldn't I have known about this?"

"Do you check your credit reports?"

"No." The smell from the French fries was making her nauseous.

Mel looked at the sidewalk. He shrugged. "I'm sorry, Nina. I don't know the details. I only know they turned you down. This is a job for the authorities to untangle. I hope you can work this all out. It looks like a mess. But our bank can't risk the loan."

Mick came back from the record shop to find Nina sitting on the curb, her head in her hands.

He sat down next to her and put his arm over her shoulders. She told him the story of the house disaster.

"There's no money, Mick. There might not even still be a house. I can't help you. You stayed all this time for nothing."

"Not nothing," he assured her. He could feel her pain as if it were inside his body, and there wasn't a thing he could do about it. "The furthest thing from nothing."

"But Bella."

He grimaced, thinking of his sisters. That was a phone call he wasn't looking forward to making. "It was a long shot for me to come out here. I always knew that. And Nina, even though this is awful, I'm a little glad I'm not taking your money. It felt lousy from day one." The truth of his words hit him in the gut.

"Maybe the records Bobby found in the loft will bail us out," she said, only half-joking.

He shook his head. "Doubtful. The guy at the shop said that Bobby was full of shit." As soon as he said it, he was sorry. Why did he always have to burst her bubble? All of this was his fault.

"Oh, Mick. I'm so sorry about all this."

"It's not your fault. It's not anyone's fault. I'll figure it out somehow," Mick said.

"We'll figure it out," Nina insisted.

"We'll figure it out," he repeated. He took her hand and gave it a squeeze.

• • •

Nina wanted to keep working on the wall to keep her mind busy while she tried to think this whole thing through. She and Johnny had sketched out the words *Duty, Honor, Country* in huge letters across the wall. The space inside the *D* formed one blank white "screen" where they'd project videos. The *O*s in *Honor* and *Country* formed the two others. They would illustrate in the space left over around the words.

Mick tried to think through what to do now that the money wasn't going to come for Bella. He hated that he'd made Nina feel responsible for his mess. He hated that he'd have to call Sandy and tell her the bad news. He hated that he'd wasted so much time, even if it was no one's fault but a scam artist who called herself Mary.

"We need more black paint," Johnny called down from the ladder.

"That's my job," Mick said. "I'm the go-fetch guy. I'll go back to the house and get it." He was relieved to have something to do besides sit around and feel miserable.

"Okay. Bring a snack too, while you're there," Johnny said.

"Bring whiskey," Nina joked. The look on her face told Mick that she might not be joking.

Mick opened the barn door carefully, looking behind him as he entered to be sure Sylvia wasn't sneaking up on him. He stepped into the darkened space, flicked on the lights, and froze.

The barn was trashed, every bin overturned, canvases thrown everywhere.

In the corner stood Bobby Ridale.

He was holding a red metal box.

"Well, hi, Mick," Bobby said, as if they were meeting by chance in a public park.

Mick held his ground, his heart pounding. Where had Bobby gotten that box? It looked just like the box that was growing barnacles at the bottom of Galton Lake.

"See your mind is zinging, son," Bobby said. "I am sorry you had to see this. Quite the shame."

Mick advanced toward the other man. "You were the one who trashed Nina's house," Mick said, the pieces of the last weeks coming together in a rush. "You were blabbing on about all those prison stories so your thugs had time to go through Nina's house, looking for this." Mick was so surprised at his discovery, he almost forgot to be angry. Almost.

Bobby shrugged. "Such a smart guy you are."

"I found the wrong box," Mick said. He remembered the line in Walt's letter: *There's a couple of them... you'll know you've got the right one if the key fits...* The truth rushed over Mick in a sickening wave. His key must have fit two boxes.

"You get the grand prize," Bobby said. "Now, how about being even smarter, and forgetting you ever saw me. Let me leave with this, Mick. You don't want to know what's in here."

Mick crossed the barn. They were face-to-face.

"Let you leave?"

Bobby said, "Look, Mick. This is all, in fact, very simple. I have what I've been looking for. I'm leaving today. You be smart and do the same."

"You don't love Georgia," Mick said. "You came back to Galton just to find the box. You faked loving Georgia so you could have access to Nina, access to her house, to her life. I was right about you all along."

"It's not that simple," Bobby said. "But it's none of your business."

Mick was ready to punch Bobby, but just as he was about to let one loose, Bobby held out the box to him. "You want it? I'm not going to fight you for it. Take it."

Mick couldn't swallow. His mind was racing. What was this guy up to?

"Look at it this way, Micky. This is your second chance to do the right thing," Bobby said. "And the right thing is letting Nina think that Walt was a good guy. She's working on that memorial right now, isn't she? The memorial to her heroic brother? Let her keep that fantasy, Mick. We'll both split—and get on with our lives without ruining the lives of these two beautiful women we've so badly used. Everyone will have their happily ever after."

"Walt was more of a hero than you could ever hope to be," Mick said. "You have no right to say anything bad about him."

Bobby waved the box. "You sure?"

Mick was sick to his stomach. What was in the box? Did he want to know? Or could he let Bobby leave now? He could straighten the barn, pretend that none of this ever happened.

Bobby said, "You came into this kind, sweet, beautiful woman's life and ripped it apart, didn't you, Mick? You should stop this nonsense, let me leave with this box, and let Walt and his little sister rest in peace."

Mick considered his options. "Give me the box."

"Okay. But before I do, I want you to consider this— Georgia didn't throw that rock. I was there too when her parents died on that bridge. Georgia lied about being the one who threw the rock."

"You threw the rock?" Mick asked.

"No, dummy. Walt did. Walt killed them."

"I don't believe you."

"Go ask Georgia. She's Nina's friend. She was covering for Walt because she thought it was better that way. That's a little lesson for you, see? Do the right thing, Mick. Let me go, and forget you ever saw this. Protect Nina from the truth about her brother."

Mick considered. He looked around him at the destruction, at the man who couldn't be trusted. One of the earlier studies for the canvas for Super-Walt lay in the middle of the barn at his feet. He felt an overwhelming desire to make this all right, but he didn't know what right was anymore.

He looked at Bobby. "You're leaving town forever with Walt's secrets?"

"Soon as I can."

"Never coming back?"

"Never."

"Come with me to Georgia's. Right now. I need to know you're telling the truth about what happened on that bridge."

Bobby smiled a wicked smile. "Only if you keep my secret from her."

"Okay," Mick said. It was a deal with the devil if there ever was one.

Georgia was getting into her white Lexus when Mick pulled into the drive, followed by Bobby in his black Cadillac. Georgia climbed back out of the car, obviously shocked to see the two men together.

Mick could feel sweat soaking his T-shirt, dripping

down his back. What a day it had been. "Let's go inside," he said.

She let them into the house without a word.

As soon as the door closed behind them, Mick began. "Okay, tell me the truth about the accident," he said to her.

"Did you tell him, Bobby? Why?" Georgia asked.

"I—," Bobby began.

Mick cut him off. He didn't have time for nonissues. "It wasn't his fault, Georgia. I figured it out," he said. "Just tell me the truth, Georgia. I won't tell Nina."

"I don't want Nina to know," she said.

"Okay," Mick agreed. He was feeling restless, unsettled.

She took a deep breath. "Walt caused the car crash," Georgia said. "It was an accident."

Mick's head began to ache. What Bobby had said was true.

She went on, "I took the blame, but it wasn't me. I didn't want Nina to know it was Walt. He didn't mean to do it. It was an accident. He was on the bridge with Bobby. I was behind them, walking home from school. I was nine, remember. A little kid. I had stayed late for help with a math assignment."

Mick was speechless, the information tumbling around his brain. *So much darkness . . .*

"Anyway, Walt had a stone and he winged it at a car down below us, and it just bounced off with a ping. Then we saw another car coming on the left side of the bridge, and he said, *It's my parents,* and he ran across to the right side, to wait for it. He didn't realize that the driver's window was open. The stone hit Mr. Stokes. He yelped and practically jumped through the roof. The car went off the road, and they screamed, and we screamed, and, well, you know the rest."

Mick felt like he'd just gone off a cliff. "And you saw it?" he asked.

"I did. The whole thing."

"Why didn't you tell anyone?"

"Because I was nine and I was in love with Bobby. He was twelve. Very dreamy. I promised him I wouldn't tell. He told me that Walt was mad at his parents for agreeing with the principal that he should get kicked off the football team for his low grades. Walt was so mad, he had refused a ride with them, had said he *wanted to kill them*. He and Bobby and I just happened to be on the bridge when their car passed below. Walt happened to be tossing a little stone in his hand. It was an accident even though he was mad. Walt was just that way. We were kids. We thought they'd send Walt to jail." Georgia shook her head and Bobby crossed the room to her.

Mick stiffened.

Sticks and stones can break your bones, but words can never hurt me...

It was wrong. Words could hurt worse than stones. The truth could ruin everything. Mick thought back to how upset Nina had been over his letting slip that Walt was a reckless soldier. Now this. This and whatever was in the box that was locked in his trunk—

"Walt thought the stone would hit the car," Georgia insisted. "It was supposed to bounce off and that would be it. But it didn't work out that way. Walt held that secret his whole life. I think it was why he joined the army. I truly believe he didn't mean anything more than to hit their car with a little ping. What happened shocked him. It shocked us all. But he always believed it was his fault. He had said that he wanted to kill them, and he did. He took that very, very seriously. We all did."

Mick tried to get his head around what she was saying, running the scene through his mind.

"He joined the army to get killed," Georgia insisted. "He lived his whole life on the wild side, trying to get killed. The guilt was too much for him. And it'll be too much for Nina."

Mick shook his head, reimagining Walt through this new prism of information. "That's why you never told Nina you saw the accident."

"Right. And I never will tell her the whole truth and neither will you—either of you! It's a terrible thing to know about your brother. What difference does it make? Walt's gone. Her parents are gone. It would be cruel."

"She's downtown, painting a mural to him," Mick said, the truth of what that meant sickening him. Mick needed to get out of there, to think this all through.

"Nina's happy," Georgia said. "She believes that the world's a decent place. I really envy that about her. I don't want her to lose that because a couple of macho guys can't keep their mouths shut."

Mick and Bobby left. They drove to the lake and got out in the parking lot. Mick leaned against his car. Bobby lit a cigarette. All around them, families were out to enjoy the beautiful day. Little kids in swimsuits headed for the small beach, their mothers following with coolers stuffed with supplies.

Life was good here.

And then there was him and Bobby.

Mick watched a redheaded kid play in the sand. "I want you to decide that Georgia's too good for you," he said to Bobby. "I don't ever want to hear that she knows you used her," Mick said.

"You got it. That was my plan anyway. I was going to tie up all the loose ends."

"Let her down easy, then split," Mick said.

"Yes, sir." Bobby saluted. "Now, are we agreed? It's best that we both split. So can I have my box back?"

"Tell me something first. How did you know about the box?"

"Because it's mine. Walt had smuggled it back for me during his last leave. But I was stuck behind bars, upstate, and I couldn't come to get it. Then I finally get out, I come back here to get it, and you're also searching for the damn thing. I couldn't believe it. Guess Walt had a change of heart."

"I knew you hated me," Mick said. "I knew you weren't right."

"Yeah, well, it was my box."

"You must have been laughing your ass off when we found the wrong box."

"It was pretty funny," Bobby admitted.

"Hilarious." A family passed close by and the two men stopped talking until they were out of earshot.

Mick went to his car and got out the box. He handed it to Bobby.

"You wanna know what's in it?" Bobby asked.

"No." Then he stopped. "Yes. If it's worth money. Then I want you to split it with me."

Bobby smiled a demented grin. He had finished his cigarette and he threw it to the ground and stomped it out. "Open the fucking box."

Mick pulled out the key that was still on his ring. It worked easily. "Fuck me." His body went numb. *Leave town today and don't come back.* "Walt was smuggling antiquities?" He shut the box quickly, looking around to be sure no one had seen the gleaming gold and gems inside the rusty box.

"I told you you didn't want to see," Bobby said. "It's the real deal. Worth a couple hundred thousand. Walt got it out for me so I could get on with my life. Only catch was, I couldn't tell Nina. Problem was, he couldn't bring it to the prison. So he stashed it at his house for when I got out. Only, he hadn't thought it through so good. How could I tell her I was looking for the damn thing?"

It couldn't have been worse. This wasn't reckless behavior; this was criminal. He couldn't believe that Walt would have done this.

Duty. Honor. Country.

Screw that. He was done with doing the right thing for society, for other people. He was going to do the right thing for Nina.

"I want a hundred thousand," Mick said. He hated himself for saying it. He wasn't sure he could do it. But Bella—he had to think of Bella.

"No problem. That's nothing," Bobby said.

Mick shut the box. He tossed it back in his trunk and slammed it.

"Hey," Bobby protested.

"First, let Georgia down easy. I'm keeping the box till you do it."

Bobby considered him. "I could beat your face in right here and take the box myself."

"I know. But you won't. Because you want a clean get-away. You know if you do the right thing by Georgia by never telling her the truth about what a scumbag you are, I won't snitch and you'll be home free. Soldier's word of honor," Mick said.

Bobby considered him. "Okay. It's a fair deal. Give me two hours. Where will you be? At Nina's?"

"Call my cell." He gave Bobby the number.

"What are you going to do about Nina?" Bobby asked him.

"What do you care?" Mick asked.

"I care about Nina. She's a good kid. That's why I'm keeping my mouth shut. Why I went to all this trouble to get out without her knowing."

"You're the hero, huh?"

"Guess I am," Bobby said.

Mick went back to the wall with the black paint and sandwiches. He didn't bring the whiskey, but he wished he had. He helped out as best he could, considering how distracted he felt.

Nina's cell phone rang before his did.

"Can you hand me that, Mick?" she called down to him from her ladder.

He saw on the caller ID that it was Georgia.

Nina listened for a while. "Oh, honey, I'm so sorry," she said. She climbed down the ladder.

Then his cell rang.

"The deed is done," Bobby said. "I let her down easy like we agreed. I said she was too good for me, yadda yadda yadda."

"You told her the truth," Mick said.

"Yeah, asshole, I told her the truth. Now, give me back my box."

Mick waited an hour; then he got in his car and went back to the house.

Finally he understood what he owed to Nina.

What he should have done on day one: get out with Walt's secrets and never come back. This was his second chance, and he had to do the right thing this time.

She deserved rainbows.

She deserved to know that her brother was a hero, and that was the end of the story. If he stuck around, he'd have to tell her the truth. And the truth, like most truths, was better off buried.

Bobby drove up a few minutes later. Mick gave him the box. "Forget the money," he told him. "I don't want your dirty money."

Bobby didn't protest. "Suit yourself." He drove away, leaving Mick at the empty house.

He hesitated outside the door, his small bag slung over his shoulder. He couldn't bear to be in the house, and he'd left everything behind but what he needed for the drive back to California. He found a pen and wrote Nina a note.

He tucked it into the flower-covered mailbox.

Then he drove off, not looking back.

Chapter Forty-eight

When Nina got home after suppertime, Mick's car wasn't in the drive.

She checked the mail and found Mick's letter.

Dear Nina,

I love you and I'll always love you. But I had to go. It's for the best, I promise. I'm sorry and I'll never forget you. Please believe that I never wanted it to be this way. Be happy, be optimistic, and know that you're loved.

Love, Mick

Chapter Forty-nine

Jill, Lizzie, Georgia, and Nina were getting a little tipsy in Nina's living room. Lizzie, as usual, had called the emergency Enemy Club meeting, the third this week, and brought the wine. Georgia and Nina were eating the M&M'S like, well, candy. Jill and Lizzie looked on with grim faces. Mick had been gone six days and they hadn't heard a word. Bobby had split too, claiming he couldn't live up to Georgia's standards. He said he was going back to his life of crime.

"Men are all cowards," Georgia said.

"Now, now. Not all of them," Lizzie said.

"You got the last good one," Nina conceded. "How could Mick just leave without saying good-bye? Without explaining? I just can't believe he was only after the money. Scamming me the whole time."

Jill shook her head. "You don't know that he was scamming you."

Nina scowled. "He left the day I told him that there

was no money, Jill. Don't be a Pollyanna. Of course he was scamming me."

Nina hadn't anticipated how much she'd miss him. "You know what's sick? Even though I know the truth about him, I still want him back." Nina hung her head and ate another M&M. "The worst part is, he just wrote a stupid note, like I was the cat-sitter or something." She threw herself back on the couch. "At least Bobby had the balls to say good-bye in person."

They all nodded in understanding. They had believed in Mick too. Bobby, not so much, but at least he'd had the honor to admit he was in over his head.

They drank more wine.

Nina went on. "He even left a bunch of his clothes. And I washed them. Folded them. Put them on the stupid bed in the guest room like maybe he'd come back and then he'd get pissed at me for doing his laundry again and I could get pissed right back at him. Why did I believe that he could be anything but a scam artist? Why, after everything, was I such a fool?"

"Because you're you," Lizzie said. "You're hopeful. It's what we all love about you."

"What a mess," Nina said.

They got through the rest of the bottle of wine and opened a second. Then Lizzie's eyes lit up. "I have an idea. No. Forget it. Never mind."

They all sat forward. "What?" Nina asked.

"It was terrible," Lizzie said.

"Tell. You have to," Jill insisted.

"Let's burn his stuff. Let's have a ceremony to be rid of him. Did Bobby leave anything, Georgia? We could burn his stuff too."

Georgia shook her head. "No. Nothing. Wait—his striped bathrobe. God, I hated that thing. It was so mafioso."

"It just seems so final," Nina said miserably.

"We could have a huge bonfire. A good-bye to the summer of asshole men."

"I have a better idea," Nina said, warming to the idea. "Let's drive out to the lake and dump their stuff in the lake. Then after, we could skinny-dip. We haven't in years."

"I never have," Georgia said.

"Well, that we have to fix," Jill declared.

"You're drunk," Lizzie warned.

"Just tipsy. I really want to do this. I swear. It would help me get over him."

"It is a nice night," Jill said. "And I've been sipping club soda. I can drive."

Nina went upstairs to gather Mick's things. She shoved his tattered T-shirts and jeans into a plastic bag. This would be perfect. It would be good. It was the exactly right thing to do. All that talk he'd done about facing the truth was just that: talk. Sleeping in a tent and refusing to let her do his laundry didn't make him a man. It just made him a coward. How could he have been scamming her all along? How had she believed in him? How could she have made love to him?

She scanned the room for anything she'd forgotten. Sylvia sat on the end of the bed, watching her. She stroked the cat. "Sorry, hon. He's not coming back."

The cat didn't seem to care either way. Lucky cat.

She looked into the closet, expecting it to be empty

except for the extra linens she stashed there. But instead she found Mick's shirt that they'd bought for him to wear to Georgia's dinner party. Her heart beat a little faster. The shirt felt like hope, which was ridiculous. She grabbed it and stuffed it in the bag. She had to stop looking for rainbows.

She opened the drawers on the bedside table. Nothing in the top one.

Emotion caught in her throat when she opened the second drawer.

It was the orange bandana. The one she'd tied around the porch rail the first day he'd come.

She had an urge to stuff it in the bag and an equally strong urge to tie it around the rail.

God, she was still an idiot after all this time. Here she was, weeping in an empty room over a bandana that represented a man who was too stupid to know a good thing when it smacked him in the face.

She put the bandana back in the drawer and went downstairs.

They stood on the end of the pier, giggling like schoolgirls.

Tipsy schoolgirls.

The moon was full, reflecting in the black lake like a spotlight. Cicadas chirped from the shore. The air was warm, but Nina still felt chilled. She held the bag of Mick's stuff over the water. Lizzie offered the depleted wine bottle, but Nina waved it off.

"Enemies," she said. Then she amended, "Friends. We are gathered here today to celebrate the end of summer. And the end of—" Her voice chocked up a little bit, and

Lizzie touched her shoulder. "The end of a relationship with a man who I thought was—" She stopped again. "Oh hell, never mind. I cast these clothes to the bottom of the sea."

"Wait," Georgia said. "You can't put a plastic bag in the lake."

"That's true," Lizzie said. "Think of the wildlife." Lizzie loved birds more than she loved people.

"And it might not sink if air gets stuck in the bag," Georgia observed.

Nina rolled her eyes. She loved these women, but they didn't have much of a sense of ceremony. She dumped the clothes out of the bag and handed the empty bag to Lizzie, who, like a good mother, accepted her trash.

"Friends," Nina began again. "We gather here—"

"The individual clothes definitely won't sink," Georgia said.

Lizzie and Jill scuttled around the shore, scavenging for rocks. They lugged them back to the deck, then tied the clothes around them.

"Friends," Nina said for the third time. "Enemies," she added, just to show a little of her annoyance at their inability to just get this done. "I've learned one very important thing this summer. I've learned that life isn't all rainbows and pretty flowers. In fact, I think I've learned that life isn't even *mostly* rainbows and flowers. But it doesn't matter. Because when times get hard"—she raised her hands to motion to the three of them—"that's when your friends show up. If there weren't hard times, we might never realize how important our friends are. When my house was wrecked, you all showed up. When I couldn't do my memorial, the whole world came together and sent material and saved the day. So, ladies, I commend these clothes to the depths of Galton Lake in honor of taking the bad times and turning them into opportunity. The opportunity to be with my friends."

She tossed each piece of rock-laden clothing into the lake. They observed a moment of silence as they splashed one by one into the water, then disappeared with a trail of air bubbles.

And then Nina stripped off her own sundress and panties and threw herself into the lake.

The exquisite cold of the water hit her skin like a slap. She let herself sink under; then she rose to the surface. Three more splashes echoed around her as Jill, Lizzie, and Georgia hit the water.

Nina lay on her back in the water, letting the sound of the lapping waves block out all other sound. She looked up at the stars and the moon and wondered what Mick was doing right now. Was he in Tel Aviv, having his nightmares alone in a foreign hotel room? Was he already on his way back to some war zone somewhere to do another tour of duty?

Wherever he was, she wished him well.

She wished Bella well.

As for herself, she knew she was going to be okay.

Even if it stunk, it would be okay, because she had people who had her back. She had friends.

Despite stupid Mick, she was and always would be a hopeless optimist.

The next day, Nina decided that she was done with wallowing in self-pity. She had to get back to work. She called Johnny and told him to meet her at the wall. They'd finish the job.

She took a shower and got dressed. She felt good as she crossed the lawn to get some extra supplies from the garage.

But then she threw open the door and gasped.

The place was trashed.

Tommy and two other officers surveyed the wreckage of Nina's barn. "Nina, you sure nothing is missing?"

"Nothing. I mean, there wasn't much out here."

"Two break-ins in a month with nothing taken is odd," Tommy said. "It could be a coincidence, of course. But it isn't like this is a high-crime area. Plus, with Mick and Bobby taking off at the same time, it doesn't add up."

"You think they both had something to do with this?"

"It is weird that those two guys showed up in Galton at the same time, isn't it?"

"Are you implying that Mick is somehow connected to this?"

"I have no idea," Tommy said. "It's just so odd. I wish you'd get someone to stay out here with you," he said.

"I'm fine, Tommy. It was probably kids, hoping to find glue to sniff. I keep that stuff in my inside studio, so they couldn't get it out here."

Tommy's lips were a thin, pale line. "Okay. If you say so. But I still don't feel good about this. Maybe Lizzie can come out and stay with you. Or you could go and stay with her for a few days."

"You know how she feels about cats." Lizzie had an obsession with bird feeders. No way could Nina go out there and lock Sylvia and Roe inside without them tearing Lizzie's house to pieces. Plus, Lizzie had a husband and a kid—a life. She couldn't intrude with all her sadness.

She could go and stay with Jill or Georgia, but then what? Hide out forever? "Anyway, it's fine. There's absolutely nothing to worry about."

"I can't force you to be safe. But I wish you'd talk it over with Lizzie or Jill or even Georgia."

Tommy left a half an hour later when his report was done, just as the gang showed up to help her clean.

"This is getting to be a habit," Jill said. "I'm starting to think you're doing this yourself just to get us to help you with your summer cleaning."

"I wish," Nina said. "Look at this mess. Every shelf pulled down. And who knows how long it's been like this?"

"I think you should listen to Tommy," Lizzie said. "I don't feel good with you out here alone."

"I'll lock the doors," Nina said. "I'm fine. Nothing's going to happen to me. It's just a couple kids, that's all."

"Well, let's hope so."

Jill helped as long as she could before she had to run off to a client. She promised to bring the rest of them dinner. Georgia had an hour; then she had to leave too.

"You're darn lucky this was my day off," Lizzie said.

"Thank you, honey," Nina said. "I couldn't face this alone."

They put on some music and worked all afternoon. At three, Lizzie had to go too, to drive her daughter, Paige, to the dentist, leaving Nina alone in the barn.

And that was when she started to cry.

Damn you, Mick, for leaving.

But no matter how hard she tried to believe it, she couldn't believe that he had anything to do with this.

But why had he left? Why wouldn't he answer his

cell? She was doing exactly what she'd done for two years before she met him. Trying to reach the man who was unreachable.

She ought to just admit that he was a scam artist. Maybe he was even off with fake Mary, luxuriating on some beach in Mexico with Walt's money.

Later that night, alone in the house, she lay in her bed and tried to sleep.

She missed Mick so badly, it hurt.

Finally, after hours of tossing and turning, she got up, went to the empty guest room. She got out the orange bandana and tied it around the front porch rail.

She couldn't help herself; she still believed.

Chapter Fifty

Summer was winding down.

Nina finished the last painting for *The Vegetable Virgin* and mailed it off to her publisher. Johnny was spearheading the work on the memorial; he showed up once a week at the house to show her what was going on with it, but only to be polite. He was doing most of the hands-on work himself. She'd go once a week to paint the artwork on the walls, but they were almost done everything on the physical project.

The chill in the air was getting hard to deny. Fall came early in upstate New York; then the seasons moved on to winter before you blinked. Mick had been gone a few weeks, but it felt like longer. Some nights, it even felt like he had never been here at all.

Other nights, she felt as if he'd grabbed her heart fresh the night before.

Every day, Nina would check the mail, wondering if he'd send a letter, and if he did, where in the world it would be from.

Nothing arrived except bills and catalogues.

Nothing helped the ache that was still in her heart.

The one happy spot in her haze of longing was the progress of the memorial project. It kept growing exponentially. The media loved it, and every time it was featured on a newscast or in a magazine, an influx of pictures, videos, and donations would flood them.

Lots of donations. So many, Nina didn't know what they'd do with them all.

At Georgia's urging, Nina hired a lawyer to set up a trust for the money. She also brought together a board of directors so that everything could be handled honestly and publicly.

Tonight, she had gathered the board in her living room: Mr. Garcia, Johnny, Tommy, two decorated veterans from the town, and of course, the Enemy Club.

After they'd eaten Nina's vegetarian chili and Lizzie's peach cobbler for dessert, Nina brought the meeting to order.

"So we have over two hundred and fifty thousand dollars in the trust. We have to decide what to do with it."

They all nodded, congratulating Johnny and Mr. Garcia.

"We should give the money to wounded vets," Mr. Garcia suggested.

"But how do we decide who gets it? We need a process."

"People could apply. Someone could be in charge of the applications. A committee," Lizzie said.

"There's more and more coming in every day," Johnny said. "It's crazy. It's like an avalanche."

"I like the idea of a committee," Nina said. "But I want

to make one executive decision. I think the first disbursement should go to someone special."

They all quieted.

"To Mick's sister."

"Nina!" Georgia gasped. "Why?"

"Look, I've thought this through a lot," Nina said. "Without Mick, this wall would never have happened. I don't know where he is and I don't know what he's doing. But I do know that he can't get the money himself. I know that he hurt me—" She took a minute to let that settle. Lizzie touched her arm. "But this isn't about me. It's about giving back to veterans. I think we should all vote to make the first payment to Mick's sister because she was as much a victim of the war as others. Mick could have helped her if he hadn't been off fighting. He could have saved her with my money if I hadn't been scammed. This shouldn't just be about helping the vets, but also helping their families."

They voted unanimously to give Bella the money.

"I'll call the lawyers to see how we get it done," Georgia said.

Later, as Lizzie and Nina cleaned dishes in the kitchen, Lizzie said, "You forgave him, didn't you?"

"I just don't believe he's bad," Nina said. "Despite everything, I don't think he was scamming me."

"That's because you always look on the bright side."

"Yeah, I guess I do. And you know what? I don't care. I'm glad Mick will get help for Bella, whether he likes it or not. Maybe one day he'll come back and explain everything."

Three weeks later, it was time to take down the tomatoes.

Nina ripped the cages out of the dry earth one by one, untangling the overgrown bushes from the metal.

And then she heard it.

She didn't even need to look up to know what it was.

Mick's ridiculous red car, roaring up the drive.

He stopped halfway.

She ducked behind the tomatoes, then scolded herself and stood up straight and marched for the drive. She wasn't hiding from anyone ever again.

Mick unfolded himself from the front seat, as gorgeous as ever.

She steeled herself to resist him, promised herself that she wasn't going to forgive him, even if he took off his shirt.

Luckily, he didn't.

He met her in front of the garden, now mostly put to sleep for the fall. "Hi."

"Hi."

"Where the hell have you been?" she asked.

"Being an idiot."

He came close and he raised her chin with his finger, and she knew she was lost even if she was determined not to be. *He will not just waltz back in and be forgiven.*

"I understand that a certain memorial project of Galton donated a hundred thousand dollars for Bella's care," he said.

So he'd come back to thank her. She kept her voice firm. "You understand right."

"Why, Nina?"

"Because, despite your inability to act like a good guy, I still believe that you are one."

"So you're still a hopeless optimist?"

"Yes." She shrugged. "I'm even optimistic about fixing this thing with the house. I hired a lawyer, and we're going to get it unraveled. But not in time to help Bella. So what could we do?"

"Good for you."

"Mick, where the hell have you been?"

"I had to get something for you," he said. He held out the rusty red metal box.

"Did you get that off the bottom of Galton Lake?"

"No. Nina, we had found the wrong box. Bobby had found the right one."

She could feel her insides shift. She sighed. "You should be in Tel Aviv."

"I should. But I had to take care of this first. Bella's fine. Especially now that the town of Galton came to her aid."

Nina stared at the red box in his hands. "Come inside," Nina said. "I'll put on tea."

"I was a moron," he said after they were settled in her living room, the tea steaming on the coffee table between them. He couldn't bear to touch it. She invited him in as if she still trusted him. The box sat on the table. He could hardly bear to look at it. It hadn't escaped his notice that the orange bandana, faded and rain soaked, had been tied around the rail. But instead of it making him feel good, it made him feel even more in the wrong than he already did. "I left because I found out something about Walt that I didn't want you to know. I couldn't let his memory get messed up in so much darkness."

She watched him, waiting.

"But you giving Bella that money." He struggled to

keep his voice steady. "I knew, when you'd done that, that there was absolutely nothing in this world that could make you lose your spirit. Even me being a big enough jerk to leave you without explaining. Without saying good-bye."

"I could have told you that." She stared at the box that he'd put on the table between them. "So this is the thing you didn't want me to know about?"

"The second box."

"How did you find it?"

"I caught Bobby trashing your garage the day I'd gone back for paint."

"The day you left."

"Yes. He found it. It was actually his." He told her everything about Bobby, about the second box. He left out the part about Walt throwing the stone. That could wait until later. "The box was in the garage the whole time. It had fallen behind the shelf at some point and had gotten wedged against the back wall. It took Bobby's ransacking to uncover it."

"So he was the one who destroyed the garage."

"And the house, before that. At least, his thugs had done the house while we were at Georgia's."

"I don't ever want Georgia to know he was using her," Nina said.

Mick agreed. "Some secrets are probably worth keeping." He looked her in the eyes. He had missed her like mad while he was gone, and it took all his strength not to dive across the table and take her in his arms. But he didn't know if she would forgive him. "So do you want to open it?" Mick asked. He took out the key and put it on the table next to the box.

"How did you get it back from Bobby?"

"I left here, planning to go to California to re-up. But then I came across Bobby's car in the parking lot outside a bar on the way to the highway." He shrugged. "I stole the damn thing back. Broke into his trunk. It wasn't that hard."

"I'd love to have seen the look on his face when he saw it was missing," she said.

"Me too," Mick agreed. "Then I got back on the road and drove for three straight days. I didn't know what I was going to do. I was a little out of my mind. I was even thinking of trying to sell what was in the box. For Bella, of course. And I almost did."

She stared at the box. "Did you re-up, Mick?"

"No. I couldn't. I've done my duty. I can't go back there, Nina. That was part of the problem I was struggling with. I was driving toward nothing, and away from everything."

They stared at the box some more. She looked so beautiful and so sad. Would she ever forgive him? "I should have never left," he said. "I was an idiot."

"A moron," she agreed.

"A coward," he added.

"True."

"Nina. I can throw the stupid thing in the lake. We can go right now to the lake and throw it in together. Pretend it never existed."

She looked wobbly, but she shook her head and picked up the key. "I want this over with. Now."

Nina knelt on the floor. She could hardly breathe as she turned the key.

She opened the lid.

She peered in.

"Oh my God, what is it?" She carefully lifted a small gold, domed container out of the box. It wasn't more than two inches high. It was made of the most luscious, beautiful gold Nina had ever seen. A wavelike pattern was etched into the surface that was so fine, it gave her goose bumps just to be in its presence. A pinnacle rose from the center of the case's dome, a spire so delicate, Nina didn't dare touch it for fear it would turn to dust. "Oh my God," Nina repeated. "What the heck was Walt doing with this?"

"I looked it up. I think it's a first-century reliquary. Solid gold. Gorgeous craftsmanship."

Nina felt the floor beneath her. She tried to keep her breath steady. "Walt was stealing antiquities?" Nina asked, letting herself fall back on the couch. She couldn't take her eyes off the exquisite piece. "I can't believe it. He wouldn't. Not him. Oh hell."

Mick picked up the reliquary. "Well, you can look at it that way. Or you can see it in a more positive light."

Nina raised her eyebrows at him.

"Say some poor farmer found it in the cave above his fields. Crazy place, Afghanistan, poor farmer getting ahold of something like this. The Afghan government has nothing for this guy. His family is starving. Maybe Walt helped him by buying it off him. Maybe he saved the guy's family."

"It's wrong," Nina said. "Looting a country we're supposed to be protecting. Illegal. There's nothing good about it."

Mick sighed. He put the reliquary back into the metal box and shut the lid. "Well, tell that to the farmer whose wife and ten kids are starving to death. Maybe Walt saved that farmer's life, saved the whole village for a few weeks." Mick went on. "Do you protect the people you love or protect some fancy knickknacks that would probably go to corrupt government officials anyway?"

Nina frowned.

Mick went on. "Divided loyalties. Who do you do right by—society or your family? You can't do right by both of them, can you? Because life isn't simple like that. It's not black-and-white. Duty is complicated. So who's more important? A museum that doesn't even exist yet, run by a government that barely exists, or feeding your family for another few months?"

She didn't answer.

"I know, I'm grasping here," he said. "That's why I didn't come back, Nina. I didn't want you to know this about Walt. And then I remembered something. Something important."

She waited.

"I had to know if my hunch was right. To know, I had to find Bobby again. That wasn't easy," Mick said. "But I let word get out that I had his box, and funny, he found me." He paused. "And I was right. Bobby was blackmailing Walt."

"With what?" Nina asked, her heart in her throat.

"The bridge," Mick said between clenched teeth. This was going to be the hard part. The part that he never wanted to tell her. The part she might never forgive him for telling her.

"The bridge? What do you mean?" Nina asked.

So Mick told her the story of Walt throwing the stone. He tried to ignore the look of pain in her eyes so that he could keep going. "I'm sorry, Nina. But it's important that you know. Bobby blackmailed Walt to bring the reliquary back in return for keeping what happened on that bridge a secret from you."

He watched Nina assimilate all this bad news. "So what do we do now?" she asked.

"Well, that's up to you. Either we throw the box in the lake as if it never existed. Or we turn it in to the authorities. But, Nina, if we turn it in, it doesn't make Walt look good. It's an international crime, smuggling antiquities. We don't really know how Walt got the box, and we probably won't ever know. But Walt brought it back from Germany for Bobby and agreed to hold it all this time. If we turn it in, Walt's good name will be messed up in this, even if it was blackmail, which I don't know if we could ever prove."

"We could turn it in anonymously," Nina said.

"We could," Mick agreed.

"But it feels kind of lame," Nina said.

"It does," Mick agreed.

For the next few days, they discussed the box while they got their relationship back at least a little closer to where it had been before Mick left.

Over a dinner of chicken enchiladas that Mick had cooked up, as usual making enough for the next month, Mick said, "On the one hand, Afghanistan is lousy with priceless artifacts like these. They're like potatoes that farmers dig up in their fields."

"It'll disappear forever," Nina said. She felt as if she might cry. The reliquary was so achingly beautiful, it deserved to be in a museum.

"Nina. Let it go. It's not our battle. We have to protect Walt. I have to protect Walt. His memory anyway. And you and me, we have each other. That's all that matters. Haven't we learned that love comes before duty sometimes? That sometimes we have to choose love?"

"But sometimes it doesn't," Nina said. "This thing is the property of the Afghan people. This is bigger than us. This is bigger than Walt." She stood up. "Mick, I can't do this another minute. I'm calling the police."

Chapter Fifty-one

$\mathcal{M}$ick felt a sense of peace descend on him as he watched Nina dial the phone.

"I'd like to report some stolen property that I've uncovered—"

As hard as he tried, Mick didn't give a damn about the reliquary. But Nina was spectacular. He felt a new kind of awe for her as all the pieces of the puzzle came together for him. It was her duty to society to return the box, and she took it, headlong, reckless, not caring about the consequences. Because she loved what it stood for.

If there'd been cash in the box, weapons, drugs, things might have been different. She wouldn't have cared about any of that. But no. It had to be art in the box. Something beautiful and irreplaceable that transcended petty concerns like money. "Nina, that was the best thing I've ever seen anyone do," Mick said. He sat down next to her.

Her arms were limp at her sides. She said, "I had no

choice." She shot him an annoyed look. "Why are you grinning?"

"You did have a choice. And you chose something bigger than yourself. Not many people would have done that."

The sounds of a police siren echoed in the distance.

"Yeah, I guess. I feel like a traitor to Walt."

"I love you, Nina."

"Well, you better. Because once we give this thing away, you're all I've got."

"I hope I did the right thing," Nina said when Tommy had taken their statements and the reliquary.

"You saved a priceless piece of history," Mick pointed out. "It was the right thing to do."

"Maybe. But I didn't think it through. I was reckless again, Mick."

Mick took her hand. "Be reckless one more time."

"What?"

"Tell me that you'll marry me. Don't think; just do it. Rush in. Marry me. And we'll honeymoon in Tel Aviv."

She stuttered something, stopped, tried to start again and failed. "This is very reckless of you, soldier."

"To hell with sanity. Soldiers and artists and lovers have to dive in no matter what. It's bigger than us, isn't it, Nina? It's unavoidable. It's not right or wrong; it just is, and there's not a damn thing we can do about it; even if we don't want to love each other, even if we remind each other of the worst things that might happen in life, there it is, in the air. We're making history, caught up in this moment of life. So let's finish this thing. Marry me."

"No more secrets?"

"Well, one." She watched as he pulled up his sleeve. "I've been waiting for the perfect moment. But since I haven't managed to get you into bed yet, I guess I ought to just show you this now."

"Oh, Mick. I love it. Yes, yes, let's get married." She took the plunge and it felt divine. Like the cold water of the lake over her skin. Like the joy of doing art and getting it right. Like being in Mick's arms.

"Don't you want to think about it a bit?"

"Nope."

He grinned.

She leaned down and kissed his modified tattoo.

Duty. Honor. Country.

Then, underneath, he'd added another word.

Love.

Chapter Fifty-two

The story about the reliquary was the lead piece in the next *Galton Daily*. An article ran on the front page and three follow-up pages, alleging Walt's role in the fiasco, accompanied by a picture of the reliquary, of Walt, of Nina, of Bobby, and even of Mick.

Nina couldn't force herself to read a word of it. The headline, "Local Soldier Accused of Antiquities Smuggling," made her sick to her stomach.

The Enemy Club came by one by one and sat with her. They all offered sympathy and baked goods, but this time, there was no broken glass they could sweep up or pictures they could put back on the wall.

"I think I made a terrible mistake," Nina would whisper to Mick in the middle of the night, when neither one of them could sleep.

"No. You did what you had to do," Mick would whisper back. "You went in full guns blazing. The Walt way. He'd be proud."

In the full light of day, they'd talk about what had happened, running it over and over from every angle.

The men from the army's internal affairs department came with briefcases, in full uniform, and Mick and Nina each gave statements, unsure where all of it was heading, but unable to stop it. Everything had been set in motion.

The only good thing about all the chaos and attention was that it forced Nina's attention away from what had happened on the bridge when her parents died. "I'd give anything to talk to Walt, to tell him that I forgive him," Nina said. She and Mick were sitting in the park, watching the lake. They hoped that this would all pass over soon so they could elope, then go to Israel to be by Bella's side.

The second stage of her treatment would start in a week.

"Do you forgive him?" Mick asked. "Is it that easy?"

"Yes. It was an accident," Nina said. She watched families go by and she wondered if she and Mick would ever have a family. "He was a kid. I could have helped him if he'd told me."

"You always see the sunny side," Mick said. "That's why I love you."

"And you always have my back," Nina said. "Looking out for me in a dangerous world. That's why I love you."

"We make a pretty good pair," Mick said.

"I guess we do," Nina agreed.

Chapter Fifty-three

𝒩ina was surprised to see Mr. Garcia outside by the mural when she and Mick drove up in her Subaru. Mr. Garcia was talking to a man with a prosthetic leg. They were deep in discussion, and Nina thought that maybe she had even seen a slight sheen of tears in Mr. Garcia's eyes.

She and Mick unloaded their supplies alongside the wall. This was the final piece of artwork before the wall was officially finished. Walt's case had been cleared by the authorities: he'd been found not guilty by reason of blackmail. The police were still after Bobby, but Nina didn't care about him. She didn't care much about anything now but Mick.

They'd elope at the Galton Town Hall, then leave for Tel Aviv in two days.

Mr. Garcia waved and came over to shake their hands.

"So where's Johnny?" Nina asked. "Is he out of town?"

She had tried to get in touch with Johnny all week, but he hadn't been answering his phone.

"Yep." Mr. Garcia blushed a little.

Nina threw the drop cloth while Mick brought the ladder.

"At a family event? Football?" Nina asked. She had really been hoping for the kid's input. She knew the change she wanted to make on the wall, but she felt a little odd doing it without Johnny's approval. She felt as if the wall was more his than hers.

The man with the prosthesis came over to say good-bye to Mr. Garcia. "You take care, now," he said. "Your boy sure done good. I came across three states to see this memorial last night, and boy was it ever worth it."

Nina and Mick watched as the man got into his car and pulled away. Mr. Garcia waved good-bye.

"What?" Mr. Garcia asked. "Happens all the time. I can hardly run my store anymore. I have to always be out here, chatting up the vets." He paused. "Anyway, Johnny's off with his mother touring art schools. You know, if he's going to get into a good one, he's got to do his homework now."

Nina threw her arms around Mr. Garcia. "Oh, the boy is going to be brilliant," she said.

"He can still be a soldier," Mr. Garcia said, pulling away a little stiffly. "But later. After he does some good here, you know? Our boys deserve his good work."

"Exactly right," Nina said, more guarded. She didn't want to embarrass Mr. Garcia again.

She went to work on the wall while Mick held the ladder for her. It took about an hour, but when they stepped back to see the results, there were tears in both of their eyes.

Duty. Honor. Country.

And then, below, *Love*.

Their job here was done.

Lizzie Bea Carpenter
is an independent
woman with a lock
on her heart.
Will she see that sexy
Dante Giovanni is
holding the key?

Please turn this page
for an excerpt from

How Sweet It Is

Chapter One

*F*or over a week the envelope sat on the dining room table unnoticed, buried under a stack of birdseed catalogues and household bills like a bomb waiting to go off.

Life went on around it. Work, grocery shopping, and housework for Lizzie Bea Carpenter. School, babysitting, and friends for her fourteen-year-old daughter, Paige.

Tick tick tick.

Normal life. A good life. Maybe not great, but fine. Galton, New York, *centrally isolated,* the locals liked to say, wasn't exactly the kind of town where momentous things happened.

Until Saturday, September 8, 8:22 in the evening, when Lizzie's world turned upside down.

"Who do we know in Geneva?" Paige asked, coming into the kitchen, holding up an envelope covered in foreign stamps. It had been Paige's turn to clean the dining room after dinner. She'd swept the crumbs under the thread-bare Turkish rug, pushed around the ragtag assortment of antique chairs until they looked more or less orderly, and tossed most of the pile of mail, including an ominous-looking letter from her middle school, into the overflowing recycling bin with a quick, guilty second glance.

Lizzie turned off the faucet, put down the mac-and-cheese pan she was scrubbing in the sink, saw the handwriting, and said, "Ratbastard." She backtracked quickly, her throat constricting. "I mean, Geneva? Ha! No one. Let me see that." She grabbed for the letter, but Paige was too quick. Lizzie's heart was pounding. Her throat was dry with dread.

"Who?" Paige tore the letter open while dodging around the counter.

"Don't," Lizzie said, but the word came out listlessly because she knew it was too late. Everything was about to change, and there was nothing she could do to stop it.

"It's addressed to both of us," Paige said, unfolding the single sheet.

Lizzie didn't know that she knew anyone in all of Europe, much less Geneva, but apparently she did, because she recognized that handwriting at a glance, even after fourteen years. Her traitorous body knew it, too, and was responding as if it were still sixteen and stupid. This couldn't be happening. *Oh, Paige...*

Paige read the letter. She stopped, frozen, on the other side of the counter. "Oh. I see," she said, letting the letter fall to the counter. "Ratbastard." She said it as if it were an ordinary name like Steve or Joe.

Lizzie wiped her hands on the dishrag, trying to look like a mother in control. "Well. He could have changed," she said as carefully as she could. "We shouldn't jump to any conclusions."

"He wants to come here, Mom."

Lizzie cleared her throat. "That's lovely," she managed to get out.

"On Christmas Day."

"Ratbastard! Sorry. Lovely. Hell." *Nice work.* Lizzie needed a few minutes to pull herself together. She needed to sit and to breathe and definitely not to cry. She wanted to hit something but she couldn't. Not now, in front of Paige. At least, not anything that would break. Not that there was much left to break in their kitchen, which was clean, but failing. Two burners were dead on the stove. The icemaker had quit eleven months ago. The radio worked when you banged it. Hard. Couldn't do much damage in here, even if she tried.

But that letter had done damage.

Paige looked as if she'd already been pummeled. Her face was blank and pale. Her new black, chin-length Cleopatra haircut made her face seem rounder and her brown eyes even huger than usual. She looked like an eight-year-old and an eighteen-year-old simultaneously, a special effect in a bad after-school movie about girls growing up too fast.

Lizzie picked up the letter. She imagined Ratbastard walking into a store and asking for the stationery that screamed *I'm rich and arrogant* the loudest. The cream-colored paper was heavy and stamped with a fancy watermark. The handwriting was neat, the tone straightforward. He spelled realize like a Brit, even though he had been born and bred in Michigan—*I realise this is out of the blue. But I'd like to meet my daughter. I'll be in the States over the holidays, and will stop by then. Twelve o'clock Christmas day? I hope she'll be willing to see me.*

There was no return address, no phone number, no e-mail contact, nothing but a breezy signature—*Ethan Pond*. Then, in parentheses, *Dad*.

Lizzie excused herself, climbed the stairs, turned on the water in the bathroom sink to muffle the noise, and threw up.

Ethan Pond, Paige's father, the boy who'd changed Lizzie's life forever in the back of his Lexus during her senior year of high school, was coming back.

This was a matter for the Enemy Club.

Chapter Two

*T*ay Giovanni sipped his coffee, wishing he could taste it. It was 7:27 in the morning, and he was hunkered down on a stool in a chrome-and-mirrors diner in a nowhere town waiting for Candy Williams, the woman who hated him most in this vast, frozen world.

Was this bottom?

A hum of activity from four women at the end of the counter distracted him from his dark thoughts. The buzz grew until it exploded into shouts.

"Ratbastard."

"Pondscum."

"Ninnyhammer."

"Ninnyhammer?"

"What's wrong with 'ninnyhammer'?"

"Fuckface is better."

"You know I won't say that word."

"Face? Why not? We all have one. C'mon. Just once? For Lizzie? This is Ethan Pond we're talking about."

"He's a fartface, Liz."

"Oooh! She said 'face'!"

A wrinkled, gray-haired man on the stool next to Tay nodded to indicate the women. "That's the Enemy Club."

Was the man talking to him? Tay looked around, hoping someone else was nearby.

No such luck.

The old man went on. "I come in Wednesday mornings just to watch them." The man's baseball hat read *John Deere Tractors*. He was missing two fingers on his right hand. These two facts combined rocked Tay's already rocky stomach. The man lowered his voice as if telling a juicy secret. "They used to be the worst of enemies. Now they're the best of friends. But friends with a difference. They tell each other the truth, the whole truth, and nothing but the truth the way only natural-born enemies can. I could sell tickets!"

Natural-born enemies.

The words stuck in Tay's gut. If any words described his relationship to Candy—to the world in general—those about nailed it. He wondered if the Enemy Club had openings.

The old man elbowed Tay good-naturedly, then chomped into his chocolate-covered doughnut with pink sprinkles. "But now look at them. Best friends forever. Right, Lizzie Bea?"

The waitress had come down the counter to top off their coffees. "Best *enemies* forever. Leave that poor man alone, Mr. Zinelli." She poured more coffee into Tay's mug, even though he'd barely touched it. "Ignore him."

One of the women stuffed a cream-colored piece of paper into a matching envelope and held it above her head. The address was handwritten, *Elizabeth and Paige Carpenter, 47 Pine Tree Road*. "I say we burn it."

The waitress hurried back down the counter. "Put that lighter away, Jill!"

Tay tried not to watch, but he couldn't tear his eyes away. Were they really enemies? They certainly didn't look like they had anything in common, but they were completely at ease, the way they moved, touched, threatened to burn each other's possessions.

The old man leaned in close, pointing as he spoke. "The princess, the oddball, and the brainiac. Oh, and the waitress—she's the good girl gone bad. All leaders of their packs back in the day. Look close, and you'll see. They don't look like normal friends, right?"

Tay didn't need a close look; it was obvious they didn't have anything in common without a second glance.

Jill, the woman with the lighter, was a bottle blonde, her hair pulled back in a brain-pinching bun, her earlobes dripping with diamonds. She drank from a takeout coffee cup that read *Brewhaha*, the hopping, trendy coffee joint across the street that Tay had gladly passed by for the quiet neglect of the diner. *Friends don't let friends bring takeout to other friends' restaurants.*

A pixie of a woman in an orange flouncy sweater, coral beads, and short-cropped, orangish hair snatched the blonde's lighter and slipped it into her canvas bag. Her nose was covered in orange freckles.

"I have to go," a third woman in itchy-looking tweed said, obviously annoyed by the other two's jostling. She was short, her brown shoes nowhere near reaching the ground. How she'd gotten herself up on the stool, Tay couldn't imagine. The muscles in his arms twitched, jonesing to help her down.

He clenched his teeth until the urge passed.

Ever since the accident, he'd been like this, possessed by the soul of a souped-up Boy Scout, needing to jump in and save the world, or at least the part in front of him. When the urge hit him, it was like an epileptic fit, unexpected and uncontrollable.

As if a million good deeds would even out his karma.

Not that he believed in karma.

Or, in his case, in the possibility of even.

Hell, he had no idea what he believed in anymore.

"Wait, you can't go, Georgia," the waitress said. "Not yet." The other women treated the waitress with deference, as if she were the leader of the group, or maybe it just seemed that way because she was standing, moving, while they sat and watched. Tendrils of wavy brown hair had escaped her bun, softly framing her round cheeks. Her waitress uniform was simple, with no necklace or earrings or any adornment to make it appear anything more than what it was. Minimal makeup, just a bit of faded color on her lips, a touch of blush on her cheeks. *The truth, the whole truth, and nothing but the truth . . .*

The blonde caught him staring at the waitress, so he trained his eyes back on his coffee. The old man had taken up with his doughnut, and the Enemy Club quieted to a low murmur. Tay tried to focus on his situation. He glanced at his watch: 7:28. Candy would be here in two minutes.

Or not.

The women's conversation drifted in and out until the freckled one's calm tone silenced the others so that Tay could hear clearly, no matter how hard he tried not to. "Lizzie, if you want something, you have to face it, admit it, then wish for it with all your soul. That's how the universe works. It will hear your wish, and if it's sincere, it will answer."

The waitress crossed her arms, leaned back against the service counter, and said, "Don't get me started on the universe granting wishes. I love you, Nina, but that's nuts."

Tay tried not to smile. He liked that waitress.

"But if it could?" the freckled one persisted.

"Then I wish for the perfect man."

Despite the blackness that was numbing him, Tay stilled, hoping to hear better.

The blonde said, "No such thing," and they all exploded into an uproar over the possibility of a half-decent man ever appearing in Galton, New York.

The waitress held up her hand for silence. "The perfect man is one who'll show up once a week, fix stuff around my house, and then split. That, O great universe, is what I wish for."

And they were off again. Tay looked down at his mug, trying to clear his head of waitresses and wishes. Candy would walk through those doors any second.

...if you want something, you have to face it, admit it, then wish for it with all your soul...

He agreed with the waitress—nuts. But he couldn't help himself.

He wished he wasn't in this Podunk college town in the middle of nowhere, waiting for Candy to rip him to shreds.

But that was a coward's wish, so he tried again: He wished with the few pieces left of his soul that Candy would show up and take the money and then maybe, just maybe, he could taste his coffee again, feel the cold, sleep at night.

The old man was staring intently at him, his gray eyes narrowed. Tay wondered for a sickening second if he'd said his wish out loud.

The blonde threw her arms out and proclaimed, "I wish for the perfect man—one with good pecs!" She lowered her voice and looked right at Tay. "And beautiful green eyes." He concentrated on the pies in the case across from him. Cherry, key lime, banana cream. There was a time when he'd have been plenty interested in a beautiful blonde dripping in diamonds eyeing him as if he was dinner, a time when he'd have been completely at home shooting the shit with a friendly old man over coffee and doughnuts. But now, he just wanted to be out of here and on his way back to Queens. This small town where everyone knew a person's business wasn't his kind of place. Tay could imagine what the old man would whisper about him to some stranger the next stool over. *There's that man who was in that tragic accident. The woman in the other car died, you know. He hasn't been the same since. I come in every Wednesday just to keep an eye on him…could sell tickets…*

Seven-thirty-one. Tay watched the women joke and cajole, and despite his worry, a tiny sliver of hope snuck into his consciousness. *Enemies can be forgiven, can become friends.* There was a connection between the four women that mesmerized him. The freckled one touched the blonde lightly on the shoulder and secretly passed her the lighter under the counter. The tweedy one sloshed her coffee distractedly and the waitress wiped it up without a word. They all watched the waitress carefully, warily, concern evident in the way they licked their lips, pursed their mouths, caught and held one another's eyes. They leaned in across the counter that separated them from her as if it was all they could do to keep from leaping over it and whisking her away to safety.

Was it really possible to befriend your enemies? What did it take? Telling the truth, the whole truth, and nothing but the truth? *I am Dante Giovanni. I went through a red light and hit another car. No excuses, just a dumb accident, a distracted moment that I can never take back. A woman died. There's no way to make it right. No way to fix it. But she left behind a daughter who needs help. I will find a way to help that girl.*

For an instant, the smell of coffee, eggs, and toast hit Tay full on.

Then Candy walked in the door, and his senses went dry.

THE DISH

Where authors give you the inside scoop!

♥ ♥ ♥ ♥ ♥ ♥ ♥ ♥ ♥ ♥ ♥ ♥ ♥ ♥ ♥ ♥ ♥

From the desk of Caridad Piñeiro

Dear Readers,

I want to thank all of you who have been writing to tell me how much you've been loving the Carrera family, as well as enjoying the towns along the Jersey Shore where the series is set.

With THE LOST, I'm introducing a much darker paranormal series I'm calling *Sin Hunters*. The stories are still set along the Jersey Shore and you'll have the beloved Carreras, but now you'll also get to meet an exciting new race of people: The Light and Shadow Hunters.

Why the change? There was something about Bobbie Carrera, the heroine in THE LOST, that needed something different and something very special. Some*one* very special. Bobbie is an Iraq war veteran and she's home from battle, but wounded both physically and emotionally. She's busy trying to put her world back together and the last thing she needs is more conflict in her life.

But I'm a bad girl, you know. I love to challenge my characters into facing their most extreme hurts because doing so only makes their happiness that much sweeter. I think readers love that as well because there is nothing more uplifting than seeing how love can truly conquer all.

Bobbie's challenge comes in the form of sexy millionaire Adam Bruno. Adam is different from any man she has ever met and Bobbie feels an immediate connection to him. There's just one problem: Adam has no idea who he really is and why he possesses the ability to gather energy. That ability allows him to do a myriad of things; from shape-shifting to traveling at super speed, to wielding energy and light like weapons. But these powers are challenging for Adam: as his abilities grow stronger, they also become deadly and increasingly difficult to control.

Enter Bobbie Carrera. Bobbie brings peace to Adam's soul. Adam feels lost in the human world, but in Bobbie's arms he finds love, acceptance, and the possibility for a future he had never imagined.

But before he can reach that future, he must deal with the present, and that means battling the evil Shadow Hunters and facing the shocking truth about his real identity.

I hope you will enjoy the *Sin Hunters* series. Look for THE CLAIMED in May 2012, which will feature someone you meet in THE LOST. Not going to spill who it is just yet, but keep in mind I just love stories of redemption. . . .

Thank you all for your continued support. Also, many thanks to our military men and women, and their families for safeguarding our liberty and our country. THE LOST is dedicated to you for all the sacrifices you make on our behalf. God bless you and keep you safe.

♥ ♥ ♥ ♥ ♥ ♥ ♥ ♥ ♥ ♥ ♥ ♥ ♥ ♥ ♥ ♥

From the desk of Jennifer Haymore

Dear Reader,

When Serena Donovan, the heroine of CONFESSIONS OF AN IMPROPER BRIDE (on sale now), entered my office to ask me to write her story, I realized right away that

I was in trouble. Obviously, there was something pretty heavy resting on this woman's shoulders.

After I'd offered her a chair and a stiff drink (which she eyed warily—as if she's never seen a martini before!), I asked her why she had come.

"I have a problem," she said.

I tried not to chuckle. It was obvious from the permanent look of panic in her eyes that she had a very big problem indeed. "Okay," I said, "what's the problem?"

"Well—" She swallowed hard. "I'm going to get married."

I raised a brow. "Usually that's reason for celebration."

"Not for me." Her voice was dour.

I took a deep breath. "Look, Miss Donovan. I'm a romance writer. I write about love, blissful marriages, and happy endings. Maybe you've come to the wrong place." I rose from my chair and gestured toward the door. "Thanks for stopping by. Feel free to take the martini."

Her eyes flared wide with alarm. "No! Please . . . let me explain."

I hesitated, staring down at her. She seemed so . . . desperate. I guess I have a bleeding heart after all. Sighing, I resumed my seat. "Go ahead."

"I do respect and admire my future husband. Greatly. He's a wonderful man."

"Uh-huh."

"But, you see, he—" She winced, swallowed, and took a deep breath. "Well, he thinks I'm someone else."

I frowned. "You mean, you told him you were someone you're not?"

"Well, it's not that simple. You see, he fell in love with my sister."

"O . . . kay."

Her eyes went glassy. "But, you see, my sister died. Only he doesn't know that. He thinks I'm my sister!"

"He can't tell that you're not her?"

"I don't know . . ." Her voice was brimming with despair.

"You see, we're identical twins, so on the outside we're alike, but we are such different people . . ."

Oh, man. This chick was in big trouble. "And you want to fashion a happy ending out of this, how?" I asked.

"But I haven't told you the whole problem," she said.

I thought she'd given me a pretty darned enormous problem already. Still, I waved my hand for her to elaborate.

"Jonathan," she said simply.

"Jonathan?"

"The Earl of Stratford. He's a friend of my fiancé and the best man," she explained. She looked away. "And also, he's the only man I've ever—"

"That's okay," I said quickly, raising my hand, "I get it."

She released a relieved breath as I studied her. I really, really wanted to help her. She needed help, that was for sure. But how to forge a happy ending out of such a mess?

"Look," I said, flipping up my laptop and opening a new document, "you need to tell me everything, okay? From the beginning."

And that was how it began. By the time Miss Donovan finished telling me her story, I was so hooked, I had to go into my writing cave and write the entire, wild tale. The hardest part was getting to that happy ending, but it was so happy and so romantic that it was worth every drop of blood and sweat that it took to get there.

I truly hope you enjoy reading Serena Donovan's story! Please come visit me at my website, www.jenniferhaymore.com, where you can share your thoughts about my books, sign up for some fun freebies, and read more about the characters from CONFESSIONS OF AN IMPROPER BRIDE.

Sincerely,

Jennifer Haymore

From the desk of Sue-Ellen Welfonder

Dear Reader,

Does a landscape of savage grandeur make your heart beat faster? Do jagged peaks, cold-glittering boulders, and cauldrons of boiling mist speak to your soul? Are you exhilarated by the rush of chill wind, the power of ancient places made of stone and legend?

I love such places.

TEMPTATION OF A HIGHLAND SCOUNDREL, the second book in my Highland Warriors trilogy, has a truly grand setting. Nought is my favorite corner of the Glen of Many Legends, home to the series' three warring clans. These proud Highlanders prove "where you live is who you are."

Kendrew Mackintosh and Isobel Cameron love wild places as much as I do. Kendrew boasts that he's hewn of Nought's soaring granite peaks and that he was weaned on cold wind and blowing mist. He's proud of his Norse heritage. Isobel shares his appreciation for Viking culture, rough terrain, and long, dark nights. She stirs his passion, igniting desires that brand them both.

But Isobel is a lady.

And Kendrew has sworn not to touch a woman of gentle birth. Isobel is also the sister of a bitter foe.

They're a perfect match despite the barriers separating them: centuries of clan feuds, hostility, and rivalries. Bad blood isn't easily forgotten in the Highlands and grudges last forever. Kendrew refuses to acknowledge his attraction to Isobel. She won't ignore the passion between them. As only a woman in love can, she employs all her seductive wiles to win his heart.

The temptation of Kendrew Mackintosh begins deep in his rugged Nought territory. In the shadows of mysterious cairns known as dreagan stones and on the night of his clan's raucous Midsummer Eve revels, Isobel pitches a battle Kendrew can only lose. Yet surrender will bring greater rewards than he's ever claimed.

Kendrew does open his heart to Isobel, but they soon find themselves caught in a dangerous maelstrom that threatens their love and could cost their lives. The entire glen is at peril and a brutal foe will stop at nothing to crush the brave men of the Glen of Many Legends.

Turning Kendrew loose on his enemy—a worthy villain—gave me many enjoyable writing hours. He's a fierce fighter and a sight to behold when riled. But beneath his ferocity is a great-hearted man who lives by honor.

Writing Isobel was an equal joy. Like me, she feels most alive in wild, windswept places. I know Nought approved of her.

Places do have feelings.

Highlanders know that. In wild places, the pulse beat of the land is strong. I can't imagine a better setting for Kendrew and Isobel.

I hope you'll enjoy watching Isobel prove to Kendrew that the hardest warrior can't win against a woman wielding the most powerful weapon of all: a heart that loves.

With all good wishes,

Sue-Ellen Welfonder

www.welfonder.com

From the desk of Sophie Gunn

Dear Reader,

Some small-town romances feature knitting clubs, some cookie clubs, and some quilting clubs. But my new series has something else entirely.

Welcome to Galton, New York, home of the Enemy Club.

The Enemy Club is made up of four women who had been the worst of enemies back in high school. They were the class brainiac, the bad girl, the princess, and the outcast. Now, all grown up, they've managed to become the best of friends. But they're friends with a difference. They've promised to tell one another the truth, the whole truth, and nothing but the truth so help them Gracie (the baker of the pies at the Last Chance diner). Because they see things from their very (very!) different points of view, this causes all sorts of conflicts and a nuanced story, where no one has a lock on what's right or wrong.

In *Sweet Kiss of Summer*, Nina Stokes is the woman with the problem, and she's going to need everyone's help to solve it. Her brother lost his life in the war. On his deathbed, he asked a nurse to write Nina a letter, instructing her to give his house back in Galton to his war buddy, Mick Rivers.

Or did he?

How can Nina know if the letter is real or a con? And even if it's real, where has Mick been for the past two years, during which Nina tried everything to contact him to no avail? How long should she be expected to keep up the house in this limbo, waiting for a man who obviously takes her brother's last wish lightly?

So when a beautiful man claiming to be Mick roars up Nina's driveway one summer afternoon in a flashy red car, demanding the house that he feels is rightfully his, every member of the Enemy Club thinks that she knows best what Nina should do. Naturally, none of them agree. The themes of friendship, duty, and honor run deep in Galton, and in *Sweet Kiss of Summer*, they are all tested. To whom do we owe our first duty: our family, our friends, our country—or ourselves?

What I loved most about writing *Sweet Kiss of Summer* was that there was no easy solution for anyone. As I wrote, I had no idea what Nina would do about her dilemma. Mick struggled with an even thornier problem, as his secrets were bigger than anyone in the Enemy Club could imagine. I could understand everyone's point of view. There is just so much to consider when you're not only out for yourself, but for your country, your community, your family, and ultimately, something even bigger.

I hope you'll enjoy reading about these characters as much as I've enjoyed writing about them. Come visit me at SophieGunn.com to learn more about the small town of Galton and the Enemy Club, to see pictures of my kitties, and to keep in touch. I'd love to hear from you!

Sophie Gunn

www.sophiegunn.com

Find out more about Forever Romance!

Visit us at
www.hachettebookgroup.com/publishing_forever.aspx

Find us on Facebook
http://www.facebook.com/ForeverRomance

Follow us on Twitter
http://twitter.com/ForeverRomance

NEW AND UPCOMING TITLES

Each month we feature our new titles
and reader favorites.

CONTESTS AND GIVEAWAYS

We give away galleys, autographed copies,
and all kinds of exclusive items.

AUTHOR INFO

You'll find bios, articles, and links to personal websites
for all your favorite authors—and so much more.

GET SOCIAL

Connect with your favorite authors, editors, and
other Forever fans, and share what's important to you.

THE BUZZ

Sign up for our monthly romance newsletter,
and be the first to read all about it.